LAST STOP

EERIE RIVER PUBLISHING

www. EerieRiverPublishing.com

LAST STOP
HORROR ON ROUTE 13

ORIGINAL STORIES BY

Holley Cornetto
L. T. Emery
Peter J. Foote
J.W. Garrett
David Green
Stephen Herczeg
Abigail Linhardt
Beth W. Patterson
Lynne Phillips
Austin Shirey
Joshua D Taylor
V. A. Vazquez
Patrick Winters

Stories

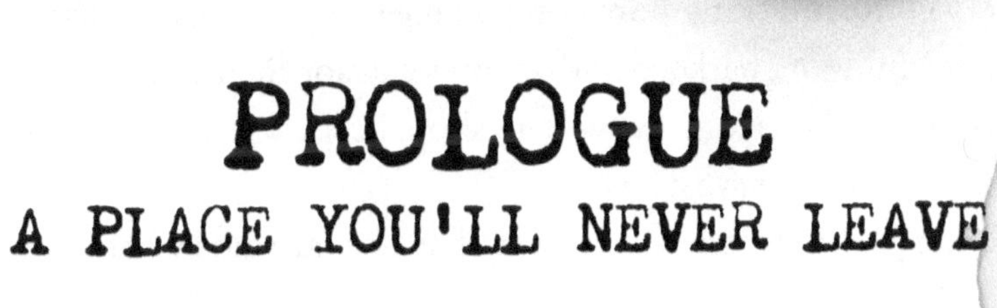

PROLOGUE
A PLACE YOU'LL NEVER LEAVE

BY DAVID GREEN

You ever heard of it? Route Thirteen?

No, not the one in North Carolina. The *real* one.

You won't find it on no map, won't come across no tourist guides urging you to travel it. Oh no. Not old Route Thirteen. You dig around though, you unearth secrets best left buried, best left forgotten…

But you're a curious sort. Can tell by that twinkle in your eye. Well, lemme tell you a little 'bout what you might find.

Our Route Thirteen runs through Idaho; a winding, forgotten dirt road making its way past a one-horse town called Chevron and a canyon of ill-repute named Devil's Ladder.

Yeah, you heard me. Devil's Ladder. County's that kinda place.

Let's say some Godforsaken urge takes you, makes you drive that road. You'll come across a place, eventually—it'll find you when the time's right, don't you worry 'bout that—name of Whiskey Pete's. Looks like any old bar and motel stranded alongside a road in the middle of nowhere, till you peer a little closer.

I suggest you do, take a real good look at it, then get back in your vehicle, and keep right on truckin'.

Say you don't.

Say you've taken leave of your senses, and you take a stroll inside. I'd put every goddamn thing I own on you meeting this cast of characters:

Con Muldoon, barkeep and grunter extraordinaire.

Lorne W. Peterson, Canadian shop keep, has a name-tag reading 'Dale'. No one knows why.

Young Joel Masterson... Inspect that one, all's not what a first glance might tell ya.

Old Melvin Washington. Some say he knew his more famous name-sake, not least hisself.

Last, but not least, Stacey Jenkins. Well, the less said about her, the better.

Now. Let's say you wandered on in there, laid eyes on the folk I just mentioned. You hightail it out of there, and don't ever think of coming back; don't stop till your ride's running on fumes. That's my advice, given free. Take it or leave it.

It's the kinda joint where time don't run straight. Things, places, names, even the goddamn furniture don't act the way they're s'pose to. It changes. Twists, like it's-a molding itself to whatever's in your noggin', fitting into memories best left forgotten.

Just like Whiskey Pete's.

How'd *I* know about Whiskey Pete's on Route Thirteen? Now you're asking the right questions!

Hmm... It's not a place the unlucky folk who darken its door often leave, and if you're fortunate to get out, never make the mistake of thinking you escaped. Their reach is long.

No one ever really leaves Whiskey Pete's...

NIA AND JAMIE
By Patrick Winters

It was 2:07am, and Jamie was getting jittery as hell.

He twisted his head around, glaring out the back window and scanning the street, looking over all the neighboring house-fronts with a wary eye. Households were quiet all along the block, not a single porch light on and nary a glow in any window, where an insomniac or night-owl could be staring out from, taking note of the young man sitting in his car. But darkness keeps secrets well. Maybe someone was watching him—peeking out through a curtain, hiding away in the dark.

He eased back into his seat, staring up to Nia's second-floor window, urging it to open and for her to come out.

Come on, baby. He was getting so paranoid, even the thoughts in his head were whispering. *Where are you?*

Jamie forced himself to loosen his death-grip on the steering wheel of his '77 Aspen. Another minute passed—or several—and he was starting to sweat up a storm.

He ground his teeth and wiped an arm across his forehead. He debated rolling down the window, arguing with himself as to whether the whirring of the glass could wake the neighbors. He finally found the nerve, and put the front windows all the way down. A slight breeze wafted in, cooling and calming him some. Not nearly enough.

They found out. Her folks have got her locked up tight. Daddy probably called his buddies on the force. They've got squad cars coming over right now, ready to drag your ass away...

He could hear the echo of their sirens now, ringing through the fear, closing in on him. His hands started wringing the steering wheel again, and that voice in his head grew traitorous. *Go. Now. Forget this crazy idea and get the fuck out of Dodge.*

Jamie strong-armed that thought away, shaking his head. "Fuck that."

"Fuck what?"

The whisper from his right sent a chill down his spine, and he whipped his head around to see who had discovered him. His dread washed away when he saw it was Nia, looking in at him with a bemused smile on that gorgeous face.

Jamie gave a nervous laugh. "Jeez, babe. You about scared the shit out of me."

Nia tossed a bulging duffel bag through the window. It smacked against Jamie, and he set it in the backseat as Nia slipped into the passenger's side. She was careful to ease the door closed, quiet as possible.

"What took you so lo—?"

Jamie's concern was cut off as Nia slid up to him and kissed him full on the lips. Her embrace instantly worked its magic on him, as only hers ever could. The tension in his muscles eased, his fears crawled back into their dark hideaways, and any doubts of what they planned to do were cast aside, if only for this one serene moment.

This. This feeling between them. This was what they were fighting to keep alive, what they would ensure was theirs, at the cost they were about to pay. And to preserve that blissful bond, the cost was well worth it.

Jamie pulled Nia in closer, holding the kiss a moment longer. When she pulled away, he was left wanting more.

"Sorry I'm late," she whispered. "I thought I heard dad down in the kitchen. Didn't want to risk coming out until he was back in bed."

Jamie set a hand on her forearm, rubbing at it gently. "For a minute there, I was thinking we were done for."

"No way." Nia said, setting her hand on his. Jamie found some extra resolve in how steady and gentle that touch was. "We're just getting started."

They shared another quick kiss—a peck of reassurance—before Nia slid back and buckled herself in. Jamie started up the car, jaw rigid with renewed anxiety as the engine grumbled to life. He put the car in gear and slowly pulled it away from the curb, keeping his headlights off until the next block.

"Okay," Jamie sighed, eyes darting about as he drove. "Here we go."

Nia gave him a small smile of confidence. But as she left behind the only home she'd ever known, Jamie saw that smile fall away, and she looked out to the dark night with uncertainty on her beautiful face.

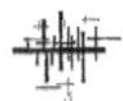

It was the third morning of the young couple's great escape. So far, so good.

There was no plan. No predetermined routes or timetables to adhere to. The only concrete destination they'd ever had in mind was 'away,' and that suited Jamie and Nia just fine, for the time being. Once they'd left their hometown of Astoria behind, they'd headed southeast, saying fare-well to the waters of the Pacific, which they'd known and swam in all their young lives. From there, they'd taken Route 30, which could have delivered them all the way to the other side of the country.

But, once they reached the hustle and bustle of Portland, the allure of major routes and highways faded quickly. With their newfound, flexible lease on life, they could take whatever path they wanted, wherever they wanted to take it.

So it was no big decision when Jamie opted to get off US Route 30 and head on down Route Thirteen, which neither of them had ever heard of before.

The traffic dried up, and it looked like it would give them free rein of more back road options. Nia agreed to try some out-of-the-way areas, which held a certain adventurous—even romantic—charm.

They made stops when they needed to, to stretch their legs or grab a quick bite to eat. Something simple and cheap. They'd enough forethought to bring food along for the trip, but it was mostly snacks and junk food.

They'd accepted that true, warm meals would be few and far between, at least until they settled down somewhere. Motel rooms would be just as scarce. They could afford one now and again, if conditions were rough, but they figured it would be best to save their money whenever they could manage. With the pleasant spring weather setting in, their nights and days of travel were more than comfortable, and Jamie's Aspen was roomy enough for them to sleep in. That's what they'd done every night thus far, pulling off to the side of the road or into abandoned lots in the many towns they passed, one sprawling out in the backseat and the other in the front to catch a few winks—though there was enough room for two in the backseat, at least on certain occasions. It made for a modest home, to say the very least, but they didn't mind it.

That home carried them across the Oregon-Idaho state line, and Jamie saw the crossing as a cause for celebration. He cranked up the radio, which happened to be playing *Around the World* by the Red Hot Chili Peppers. Nia knew they were one of Jamie's favorite bands, but his appreciation didn't match the performance he gave as he started to sing along to the tune. His memory failed him as he mumbled over the rhythm, and what lyrics he could remember were lost to his own laughter as he gyrated and grooved behind the wheel. Nia cracked up alongside him, tears welling in her eyes as she laughed and laughed.

But, once they turned the radio down low and the conversation ran sparse again, her mind began to wander. No matter how much she believed in what they were doing, no matter how she told herself it could actually work out for them, the rational, fearful part of her had to throw the insanity of it back up in her face. And though her sight was on the road's edge, her mind's eye turned back to the past.

She'd first met Jamie at a party, a little over a year ago. A friend of a friend, and when they'd first been introduced, she was smitten, no doubt. Not head over heels for him—that would come later—but his charms, and how he'd made her laugh that night, made her want to see more of him by the party's end. Plenty more.

He became a permanent fixture in her young mind, And that fixture became a star she'd wished upon, after the hangouts that followed, and the outright dates, where they became so close so quickly. She wished to be with him, totally and truly, as only those old, classic love stories would allow. Living their lives together as they saw fit.

The trouble was, Nia had been a fresh sixteen at the time of the party, and Jamie had already turned twenty. And considering where the relationship had turned in recent months, there was a name for what their case was.

Their families—specifically, the difference in their races—provided a whole other problem. Jamie was from a working-class white family. His mother had died when he was thirteen, leaving him to raise himself, taking up two jobs by the time he'd finished high school to keep himself afloat. His father had been a hard-nosed dockworker since before Jamie was born, and he didn't much care about Jamie's school work, or his jobs, or much of anything else regarding his son. When Nia had broken down and asked how his father would react to him being with a black girl, Jamie had averted his eyes and shrugged, simply saying: "He'd take it or leave it." And she knew well enough to realize what that meant.

Then there was her family, and therein lay the greater fallout. Her family was higher up in the Astoria chain, so much so that a few small businesses had their last name plastered across spots in the city. And her father had 'connections', which were occasionally alluded to by friends and family but never given much elaboration for her understanding. Some in the police, some in other places.

It wasn't snap-your-fingers-get-your-way kind of clout, but it was clout all the same, and her parents held their good name to a high standard. As good-hearted and community-minded as they often were, they had drawn dividing lines in the sand when it came to dealing with 'the majority', as Nia had often heard it put through the years. The idea of her even *dating* a white man would have been met with her parents' criticism.

And if they'd even suspected, much less known, about Jamie and just how far their relationship had gone...

The connections would have come out, and Jamie and Nia's time together would've been snuffed. They'd end up the whispered subjects of small town gossip, and Jamie would live the next stint of his life behind bars on a statutory rape charge, if her father pulled enough of those strings.

When Jamie first mentioned the idea of their running away, he'd passed it off as a joke. But she hadn't laughed, because from the first mention, it held a certain temptation. A temptation that went past the youthful angst of wanting to get away from whatever held your wild soul down.

No, this was something stronger. Truer. And for them to be together—with no more facades, or doubts, or waiting—it would be worth it.

They'd hatched their getaway for about a month, getting things ready, trying to plan for the realities that would hit them on the road. Jamie had a decent amount saved from his jobs, and Nia's token position at McDonald's added a little to their collective wallet. They would go wherever they felt like going, do whatever they felt like doing, until they found a place they felt was suitable for them. And once there, they'd settle down. Get an apartment or whatever they could afford, take up any jobs that presented themselves, and make a life that was all their own.

It wouldn't be easy, by any means, but it would be of their own choice, and that was something.

There were plenty of opportunities ahead of them. Plenty of pitfalls, too. And while their journey thus far had shown nothing but opportunity, Nia wondered when the first pitfall would present itself.

"How you doing over there, sweet cakes?"

Nia snapped out of her thoughts and turned to Jamie. She'd been massaging her knuckles across her lips without realizing it. A habit of hers, whenever she was feeling doubtful.

"Doing fine, sugar lips." She put her hand in her lap, hoping Jamie didn't pick up on the tell. "Taking in the view."

He nodded, looking back to the road with a ponderous expression on his face. "Hey. What did the prostitute say to the potato?"

Nia shook her head and held back a grin. "I have no idea."

"Idaho."

She couldn't hold back the snort that came, and as he chuckled at her, she gave him a punch to the arm.

"God, you're awful!"

"Awful? Hmm... That German for 'comic genius' or something?"

"Or something, for sure."

Jamie gave her a loving grin and a wink. Nia, still shaking her head, looked out the window again, taking in the scenery for real this time. Eventually, she turned her attention to the radio. She started searching for something else to listen to.

When she happened upon a station playing *Blinding Lights* by The Weekend, she cranked it up, and it was her turn to serenade Jamie. Both would have agreed she did a better job of it.

Four hours later, they were still on the road. They'd gone a good distance, zipping on through the Payette National Forest and making a single stop in that time, taking advantage of a rest area to relieve themselves and stretch their legs. The mood had been up. More sing-alongs, more ideas of where they'd go and what they'd do when they got there.

So, when Nia started to groan, bracing her hands against her knees, Jamie knew something was up.

"You okay?" he asked.

Her eyes rolled before she squeezed them shut, breathing quickly in and out through her nose. "No," she said. Then her cheeks bulged, and her throat gave a lurch. "Pull over, please!"

Jamie made certain there was no one behind them—and there wasn't, just as there hadn't been for most of the trip down Route Thirteen—then pulled the Aspen over just as Nia threw off her seatbelt. She had the door open and was out of the car before he could even put it in park. When he cut the engine, her composure broke and she vomited.

Jamie got out and made his way around to her, sparing a glance at the flanks of pine surrounding them on either side of the road. Some bird cawed from atop all the green, and the faint trickle of a nearby stream could just barely be heard beneath that. It would've been a pleasant enough scene, under different circumstances.

But as Nia retched again, with force, the tranquility was lost.

Jamie paused a couple steps behind her, wanting to comfort her and give her some space at the same time. His own stomach remained steadfast as he saw the muck that was making its way out of her—the snacks she'd eaten here and there today, or what remained.

"It's okay, baby," he cooed. "Just let it out. Take deep breaths when you can."

She let loose again, then righted herself some, spitting and catching her breath. He eased on up to her and set a hand to her back, ready to hold her up if she started to get lightheaded. After another moment of catching her bearings, Nia turned about, revolving slowly, eyes down. She looked embarrassed, or maybe she was still holding back whatever was wrestling in her stomach.

"You okay?"

"Yeah," she said weakly. "Better, at least."

"Seemed kind of sudden."

She shook her head. "Started feeling sick a little bit ago."

Jamie tried to sound caring, not demeaning. "You should have told me."

"Sorry." She reached out a hand to him as they made their way back to the car. "Hoped it would pass."

"Nothing to be sorry about. Here we go, sweet stuff."

He helped her ease in before he got back behind the wheel. He shut the door, and they sat there for a moment, relaxing.

"Feeling better?" he asked.

She gave the smallest of reassuring smiles. "Yeah. My stomach's settled."

"What do you think brought it on? You been feeling sick at all before now?"

Nia shook her head and set her eyes to the glove compartment, clearing her throat and staying quiet. Jamie wasn't sure he believed her.

Maybe it's nerves. Maybe she's getting doubts and the pressure of this whole thing of ours is literally making her sick to her stomach. Maybe we were wrong, after all.

But he didn't want to believe that. Couldn't believe that.

"Maybe it was the fast food from yesterday?" But he shook his head as soon as he said it. "I haven't been feeling bad though, and we had the same thing."

Nia shrugged after another moment of mulling things over. "Well, I used to get some motion sickness in the car when I was younger. Sometimes it was pretty bad. But I haven't had that problem for a long time..."

Jamie thought it over. "Yeah, maybe. We can stop at a pharmacy sometime. See if we find anything for that, just in case. You feel good enough to keep going?"

Nia nodded, but didn't seem very certain. She still looked dazed and worn out, leaning against the passenger door.

Jamie thought about the most recent miles of their journey, and what to do next. The last town they'd passed through had been a good forty miles back. They'd gone past a spot for a hiking trail just a short while ago, a place called Devil's Ladder, but there hadn't been very many other turn-offs or signs of civilization other than that. They seemed to be out in the sticks. Plenty of niches in the woods where they could pull off into and rest, but he wasn't sure that's what they needed right now.

"How about we drive a little bit further?" Jamie suggested. "Until we find a town, or a restaurant or something. Somewhere we can go into, rest for a bit. Maybe get something to drink and something to eat, if you feel like it? Then see what you feel like doing from there?"

Nia eased back into her seat, seeming more composed now. "Sure. Sounds good."

"You sure you're okay?"

"Yep. I'm good."

"Because if you hurl on me, I'll take it personally."

Nia narrowed her eyes at him as he buckled back up. Then they were back to it.

It seemed that fate was on their side, because it wasn't very long before an old sign rose up and over the road ahead.

WHISKEY PETE'S

"Here we go," Jamie said, smacking the wheel. "Looks like we're in business."

Although he wasn't sure if the same could be said for the establishment that came into view. As the road curved into a slight bend, Whiskey Pete's presented itself with all the fanfare of a blown raspberry. It was, in a sense of character, just there. Functional, at best. A rat trap, at worst. The main building—the bar area—was attached to a modest storefront, and both looked like they'd seen better days, sometime in the previous century. A few gas pumps sat out front, looking equally antiquated. And round the bar's back was a two-story motel, with a swath of dense forest behind it. Jamie couldn't speak for the parking of the motel area, as it was out of sight, but the gravel lot of the store and bar was devoid of vehicles.

But their lights were on, and so long as they were serving, the place would suit their needs well enough.

"Be careful parking," Nia said, as he pulled into the lot. She looked and sounded like she was coming around from her nausea. "Wouldn't want to ding anybody."

Jamie grinned at her as he parked. As they got out, he rushed around and kept to Nia's side, in case the nausea returned or she got dizzy.

The air in Whiskey Pete's was musty and heavy, clinging and hanging over the couple the moment they entered the joint. Their eyes had to adjust to the dimness of the place, the lighting subpar and casting the room in a haze. It was as modest within as it was without—a small collection of booths and a suitable stretch of bar, a jukebox playing something by Credence Clearwater Revival, if Jamie's ear for music served him right. Stuffed animal heads on the walls, pool table, restrooms near the back. And not much else. A cozy kind of place, to a certain sort.

Contrary to what the bare lot indicated, there were a few people already inside. A bartender, wiping some glasses at his station; a young man, circling about the pool table and gauging his next shot; and a much older, hunched gentleman sitting and sipping at the bar. Perhaps their cars were parked somewhere around back.

The guy playing pool was the first to acknowledge them. He turned a handsome smile up at them as he paused at a corner, taking the couple in a moment before leaning over and sending the cue ball bouncing.

Jamie and Nia trudged up to the bar, Nia crossing her arms over her stomach and hunching her shoulders in what Jamie took to be a show of uncertainty. He couldn't blame her. The place didn't exactly exude an open arms kind of feel.

They stepped up to the bartender, who kept his attention on his glasses. He was a bulky fellow, sporting the kind of heft a retired wrestler or linebacker might have, and was decked out in denim.

"Hey," Jamie said, easing a hand up to the bar and offering a smile.

It took a moment for the bartender to acknowledge them, and when he did, the look he gave was one of pure indifference. His eyes, oddly enough, were different colors—one green, one blue. It was an outstanding trait that didn't gel with his working stiff, salt-of-the-earth look.

"Could we get a couple of drinks, please? I'd like a soda. Coke, if you have it. Babe?"

Nia shrugged. "The same, I guess."

The bartender turned those mismatched eyes to her, giving her a look-over. They hovered on her face for a minute, then turned down to where her arms were crossed over her stomach. His hands slowed, the glass and washcloth in them going still. He stood, absolutely still, his focus on Nia's abdomen. Then, just when it was about to go from odd to awkward, he glanced back down and went back to his work with a grunt.

"Anything else?"

"Uh, you serve food?"

"I don't want anything," Nia added, rather quickly. She shuffled her feet, glancing down as Jamie reconsidered.

"In that case, I think we're good," Jamie said, getting out his billfold and handing over some cash. "Just the drinks, please."

The bartender scooped up the money and popped open the nearby register, giving back the change. "Be right up," he grumbled.

The pair moved over to a booth, sitting across from each other, Jamie facing the bar and Nia the door. Jamie leaned over the table and whispered: "You okay?"

Nia gave a slight shake of her head, eyes scanning the nooks and crannies of the joint. "This place is kind of creeping me out. Feels like... I don't know, like the air is pressing in on me. Sort of claustrophobic."

She glanced over her shoulder and was surprised to see the old man at the bar had half-turned about, sunken eyes set on her. But he wasn't looking out of curiosity, as one stranger regards another. He was glaring, mouth turned down in a scornful frown, nostrils flaring.

Then he turned back around, shaking his cotton-top head and mumbling something. It sounded like: "General Forrest would roll over in his grave."

Nia turned back to Jamie. "And the people are *so* pleasant."

Jamie reached a hand across to hers, palm-to-palm. "We'll only stay long enough to finish our drinks and give us time to relax."

Nia raised her eyebrows in doubt. But if she was about to say anything else, it stayed put as the bartender lumbered into view. He set their sodas down and turned right back about.

"Thank you," Jamie called to his back. The bartender simply grunted and moved back behind the bar.

The couple started sipping at their drinks, each crinkling their noses at the initial taste. If it was Coke, it didn't taste like it. Watery as hell and flat. Still, they drank, Nia working hers over quicker than Jamie.

They sat for a few minutes, quietly drinking as the jukebox played on, tunes punctuated now and again by the smacking and sinking of balls at the pool table. Occasionally, one of them would glance up and over to the pool player and realize he was returning the look, showing them that same smile every time. Jamie would give a nod in acknowledgement; Nia would just turn back around, focusing on her glass again.

A while later, Jamie felt nature calling and slipped out of the booth. "Need to take care of business."

"Hurry back," Nia said quietly.

Jamie gave her a playful salute and made for the restroom. After a cautious knock on the men's door, he slipped inside, flicking on the nearby light. The joint's modesty carried over to the restroom; it was small and cramped, with a single toilet, a crud-covered sink and mirror, and a full wastebasket in the corner. Each wall was covered in a combination of filthy smudges and the classic latrinalia.

He stepped up to the porcelain and started going with the flow, looking over the chicken scratch on the walls as he went. Most messages he couldn't make out, save for one scrawled in large, crooked print over the toilet.

Pete's got his eye on you.

Unimpressed with the attempt at roadside creepiness, Jamie zipped up and washed his hands. As he stepped back out and headed for their booth, the old man at the bar turned about, lifting a long-nailed hand in admonishment.

"I didn't fight in the War of Northern Aggression to see such pairings, boy!" he chastised. "You ought to know better and stick to your own!"

Jamie's disbelief must have been evident as he stared at the old man, processing what he was getting at. Even if this guy was senile enough to believe he'd been a part of the Civil War, Jamie didn't have to put up with the bullshit he was selling.

"Just mind your beer and your own business, sir," Jamie said, trying to keep an even tone. The old man sneered at him, but turned away all the same, and Jamie stomped back to the booth.

"What did that guy say to you?" Nia asked, looking concerned.

"Nothing. Just bragging about a date he had with Cleopatra."

Nia grinned around her glass as she took another drink, and Jamie looked down to the tabletop. They kept on nursing their drinks as *Take It Easy* by The Eagles started playing, filling Whiskey Pete's with calming, soft rock vibes.

Eventually, the jukebox went quiet, and so did the sounds at the pool table. The pool player stepped up to their booth, balancing his cue across his shoulders and draping his arms over each end. He had the air of a Roadhouse extra about him, standing there in his cowboy boots, tight jeans, and plain white t-shirt. He must have been in his mid-twenties, though the fluff on his chin and cheeks looked like it belonged on a younger sort who'd just stepped into puberty.

Up close, his sheen of handsomeness lost its luster; in truth, he was somewhat dopey looking, his dark hair fine and hanging loosely about, his teeth yellowed and crooked.

"Hi there," he said, pleasantly enough.

Jamie returned the greeting, and Nia offered an obliging half-smile.

"I'm Joel. Pleased to meet ya."

"Same," Jamie said, not feeling inclined to give him their names in return. Something about the guy led him to believe this conversation was going to be an awkward one. He could feel it.

Joel looked them both over, but his gaze seemed to linger on Nia for a second or two longer. "Where do you and this pretty little miss hail from, if ya don't mind me asking?"

"Oregon," Jamie said, the politeness of his smile becoming forced. "Up north."

"And where ya planning on heading off to?"

"Oh, nowhere in particular. Just driving around, seeing the country, what it has to offer."

Joel nodded knowingly. "Sort of a vacation, huh?"

Jamie shrugged. "Something like that."

Joel gave an "mm-hmm" of appreciation and looked back over to Nia. "Fine company to be on vacation with."

Jamie sighed and glanced at Nia. They shared a look that said, *Can you believe this creep?* before Jamie worked up a response. "So, are you from around here? Or are you just passing through too?"

Joel turned back to him with a bitter laugh. "Naw, I stick to these parts." His voice picked up cheer as he faced the bar and spoke louder. "After all, someone has to make this place a little bit interesting!"

The bartender didn't bother to respond, his attention on the contents of the register, and the old man just flicked a bony hand up in dismissal, without turning around.

Joel deflated a tad at their indifference, but managed to keep some mirth in his tone. "Stubborn bastards would be lost without me." Then, to Nia: "I'm the only one around here who knows how to have any real fun."

The conversation faded out after that, but Joel kept his eyes on Nia while she looked down at the table, squirming ever so slightly in her seat. Jamie noticed it and knew he had to act. "Well, it was nice talking to y—"

"You two an item?" Joel cut in, eyes narrowing at them in curiosity.

"Yes," Jamie answered. His smile had finally gone away. "Yes, we are."

"Shame," Joel sighed, shaking his head and focusing on Nia again. "What I wouldn't give to know a sweet, young thing like you a little better. And if only ya knew me a little better too! Might just be able to tempt ya away from your strapping sweetie-pie here." Then, towards the bar: "I've wooed more than a couple of fine girlies in my time, haven't I, fellas?"

The bartender finally looked up, sneering and shouting: "JOEL, SHUT YOUR GODDAMN HOLE!"

Joel shifted his feet, looking wounded. Taking advantage of his silence, Jamie spoke up. "Look, man, we'd like to be left alone now. Okay?"

The cue slipped from Joel's shoulders as he turned around, holding the stick at his side. "I'm just trying to be friendly," he said to Jamie matter-of-factly. Then, back to Nia: "Hell, you can't blame me. Never had a chance to be...friendly...with a colored girl before. I'm curious what it's like."

Nia looked up at him in disgust, and he grinned back at her. As Jamie shot up out of his seat, Joel turned the grin on him.

"Fuck off, asshole," Jamie grumbled. His jaw went rigid, and his fists clenched at his sides as he stared Joel down. But the crude creep rose to the challenge.

"And what'll you do if I don't, hero?"

"I'll shove that cue down your throat and make you swallow every one of those crooked fucking teeth!"

Joel's show of mockery crumbled after that, and he glared at Jamie with utter hatred. He made to step forward, and Jamie the same, but Nia was quicker than both. She slipped out of the booth and got between them, grabbing hold of Jamie's arm and trying to drag him towards the door. "Let's go, Jamie!" she begged. "Let's just go!"

He struggled against her for a moment, but slowly gave in, walking backwards and keeping Joel in his sights. Joel, meanwhile, stayed put, wringing his pool cue in his hands and watching them go.

"Drive safe, shithead!" he hollered as they went out the door.

They got back into their car in silence. Jamie broke it when he slammed his door shut and smacked the steering wheel. "Asswipe!"

Nia sighed and rubbed her temples as Jamie sat there a moment longer, letting his anger die out. "I'm sorry," he eventually said. "I'm sorry for suggesting we stop here and I'm sorry for what he said to you."

"It's okay." She set to putting her seatbelt back on, eyes downcast. "Let's just forget about it and move on."

Jamie cocked his head and looked out the window, up to the sky above. Only a few golden streaks still arced across the cloudy heavens; night was setting in, and it would be dark within the hour. "Do you want to stay at the motel around back tonight?"

"No," Nia said, with certainty. "I don't want to be around this place or these people any longer."

Jamie had to agree with her, and he checked the gas gauge after starting the car up. They'd refilled the tank in the last town they'd passed through, and they were still good for a fair stretch of travel. The trouble was, he didn't much feel like being on the road anymore tonight.

"How about we double back?" he suggested. "I saw plenty of places around that 'Devil's Ladder' turn-off where we could pull off into the woods. Call it an early night and sleep in the car again?"

Nia nodded. "Works for me."

Jamie resisted the urge to flip off Whiskey Pete's as he put the car in reverse, opting instead to just get away from the place as quickly as he could. They got back on the road and gratefully left the joint behind, retracing the miles back to Devil's Ladder. They went past the trail's parking area once more, and after going a little further, Jamie pulled off and slipped the Aspen into a suitable niche in the woods, guiding the car along and bringing it to rest far enough into the trees that they'd be out of sight from the road.

He shut the car off and leaned back. "How about you take the back-seat tonight?"

Nia nodded appreciatively and got out, slipping into the back and resting herself against the opposite door, facing Jamie. She set her hand over the front seat, and he took it in his.

"Sorry again for what happened back there. You feeling any better, at least?"

She gave him a tired smile. "Don't worry about it. That's the beauty of being on the road. You can drive away from anything. And yeah, I'm feeling better."

"I love you, you know."

"Yup. I love you too."

With that, the mood started to change, and they chatted and laughed well past nightfall before sprawling out and wishing each other good night.

It was the chill that brought Jamie out of sleep. A breeze wafted over his skin and nudged him awake.

He sat up, rubbing his eyes, and looked for the chill's source. It came from the open back passenger door of the car.

Nia was nowhere in sight.

"Nia?" he called out, glancing out the windows and into the night. But whichever way he looked, she was nowhere to be found. Had she got-ten out to go to the bathroom?

Concern beat back his lingering weariness, and Jamie groaned as he got out of the car.

"Nia?" he called again, more forcefully this time.

Still no answer. Peer as he did into the trees and around the nearby bushes, he couldn't spot her. That was when the fear really set in.

"Nia?"

Why wasn't she answering? How could she have gotten so far away from the car that she couldn't hear him?

He gave another call and then listened to the night, hearing nothing but the wind in the pines and the murmur of insects. Then, muffled yet discernible, he heard a woman's cry of fear, somewhere off in the distance.

"Nia, I'm coming!" Jamie shouted, and he hauled ass into the woods without a second thought, trying to pinpoint where the call had come from.

His heart pounded in his chest as he ran, hitching worrisome breaths with every step. The woods stretched on before him. She could have been anywhere out there, hurt and lost and needing him. Another quick and wordless call came from somewhere ahead and to the right, and he followed it. He kept calling for her, hoping for a clarification of direction, but all he ever got back was a sporadic shout, steadily growing louder.

He went deeper into the woods, the road and the Aspen now completely out of sight behind him, and he kept on going. The darkness played tricks on his troubled mind, casting shadows that moved and distracted, repeatedly making him question if that might have been Nia stumbling around just ahead of him or another trick of the light.

As he went, the trees he passed seemed to become more gnarled, more ancient, stretching up high like silent, black giants, mocking the fearful little man scurrying about their feet. Here and there, marring their bark, were unsightly scratches made by some great animal's massive claws. Then there were the noises that started to strike up: grunts and chattering that came scattered from the woods, calls of creatures he couldn't place, as though some strange menagerie lay just out of sight, stirred to action by his intrusive presence. In his ears, the sounds mocked him.

Then another cry came—one of great, drawn out agony—and it made Jamie's blood run cold to hear it.

"Nia!"

He made for the sound, which came from a few yards ahead, where the flickering light of fires could be seen through the trees. As he drew closer, the flames grew more pronounced, and he came to realize that they were torches, and they were being held by darkly clothed figures.

Launching himself into a small clearing, Jamie came across a scene that made him stop short.

Before him were a dozen or so people, dressed in black robes that caught and reflected the moonlight and the glow of their torches. They stood in a circular pattern with their arms aloft, chanting words that he couldn't make out, faces hidden beneath the hoods draped over their heads. Another of their number kneeled in their center, hands working at something that lay stretched out before them.

That something was Nia, lying still upon the ground, lips parted, eyes open, unblinking. Unfeeling. Her shirt had been pulled up, her belly exposed and cut wide open, blood pouring from the wound as the robed person hanging over her rooted through her stomach. The ceremonial knife they had used to kill her lay in the dirt beside her head.

Tears came to Jamie's eyes. Try as he might, he could neither reconcile nor bring reason to the horrific sight before him. His chest seemed to cave in of its own accord as grief befell him, and he struggled to breathe under the terrible pressure.

Then, rooted in his terror, he watched as the robed figure pulled their hands out of Nia, tearing away something that had been inside her. They held it aloft in twisted reverence, cradling it in their palm for the gathering to see.

At first, it looked like an organ of some sort, soaked in scarlet and bending like a mass of tissue in the killer's hands. But it had a distinct shape to it: small and curved, with tiny nubs sticking out of the main mass, and a pronounced swelling at its top. Almost like a...

As realization dawned on him, Jamie's lips pulled back in a mixture of rage and disgust. His tears flowed freely as he screamed out his awful sorrow, and his body shook from loss.

As determination came back to his limbs, he rushed forward, charging at the chanting congregation with murder in his heart.

The robed figures turned on him as he rushed the first of them, flinging a fist that cracked into the person's skull, sending them to the ground. As he made for the next in line, two others darted forward, hands reaching out to restrain him. He put up a fight to stay out of their clutches, but despite his efforts, his flailing arms and legs were caught, and he was brought to ground by the strange group.

They held him fast, despite his thrashing and his curses, and made way for the leader of the ritual, who approached with the knife in their bloodied hand.

Jamie spat and struggled as the figure kneeled beside him, but he couldn't stop the blade from piercing his chest. Pain followed, and his body went stiff all over. As he choked on his agony, as his vision started to swim, the robed figures let him go and rose to their feet, parting and swaying as they took up their chanting once more.

Jamie gasped for air as he turned his head, looking over to where Nia lay. A memory played out in his mind, of lying on the ground beside her on one of their secret evenings, laughing together and staring up at the stars, of talking about their great escape and what all could lie ahead of them when they were finally together, on their own and free.

He remembered her smile, which he'd loved so much.

And as he took his last breath, he hoped that he might see it again sometime, in a kinder world.

CRUEL
By Joshua D. Taylor

Susan,

I once said that you were the cruelest person I had ever met. I take that back. I did not know true cruelty. Now I do. Please don't come looking for me. For your own sake.

M.

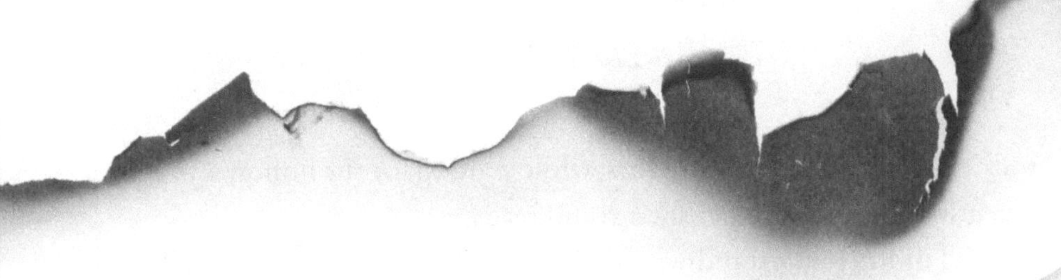

DAVE AND JILLIAN
BY JOSHUA D. TAYLOR

"A squid wank?" Joel said, crooked toothed grin accompanying his always cheerful demeanor. "You know, I used to know a girl who'd sneak out to her neighbor's horse stable at night, to spend some quality time with their prize-winning stallion. If you know what I mean?"

Con, standing stiff like a totem pole in his usual spot behind the bar, not wiped down since the day Whiskey Pete's opened, only rolled his eyes. Melvin—a withered, spindly old man with long, white hair, sitting on a bar stool at the far end of the small room—cackled. David and Jillian, sitting at the table Joel was leaning over, looked horrified.

"N-no," Dave said. "A Squiddlewonk. It's kinda like Bigfoot, but with a big bobble head, large, reflective eyes like an owl, and four long bear claws."

Joel nodded like he actually gave a damn, which he didn't, and licked his cracked lips, trying to stare down Jill's sweater. "You know what, that critter looks just like P—"

"JOEL, SHUT YOUR GODDAMN HOLE!" Con bellowed, from behind the bar.

Joel took a sip from a random, half-full beer and tried to act casual.

Jill looked away and smoothed out the map that she and Dave had spread on their tiny, round table. It was difficult, since at least one of the table legs was missing a foot, so every time she tried to fix the map the table rocked, spilling their drinks. This, while waiting for the hollow-eyed motel receptionist, Stacey, to get their room ready.

Jill didn't understand why she had to get the room ready at all. There didn't seem to be anyone else staying at the place.

"And y'all are gonna go looking around our woods for 'em?" Joel asked.

Jill took notice of his use of the phrase 'our woods'.

Dave didn't. He sipped his terrible, watered-down beer, looked around at the other patrons, and launched into his practiced spiel. "Well, these types of old-growth forests are the perfect habitat for the Squiddlewonk." He made a sweeping gesture at the map on the table. "The elevation and climate are just right. It's very shy, so these types of remote areas are ideal."

"What are ya gonna do if y'all find it?" Joel asked, probing his ear with his pool cue.

"Well, we probably won't find it," Jill said. "No one ever really finds cryptids. But we'll talk about the adventure on our podcast 'Squatching the Country with Dave and Jill'."

"Yeah, we've looked for El Chupacabra in New Mexico, Montana Deathworm, and even the Reverse Chicken of Monterie," Dave added. "Now we're out here looking for the melancholy Squiddlewonk."

"Podcast?" Con grunted, barely moving his mouth.

"Oh, it's like a radio show for the internet," Jill said. Everyone in the room looked confused. "You guys know about the internet, right?"

Dave laughed uncomfortably. "She's joking."

No one else laughed.

Joel adjusted his crotch, then leaned back against the pool table. "So, you're just gonna go out in the deep, dark woods and look for some kinda critter that you don't really expect to find?"

"Pretty much," Dave smiled.

"Yep," Jill conceded.

"No offense, but that has to be the dumbest thing I ever heard," Joel said.

Con nodded.

"Definitely," Melvin said, brushing his long, white hair off his shoulders with some equally long fingernails.

"Thanks for the input, guys," Jill said dryly. "We'll take it under advisement."

"How did you find us?" Melvin asked.

"Find you?" Jill asked.

"Pete's," he clarified.

"Well, we were on our way up to Devil's Ladder when we saw the sign and thought we'd stop and look around," David said, getting visibly excited. "Turns out this is the perfect spot."

"Lucky us," Joel said, with a smile that sent shivers down Jill's spine. Melvin giggled into his shot glass.

"Yeah," Jill said, looking around. "Strange how this place isn't on any map, and when we asked in Chevron if there was anywhere to stay along the way, no one mentioned Pete's. Any idea why that would be?"

She looked at every person in the room in turn. Con just grunted.

"Them city folk think they're better than us," Joel said.

"City folk?" Jill asked.

Chevron was barely a town. More of a hamlet. Dave started to look uncomfortable. He never was very good at confrontations.

"You sure do ask a lot of questions, girly," Melvin wheezed, in a long, slow Southern drawl that Jill and Dave had to focus on to understand.

Dave knew what was coming before it happened. In their adventures around the country Jill had been talked down to by enough dirty, old men and white trash shitkickers that she went straight berserker at the slightest hint of disrespect. Dave understood how she felt. He just wished she'd pick her battles.

"Excuse me?" Jill said, standing up with enough force to knock her chair over.

Dave leapt to his feet to step between them. Joel smiled a wicked grin, gripping his pool cue hard enough to turn his knuckles white. Con just refolded his arms.

"Oow, this one's got fire in her loins," Melvin cackled.

Jill pushed Dave aside, ignoring his weak-willed objections. The slam of the door interrupted the brewing conflict. Everyone's head turned, breaking the moment's tension. Stacey stood there. Without a coat.

Jill had found the young woman unsettling from the moment they met her, sitting behind the desk in the motel office. It was as if the emptiness of her eyes betrayed an emptiness inside her. Uncanny valley went hand-in-hand with cryptid research, but Jill had never seen so textbook a case as in Stacey. She looked like a mannequin had come to life, but didn't really know how to be human.

"Room's ready," she said, seemingly oblivious to the tension she had walked in on.

"Great," Jill said, folding up the map and shoving it into her oversized travel backpack. "Get the rest of the bags."

She nudged Dave, who was staring at Stacey, who didn't seem to notice the attention. Dave picked up the backpacks, dropped a few dollars on the table, and followed Jill. Stacey let the door slam behind her before Jill could reach it. Jill threw the door open hard enough to dent the wall.

Gravel crunched under their feet as they followed the other woman across the parking lot to the two-story strip of motel rooms. Only three or four rooms had working lights out front, and all the forecourt lights seemed to be out. The darkness made the quick walk seem to drag on. Dave's beat-up, old Corolla still sat where he'd left it, outside the motel office. A dull, yellow light shone through broken mini-blinds.

Stacey stared off into the darkness when they finally caught up with her on the first floor in front of an unlabeled room, the number having long-since fallen from the door. It was sandwiched between rooms six and eight. Stacey stood unresponsive for a long moment, looking off like there was something on the horizon only she could see. Dave made a very obvious attempt not to stare at her breasts. It was so cold that they could see their breath, except for Stacey's.

The moment dragged on for so long that Jill was about to turn around to see what she was staring at. Then with a sudden motion, Stacey punched her hand out. Both Dave and Stacey flinched, almost screamed.

Jill wondered if the strung-out looking woman was about to attack them until she realized that a room key dangled from Stacey's clenched fist. Before Jill could take it, Dave slipped his hand around Stacey's and took the key, spending far too much time touching her. Jill rolled her eyes. The action seemed to have reawakened Stacey, who moved out of the way so they could unlock the door.

She stood aside while Dave unlocked the door, then began to bring in the remainder of their gear.

"Thanks," he said to Stacey, who simply stared off.

Jill puffed herself up, trying to fight off the winter cold, and headed for the room. As she was about to step inside and slam the door in the face of the braless zombie innkeeper, Stacey's hand shot out again, grabbing her by the wrist. Stacey's hand wasn't ice-cold like it should have been, but warm and clammy. Uncomfortably so.

This time, Jill did scream. Dave spun around, dropping his luggage, but unsure of what to do. Jill tried to pull away, but Stacey held tight. Despite her iron grip, Stacey's thumb caressed Jill's skin with tender affection.

"Let me go!" Jill demanded.

"You have nice skin."

"Um, thanks, I moisturize."

Jill finally managed to pull her hand away and stumbled backward into the room, almost falling over. Now the door was out of reach. She stepped forward and grabbed the door, *then* slammed it in the receptionist's face. She locked it and put a chair under the handle. They watched as Stacey's shadow walked away on the other side of the faded, puke-green curtains.

"What a fucking weirdo," Jill said, wrapping her arms around herself. She could still feel Stacey's hand on her wrist. Dave stood by the twin beds, searching for a phone charger in his backpack, trying to pretend like everything was fine.

"Uh, at least she said you have nice skin."

Jill spun on her heels, taking in the room for the first time. The cracked seashell wall sconce, peeling floral wallpaper, and carpet worn so thin that subfloor was almost visible did nothing to improve her mood.

"Well, you can go and fuck her if you like. I know you have a thing for redheads."

Dave winced. "You know I would never do that. Besides, I have three more months left on spiritual cleanse and I won't be swayed by the temptations of the flesh."

"Oh yeah, that's not what you told those twins in Houston."

Dave flushed red. "That...that was different. We were on the same path of enlightenment," he muttered.

Jill bit her tongue and decided not to tell him that the only path he'd been on with those two was a path to the free clinic to get penicillin. She was glad she and Dave had never been a couple. It had been a close call, but she had definitely dodged a bullet. He was good company, if a doofus, and fiercely dedicated to their ridiculous podcast. But he was too gullible, too much of a pushover, to be a romantic partner.

She picked up her backpack and began to empty it on the other bed. The sheets were not so much a single color but a collage of different faded stains. They were so thin that Jill could see the protruding bed springs through them. "If I get bed bugs, I'm leaving you in the woods."

"Come on," Dave said. "I know it's a little outdated, but let's try to make the best of it. I think we have a real chance of finding evidence of the Squiddlewonk tomorrow."

She peeked inside the chipped ice bucket to find a dead cockroach, legs up. "David, this place was outdated when our parents were our age."

"Well, let's just get to sleep. We're going to need to be well-rested for tomorrow. Those woods look dense."

Before Jill could tell him that he was the only dense thing around there, a strange sound reverberated through the room, shaking the clouded, single-pane window.

"Hoot-Hoot-Hoot-HOOOOOOOOOONK!"

The two friends spun around in opposite directions, looking about wildly. "What the hell was that?" Jill asked.

Dave gave her a puzzled look, excitement clearly written on his face. "It's a Squiddlewonk call. This is fantastic. I wish I'd brought the recording equipment in from the car."

"That's not at all what Indrid Cold said they sounded like."

Dave's face fell. "Well, it sort of is. I mean, it could be a regional variant."

Jill thought it sounded more like two drunken farm animals of different species trying to have sex, but she did not have the energy left to crush Dave's hope.

"Sure, we'll check it out in the morning," she said, turning off the light.

Early the next morning they packed up their hiking gear and headed into the forest that surrounded Whiskey Pete's and blanketed the surrounding countryside. Jill had refused to go back into the bar or the small convenience store, so they ate a meager breakfast of granola bars and smoked half a joint split between the two of them.

The cold morning sky was clear and merciless. Dave squinted in the bright light as Jill donned a pair of aviator sunglasses that she'd stolen from an ex-boyfriend. The ground was frozen beneath their feet. He kicked at it.

"This is gonna make it impossible to find fresh tracks. Let's hope we find some scat."

"Yes, let's hope for scat," Jill said, not caring if Dave noticed the edge in her voice or not.

She had suddenly found herself distracted by the tree line they were dutifully marching toward. They felt less like a couple of hikers going to stumble around in woods for a few hours and more like the conquistadors who set out to explore the Amazon basin, thinking they knew the score because they came from 'civilization'. But in the end, they were woefully under-prepared for what they were about to undertake. She felt like that, minus the genocide of the indigenous peoples.

She caught Dave staring as well. The night before, it had been so dark all they could see were trunks of giant trees in the Corolla's single, functioning headlight. Now the treetops seemed to reach almost to the sky, naked branches like thousands of skeletonized hands raised in prayer. It made them feel small, insignificant, which was a feeling both of them were familiar with being indie podcasters.

Dave unconsciously tightened the straps on his backpack in response to an unexplained feeling of vulnerability. Jill fidgeted.

Despite the blinding sunlight and bare treetops, the understory was as dark as night. Somehow all the light and sound were swallowed up by the forest floor, leaving it cold, dark and silent, like the vacuum of space. Jill did not find this reassuring, but it still seemed better than hanging around the motel with its doll-eyed manager and collection of creepy bar flies.

"Let's go," she said, bumping Dave with her shoulder before heading for the tree line.

He stumbled a step, then followed. They only progressed a dozen feet before they stopped again, this time at the very edge of the forest. The outskirts stretched out left and right to form a wall. They stared down at a deer skull sticking out of the frozen ground. Jill wouldn't have been surprised if it started talking to them.

It didn't, but Jill could imagine it quoting the gate to Hell in Dante's Inferno—'Abandon all hope, ye who enter here'.

"I mean, deer die all the time, right?" Dave asked.

"Sure," Jill said.

Dave stepped over the skull, maneuvering between the brambles that grew at the edge of the forest as they tugged at his clothes. Without a word, Jill followed suit, then they disappeared into the darkness, leaving only the sound of breaking branches.

As the forest enveloped them like a fish swallowing worms, Jill wondered how she ended up here, chasing down off-brand Bigfoot behind a redneck bar for a podcast no one listened to with a guy she'd met at the Skunk Ape convention. Then she remembered driving through the rain, sudden impact, the blood, fleeing the scene, leaving town and changing her name. She reminded herself that things could be worse.

They were only a few feet into the forest when they glanced back to find they could no longer see Whiskey Pete's. Everything outside the forest was obscured by the trees and the underbrush. It was like they had stepped into another world.

"I wish we'd brought some glow sticks," Dave said.

"Or flashlights," Jill muttered.

They struggled through the forest until they found a game trail of mostly cleared bushes and went with the path of least resistance. The interior of the forest was still, even for the daytime. Jill kept looking up through the branches to remind herself that the sun was out, but even the sky above seemed to have darkened.

Everything looked the same, barren tree trunks and leafless bushes. It felt like they were trudging across the frozen dirt and rocks for hours, but whenever Jill looked at her watch, only a few minutes had passed. The same landscape continuing to pass by over and over caused her to lose track of time. She was getting ready to tap Dave on the shoulder and call the whole thing off. They could go back to the sleazy motel, get their stuff, then drive the rest of the way up to the Devil's Ladder and look around there.

Then she heard Dave take a sudden breath. Jill was certain that he must have stumbled upon a dead body. "What is it?" she asked, trying to look over his shoulder.

He leaned over and began to inspect the trunk of a tree. Jill let out a sigh of frustration.

"It's just a tree, Dave. The same as every other tree in the dark, freezing forest."

"No, no, Jillie, look at this," he said.

His excited toddler voice worked on her every time. He stepped aside, moving off the trail to make room for her. A stray beam of sunlight managed to make its way to the forest floor and illuminated a few feet of trunk. The texture of the bark seemed odd. Its regular pattern was disrupted by several horizontal bands. There were four of them, lighter in color than the bark and evenly spaced.

"Okay, what am I looking at?" she asked. Her interest was piqued, but her patience was still running short.

"Step back," Dave said, self-satisfaction saturating each word.

Jill did as instructed, but the heel of her hiking boot caught on a tree root. She fell, arms flailing. Before the back of her head hit the frozen forest floor, Dave's arms scooped up under her armpits and caught her.

"Crap!" she shouted.

"I got you. You're okay."

She kept struggling for a moment, before she realized she was safe. Her breath came in short, ragged puffs. Jill stood fully upright again with Dave's help. She glanced down at the ground, searching for the offending root, but the forest floor was covered in too many leaves.

"That was close," Dave said. "I don't know what we would have done if I'd have had to carry you out of here."

Jill glared at him. "Cause I'm fat?" she spat, even though she knew she barely weighed more than a hundred pounds.

"No, cause I have the upper body strength of a toddler."

He pretended to flex. Jill couldn't help but laugh. Dave's sense of humor was simple, but his heart was in the right place. With his mission of levity accomplished, Dave pointed back to the tree.

"Claw marks," he said.

Jill's eyebrows shot up her forehead. Sure enough, the lighter horizontal marks were gouges in the wood. They went clear through the bark into the lighter-colored wood underneath.

She adjusted her backpack, which had shifted when she tripped. "Are you sure it's not from a bear? Are there even bears around here?"

She looked around, concerned. The forest had seemed so dead from the moment they set foot in it that it had never occurred to her there might be dangerous animals.

"No way. Look at these claw marks," he said, spreading out his fingers and holding his hand in front of the markings. Each mark was at least eight inches apart. "These are way bigger than any bear."

"That's not comforting. And you didn't answer my other question."

Dave just shrugged. "Let me get some pictures, and then we'll keep moving. I bet we're getting close."

He took out his camera and began snapping photos from different angles, several with his hand for scale. Jill kept scanning the forest around them, only able to see a short distance through the darkness and encroaching tree trunks. It seemed like the further they went, the closer together the trees became.

There was nowhere for them to walk except along the trail. The forest had become so tight. It felt like they were being herded down a cattle chute to the killing floor. It was too convenient that they had found the exact evidence they were looking for along the only path. Perhaps the Squiddle-wonk used the trails too. The idea of a creature with those claws hurtling down the trail at them made her sweat under her coat and hat.

"Maybe we should just head back, this is more evidence than we usually get." At this point, bizarre sexual harassment from Stacey seemed downright quaint.

"No, come on!" he said, grabbing her arm to pull her forward.

So, they went further into the forest, winding around fallen trees and climbing rocky slopes. The day never seemed to warm up below the canopy and frost clung to leaves and trunks, even at midday. Dave's enthusiasm kept them chugging along for a while until hunger and cold won out. With sore backs, cold noses and blistered feet they found that they had slowed to a crawl.

"Okay, I guess we should head back and get something to eat," he said. "Maybe we'll see something we missed on the way."

"Which way is back?" Jill asked, looking at the uniform forest that had nothing even resembling a milestone.

"Oh, did you forget to leave a trail of breadcrumbs?" he asked, unable to hide a dopey, ear-to-ear grin.

Jill gave him the most unamused glare she had in her considerable arsenal of facial expressions.

"Okay, okay, that was lame, I admit it," he said. "But seriously, we just turn around and head back. We've been on this same path the whole time. There's nowhere else to go."

"I hope you're right."

Jill began to slowly turn around, joints stiff from late winter cold and the impact of having walked on frozen ground for what felt like hours. The path was too narrow for Dave to pass her, so she took the lead position.

Her body was tired, and her skin ached from the biting chill, but with each step forward the heavy feeling of dread that had blanketed her since she first laid eyes on the forest began to lift.

After exactly three steps, Dave spoke. "Hang on. I have to pee."

"Are you serious? You never drink water."

"I'll just be a second. I'll go behind a tree."

"Well yeah. Not like there's a random port-a-potty out here." She waved her arms at the claustrophobic forest. "And if we come across a lone outhouse, *I'm* not using it."

Dave had already disappeared around a tree trunk that was thicker than a stone column.

"Don't let that thing get frostbite," she called, rubbing her hands together for warmth.

"Jill, come here," he called from behind the tree.

"I don't think so. I haven't fallen for that one since college."

"No, seriously. You have to see this."

She exhaled a cloud of steam that floated off amongst the trees. "Okay, but if your dick is out, I'm gonna spray mace in your urethra."

She stepped gingerly. The memory of what happened last time he showed her something was still fresh in her mind. She stopped dead in her tracks as she rounded the enormous tree trunk and saw Dave standing at the mouth of a hole in the ground large enough to drive a motorcycle into.

"What the hell is that?"

"Squiddlewonk tunnel."

"Do they make tunnels?"

"Looks like it," he said, bending over to peer down the unlit shaft.

There were mounds of dirt on either side of hole, which descended into the earth at a steep angle. Jill could only see a few feet in.

"How do you know it's not a bear den or a sinkhole?" she asked, taking a step back to place a hand on the tree for support. The last thing she wanted was to lose her balance and go tumbling inside.

She pulled her hand away from the bark as she felt something rough and jagged under her palm. She looked at the trunk to see four claw marks above a wet spot where Dave had peed.

"That's how," Dave said, looking back at her.

"Okay." Jill, despite the cold and the possibility of being near a large, undiscovered wild animal, started to get excited. "This is it, isn't it?" Dave was too busy taking pictures to respond. "This is the real deal. Nothing else could have done this."

"This is way better than those guys from Norfolk that found that Big-foot loincloth. We're gonna be famous," he said.

She was elated. All their hard work, driving back and forth across the country chasing footprints and drunken stories, had finally paid off. This was going to hit the online cryptid and paranormal community like a pipebomb. She couldn't wait to leave the forest and return to civilization so they could upload and edit their pictures.

"Okay." Dave stood up. "I got some good photos of the outside of the hole, so let's head back to the room. We'll fetch some lights so we can explore the interior."

Jill's excitement blew away like a cold breeze between the branches. "Oh, hell no! When we get back to the motel, we are getting in the car and driving the fuck away from this god-awful place."

Dave's jaw dropped. He stood up straight and took a deep breath. The freezing January air almost made him cough, but he stifled it. Digging his heels, he opened his mouth when a reverberating bellow erupted from the Squiddlewonk tunnel.

"HOOT-HOOT-HOOT-HOOOOOOOOONK!"

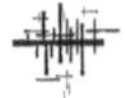

It was so loud Dave could feel his fillings rattle. He was glad that he had just emptied his bladder. Jill clasped her hands to her ears. The bellowing went on, as if they were standing at the end of a great, earthen air horn.

Dave started to open his mouth again, to ask her what to do, but he knew exactly what had to be done. He grabbed Jill's hand and pulled her back to the path. He ran as fast as the small, uneven trail would allow.

The icy air burned his lungs as he felt blisters pop in his boots. He was about to stop and turn back to Jill when he unexpectedly burst through the forest into the empty lot behind the motel. He brought a hand to his face as the bright light stung his eyes.

"Ah, what now?" he shrieked, disoriented.

As his eyes adjusted to the merciless daylight, he realized where he was. Elation filled him and he threw his arms in the air. They had made it out of the forest. He struggled to catch his breath before he spoke.

"Holy shit, Jill, that was crazy. But it's going to make for a great story on the podcast," he said. A moment of silence ticked by. "Jill?"

Dave turned around, but found himself standing alone next to the forest. Jill was nowhere in sight. The lone deer skull looked up at him with contempt from the frozen ground.

"Hoot-Hoot-Hoot-HOOOOOOOOOONK!"

The call from deep within the forest was the only reply.

The door to Whiskey Pete's slammed against the wall as Dave burst in, beet red and covered with sweat. His hands trembled as his gaze swung wide around the room. The occupants of the bar were very similar to the night before—Con standing stiff behind the bar, Melvin perched on a stool in the corner, and Joel playing pool with the only unbroken cue. The only difference was that Stacey sat by the bar, paging through a faded, thirty-year-old copy of People Magazine featuring a young Oprah Winfrey on the cover.

Before Dave could catch his breath enough to say anything, Joel spoke. "The hell happened to you?"

"The forest—" Dave said, between gasps of air. "The Squiddlewonk took Jill."

"You actually saw it?" Joel asked.

"No, but there was a hole...and markings."

Joel waved a dismissive hand. "That's ridiculous. She probably just fell down a hill and broke her neck. Con, pour this man a drink, he looks like he needs it."

Con didn't move. Melvin cackled to himself.

"Someone, please help," Dave begged in desperation. He couldn't believe that no one was listening to him. The whole situation seemed too crazy to be real. Like some awful nightmare. Dave looked over at Stacey, who had put her magazine down on the sticky bar top. "Please!"

Stacey held out a hand and carefully examined her heavily chipped nail polish, as if it held the secrets of the universe. "She was rude to me," Stacey said, with finality.

"Sorry buddy, we told you it was a stupid idea," Joel said.

"Yep," said Melvin.

"Stupid," Con agreed.

Out of options, Dave headed back into the forest on his own. No one in the bar would help him and even if he could call for help, he was pretty sure that the people of nearby Chevron would not be coming to his aid. He couldn't wait, so he refilled his water bottle, retrieved the first aid kit from the back of the car, and returned to the forest. The exhaustion that had crept into every inch of his body meant nothing. He had to find Jill.

She was like a sister to him. A bossy older sister that he'd never asked for. They had been through thick and thin together. The podcast, his life's work, would not exist without her organization and planning. He was not going to leave the forest without her.

Dave flew through the trees like a man possessed. His feet barely touched the uneven ground as his hands guarded his face from branches and thorns that grabbed at his clothes and tore at his skin. The forest seemed to be trying to push him back out, like an anus unwilling to accept a thermometer. It felt entirely different this time. It had never been welcoming, but now it seemed openly hostile. As if it intended to stop him from finding Jill.

He tripped and fell repeatedly, and multiple times became so entangled in brambles and vines that he had to cut himself free with a pocket knife.

The path that had once been a single, narrow trail now continued to branch and split, going off in a myriad of different directions. Dave had no idea which way he had gone before. The entire forest looked the same. Leafless shrubs and bare, grey tree trunks packed together like tombstones in an overcrowded cemetery.

The only thing guiding his desperate venture back into the recesses of the forest was the occasional 'Hoot-Hoot-Hoot-HOOOOOOOOONK!' calling him to follow. Telling him which way to go. The strange call pulled him forward. If he could find its source, maybe he could find Jill.

He was trudging through an unusually well-lit, straight path when a deafening crack came from Dave's right. The enormous passing shadow gave him just enough warning to throw himself out of the way of a falling tree. The noise was tremendous as the giant oak smashed through the undergrowth and knocked over several smaller trees on its way to ground, barely missing Dave.

Dave landed the same time the tree did, smacking the right side of his face on a large stone, splitting his cheek. He saw a small splatter of blood on the stone as he pushed himself up. When he was again on his feet, he surveyed the destruction. The falling tree had left a hole in the forest and effectively blocked his path forward. He took a moment to catch his breath and wipe the blood from his face with his sleeve.

Both ends of the tree were too embedded in the brush for him to go around it. So, it was either over or under. He tried to pull himself up onto the horizontal trunk, but it was too wide for his exhausted body to manage. Bending over, he saw there was a little clearance between the trunk and ground. Without hesitation, Dave shrugged off his backpack and crawled through the leaves to the other side of the path.

Upon emerging from under the trunk, he rose and turned around to see something that disturbed but did not shock him. The bark closest to the bottom was covered in long Squiddlewonk claw marks. There were dozens of them, in a variety of sizes, suggesting an entire family of the creatures.

From nearby the call came again.

"Hoot-Hoot-Hoot-HOOOOOOOOONK!"

He spun around. This one was much closer than the other calls. It seemed to come from right behind him, but the trees were so dense that the Squiddlewonk could be standing a few feet away, dressed as Santa Claus, and Dave would never see it.

Then a dark figure dashed between two trees, off to the left. Dave turned, but there was nothing there. There was a loud rustling of dried leaves behind him. Dave spun around in time to discover a large shadow disappearing behind a tree. Then, from another direction he heard the call.

"Hoot-Hoot-Hoot-HOOOOOOOOONK!"

They were stalking him. Now he knew how Muldoon in Jurassic Park had felt.

Without making any sudden movements, Dave squatted down and picked up a broken branch from the fallen tree. He stood up slowly, careful not to make any threatening gestures. He tried to slow his breathing. He waited until another dark form flitted by in his peripheral vision—this one was close, just off the trail—then flung the tree branch at it hard enough to dislocate his shoulder.

The instant the branch left his hands, he charged down the path, hoping the diversion would throw the animals off long enough for him to make an escape. Everything was going smoothly for a few moments, then the ground dropped out from under him. For a brief moment, he felt like Wile E. Coyote, running in space, but then he felt the pull of gravity. For a few terrifying seconds, he thought that he'd fallen into another Squiddle-wonk tunnel. Then he smashed into the ground at the bottom of a slope next to a small stream. It was not a very comforting realization.

He lay there, stunned, until he managed to roll over, dunking his head into the muddy stream. The cold water jolted him awake. He rolled away from the water onto his back, gasping in pain. He saw the blue sky above, shining through the break in the canopy above the stream. Clarity came to him just as the dark, blocky form of a Squiddlewonk leaned over him.

Back-lit by the sky, it was difficult to see any details other than its enormous bobble head, almost as wide as its shoulders, and its dinner plate-sized reflective eyes.

It let out a few gentle hoots before it began slashing down at Dave with its long, narrow claws. They sliced through his thick winter coat and lacerated his chest. He screamed and held up his arms in a vain attempt to fend off the beast, but the attack continued. Its claws, that had made short work of the tree's trunk, passed right through Dave's clothing and flesh. He screamed, throat raw as he felt razor edges scrape against the bones of his forearms. His sleeves were instantly soaked in blood as rivulets of red splashed onto his face, blinding him.

Panicked beyond all rational thought, Dave kicked out with his legs and landed a solid blow. The dark form of the Squiddlewonk disappeared from his limited vision. Without hesitation, he rolled over and started scrambling away without getting up. He climbed the small slope on the far side of the stream by holding onto roots and tufts of dead grass. When he reached the top and staggered to his feet, blood loss made him woozy.

He looked around for some place to hide. Instead, ahead of him, he saw a clearing in the forest, probably the first open space he'd seen since he entered. There was the form of a naked woman, swaying gently from side to side or shivering in the cold. He could not tell. The strange sight caused him to pause for a moment, unsure of what was happening. For a moment, he thought he was hallucinating from the immense physical trauma he had undergone. Then he saw a large peacock tattoo wrapping around her ribs. He knew in an instant that it was Jill.

He'd finally found her.

He lurched forward. He had to get to her. Together they'd find a way out. He tried to call her name, but he was hoarse from screaming. His arms hung limp at his sides as he shuffled toward the clearing, desperate to reach his friend. She still stood, naked, under the low-hanging branches of a spruce tree. Tears streamed down his face as he imagined all the horrific things that might have been visited upon her. He tried not to speculate on what had happened to her clothes.

He drew nearer, close enough that she should see him. "Jill," he managed to call out, in a small voice stolen away by the breeze like a loose windsock.

Something about her movements seemed off. She wasn't shivering or shaking the way a normal person would. Her whole body swayed gently about, not moving at the joints but twisting subtly all over. When he was only a few feet away, a strong breeze blew her around so that her empty, eyeless face stared at him. Her mouth hung open, devoid of tongue, teeth or a jaw to give it shape.

It wasn't Jill. Just her skin.

It was hung from a tree branch as it slowly twisted in the breeze. Shock overcame Dave. He tried to lift an arm to touch it, to see if it was real, but his arms had gone numb. Most of his body had lost feeling. He couldn't imagine how or why the Squiddlewonk would do such a thing. It was not the work of any animal. The impossibility of it prevented truth from fully sinking in, prevented the full horror of it from reaching his conscious mind.

As he fought to clear his head, a dark bobble-headed shade with shining eyes dashed out into the clearing, razor-sharp claws spread wide. Dave stumbled back, but was far too slow. The beast's claws sliced through his abdominal wall, right below his navel. His steaming entrails spilled out onto the ground effortlessly, like they had been waiting for the opportunity to escape. Even the Squiddlewonk seemed surprised as it paused in its attack for a moment.

Dave's abused and exhausted body, brain low on blood, barely registered what happened. He felt the pain, then a strange sensation of things sliding out of his stomach. His body was out of adrenaline and his mind was too fogged to think. So he ran.

Across the clearing and back into the forest, he ran with his guts trailing behind him, leaves and dirt sticking to them, while his arms hung uselessly at his sides. His vision had gone monochrome, and he could barely register the trees enough to avoid them. He stumbled, nearly falling, his entrails snagging on branches, tearing, leaving a convenient trail of blood and bile.

From behind a tree trunk, another claw slashed out, cutting his throat so deeply it nearly severed his head. His body fell to the ground on the spot. He continued to kick his legs helplessly, still trying to run as the last little bit of his blood leaked from his throat and the sewer smell of feces from his torn intestines filled the cold air.

Two Squiddlewonks ambled over to Dave's body and stared down at it. One of the beasts reached up with its great claws and undid a hidden latch under its giant chin. It lifted the oversized mask off its shoulders and said, "Man, that was fun. I love getting dressed up in these costumes."

It poked Dave's body with the pointed toe of its outsize shoe.

In a muffled, human voice, the other Squiddlewonk said, "They're too damn hot."

WHO'S DALE?
By Lynne Phillips

Mom,

Having trouble with my van. It broke down at a place called Whiskey Pete's, down Idaho way.

Some old dude called Lorne is helping me fix it. I walked twenty miles into Chevron for a part from a motor dealer. Will post this here. Should be on my way tomorrow. Don't want to spend any more time here. This place gives me the creeps and the beer's like piss.

See you soon,

Dale

TOOMBS

By Austin Shirey

There's always a rational explanation.

Franklin Toombs lived by that mantra. And right now, he was clinging to it like a drowning man to a deflating life preserver.

He breathed heavily, sending a rush of cloud into the cold December air. He was slick with sweat, blood and dirt. Digging five graves in the winter earth, dragging five bodies to those graves, wasn't easy work—especially with only one good hand. He shook with exhaustion. And he'd ruined a perfectly good suit!

Good news was, he wasn't cold anymore; the night's grisly work had seen to that. But his mind felt frayed at the edges, and he needed a drink. Bad.

The sick feeling in his stomach, the one that had been growing worse since he'd first turned down Route Thirteen, threatened to overwhelm. Somehow, this place—with its pockmarked, two-lane dirt road, its dump of a bar, greasy gas station, and moldy motel surrounded by thick pine forest—was testing his resolve, the steadfastness of his personal philosophies. Just for the hell of it...

Toombs shook his head. *No. Don't think like that. Just get a drink, calm your nerves, and get yourself out of here.*

He took another deep breath to steady himself and glanced up at the night sky. Bad idea. The stars were still winking out one-by-one as the impossibly vast, multi-angled behemoths he'd seen earlier continued surging across them. His stomach clenched again; he couldn't explain why, but the twinkling lights darkening in the wake of those...things made him feel utterly alone. Like the stars were a million eyes closing, not wanting to witness.

No. What he was seeing, hearing—it wasn't there. It couldn't be. He'd lost so much blood, taxed himself killing the cultists up on the mountain, burying them in those freshly dug graves, stumbling through dark woods all the way back here. He was in shock, hallucinating.

There's always a rational explanation.

Toombs crossed the empty road, a specter in the fog, drawn to the gaudy neon lights of Whiskey Pete's bar like a skeeter to a bug zapper.

He kicked open the door, leaving a muddy boot-print on the worn wood. The hinges squealed like a slaughtered pig.

"'And lo, I beheld a pale horse...'"

The lilting voice froze Toombs' blood in his veins. A wave of light-headedness surged through him as his eyes settled on the five people standing at the bar, wiping dirt off their clothes.

But... But that's impossible.

The old man in the red mechanic coveralls, the name Dale stitched into the chest, spat a clump of dirt out his mouth, examining another gob on the end of one of his gnarled, grime-black fingernails. "'... and Hell followed with him.'"

Toombs had a sudden desire to lie down, to sleep the sleep of the dead. None of this could be happening.

There's always a rational explanation.

He'd gone insane; that's what this was. His mind had shattered; his brains were leaking out his ears. That was it.

The five Whiskey Pete's regulars stared back at him as they continued wiping themselves clean of the muck from their graves. Their clothes—their skin and bones—were intact. No severed limbs, no gaping, bloody wounds, no hamburger mash of flesh and splintered bones. Like nothing he'd done, only hours before, had actually happened. Except for the dirt, the mechanic, the big man with mismatched eyes, the red-headed Stacey, the raven-haired Joel, and the decrepit old-timer all looked much as they had when he'd first met them several hours earlier: very much alive.

But he'd killed them. Torn through each and every one of them with a knife and shovel. Toombs looked down at his clothes: his Armani suit was still stained with their blood.

Somewhere out of sight, a door creaked open.

"Well, shit," Toombs said.

Route Thirteen, the worm ouroboros. Never-ending.

Toombs had turned off Route 30 and onto Thirteen early that morning, a little while after he'd gotten out of Portland, but that had been several hours before. Around noonish, he'd already passed Payette National Forest. The day was cloudy, and from inside his pristine, matte black 1967 Pontiac GTO, Toombs could tell it was a cold one. It had that blue winter look to it. No matter. Inside the GTO, the heat was on, and Nine Inch Nails' *The Downward Spiral* was pulsing from the speakers.

If someone had asked him why he'd left the state-maintained smoothness of Route 30 for the long-neglected, seemingly forgotten—and, if the GPS on his smartphone was to be believed, apparently nonexistent— puckered dirt path of Route Thirteen, Toombs probably wouldn't have been able to answer.

He was following a hunch.

And in all his years of work, finding people that didn't want to be found, cleaning up messes and tying up loose-ends for anyone that could foot the bill, Toombs had learned to trust his hunches. After all, they'd kept him alive and kept him paid.

Another question Toombs wouldn't have been able to answer: why in the hell the car's stereo had burst into static and his stomach had begun cramping as soon as he'd made the turn.

He told himself it was probably a mixture of the uneven road messing with the stereo wiring and bad fast food. Had to be. There were no other explanations, and if Toombs was anything, he was pragmatic. A man of reason.

He forced his mind back to the job.

The kids he was tracking—one Nia Lewis, 16 years old, and Jamie Walsh, 20—hadn't been staying in hotels, based on the information he'd received from her father. Jerome Lewis' impressively wide web of both legal and extralegal connections had been keeping tabs on Nia, at least until she and her boyfriend disappeared off Route 30 somewhere after being spotted leaving Portland.

According to some of Jerome's police connections, Nia and Jamie had been foregoing hotels in favor of parking their getaway vehicle—Jamie's crappy, 1977 Dodge Aspen—in Wal-Mart parking lots or wooded areas just off the main road, probably to save what little money they had and keep a low profile. Poor, love-struck Nia didn't realize just how far her daddy's reach really was.

The stark reality was, Jerome's reach was both wide and powerful enough that he could have his police connections keep a watch on Nia and have someone like Toombs come along to sweep this little family embarrassment under the rug as quickly and quietly as possible.

"What do you want done with Jamie?" Toombs had asked Jerome, in the alley behind the man's house in Astoria a couple nights before.

"As far as I'm concerned," Jerome said, "that man is a rapist. Do whatever the hell you want to him. I don't want to know about it. I don't want to hear about it on the news, or see it in the papers. Just bring my baby girl home, with as little fuss and muss as possible. I'll make it worth your while."

And Jerome Lewis *had* made it worth Toombs' while. He'd paid triple the normal front-end fee Toombs charged, with a promise to triple the remainder upon completion of the job. With the amount he'd make from this one job, Toombs could buy enough Armani suits to wear one every day of the year. If Toombs loved anything more than his job, it was Armani suits. They were the only thing he felt a man should wear.

The sun was beginning to set when he saw the road sign. He pulled the GTO to a stop next to it. The thing was old, made of splintering, mildewed planks of wood, the words looking like they'd been carved by an unsteady hand:

DeVIL'S LAdDEr

wHiSKEy PEtE's

Toombs snickered. The sign—and the place names, even the handwriting—looked like a leftover prop from some old horror flick. Devil's Ladder? Whiskey Pete's? Really? Names like that didn't belong to real places; they belonged to places where cults practiced human sacrifice, or where inbred cannibals preyed upon bumbling out-of-towners. In movies.

And yet, even as he snickered, his stomach was doing kick-flips. A band of static buzzed through the stereo, stuttering the chorus of *March of the Pigs*.

Must've been the In'N'Out. And he'd probably knocked something loose on this damn cratered road...

There's always a rational explanation.

He sat staring at the sign, readjusting his seatbelt as the car idled in the gathering gloom. If he were two love-dumb kids making a run for it, where would he pull off for the night?

Toombs stepped on the gas.

It was a 50-50 shot they'd stopped at either place.

Eight miles later, Toombs found the car.

Well, what was left of the car.

It was maybe a mile and a half past the parking area for the Devil's Ladder hiking trail, pulled into a copse of pines that would've given the young lovers plenty of privacy. Toombs would've probably driven right past if the immediate area hadn't been burned to a black crisp. The trees were nothing but mangled, black skeleton fingers grasping at the sky.

The GTO's headlights had caught the burned-out husk of the car as he gently fish-tailed up the dirt path that he assumed was the hiking trail. He pulled up to the scorched pocket of trees, headlights illuminating the charred vehicle at its center, and put the GTO in park. He turned down the music and stepped out into the night.

The site reeked of gasoline. Except for the idling of the GTO's engine, the night was quiet; the kind of quiet that made him uneasy. Even in winter, this kind of wooded area should've pulsated with the noise of nocturnal wildlife. Hell, he didn't even hear crickets. There should at least be crickets.

Toombs stepped up to what was left of the vehicle and examined it. The husk looked like the right shape for a 1977 Dodge Aspen, but he needed to be sure. He stepped around to the driver's side and pulled his phone out of his jacket pocket. He tapped open his file on Jamie, scrolling with his thumb until he came to the Aspen's VIN.

He turned on the phone's flashlight and hovered the beam over the blackened car, just under where the windshield had been, and wiped away the ash gathered there with his other hand.

The VIN was faded, but still readable. This was Jamie's car.

Toombs slowly walked the phone's light around the car, searching for any sign, any indication that Nia and Jamie had been in the Aspen when it was torched.

Nada.

He'd need to come back in the daytime to be sure, make a more thorough examination, but he didn't think the kids had been in the car when it was set aflame.

Something nagged at him, though. Had Nia and Jamie set the fire themselves? Or had someone else? Did the kids ditch the car here, then steal another hiker's car? Or maybe they'd hitchhiked or backpacked somewhere nearby?

There's always a rational explanation.

Toombs vaguely remembered seeing a sign for a town called Chevron a while back, but his gut had told him to keep on driving. Had his hunches finally failed him? Or had the bad food he'd eaten messed up his gut to the point he couldn't tell a hunch from a bad case of gas?

No, that couldn't be it. His stomach might be dancing in his belly, but he could still read his hunches.

And right now, his hunch was saying—

"Hoot-Hoot-Hoot-HOOOOOOOOONK!"

Toombs froze. What the hell was that? He'd never heard anything like that in his life before. It didn't even sound like an animal. It sounded more like—

Something massive eclipsed the GTO's headlights, plunging Toombs into darkness.

"Hoot-Hoot-Hoot-HOOOOOOOOONK!"

Toombs whipped around, exchanging his smartphone for the SIG Sauer P320 he kept in the shoulder holster beneath his jacket.

Backlit by the headlights, the thing was a blocky shadow, but Toombs thought he caught flashes of something reflective on the large, bobbling head that could have been eyes.

"Yeah, no," he said.

Long, knife-like claws slashed at him. "Hoot-Hoot-Hoot—"

Toombs got three shots off. Muzzle flashes lit up the night like lightning, the suppressor Toombs used religiously making the gun sound less like thunder and more like a hydraulic piston.

Even as he heard the thud-thud-thud of the bullets hitting their target, the thing's claws met the hand holding the gun and slashed through flesh, tendon and bone like they were toilet paper.

"Shit!"

His hand, his gun, and his monstrous attacker crumpled to the ground. Toombs was only vaguely aware of the all-too-human voice screaming from the blocky shape at his feet, his eyes fixed on the jagged stump where his left hand used to be.

"Holy shit!"

Blood sputtered forth like a faulty spigot. Before he could think about what he was doing, Toombs pulled his tie loose with his right hand and used a combination of his teeth and his good hand to tie a makeshift tourniquet around the forearm above his severed wrist.

He staggered over to the GTO, blood pumping in his ears in time with his heart. He released the brake with his right hand while the bleeding stump of his left flopped around like a dying fish on the steering wheel, painting it slick with blood. He got control of himself, put the stump in his lap. With his good hand, he threw the car into reverse and grabbed the steering wheel as he slammed the gas pedal down, and then he was speeding backwards along the trail, back toward the parking area.

The GTO reverse-fishtailed onto Route Thirteen, and just as Toombs thought he'd made it, he hit a pothole and the back passenger-side tire blew. The car careened over into a ditch on the left-hand shoulder, slamming to a metal-crunching stop against a strand of whispering pines.

Toombs came to on sticky carpet. Four human-shaped blurs stood over him, talking. Only one eye seemed to be working, and even that was hazy, like he was looking through a dirty glass; the other eye refused to open, puffed up and glued shut. His head felt like it had been scooped out and stuffed full of broken glass. His body ached, and his left stump throbbed and buzzed painfully, like someone was sawing at it with a blazing-hot blade.

"...find Joel?" the blur standing near his feet asked.

The vision in his good eye cleared some, and he could make out more of the people talking above him. The man who had spoken was dressed in denim, heavily muscled but leaning toward fat; his craggy face was too big, his nose too bulbous. Toombs thought his eyes were a different color—one green, the other blue—but figured that was just a trick of the light.

Toombs moved his eye slightly, trying to get his bearings. Behind the big man with the mismatched eyes, he could make out a bar to the right, the shelves on the wall behind it dotted here and there with dusty liquor bottles. On his left, near his shoulder, just behind the pretty redhead with the green eyes standing over him, a jukebox that had seen much better days—Toombs doubted it even worked—leaned long-neglected against a dirty wall. The place smelled musty, old and sour, like it was rotting. He had the urge to leap to his feet—this was one of those dives you'd never want to take a piss in—but his body was too battered to respond.

The redhead nodded at the big man. She kept her arms folded protectively across her chest. "He's out back, gettin' cleaned up." Her voice was flat, lifeless; Toombs found it incongruent with her shapely lips. She dipped her head slightly toward him. "Shot him coupla times."

The big man grunted.

The scrawny man standing over Toombs, across from the woman, laughed. He wore ill-fitting red mechanic's coveralls with a nametag Toombs couldn't make out. The man kicked him. "Not much of a shot, eh, asshole?"

Toombs noticed pictures tacked to the wall behind the bar, and the wall directly to his right. Old, black and white, and from his angle on the floor, he couldn't be sure, but he thought the big man with the mismatched eyes and the redhead were standing on either side of another man in a checkered shirt and dark pants—a man not currently present—but this man's face was blurred, like he'd turned before the camera had finished taking the picture.

Directly above Toombs, a third man, gaunt and disheveled and dressed like a soldier in a Civil War documentary, bent closer. The man's breath was rancid, his teeth black and likely rotting in his mouth.

"Yew for the Gray or the Blue, boy?" the man wheezed in a thick, Southern drawl.

"Ah shaddup, you old coot," the mechanic said, waving the man away. He had a lilt to his voice—Canadian, maybe?—and the dirtiest fingernails Toombs had ever seen.

The old-timer straightened and mumbled to himself; Toombs thought he heard the words 'war' and 'Northern Aggression', but he wasn't sure.

"He by himself?" Big Man asked. Toombs thought he heard the hint of a New York accent.

Redhead shrugged. "Ask Joel."

"He didn't say?"

"Other than bitchin' he got shot by some dandy in a suit pokin' around that burned car, no, he ain't said nothin.'"

"I told ya we shoulda done something else with that car," Mechanic said. "Told ya somebody come looking around for them kids."

Big Man grunted.

"Well, Con? Whadda we do?"

"Hang 'im," Old-Timer mumbled. "For treason."

Big Man sighed. "Gotta talk to Joel, first."

"An' then?" Mechanic asked. "As gooda night as any, ask me..."

"Been a while, too," Redhead muttered. She glanced at Toombs with something like hunger in her eyes—a look that both aroused him and made him sick.

Big Man grunted. "Lock him in the motel. Then we talk to Joel."

Toombs passed out again as soon as they jerked him up from the carpet with grimy hands.

He awoke to the sound of a door locking shut.

It took a few moments for Toombs' good eye to adjust to the darkness. The other side of his face pounded terribly, as if his heart had switched places with his right eye.

When he was finally able to see his surroundings in the murky twilight, he found himself tied to a bed in an old, run-down motel room. Stained wallpaper curled from the walls, and the musty, rotten, mildewed smell that he'd first sniffed in the bar was worse here. The bed itself had no padding, and the springs poked up through the mattress and into his back.

Something moved at the foot of the bed.

"Who's there?"

"Stacey," came a soft, monotone voice. Toombs remembered it from the bar. The redhead.

He was having trouble seeing her. There was a deeper shadow near the end of the bed, gliding closer now, but between the darkness of the room and the limited use of his one eye, Toombs still wasn't clear on her position.

He heard a zipper slowly pulled down, then the sounds of various bits of soft things dropping to the floor.

Toombs swallowed. Sure, Redhead—Stacey—had been somewhat attractive, but this was neither the time nor the place. He wasn't into the kinky stuff, and anyways, none of this was consensual. He felt like hot rocks were sizzling in the pit of his stomach.

Stacey appeared at his left side, a sliver of light streaming through the curtains across the room draping her naked body in lambent moonlight.

"You look good enough to eat," Stacey said, as she leaned over Toombs.

His heart was beating fast, and the pain behind his right eye and where his left hand had been intensified. His vision grew hazy.

"Listen, lady—"

Toombs' mouth went dry as Stacey brought her hand up suggestively between her breasts.

He looked at her eyes—and his blood went cold. They swirled like black holes, impossibly deep and dark, getting darker, deeper, wider as he gazed into them. Then the darkness in them threatened to spill over, to eat up the room—maybe even the world.

Her fingers went ballistic, digging, ripping into the skin of her chest, and she was pulling herself open, blood spilling upon the floor and spraying across his face, and still she was digging, pulling, stretching the skin to impossible lengths like it was a linen sheet she was ripping apart.

A towering swarm of cockroaches exploded from her.

He screamed, writhing in terror and disgust, unable to wrench free from his bonds as the roaches descended upon him and millions of little, sickly, sticky legs scuttled over him. He tried to tell himself this was only a hallucination brought on by blood loss—*there's always a rational expla-nation, dammit!*—but then he was choking on roaches as they forced their way down his throat and into his ears and his eyes and his—

Toombs woke screaming in a dark, musty room. He tried to move and found he was tied, spread-eagled, to an uncomfortably springy bed by his right hand and both his feet, clothes wet with sweat. His stump flopped uselessly at his side, burning, always burning. He gasped for breath, his head swimming in a hazy mist of pain and terror.

And then, mercifully, he passed into a dreamless void.

On the edge of consciousness...

"... shouldn't we bind him or somethin'?" Redhead again.

"Man's got one good hand, one eye stopped shut, and he's lost enough blood to fill a bucket. He's half-dead, Stacey." The Mechanic.

"Joel'll feel more like a man gutting him if he's not bound." Big Man.

"Fuck you, Con." Something familiar about that voice...like he'd heard it in pain, somewhere...making strange birdcalls, maybe?

Chanting, rhythmic and baroque, filled the air, a choir of voices melting together into a haunting, brooding hymn.

A breeze caressed Toombs' face as he slowly regained consciousness. His eye opened. He was on his back—again—but this time, outside, laid out on some kind of stone, surrounded by grass. Orange light flickered at the edge of his vision, seemed to curve around him like he was the center of something. He was staring up at the starry sky, except—except something was terribly wrong. There were massive...things moving across the sky, darker than the void between stars, consisting of angles that made his head feel on fire, roaring in languages that made his ears bleed. The stars winked out one-by-one in their wake.

There's always a rational explanation, he reminded himself, as tears tumbled from the eye that was not gummed shut by blood and pus.

"'Madness rides the star-winds,'" the Mechanic said nearby. "'Claws and teeth sharpened on centuries of corpses...'"

Four hooded figures approached Toombs from all points. Their cloaks were black as pitch, hoods so wide and deep their faces were permanently lost in shadow, but he could feel their eyes piercing him as his vision flicked from one to another. The chanting continued from all around, from others outside the range of his limited vision.

A fifth hooded figure approached, kicking Toombs' feet apart and walking right up to his crotch. This figure withdrew the most evil-looking knife Toombs had ever seen in his life—wickedly curved, with an obsidian cross-guard that looked like it had been made of molten darkness—and his balls retreated into his stomach. The light of what little stars remained in the sky flickered across the silver blade, morphing with the reflected lights of torches and creating infernal fractals that burned themselves upon Toombs' retina.

"Shoot me, leave me to bleed out in the woods," that familiar voice said again from within the cloak looming over him. The figure pulled back the hood, revealing a raven-haired man with a crooked, yellow smile. His eyes blazed with menace. "I'm gonna enjoy this."

The raven-haired man brought down the wicked knife in a flash, but Toombs' right hand snapped up to block it.

"No," Toombs said, barely a whisper.

The knife speared his palm, jutting out the back and spraying his face with his own blood.

"Shee-it!" someone cried.

The shock of pain, the coppery smell of blood, woke something in him that had been sleeping since he'd lost his hand and crashed his car earlier that night.

It came roaring back to life.

Toombs roared.

Suddenly, he was lurching forward, sinking his teeth into the raven-haired man's nose and ripping violently backward. The man screamed as hot blood erupted from where his nose had been, and he let go of the knife stuck in Toombs' hand.

Then Toombs was on his feet, kicking the raven-haired man onto his back and yanking the knife out of his own hand with his teeth, growling around the hilt as pain lanced through his nervous system. He grabbed the knife's handle with his wounded hand and spun.

Hooded figures lunged at him, throwing wild punches and screaming to throw him off balance. Toombs stayed calm, focused on each punch, each kick that came his way, expertly deflecting them.

He sliced through flesh, opened veins, drenched the grass at his feet in blood. With his injured arm, he threw elbows, clubbed with his forearm, rammed with the shoulder.

Someone came at him with a shovel. Toombs ducked under the swing, lunging forward with the knife, sliding it through black robes and into soft flesh, yanking it up and then to the side. He twisted and withdrew, then dropped the blade and caught the shovel—it was all about reach—as his attacker screamed and clutched at the steaming coil of intestines unspooling into a slop upon the earth.

Stacey was on him then. He recognized her voice as she threw herself onto his back, wrapping her thin arms around his neck. She thrashed and screamed, bit at his neck and face and his stump as he swatted at her again and again.

He wrapped his left forearm around the back of her neck and pulled, flipping her off him and onto the ground.

He cut off her raging scream with the shovel, severing her head at the neck.

And then, it was done.

The only sound, besides Toombs' ragged breaths, and the ear-piercing shrieks from the star-things that loped across the heavens, was the sound of dying cultists, gurgling in growing pools of their own blood.

"Goddamn cannibal hillbillies," Toombs mumbled.

He limped among the bodies, staving-in skulls and severing heads with the shovel, until the only one still crying and choking was the raven-haired man. He was on his back near the stone they'd placed Toombs on, clutching at the mangled mess of his nose.

Toombs slammed a foot down on the man's testicles, applying pressure until he heard a wet pop, and the man screamed the most blood-curdling scream Toombs had ever heard. He brought the shovel point down to sever the rest of the man's genitals, then stepped around to his head, kicking away his hands from his nose and placing the shovel at his bobbing Adam's apple.

The man gagged on tears and blood. He spat at Toombs. "You're dead, man! You are so fucking dead!"

"Nia Lewis," Toombs said. "Where is she?"

The raven-haired man looked confused. "Who?"

"Nia Lewis. She came here with her boyfriend, Jamie Walsh."

"Don't know who you're—"

Toombs whacked the man's destroyed crotch with the shovel, then brought it back to his throat.

"Black girl, white boyfriend."

The raven-haired man laughed. "That bitch? She dead, man. They both dead. Their baby too."

Toombs hesitated. Baby? That was unexpected. But there was nothing he could do with that information. Not now. Nia Lewis was dead, and so was Jamie. Jerome wouldn't be happy, but what could he do? The dead don't come back.

The raven-haired man's laughter grated on Toombs' nerves, and he raised the shovel over his head.

"Oh, Pete is gonna love you," the raven-haired man said.

Toombs brought the shovel down, splitting his head in half.

Somewhere out of sight, a door creaked open.

"Well, shit," Toombs said.

"Look at him," the raven-haired man said, smiling his crooked, yellow smile. "He still don't get it. I told you he wouldn't figure—"

"—Joel," the big man said in an exasperated sigh, "shut your—"

"'—goddamn hole," Joel finished, rolling his eyes. "Get a new fucking catchphrase already, Con. It's getting old."

Con glared at him and grunted.

"It's all gettin' old," Stacey said, eyes vacant.

"Don't talk to me 'bout old," the old-timer said, words trailing off into incoherent mumbling.

This...this wasn't right. There was always a rational explanation for everything. He had to believe that. This... It couldn't... It didn't...

Toombs took a step backwards. He had to do it all again. Kill them all, and make sure it stuck this time, that they stayed dead and buried. The very thought of expending the amount of effort he'd already expended on these five assholes was too much for him, and something in his head finally just broke. The stump of his left wrist throbbed.

Had any of it been real? Or had he gone mad somewhere on Route Thirteen, crashed his car, and now he'd spend his existence looping in this god-awful redneck hell?

A roiling darkness burned on the periphery of his vision and suddenly Toombs realized there was a sixth person standing at the bar with the others. He wore a checkered shirt and dark jeans. Where the hell had he come from? Had he been there the entire time, and Toombs had just passed over him?

He couldn't be sure, but as he looked at the man, something about him seemed...familiar. Everything, except for his face. Like Toombs had only seen the man from the neck down somewhere before. But where—

His eyes flicked to an old, creased photograph tacked to the wall behind the bar, then back to the man. He tensed.

There's always a rational explanation...

"There it is," Joel said.

"'There are more things in heaven and earth, Horatio,'" the mechanic said, a wicked smile distorting his face.

Before Toombs could say or do anything, the sixth man melted into surging tentacles of pure shadow, and then Toombs was being dragged across the floor, down into a gaping, black maw of nothingness.

Outstretched arms rose and fell in unison all around him, the chopping motions in time with the chant. He was terrified by it all: the grating sounds of the organ, the sudden screams of the masses between long silences, and he couldn't understand why there was occasionally a grown man running in circles. With each sudden explosion of voices, he cried.

In addition to his terror, he knew that he had somehow failed when he dropped the rubber foam tomahawk.

The Big Mean Man told him that real boys didn't cry. The Big Mean Man told him that real boys liked sports. It didn't matter that he was only three years old. The choleric adult finally carried him out of the stadium long before the baseball game had ended.

His mother flew into Atlanta the following day and took him on the next flight back to Oregon, comforting him the whole way. Her eyes were wide and blue like his, and he thought she was the most beautiful person in the world. She held him at night when he had nightmares after that and told him that nobody ever got chopped up at a baseball game.

"Just remember to choose the right team," she sometimes whispered, "and be a good sport." During those moments, a shadow seemed to cross her face.

Mickey Madden never saw his sire again. He found out a few years later that his parents had dropped issues of joint custody and visitation. As he grew up, he decided to become his own father figure, aggressive and controlling toward his peers. He cringed when his mom told him that boys didn't have to like sports, but listened when she sang to him the lesser-known opening lines of a famous song:

"Katie Casey was baseball mad
Had the fever and had it bad..."

Of course, by this time, he knew the chorus to *Take Me Out To the Ball Game*. His throat tightened at the memory of her voice. Mickey gritted his teeth and gripped the steering wheel. He was no mama's boy. He was—in the literal sense of the expression—free, white, and twenty-one.

And now that the Atlanta Braves' *Tomahawk Chop* was considered disrespectful to Native Americans, he could pretend to eschew it in the name of political correctness. Nobody ever had to know that it still gave him nightmares.

Deep gashes of crimson floated above his only promise of respite. Not that he had time to appreciate a proper sunrise. The car was almost on empty.

The movement of an animal dashing across the road interrupted his reflection, and Mickey instinctively slammed on his brakes. It was a tuxedo cat, vanishing like a single black-and-white movie frame onto the cutting room floor.

"Don't hit the kitty!" hollered a voice in the back seat, almost making him swerve a second time.

That would be Bruce. He tried to hide it, but the ginger dude was a total softie when it came to animals. The other two guys groaned, disgruntled at being startled into wakefulness. It was just as well.

These guys are all douchebags, thought Mickey to himself, *with no sense of logistics or direction.*

He hated having to babysit these pledges for his fraternity *Pi Tau Sigma Alpha*—nicknamed 'Poutsa'—but he felt a certain responsibility to them. He hoped that they would feel beholden to him, since he was the only person willing to trade them this trip for the severe hazing they'd have otherwise undergone. The Hummer they rode in belonged to Chip, short and stout as a teapot, now yawning in the passenger seat. Bruce's family had a shareholder apartment in the French Quarter, so they had free lodging in their final destination of New Orleans. And sly Chandler had mysteriously promised to finance the rest of the journey's expenses.

But Mickey wasn't feeling particularly grateful for these perks right now. Chip's GPS had quit working, and they'd wound up at this place, promising food, booze, gas, and even lodging. Mickey was no wimp, and could have kept driving for the next twelve hours, but he had to ration his nose candy. He scowled. He'd have to fill up, no matter what.

Beggars couldn't be choosers, even if Whiskey Pete's looked like a total dive. He slowed to a halt by the shop. Even the vintage gas pump looked like it probably wasn't working.

The pint-sized man approaching from the shop looked like some sort of derelict Christmas elf with his greasy blond hair and red jumpsuit, bearing the nametag 'Dale'. Before the boys could make heads or tails of the antiquated machine, the old man grabbed the nozzle, and without ceremony asked, "Regular or unleaded?"

Mickey sneered. "That all you've got? No super?"

The shopkeep didn't budge. "Let me rephrase that. Your two choices for miles in any direction are 'take it or leave it.' So what's it gonna be, eh?" Without waiting for a response, he punched the unleaded button and began filling the tank.

"Hey, look at this!" the self-styled ringmaster hooted. "At least we don't have to pump our own gas in this dump!" Mickey was vain about being six foot two, and he towered over the unconcerned coot. "What else can you do for us, Dale?"

The leathery-faced man squinted up at the polo-shirted kid. "The name's Lorne."

Mickey hoped that Chip didn't see the man put his hands on his car. The old crank looked like he'd been scraping the inside of a toilet bowl with his nails.

"Well, Lorne, you'd better step it up, because we're on our way down to New Or-leenz to party hard and see us some titties!"

"I'm not your step n' fetch. You boys should be in school, eh?"

"We've got it all figured out. We've told the school that Chandler here is so distraught over his dear old uncle's death that we're taking a leave of absence. Exams are take-home this year, and we've all found ourselves a few sows willing to put in a little extra work for us, with the promise that we invite them to one of our swine parties."

The others snorted and squealed. Lorne's face never moved, but Mickey doubted that he would look prettier if he smiled.

"Look, I'll drive next," said Chandler, stepping between the two. The greasy pledge was an oily smooth-talker, with the slant of his eyes and the mole on his upper lip giving him the appearance of a hyena. "But we need to rest, even if it's just for a few hours. Mickey, we're gonna get pulled over if you don't watch the booger sugar. Let's get a room, a meal, and a couple of beers." He flashed his white teeth. "Save your strength for when it's hunting time."

The wallpaper of the motel lobby looked like some sort of nihilistic paper plate with its oversized flowers in harsh black, white, and metallic gold. The thin, dark wood paneling along the reception desk appeared to have lost many a fight with disgruntled customers. Worst of all was the carpet, which looked like a moth-eaten biohazard the color of spoiled guacamole. Mickey recalled numerous Polaroid snapshots he'd seen of his grandparents, and felt like he'd just stepped into a hellish parallel dimension.

The pretty little redhead who stood at the front desk barely seemed to notice them enter, even though it seemed doubtful this place got much business.

She was still daydreaming when they reached the desk, so Mickey barged ahead of the group and banged on the bell right in front of her. Her entire body jerked in a manner that seemed half startle and half reanimation.

A smile illuminated her face like an old slideshow on a projector screen. "Welcome to Whiskey Pete's," she drawled. "How many rooms will y'all be needing?"

"Well, listen to you!" Mickey flashed the grin chicks seemed to like so much, cuing the others to do the same. "Where you from, baby?"

"Miss'ippi."

"That's so cute. I love the Deep South," he crooned, trying to turn on the charm.

He actually hadn't been there since his terrifying childhood experience, but he hoped to turn his lie into the truth before long.

"That's nice," drawled Stacey, lightly fanning herself. "Do y'all want rooms or don't you?"

"Sure, we'll take one room. We're just trying to save money, so don't think we're a bunch of fags..."

He paused as he took in Bruce's reaction to a mounted deer head on the opposite wall, and grinned at his friend's discomfort.

Stacey's gaze went vacant again, eyes fixed like crosshairs on the center of Mickey's forehead.

"What are you looking at?" Mickey asked, sniffing hard. "I guess a pretty thing like you wouldn't be interested in sports. I happen to be a sports nerd." He pointed to the logo on his baseball cap. "Do you find this baby swinging a baseball bat to be creepy? It was a minor league New Orleans baseball team, the Baby Cakes."

"That's not creepy," she mumbled, still transfixed.

"Oh, come on! You mean to tell me you've seen scarier things than an angry baby looking like he's about to beat the shit out of someone with a baseball bat?"

Stacey paused as if she hadn't heard him, then switched her smile back on. "Have a good stay, boys. The key's behind the bar. Bless your hearts."

She banged a hand on the Formica countertop and then resumed staring into the distance.

It was only a short walk through the parking lot from the lobby into the bar, but wandering from the midmorning sunlight into the near-void rendered them momentarily blind. Their eyes adjusted to a single bulb guttering over the pool table like a bug zapper, and the electric Schafer Beer sign guided them in the direction of a row of stools. Each of the pledges would have turned around and walked out the second they saw the interior, but in each other's presences, they had to tough it out.

None of them was in the mood to mouth off to the silent man behind the bar. Something in his odd eyes—one blue and one green—told them that their beer choices were as limited as the fuel. Chip ordered a round of the house IPA called Warden. Mickey coughed and spluttered at the first sip and looked like he was about to pick a fight when a voice from the opposite wall saved them. "Who's up for a game of pool?"

The voice belonged to a young man just a few years the boys' senior. There was something a bit off about him, with his dusting of limp black hair and a smile that carefully concealed his teeth, but the casual familiarity drew the quartet to their fellow patron, who introduced himself as Joel Masterson.

"Glad to have someone to talk to besides these creepy old farts," said Chip. "We had our fair share of them back home in Oregon. Chandler's dear old uncle—" He indicated his fellow pledge, "—just died, and nobody questioned his motives. It sure is a damned shame that vets have such a high suicide rate."

Joel shrugged. "Many of them are homeless or have PTSD. Trauma around here has more of a tendency to…"

"Joel, shut your goddamned hole!" barked the surly bartender.

The other three boys sniggered, and Chip barely suppressed a smirk. "Not veterans. I'm talking veterinarians. I hear that vet school is harder to get into than med school. Then they can't handle it when part of their job description is to put poor old Rover or Mittens out of their misery. Or in Doctor Murphy's case, old Seabiscuit. He specialized in equine medicine."

"And now we're gonna cheer our pal up!" barked Mickey. "Beer! Titties! Music! Beads! Parades! King cake!"

And to prove to myself that I'm not afraid of the South anymore, he silently added.

Joel began to chalk his cue. "Tell me more about this king cake," he pressed.

"Oh, it's this silly tradition of your friends sharing a ring-shaped cake, just some dough with sugar on top, dyed purple, green and gold...Mardi Gras colors, y'know?" said Mickey, with as much authority on the subject as he could portray. "Somewhere inside the cake is a plastic baby. Everyone eats a piece of cake, and whoever gets the baby has to throw the next party."

"Or in our case, gets the sweetest slice!" announced Chandler, and Mickey bristled inwardly.

"That's not what the great founding fathers of this country intended for your men to do on this soil," croaked a voice out of a dark corner that made the boys jump.

A spectral-looking man glided silently into view. Mickey recalled hearing about how corpses' fingernails and hair continued to grow after they died, and wondered if it was true, and if this man were somehow a reanimated example.

"I should know. My name is Melvin Washington, as in George. Yeah, that's my..." he paused to count on his fingers, "... not sure how many greats to being my granddaddy.

"Anyways. Don't you know the origin of the word 'carnival'? It comes from carne vale, Latin for 'farewell to meat.' It's your last chance to dine on something that was once alive before Lent. Some say it really signifies the carefree spirit of the season. Others believe it means 'a farewell to flesh'. In any case, you boys had better stop thinking of yourselves as being above the law."

"Ooo, look who's preaching to us, old man!" snarled Chip.

"Just tellin' it like it is. You boys can take my advice or get yourselves kilt. Don't ask nobody 'round here no questions and leave the critters alone."

Mickey chose that moment to take another hard sniff before hocking up a wad of snot and spitting on the floor at Melvin's feet. The hard thud of the bartender's approaching footsteps was a signal for the pack to explore the territory they'd claimed for the night.

The carpeting in the room was identical to the lobby, and perhaps even more revolting. New, it probably would have been considered retro by modern standards, but Mickey found himself wondering if some avocado forgot its safe word in the making of the color.

An unholy screech outside made them freeze where they stood.

Mickey patted the small of his back. "Don't forget I'm packing! I've had this pistol on me the whole time."

"Never mind that, cowboy," sneered Bruce. "I'm better with bludgeoning. Gonna try out for the Baby Cakes when I get to New Orleans!"

He produced a baseball bat from his own luggage, but he wasn't fooling anyone. Everyone knew the animal lover's abrupt burst of sports enthusiasm was a deliberate subject change.

"There's no such team anymore!" crowed Mickey. "I'm the sports geek around here. You couldn't get on a tee-ball team."

"Wanna bet, loser?" scoffed Bruce.

Chip broke in. "Behind the rooms, edge of the woods. Let's all find out!"

Buzzed and pumped up on one-upmanship, Mickey and the PTSA pledges charged back into the bracing winter air.

"Heyyyyy, batta-batta-batta...swing!"

Mickey pitched a heavy rock that fell short of Bruce's bat, which swished through cold air.

"Strike one!" cackled Chip. "You should have just let that one go, Bruce."

"These rocks are no substitute for real baseballs," complained Mickey.

Chandler sneered. "No, you just throw like a girl, old man."

Something in the way Mickey froze alerted the pledges that Chandler had just crossed a line.

"Have you never heard the entire lyrics to 'Take Me Out To the Ball Game'?" he said slowly. "Most people only know the chorus. The whole song—written in 1908—is about a woman who knows more about baseball than any of you fuckmonkeys combined. Better yet, the person who taught me that song was my own mom. She's the only woman I'd kill for."

He paused to sing,

"Katie Casey saw all the games,

Knew the players by their first names,

Told the umpire he was wrong, all along, good and strong..."

The back of his neck prickled. He turned around to see the entire cast of locals standing between them and the motel rooms, gathered to watch the impromptu show. The potbellied bartender—Con, was it?—staring them down with mismatched eyes. Grimy Lorne in his red jumpsuit, silently assessing them and whispering under his breath. Even the younger ones, Stacey and Joel, regarded them with unblinking solemnity. Only mad old Melvin Washington giggled behind his hand.

Mickey swung the bat in a wide, menacing arc, and the cluster of locals shuffled off to their respective corners. The four young men made a tight formation as they marched to their room with feigned insouciance.

"I don't know about the rest of you douchenozzles, but I've had so much fun giving these inbreds a run for their money in this shithole." Mickey's eyes were a little too bright, and he sniffed a few times before continuing. "I wish we could stay another year, but let's hit the road and get our asses down to where the party is!"

"Mickey, we haven't even had a chance to sleep yet," said Chip evenly. "The other guys are happy to take turns driving, but not everyone likes the same...enhancements."

"Fine!" snarled Mickey. "You can all snuggle up with each other and I'll make my own way to where the big boys party. Just don't expect me to do you any favors when we're back on campus and you're a nobody."

A knock at the door made them all jump. The door swung open without even a turn of the handle, revealing the grimy Lorne in his sagging red jumpsuit, as if he were wearing another man's skin.

"I need to have a word with a Chandler Murphy," he nearly whispered. "Ham radio announcements are pretty interested in this fella. Don't care none for the new-fangled communications, but anyone getting attention with the old ways is a person of interest to us."

Chandler smirked. "People really are just falling over themselves to offer their condolences," he told his comrades. "Carry on. I'll be back after I have a word with this human beef jerky."

The others snickered as Chandler followed Lorne out of the room.

Nobody was ready to let this interruption change the subject. "So where in New Orleans are you going to stay if you leave without us?" Bruce challenged. "You don't know where my family timeshare is or how to get in. You think you don't have to contribute just because you got us into the frat? I've got the digs, Chip has the sweet ride, and Chandler has the goods to bankroll our…"

Chandler came stumbling back in, face grey even in the weak, watery light.

"Guys?" he said. "I think I fucked up."

"What do you mean, 'we're now fugitives'?" demanded Mickey.

"Look, somebody had to get to the clinic first to take the best stuff," Chandler tried to justify. "Vet meds are expensive, and get resold before you can say 'woof'. Better me breaking into the clinic than some junkie who might tear the place apart not knowing where anything was, right?"

Silence had wrapped them into a cocoon of shock for a full twenty minutes before anyone spoke.

"How could somebody have possibly found your fingerprints?" Mickey bellowed. "Didn't you have an alibi?"

Chandler lay face up on the bed furthest from the window, still pale. "Not really. I didn't think it was a big deal, that maybe they'd think I was just...helping a family member at his job."

"You probably need to be employed as an assistant to do that. So now the school is possibly going to suspend us all for being accomplices," moaned Mickey. "And I can't even access my bank. There's no reception in this hole."

"I'll find a way to get us some money," chimed in Chip loyally. "I can sell my watch..."

Mickey sneered. "Who around here has any money for that? Bigfoot?"

Nobody said a word after that. The unspoken question remained: What are we going to do now?

With no money, no backup plan, and no remaining daylight, there was nothing for the foursome to do but go back to the bar. Chandler was too restless and finally had to step outside to clear his head in the cold winter air. A strange hooting and honking of some sort resonated from the direction of Devil's Ladder.

"They ain't real, you know," rasped a voice at his shoulder.

Chandler was almost glad to see Melvin standing next to him. Now he could pretend he had something to do.

"What aren't real? Those sounds out there?"

The old man wheezed a laugh. "Naw, I'm talking 'bout them stars up there. They're just a hoax created by the ancient Greeks to make people believe in catasterism."

"What's that?" Chandler was too intrigued by this crackpot theory to argue.

"That's when heroes on earth do such great deeds, or were so beloved by the Olympians, that the gods transformed them into constellations."

"Hmmm," was all Chandler knew to reply.

"And you don't disagree with me?" asked the old man lightly.

"Disagreeing is pointless," Chandler snarled. "I just stick to my own plans."

Melvin paused to cough into a grimy handkerchief. "Look, I get it that you want to fit in. But that tall guy in the baseball cap? He thinks he's running the show, but he needs to stay here. Any of them pills used yet?"

"How did you know…? Uh, I mean, no."

"Good. You just drive yourself right back to the clinic and slip those pills in there 'fore something worse happens."

"It's too late for that. And now we'll miss Mardi Gras."

"Your choice, boy. Get out of the way if you don't want to miss more than that."

Chandler didn't know what to do except turn on his heel and storm back into the bar, almost slamming face-first into Mickey. He wondered how much of the conversation the ringleader had heard, but he was too stressed to care.

Day two was dismal all around. Mickey and the three pledges were hungover and twice as unhappy to remember that they were officially broke, if not also potential fugitives. One by one, they filed out of the room and into the lobby to see what sort of money they could earn. Lorne seemed even less thrilled to have them staying longer than they were, but weighed their words.

"Well, you can always work off your room and board, and we might even be able to give you some extra gas money if you do good," he said at long last. "We always need firewood for the furnace under this joint." He pointed to a trapdoor in the floor. "That opens up to some stairs that'll take you right down to the tunnels."

The pile of rubble in the rear of the shop looked even less promising. It included one chainsaw that looked like it had seen better days, a heavy axe with some ominous looking notches along the blade, and a dolly that didn't seem like it would be much use carrying any cut wood. Mickey suggested the four load up the back of Chip's prized Hummer. Chip was deeply unhappy about this, so Mickey had no problem reminding him of his fraternal fealty.

Bruce was examining the axe blade, trying not to look at the ancient blunderbuss in the farthest corner, hoping the others hadn't seen it.

"Ever think of shootin' for the pot?" croaked a familiar voice. Bruce hadn't even seen Melvin approaching the group, and the old man's stealth unnerved him.

"You ain't interested in hunting? Easy way to get food, and we can roast up anything on a spit near the furnace. We sure could use a better source of protein than what the visitors usually deliver."

The young man shook his head, avoiding Melvin's eyes.

"So, we loves us some critters, do we? What would you do if you were alone in the woods and a unicorn came chargin' straight for ya?"

"That's easy," Bruce guffawed, more in relief at having something better to argue about. "Nothing, because there's no such things as unicorns."

"Zactly!" crowed Melvin. "They went extinct centuries ago. You ever seen horses fight?" Bruce gave a slow nod. "Now imagine that them stallions have long, sharp horns on their heads. One's gonna walk away alive and the other's gonna walk away dead. They got too good at fighting over who was gonna procreate, and even the stallions that prevailed didn't survive their injuries for long. Soon there was no one makin' babies, or they all became inbred and sterile. Whole population wiped itself out in the fourth century."

It was so plausible a reason for extinction that Bruce almost wanted to believe it.

"There ain't nothin' wrong with havin' a soft spot for animals. It shows you got empathy."

"It doesn't serve any purpose in the real world..." Bruce began, but the words died on his tongue as he took in his surroundings, with the harsh winter landscape and the very real possibility of going to extremes for survival.

"You know what critters could use your help? The ones that ain't got no medicines. You could return the drugs. Just let us have the guy in the baseball cap."

Unnerved, the young man jammed his hands into his pockets and turned to walk away. But something still compelled him to spin around to face Melvin.

"Just a minute! If unicorns really existed and only went extinct less than a couple of millennia ago, then why hasn't anyone found any bones or fossils? Y'know, like with dinosaurs?"

"Hee, hee!" The old man bent over double, wheezing. "You don't believe in unicorns, but you buy into that shit about dinosaurs? Boy, you better go back to school!"

Bruce was furious at having his intelligence insulted by a lunatic who looked like a living mummy. He glared around the shop, looking for some sort of tool to use on the money-earning mission. They landed on Mickey, who emerged from the corner, sniffing hard.

Bruce decided that no matter what Mickey heard, there was nothing with which to incriminate him. After all, he had not audibly concurred with Melvin's suggestion.

He closed his fingers around a hacksaw and tried not to imagine how good it would feel to sever their ringleader's head from his fat neck with it.

It had been a brutal afternoon, certainly nothing worth skipping school for. Four strapping young lads with not much in the way of muscle tone rolled back up to the storefront with a carload of timber—mostly fallen branches. No one had the strength to fell a living tree, and there was something creepy about the way the bark looked anyway.

The only thing worse than the branches tearing up the upholstery of Chip's Hummer was hauling them down the trapdoor through the tunnels.

The floor was damp and slippery, and the boys took turns lighting the way with their cell phones. They passed occasional squares cut into the walls, presumably leading to the heating ducts. Most unnerving of all were the strange symbols etched into the stones along the walls, hieroglyphs that didn't resemble any recognizable pictures or letters, but carried some sort of dire warning that transcended language. Lorne had hand-drawn them a shaky map of where the woodpile lay, which didn't seem to make sense, but they followed the source of heat until they found the macabre little antechamber that was woefully low on wood.

The smells of searing meat assaulted Mickey's nostrils. *No wonder the food's so rotten here,* he thought. *They don't even have a proper kitchen.*

The grimy showers did little to make them feel any fresher, but once they lined up at the bar, they felt a sense of structure.

"This sucks balls," muttered Chip, to no one in particular.

Mickey was on his right, slumped forward with his face smooshed onto the bar. The unexpected wheeze to his left would have normally made Chip jump out of his skin, but he was too exhausted to be creeped out by the skinny old man who always seemed to materialize out of nowhere.

Melvin grinned at the dour-faced pledge. "Well, it don't do no good to complain," he said. "Chopping wood is a skill, and you should be grateful for the opportunity to learn. Most boys work their way up in the corporate world, but they couldn't start a fire to save their lives. How you gonna stay alive when the fish start walking on land and evolution starts to happen for real?"

Chip tried to blink politely, committing this to memory so that he could tell the other guys. They'd get a kick out of it.

"Speakin' of takeovers, you could really do something to get yourselves out of this mess."

Chip was not in the mood to be lectured, but he also didn't feel like facing down his peers.

"You know, you could be back in school if you left now. You're not the one we want. The tall man and quiet man? Thems is trouble. One o' them is a control freak, and the other is a thief...and worse."

Chip went very still. "These are going to be my...brethren," he whispered. "Our motto is 'belief over logic'. No matter what improbable boogeymen you folks seem to think is out there, I'll be there to stand with my guys."

Mickey, still feigning sleep, smirked to himself.

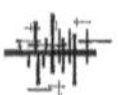

Joel was even more insufferable than usual, but the four were too tired to beat his ass at pool, or engage in any of the obnoxious rituals typical of Pi Tau Sigma Alpha. Blistered, aching, and unsure how they were going to continue earning their way out of their predicament, they fell into the twin beds, not even caring whose masculinity was threatened. Sleep hit them like a surreptitiously placed drug and they might have lain there all night if not for a mighty thud that shook the entire building.

The deep thuds in the forest grew louder, accompanied by a shriek that either could have been the rending of sheet metal or an animal.

Mickey reached for his pistol. "I'm not in the mood for some fucking bear to come knocking down our door."

"It's probably Joel fucking with us," slurred Bruce, fighting exhaustion to step up to the plate. "No need to go all Davy Crockett." The ginger man staggered to his feet, face betraying soreness and fatigue. Grabbing the bat, he ordered the others, "Just stay here. This shouldn't take long."

Mickey, who had the car keys, raised no objections.

By the time he was gone, the others were wide awake again. Whatever was out there didn't sound natural, and their basic instincts kept them on the alert. Chip reached into his suitcase and produced the last bottle of gin. It wasn't until they had nearly killed the entire contents that they noticed the noises had stopped. They waited for Bruce to return any second.

They upped the bravado to mitigate their growing unease. Mickey finally passed out in the corner, and the other two pledges curled up into a drunken slumber.

The mid-afternoon sun assaulted Mickey's eyes first when he opened the motel door. He tripped on something, swore, and drew back his foot to kick it in revenge, only to discover that it was Bruce's blood-smeared baseball bat.

There was a rusty nail driven so deeply into the wood that it had started to split in the middle. Bruce's severed, freckled hand was still wrapped around the grip and a worn piece of cardboard with the words 'STRIKE ONE' were scrawled in dark brown.

Chip would not leave the corner, shaking and sobbing.

Chandler paced the room like a caged animal. "I'm going to give him one of the horse tranquilizers I stole," he said at last. "Nobody's going to get any sleep or go anywhere until he calms down."

Mickey's head snapped up. "Wait a second! I'm not stupid! Horse tranquilizers are used as date rape drugs! What was your real agenda for robbing the vet clinic?"

"Look, it's not my fault women aren't more careful," Chandler snorted. He withdrew a bottle from his pocket. "If this stuff can calm a thoroughbred stallion, it'll be enough to make some filly too relaxed to say no. And the pills are worth their weight in gold on the street. You guys said you wanted to party, didn't you?"

"Dude..." Chip licked his lips. "That's just sick. So much for calling the police, asswipe. If we report that someone murdered Bruce, we'll get hauled in for carrying more than stolen goods. We've got contraband." He staggered to his feet, still shaking. "Mickey, I need the keys to my car. I'm going to drive to the next town and get us some real food and more booze. We can't chop wood if we live on this crap they try to pass off as food. I'm pretty sure I found a fingernail in my hamburger. You guys are supposed to be my brothers and all, but this is fucked up!"

He snatched the keys from Mickey's hand and bolted from the room, slamming the door behind him.

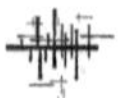

The hours that followed turned into a sort of aoristic bubble. The shadows in the room rose and fell, and still there was no sign of Chip. Hunger, exhaustion, stress and bewilderment finally snapped the last shred of the esprit de corps.

Chandler knocked a broken chair out of his path as he and Mickey squared off for dominance. Their room was already beginning to stink of sweat, piss, vomit and now blood. Somewhere deep beneath the floor, the grinding of the motel's power kicked on, droning like the gears of a giant mixer.

"Okay, buddy," growled Mickey. "Before we go on, let's be clear about something. You tell me where you've hidden those pills, and we'll find a way to go anywhere you want. You can have your fucking Poutsa membership, whatever... I don't care. We destroy the pills and never speak of this again."

He wouldn't have minded an easy piece of ass, but he had to draw the line.

"Wouldn't you like to know?" snarled Chandler. "I'll bet nobody even cares. Don't believe me? Turn on that TV and if you see us on America's Most Wanted, I'll hand over every pill with a smile on my face."

Chandler and Mickey could not get the television set in their room to work, no matter how much they twisted and manipulated the antennae. It wasn't until they ducked back into the lobby that they saw a Polaroid snapshot nailed to the wall. Details were grainy, but a tiny section of the photo revealed a vehicle burned to a crisp, unmistakably Chip's Hummer.

Emblazoned into the nearby hillside were the words: 'STRIKE TWO'.

Both young men froze, living echoes of the stuffed, senseless animal heads on the wall behind them.

After several long minutes of mute disbelief, Chandler was the first to regain his wits. "I'm telling you, it's that douchebag Lorne who incinerated the car!" he snarled. "He's the one with access to the gasoline."

The door to the lobby banged open. "If you mean me, I just woke up, so explain to me how I burned a car twenty miles away, eh?"

"What do you want with us?" snarled Mickey.

"Someone just came 'round this area looking for you boys," Lorne replied, in an even tone. "Are you interested in the details?"

"We're busy." Mickey spat, heart thudding. He turned on his heel, and Chandler followed like a shadow.

Anyone looking for them would most likely be unaware of the tunnels. The two young men only had to signal each other with a look. Back down the trapdoor they scrambled, with no real plan other than to remain hidden until the investigation was over.

There was no obvious pattern to the chthonic labyrinth, so they made their way toward the only passage they knew—the furnaces—like moths to a flame. The scent was cloyingly sweet this time, part decay and some other odor Mickey couldn't pinpoint. Cinnamon? He shook his head. The flashlights on their cell phones still worked, the drawback being that if anyone was following them, they could be seen.

And indeed, there was the distinct sound of footsteps behind them. They turned off their lights and held their breath, but the footsteps kept coming. Mickey pulled his revolver from his waistband and fired at the approaching figure.

A female cry of pain made his blood run cold. He snapped his flashlight app back on and ran to the prone figure and screamed uncontrollably at the sight of the woman blinking wordlessly at the ceiling. Her blue eyes were identical to his, only set with laugh lines like artful filigree. Mickey fell to his knees and gathered his mother in his arms. Blood-soaked bills—American and Canadian—spilled out of her pockets and the pieces clicked in his mind.

"Mickey..." She stroked his cheek with one bloody hand. "I hired a PI..." She paused to take a gurgling breath. "Traced the GPS as far as I could. They're coming for you. And I don't mean the police. You were supposed to choose the right team..."

Her body went deadweight in his arms.

Mickey had just killed the only person who had ever comforted him. And he had clearly taken on traits of his father instead.

"This was a setup!" screamed Chandler. "The only one who saw us go into the tunnels was Lorne. He's the only one who could have told your mom where to find us."

He grabbed the gun from Mickey, who was in too much shock to protest the confiscation of the weapon that had killed his mother. The last pledge took off running with the pistol, the flicker of his cell phone fading with his footsteps.

Mickey had no idea how long he sat there in the dark, alone with his dead mother. Time had no meaning, but he snapped to his senses when the tunnel suddenly flared with an orange light as someone lit the furnace. The blast of heat singed him so strongly that the only thing protecting his scalp was his beloved Baby Cakes baseball cap.

He let go of his mother's corpse, now beginning to stiffen, and scrambled away from the heat source. He would return for her body, he promised himself. But first he had to stay alive long enough to give her a proper funeral. After that, he would turn himself in. Nobody could say that he hadn't tried to face down his fears.

But now nobody alive knows what you were afraid of in the first place, chided the voice in the back of his mind.

The mechanical whir of machinery forced his mind out of panic mode and his body toward the stairs leading to the trapdoor.

He stole out of the lobby and pelted toward the room, but there was no one in sight. Mickey opened the door to find his mangled pistol on the floor, lying next to a piece of Chandler's blood-soaked polo shirt. Scrawled on the cloth in a Sharpie were the words: 'STRIKE THREE'.

The last man standing knew it was only a matter of time before Melvin approached him. The younger man sat at the bar trying to drink his raw nerves into submission as Washington heralded his entrance, singing a few bars of an old Confederate song Mickey recognized as 'Cheer, Boys, Cheer!'

The crazy old geezer pulled up a barstool beside him and croaked, "You can't escape the inevitable, son."

Mickey's pent-up terror, exhaustion, and perpetual cocaine buzz finally exploded. "But first, I'm gonna have my own little Mardi Gras right here, baby!" he wailed.

He banged on the bar and locked eyes with Con's mismatched gaze as the bartender poured a pint of Warden into the murky glass. The young man downed it in five gulps, but the drink was stronger than he was expecting.

And the voices came, as if his drink had been drugged. "Hey, baby..." they called.

Mickey followed the voices as if stripped of his will. The lights of Whiskey Pete's grew dimmer behind him as he shambled off to the tunnels. They seemed to twist and bend around him like sentient channels, neurons of the bar's rapidly changing mind.

Psssst!

He turned to follow the hiss and watched something wander angularly ahead of him. It was an arm and a leg attached by most of a torso, lumbering in a sickly bipedal gait. He trailed the grisly animated remains, helpless to his horror.

The corridor widened to a ritual chamber ablaze with candles. His addled mind could scarcely register what sat before him: a gory pentagram the length of a human body drawn on the floor. At nearly each point of the star was a head: Bruce's, sunken and drawn; Chandler's, which still retained part of his trachea; Chip's, charred with most of the hair burned away; and his own mother's, perfect and placid as if she were sleeping.

The final point at the bottom was empty and waiting.

"But first we're going to have a party," rumbled a voice that came from everywhere. "You wanted your own Mardi Gras right here, Baby Cakes!"

The world went black.

The smells that assaulted Mickey's senses were what roused him first, with the terrifying realization that he barely had any sort of ventilation. He was blind and nearly deaf, his entire body paralyzed...

No, he was encased in something. He nearly gagged on the odors of charred flesh, burnt hair, and sickly sweet cake batter.

He was a human king cake baby.

"Be a good sport," the voice whispered.

The hard thunk of something cleaving into the floor a body's length away was still audible through the meaty confection cocoon. He knew the sound of the axe. Even buried in the carnage cake, he could hear guttural laughter.

Mickey played the song in his head, hoping to invoke some burst of courage:

When the score was just two to two
Katie Casey knew what to do,
Just to cheer up the boys she knew,
She made the gang sing this song...

The second strike of the blade slicing the cake just below his feet almost made him scream. He could hear the roaring of crowds and the chant, "Tomahawk chop! Tomahawk chop!"

A second strike of the axe above his head, and his bowels voided themselves. This time he cried, knowing he had failed.

The third strike split his pelvis in two, splintering his mind into white-hot agony.

As his consciousness faded, the last words he heard were, "You're out!"

OH, THAT DALE
By Lynne Phillips

The Proprietor of Whiskey Pete's,

Hoping you can help me find my son, Dale.

I received a letter posted at Chevron six months ago. He said his van
had broken down, and an old dude called Lorne was helping fix it.

I haven't heard from him since. He is thirty years old, blonde hair,
blue eyes and works for Acme Cleaning. He wears overalls with his
name embroidered on them. Please help.

Mary Jo Samuels

Tina Belliveau pulls the Polaroid from the inside of her leather jacket and looks at it for what must be the thousandth time, her chilled and dirty fingers adding a layer of grime to its edges.

Leaning forward to keep the persistent drizzle off the overexposed picture, Tina compares the photo to the scene before her.

The only person she recognizes is Rebecca Kaufmann. She's standing intimately close to a handsome man in his early 30s with overalls tied around his waist and a wrench in his hand.

Splayed out like an awkward family around the couple are a group of characters that Tina would expect to fit into an episode of 'Unsolved Mysteries' with no problem.

God, Becca! How did you end up here, of all places?

Tina looks up from the Polaroid and sees Whiskey Pete's in the flesh, and it looks worse in person. The flickering neon sign hums at a pitch that makes a person's fillings ache, as it shines its sickly, red-orange light on the buildings. Rusted and faded gas pumps stand out in front, the closest one sporting an 'out of order' sign a child could have written. Behind the pumps is a dilapidated store attached to Whiskey Pete's itself. A small stack of motel rooms peek out from around back. Even the lack of cell signal adds to the impression that she's stepped back in time. Whiskey Pete's is carved out of an old growth forest, the trees lean as if they want to swallow the cancer infesting it.

Christ on a cracker, Tina. Listen to yourself! You're letting your imagination run wild just because it's a dark and rainy spring evening. You're here to do a job, so get started.

Shaking herself, Tina jams the Polaroid back into the jacket. She confirms that the letter that accompanied the picture is still there, and steps off the crumbling asphalt onto the gravel yard of Whiskey Pete's.

The second she does, a headache forms behind her left eye.

"Just frigging great. You better be here, Rebecca; this hunt will be the death of me."

"Can I be helping you, Miss?" a low rough voice asks from behind Tina, causing her to jump.

Twisting around, the gravel crunching under her boots, Tina takes on a fighting stance, clenched fists ready, and regards the man who surprised her.

If Tina's quick reactions surprised or impressed the old man sitting with his back to the broken gas pump, he showed no sign. He just takes another pull on his cigarette, heedless of the drizzle soaking into his red coveralls, a frayed nametag reading, 'Dale'.

Seeing that the small, elderly man doesn't seem inclined to hop up and attack, Tina lowers her arms, though her fists remain clenched.

"Sorry. You startled me. Ah, you know it's raining, right?" Tina asks, her right eye narrowing in puzzlement.

"Rain or sun, what does it matter? We're all just bags of rotting meat waiting for the world to end, anyway. Why should a little rain make a difference, eh?" says the old man, scratching his soaked and greasy looking hair.

The scent of wet dog and cigarette smoke fills Tina's nose, and she takes an involuntary step back, right into a mud puddle.

"Whatever, I had some car issues about a mile or so back," Tina says, tilting her head towards the ancient highway. "I was wondering if there might be a mechanic around here. I'm not keen on trudging the twenty or so miles back to Chevron, and I didn't see a single other car all afternoon."

The old man groans and waves off a non-existent offer of help from Tina, as he pulls himself upright, his blackened fingernails blending into the gas hose.

Hobbling past Tina, the old man mumbles, "No rest for the wicked. Man can't even get a smoke in peace with all the interruptions." He splashes through mud puddles in worn out work boots with no laces. Halfway to the rundown store, he pauses, looks over his shoulder at Tina and says, "You comin'? I figure you'll be wanting a mechanic?"

Not waiting for her reply, he resumes his unsteady shuffle that only stops when he reaches the aluminum screen door, holding it open for Tina.

"Becca, I'm starting to hope you're not here now," Tina says under her breath, gives the old man a weak smile of thanks, and walks into the store.

The dented door slams behind Tina, catching her heel and making her stumble into the store, though thankfully she didn't collide with the old . She knocks a rack of potato chips, raising a cloud of dust into the stale air of the store.

Wiping her hands on her jeans, Tina glances around the store, sees the dust, mice droppings under the chocolate bar display, and the overloaded fly strip hanging over the clunking deli cooler and puts her hands in her pockets.

As if a headache wasn't bad enough, now my stomach feels like I drank battery acid.

"Drew, ya lazy bugger, get on out here. There be a lady looking for a mechanic," the old man bellows, his voice like rocks in a tumbler.

He shuffles behind the counter and tosses his cigarettes into the cash register and slams it shut, its bell giving a hollow ring.

"Drew!" he shouts again and spits into a stained glass, leans against a rickety metal stool and picks up a battered paperback novel. The faded picture of a sad man in early 19th century clothing tugs at a memory, but fades before materializing.

Breathing through her mouth and doing her best to tune out the drone of flies coming from the deli case, in which she swears she sees the cling-wrapped sandwiches moving, Tina gives a start as a younger man walks into the store from a back room.

That's him, the guy with his arm around Becca.

Drew walks over to Tina, wiping his hands on a greasy rag. He gives Tina a nod and says, "You having car troubles?" and leans to look over her shoulder through the grimy store window.

I can see why you might have fallen for him Becca. He is rather handsome in a dumb lug sort of way. Though something is clearly up with him. Pale as a ghost, eyes kinda jaundiced, and his left cheek has a nervous twitch.

Shaking her head out of her mental musing, Tina replies to Drew. "Yeah, sorry. It's been a day. My van conked out on me a mile or so back, I still got half a tank of gas so that's not it. I'm just wondering if I could get a tow or something."

Tina's eyes narrow as she watches Drew give the old man at the till a cautious glance, but as far as Tina can tell, the old man is too busy picking his nose to pay attention to them.

Pulling his eyes back to Tina, Drew responds. "Sorry, but we don't have a tow truck here at Whiskey Pete's. Nothing roadworthy at the moment, in fact, but I'd be happy to look at your van for you. Just let me gather a couple tools."

"No vehicle? If you say so. I appreciate the help, just not looking forward to that walk in the rain again."

Drew gives a sad smile and hurries to the back room, the clunk and rattle of metal tools noticeable and a welcome distraction to the nose picking.

Minutes go by as Tina contemplates waiting outside where the air is fresher, but eventually Drew hurries out with an old canvas duffel bag over his shoulder, its contents rattling like a broken dishwasher.

"Lorne, I'm just going to go help this lady with her van, but I promise to be back. I promise, okay?"

If Lorne was paying any attention, he didn't show it. And after some unseen signal, Drew nods his head and brushes past Tina and into the afternoon drizzle.

With a quick glance at Lorne and seeing that he's attempting to get a second finger up his nostril, Tina shivers and welcomes a cleansing walk in the rain.

"Can you fix it?" Tina asks from behind Drew, who jumps as if electrocuted. He tries to hide it by rolling up the cuffs of his coveralls, but it's plain to see he's scared.

Stepping sideways so he doesn't have to come any closer to Tina than necessary, Drew slams the hood of the van, splashing rain water over them both.

"Nothing to fix. Your battery cable was just off."

"That's odd. Maybe it popped off when I hit a pothole. This road has seen better days," Tina says, and taps the crumbling asphalt with her boot.

"Maybe. Those things rarely come off without some effort. Why don't you try starting it up?"

Darn straight it was hard to get off, just about smashed my knuckles doing it, Tina thinks to herself.

Sliding into the driver's seat of the van, the cracked vinyl seat pushing her soaked jeans against her flesh, chilling her further, Tina turns the key in the ignition. The van rumbles to life, and the worn wipers squeal and stutter against the windshield.

Tina watches through the windshield as Drew stares at her with a hopeful look on his drawn face. He hurries around the front of the van as if Tina were about to dash off without him. As he scrambles into the front passenger seat, the van rocks on its abused shocks.

"How about we get some heat going? I'm chilled to the bone," Drew says and begins rubbing his hands.

Shivering, Tina does as suggested and cranks the heater to max, the blower fan howling at the unaccustomed workload.

When her shivering slows enough that some dexterity in her fingers returns, Tina pulls out the Polaroid, drops it on Drew's lap and says, "So where's Rebecca Kaufmann?"

Drew jumps as if bitten by a snake, the Polaroid falling to the floor of the cabin. "How did you? I mean... I don't know... Oh god, what's the use?"

Bending down, Drew picks up the Polaroid with shaky fingers and stares at it. Some color returns to his cheeks and his posture straightens as if a mighty weight has lifted.

"Sweet Rebecca..."

"Well, out with it, where is she? Is she alive? Is she back at the bar or is her body rotting in a shallow grave?" Tina snaps, though chattering teeth rob her voice of some fierceness.

Tears flow down Drew's face and splash onto the abused photo. Shaking his head, either to displace memories or tears, Tina doesn't know.

"Oh, for god's sake, there're tissues in the glove box, I think," Tina says, frustration clear in her voice.

While Drew sniffs and rummages for a tissue, Tina jams the van into drive and avoids slippery patches not yet melted from the April rains. She drives them back to Whiskey Pete's.

I don't know what I expected from him, but a weeping doll afraid of his own shadow wasn't it.

"Ok, enough crying. Tell me what you know, we'll be back at the bar soon."

"Back? Please, no. Let's just keep driving. Don't stop. I'm begging you, get us away from this place before it's too late."

"Not happening without Becca, so talk," Tina says, taking one hand off the wheel to fish out a folded piece of paper, which she also tosses onto Drew's lap. "Listen, I know you care for her, but others do too."

Blowing onto his fingers, Drew unfolds the letter and reads.

"'Dear Chris, I can't tell you where I am. Every time I try to write it, something stops me...' Hey, this is in Rebecca's handwriting."

"No shit, Sherlock, she wrote it," Tina snorts.

Drew continues reading aloud. "'But I hope I've found a way around that. I wish I could tell you I'm happy and safe away from the clutches of my family, but I'm not. I met a great guy named Drew; he's quiet, kind and can fix anything broken, even me. We've been traveling the country looking for an out of the way place to settle down, and for a minute we thought we'd found it. We wanted to start a life together, maybe even start a family, but we're in trouble and need your help.'"

"'I know we fell out of touch over the years, and I'm sorry my rejection hurt you so badly, but we had a lot of fun as kids. Remember the games we'd play in Mr. Dumas' theater class? I want you to remember that friendship and do what you can for us. I pray this letter finds its way to you before it's too late. Your loving friend, Becca.'"

The chilly wind invading through cracked door seals and the labored attempts of the heater to offset the loss are the only sounds for several minutes before Drew speaks.

"Becca mentioned this friend Chris several times. Parents worked for Becca's family or something."

Yeah, or something. Housekeeper and gardener to one of the wealthiest families on the east coast. But we didn't see the barrier as kids, just two lonely girls who played together until the gates of puberty changed everything, including my feelings...

"Where did you get this?" Drew says, voice raw with emotion.

"It came to me from Rebecca Kaufmann's family. I'm a private investigator looking for her, and my hunt led me to Whiskey Pete's and you. So, where's Becca?"

Drew begins shaking. Not just from the cold. Tina gives the weeping man a couple of minutes to purge his emotions and focuses her energy on navigating the crumbling road back to Whiskey Pete's.

"Okay, we're out of time. We're almost back. I can see your feelings for Becca are real, but you need to tell me what we're getting into and hurry."

Wiping his nose on his sleeve, Drew gets his sobbing under control.

He folds the worn letter and passes it back to Tina, who jams it into the inside pocket of her leather coat beside the Polaroid.

"I don't know where Becca is, honest. I assume she saw a chance to escape this place and took it without me. I should have known she wouldn't have abandoned me. I'm sorry, Becca. I knew she was trying to smuggle a letter out. She must have found a way."

Pulling into the gravel parking lot, Tina drives the van around the back of the store and in front of a two-story stack of shabby motel rooms. Throwing the van into park, she twists around to face Drew, the wet leather of her jacket creaking against the vinyl of the driver's seat.

"Okay, quit being so vague. This isn't a daytime soap opera. What is the deal with Whiskey Pete's?"

At the mention of the bar, Drew's head snaps up, and he realizes where he is. Blood rushes from his face and his voice shakes. "I can't... I just can't!"

Drew scrambles at the passenger door latch and tumbles out of the van, sprawling into the mud. Like a dog being whipped, he scrambles to his feet and dashes off towards the tree line behind the motel, disappearing in the twilight.

"Just fucking great!" Tina mutters.

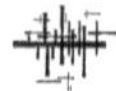

"Well, at least the heat's on!" Tina says, shaking her hair free of the rain that started as soon as she left her van and hurried into the bar. The rain and her foul mood put an end to any thoughts of chasing Drew into the dark forest.

Putting her hair into a quick ponytail, Tina flicks the wet mass over her shoulder and jumps, seeing the woman seated not three feet from her, still as stone.

"Christ on a cracker!" Tina yells, fists rising.

After several seconds of shaking adrenaline, Tina slows her breathing, stops the jack-hammering pain in her chest and lowers her arms, fists still clenched.

"Sorry, I didn't see you there. Guess I'm jumpy with the weather and all..." Tina says, then pauses when she realizes the woman still hasn't moved.

Just great, Tina. What did you get yourself into now?

"Ah, excuse me...Stacey," Tina says, looking at the name tag on the woman's retro blue dress.

Like a flipped switch, Stacey comes to life and faces Tina, beautiful lips wide in a welcoming smile, eyes staring over Tina's shoulder.

Resisting the urge to look, Tina tells herself that the cold wetness she feels between her shoulder blades is rainwater and not nervous sweat. Putting on her own best smile, which she knows is pale compared to Stacey's, Tina says, "I'd like a room, please. One night, maybe more."

Giggling as if Tina said something funny. Stacey pulls a key from the pegboard behind her, the peeling wallpaper waving from the slight motion, and slides the key stamped '3' across the chipped countertop.

"Maybe more. That's funny. You check out when you pay," Stacey says grinning.

"You mean I pay when I check out?" Tina replies and scoops up the worn, brass key.

A vacant smile is Stacey's only reply.

Becca, I hope like heck you managed to get away from this nuthouse.

Putting Stacey out of her thoughts for the moment, Tina walks into Whiskey Pete's.

God, this place looks like a set for a B-Movie. Like it's out of the pages of an old magazine that idolizes testosterone and blood sport, Tina thinks to herself, as she takes in the dark bar.

The faint haze of cigarette smoke that clings to the ceiling helps to frame the stuffed animal heads mounted on the walls. The faded photos of the bar from years past, and wooden furniture held together with sticky grime and little else.

Some guy from the back of the bar stops his solo game of pool and leans against the table. He watches Tina as if she's the first woman he's seen in ages. He places his cue on the faded felt and starts walking towards her, but freezes as a booming voice yells, "Joel, stick to your own goddamn lane!"

Joel's eyes flash towards the bar, then back to Tina, before he gives her a lopsided grin and shuffles back to the pool table as if he's being chased.

What am I getting myself into here?

Doing her best to portray a sense of confidence, Tina stomps to the bar and the man who just yelled at the pool-player, Joel.

The man looks more bouncer than bartender, but in a small place like Whiskey Pete's, it's likely they roll the two jobs into one. Built like a broken-down football player, a body gone to seed, but Tina notices the muscle under the flab and knows he's seen his share of bar brawls.

He doesn't even acknowledge Tina when she sits on a bar stool, sticky with spilled beer and God knows what else. It isn't until she slaps a twenty dollar bill beside his hand and shouts, "Whiskey", that he grunts and pulls a bottle out and snags a shot glass from a tray.

Walking as if he were a force of nature, he slams the bottle down on the wet bar top. The mixture of stale alcohol and dirty water add another layer of moisture to Tina's leather jacket.

Pouring the amber fluid flips a switch in Tina's stomach and her belly reminds her it hasn't been fed in hours.

"Thanks. Leave the bottle, okay? Any chance I can get something to eat? It's been a long, wet day."

The bartender pauses, face taking on the expression of one just tasked with bringing about world peace, and grunts.

Fucking dude is weird, and what's with avoiding eye contact? Scared I'll steal his soul or something?

"A sandwich to go will be fine. A Reuben possible?"

The bartender grunts again and stomps away.

Tina picks up the shot glass, rolls it between her fingers, grabs a handful of pretzels from the bowl on the bar top. She looks into the mirror above the bar, stealing a look at her fellow patrons, all of them in the Polaroid.

What a miserable-looking bunch, and I've been to live poetry readings on ladies' night. Tina sips whiskey that makes her eye squint and steals the breath from her lungs. She nibbles on a pretzel, shivers in disgust, and drops the rest onto a napkin.

Taking another sip of the rot-gut, Tina looks into the mirror above the bar again.

Other than the pool player, none of them have even shown the slightest interest in me. I can't believe a place like this sees many strangers, let alone women on their own. You think that would warrant a glance or two. But no, it's like they're in their own little spheres, together but not touching. Damned weird.

Tina watches as Stacey and the shopkeeper Lorne enter the bar, though they don't even acknowledge each other, heading for different tables in the poorly lit bar.

The bartender shakes her out of her musings, walking to her carrying a sandwich wrapped in wax paper.

"Thanks," Tina says, holding up another twenty and the Polaroid from her pocket. "Can I bother you for another minute? See this young woman here, who's standing six feet away from you in the picture? I'm looking for her, do you know her, or where she is?"

The twenty dollar bill waves.

"Nope," being the bartender's only reply, he scoops up the pretzels from Tina's napkin and replaces them into the bowl.

"Nope, as in you don't know her, or nope as in you don't know where she is?" Tina asks, failing to keep her tone natural.

"Yup," the bartender says, dropping the sandwich on the bar top and snagging the twenty before stomping away.

Fucking beautiful.

Sensing that tonight is not her night, Tina slides the wrapped sandwich into her jacket, grabs the whiskey bottle and walks out of the bar. Only the pool player watches her leave.

Tina has to jiggle the brass key in the worn motel door, but eventually hears the click of the locks release and looks upon her room.

"Fuck, I've had nights in the drunk tank that were nicer than this," Tina curses, as she looks into the spare and rundown space.

The duvet has a stain on it that Tina tells herself must be red wine. The olive green shag carpeting doesn't look like it's seen a vacuum since the Berlin wall went up, and the smell suggests a dead mouse or two in the walls.

A broken security latch and the general sense of unease that has settled on her since arriving at Whiskey Pete's prompts her to act. Tina grabs one of the two chairs from the side table and jams it under the doorknob. With a solid kick to wedge it tight, Tina nods. *I don't like the look of this place at all. Too many surprises by far. Wish I hadn't followed state laws and left my gun home, I'd feel more comfortable with it on my hip.*

Thumbing the thermostat to maximum, Tina gives a happy sigh as the floor rumbles below her. Hot air issues up from the two-foot square, cast iron register embedded in the carpeted floor. Wrinkling her nose at the sour smell carried with the warm air, she tosses her duffel bag she retrieved from her van onto the bed. Making sure the moth-eaten curtains are closed, she peels off wet clothes.

Wearing only her socks, not liking her naked skin touching the filthy carpet, Tina drapes her clothes over the second chair and places it near the grating in the floor. Pulling the Polaroid and letter from the inside pocket of her leather coat, Tina snags the whiskey bottle and walks into the bathroom, shutting the door behind her.

"Christ on a cracker, what is *with* this place?" Tina mumbles, face screwed up in disgust as she watches the rusty water flow from the bathtub's tap. Taking a deep pull from the whiskey bottle, she sucks on her teeth as the liquor burns her insides. She waits for it to numb the cold radiating up from the bathroom's dirty tile floor.

Minutes later, clear, hot water issues from the tap, rewarding her patience, and steam displaces the cold air. Peeling off her socks and tossing them into the sink for a wash later, Tina steps into the hot water and lets it warm her chilled bones.

Balancing the Polaroid in the empty soap tray, Tina looks at her childhood friend and takes another deep pull from the bottle.

Are you alive, Becca? Did one of these miserable bastards do something to you? Did Drew? Is that why he ran? I can't believe that. He's a big guy, but he strikes me as a gentle giant. No, my money is on one of them in the bar.

Staring at the Polaroid, Tina focuses on each face and realizes that she's seen everyone in the photo, and no one else.

That's kinda odd, isn't it? I mean, I've only been here a couple hours and everything I learned in Chevron, how they wouldn't talk about this joint, suggested this place was weird, but EVERYONE is here all the time? That begs the question...who took the photo?

A long soak and half the bottle of whiskey in her gut, Tina drags herself out of the cooling water. She turns her nose up at the moldy towel hanging from the rack and walks into the bedroom. Chaos greets her.

"Fuck me gently with a 2x4!" Tina curses as she looks upon her room.

They'd strung the contents of her duffel bag about the seedy motel room. They'd turned out the pockets of her clothes and even shredded the lining of her leather jacket. Standing naked, dripping wet, Tina grabs the lamp off the side table and searches her room for the intruder. With no closet, the search comprises looking under the bed and finding nothing but several decades of spider webs, proving no one was hiding under there. The wedged chair still secures the room, and countless layers of paint stop the window from opening. Tina circles the tiny room like a caged lion, then tosses the lamp onto the bed.

Nope, not going to happen. I don't care how cold it is outside in April, one night in the van won't kill me, I don't think I could say the same if I stayed here.

Jamming on still-damp clothes, Tina tosses her belongings back into her duffel bag, the wrapped sandwich on top. She retrieves the whiskey bottle and Polaroid from the bathroom. She scans the room one last time, kicks the chair away from the door and exits room number three. The door sways wide, the heat from the floor grating pumping away.

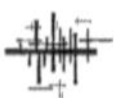

"This will do nicely," Tina says to herself, as she settles into the backseat of her van, but even to her own ears, her enthusiasm sounds hollow.

Checking for the fourth time she'd locked all the van doors, she taps the lug wrench she dug out from the back of the van that rests by her thigh and stares out into the rainy night. Her former motel room is a faint shadow against the dark.

Problem one. What were they looking for? All I can assume is that it was the Polaroid and/or the letter, since they took nothing, not even my limited cash.

The torn lining of her much-abused leather jacket lent weight to that thought. The photo and letter are now stashed in her hip pocket.

Problem two, Tina thinks as she unwraps the war-torn sandwich from the bar, *how did whoever toss my room get in and why didn't I hear anything? It was like they were a ghost?*

"Come on, can nothing go right today!" Tina whines, the limp sandwich flopping back and forth in her rage. "I said a Reuben, not a Monte Cristo! God, what did they use for meat in this thing?"

Tina smells the sandwich, before wrapping it back up and tossing it onto the front passenger seat.

"Looks like it's just you and me tonight, baby."

She takes a long drink from the whiskey bottle and squirms to get comfortable. She watches as a thunder and lightning storm moves in, the flashes casting shadows within the van adding to her sense of dread.

"Fucking perfect."

Jarred out of a broken sleep, Tina scrambles in the dark to retrieve the lug wrench, knocking over the empty whiskey bottle. Her nails scratch the floor of the van, but her fingers clasp the security of the wrench as awareness seeps back to her.

Between the rain pounding against the side of the van and the rot-gut whiskey, Tina entered a disturbed sleep. Snatches of dreams dissolve before she can grasp them, though they leave a lingering sense of unease.

"Help, please god no!"

Tina realizes the screaming woke her. It picks up volume, the terror in the voice clear through the walls of the van.

Leaning over the driver's seat, wiping the condensation from the inside of the windshield, she sees that the light in her motel room is on. Streaks of light escape through the thin curtains and the door is closed. The terrified voice cries out in primal fear.

"Drew!" Tina yells in sympathy, and scrambles into the driver's seat, lug wrench in hand.

After an eternity, shaking hands unlock the van's door and she tumbles into the gravel parking lot behind Whiskey Pete's as a fresh round of screaming begins.

Gasping to catch her breath from her fall, Tina drags herself to her feet and jogs towards the door of room number three.

A distant part of Tina's mind notices that, sometime while she was in her whiskey laden sleep, the rain had stopped. The stars are out, bringing a freshness to the air that has been missing since she got to Whiskey Pete's.

Getting her feet under her, Tina can now see shadows of movement coming from within her motel room. A last, blood-curdling cry nearly freezes her in her tracks, but she leans forward and forces her legs to pump harder. Running, Tina jams a hand into her pocket, only to realize the room key must still be in the van.

Swearing, she picks up speed and slams against the wooden door.

The door splinters easy, and Tina flies into her motel room and rolls into a drunken tumble. Using the motion, she gets to her feet, swaying as if having spent a day on a roller coaster, the lug wrench held out with her left hand.

The motel room is empty.

"What the hell?" Tina says, the adrenaline coursing through her veins displacing the alcohol and bringing the reality of her fear to the front of her thoughts.

"Come out, you bastard!" Tina yells, kicking the bed frame, metal jumping from the shag carpet and thumping back to the floor.

Nothing.

Shifting her focus to the bathroom, Tina stomps over the heating vent and kicks the door open. Bouncing off the enameled sink, the door flies back, but comes up short against Tina's boot.

"Fuck!"

Checking the small room twice, Tina swings back into the main room as if she could have missed someone.

The room has been the scene of recent violence. The side table has been reduced to campfire wood, wide streaks of blood paint the faded and peeling wallpaper, and both chairs are tossed into the corner of the room.

Taking deep breaths, ignoring the pounding in her chest, Tina lowers the lug wrench and unzips her leather jacket. She forces her mind to shift from fight to observation and looks at the motel room.

OK, a fight from the looks of it, means at least two people. So where in the hell did they go? Not through the front door and the bathroom window is too small, nor was there enough time.

Checking under the bed again, a flash of metal catches her eye. Kneeling, Tina stretches, fingers grasping through the dirty carpet and pulls out a wrench, shiny with use.

Damn. Okay, that nails it. It was Drew's voice I heard crying out. He's capable and wouldn't be a pushover in a fight. None of this makes sense. Where did they go?

Moving away from the floor grating, Tina lets the cool, outside air rushing into the motel room blow onto her face, further sobering her.

I can't be the only one who heard the screams, can I?

A quick look out the door confirms the neon sign by the road is still lit, meaning the bar is probably still open.

Do I go there looking for help? None of them seemed to care for visitors, and how do I know one or more of them isn't responsible. I think I saw an old pay phone, but would state troopers get out here before light? My gut says no.

Thinking about her stomach causes Tina's to ache in protest due to the putrid stench coming up from the floor grate.

"God, Tina. You're a fool. The heating duct!"

Dropping to her knees, Tina levers the lug wrench under the large cast iron floor grate and pries. With a groan of metal against metal, the grating rises and she flops it onto the filthy carpet. Coughing, Tina looks down into the square ductwork and sees a fresh smear of blood against the aged metal.

Sparing a glance outside, Tina looks at her van and back down into the dark hole leading beneath the motel.

Fuck Becca, what have you gotten yourself into? Tina thinks, and strips off her leather jacket. Tina makes sure the Polaroid and letter are in her hip pocket before lowering herself down into the hole and into the dark.

"God, I wish I had brought the flashlight from the van," Tina curses, trying to orientate herself in the cramped darkness of the heating ducts.

With only the light from the motel room to help her, Tina grips the lug wrench tight and waits for her eyes to adjust.

It would appear that she is in the central plenum of the motel's heating system. Which makes sense with her room being the middle one on ground level.

Mental note, next time insist on a room on the end of the complex...

Two narrowing ducts leading off at 90 degrees from her position, each filled with undisturbed spider webs and dust.

"That leaves me with only one choice then," Tina says, and stares into the large main duct, hot, putrid air hitting her in the face.

With a last look at the yellow light shining down from her motel room, Tina hooks the lug wrench through a belt loop and crawls into the duct.

Doing her best imitation of a green recruit learning to army crawl under barbed wire, Tina uses her elbows and bare feet to make steady progress down the square metal tunnel.

Breathing through her nose, Tina does her best to ignore the scratches forming on her arms, the repeated clunks as her head meets the roof of the tunnel, and the lug wrench poking her in the thigh.

I guess I should be grateful I can't see a thing, even imagining what I'm crawling through is enough to make me nauseous.

Soon, time and direction lose all meaning, and Tina just concentrates on pushing herself forward. Pausing for a breather, she twists herself to look back, the lug wrench poking her ribs, and sees the faint glow of light from the motel room.

Hell, likely only a hundred feet. How much longer does this go?

With no answer, Tina continues on down the tunnel.

A short time later, she realizes her progress has improved, as the floor of the duct is wet and the familiar, coppery scent of fresh blood fills her nostrils.

"Damn."

Tina picks up the pace when she sees a faint glow of light in front of her, and the blood coating the floor of the ductwork.

As she nears the source of the light, she hears the low drone of machinery and uses that noise to cover her own labors through the ducting. The source of the machinery soon becomes clear, as the hot air that's been cascading around her for the past while has grown hotter and more violent.

Crap, I must be almost at the boiler. There must be a way out.

Tina's fears of being trapped pass as she sees a grille in the duct. She looks down into a large furnace room filled with fermenting tanks and other equipment for making alcohol.

This must be the furnace room below the bar, I guess that makes sense.

Tina does her best to scope out the furnace room, but the slated grille limits her viewpoint. Her eyes return to what she first assumed was a pile of rags, but pale flesh comes into focus and she realizes Drew lies on the floor below.

"Fuck."

Heedless of the consequences, Tina acts. Bringing her scratched and bleeding forearms down on the grille, the flimsy grating flies off and clatters to the stone floor. Pulling herself over the hole, she lets her knees and feet fall through the opening and levers herself down. The slickness of the blood and lack of grip points sabotages her efforts and she slides out of the hole, akin to a beet meeting a food grater. The uncontrolled eight-foot fall means the young woman hits the stone floor unevenly and twists her ankle, the roar of the furnace doing little to drown out her cry of pain.

Fuck, fuck, that hurts.

Clenching her teeth until her jaw aches to keep from yelling out again, Tina has the presence of mind to pull free the lug wrench and scan the room. Except for herself and the bleeding Drew, they are alone.

Getting to her feet is an act of will. The cold stone floor helps dull the pain radiating up her injured foot. Hop-skipping to Drew, and a mere glance, she can tell he's dead—bled out from long slashes to his abdomen— but Tina forces herself to her knees and checks for a pulse.

"I'm sorry, Drew. I didn't know you well, but Becca loved you and no one deserved to end up like this."

Using the lug wrench as a cane, Tina forces herself to her feet, and in doing so, notices Drew's left hand. Smeared blood, as if he was trying to drag himself, stains the floor.

I'm amazed he had the strength to drag himself with those wounds. But there's nothing there except the stone wall, the stairs are back that way. Could it have been his rattled mind confusing him? Was he fleeing from his attacker, or something else?

With still no sign of who or what attacked Drew and dragged him through the duct, Tina stumbles to the stone wall at the back of the furnace room.

Nothing, just a boring old stone wall with cracked mortar and a piece of trash stuck to it...

Bending low, Tina pulls the piece of paper off the wall and sees it's a deli label.

"Reuben Sandwich? Wait, that doesn't make sense." Tina rubs filthy hands at her temples. "I ordered a Reuben, but they gave me a Monte Cristo, a Mr. Dumas that I don't remember as a teacher, and that weird shopkeeper's novel. The Count of Monte Cristo! A hidden door! Becca found a hidden door down here, that's what she was trying to tell me!"

Excitement lending her strength, Tina claws at the stones of the ancient cellar, looking for a latch or seam. Even jamming the lug wrench between stones does nothing. Her attacks against the wall ring throughout the cellar. Exhausted, tears running down her dirty face, she sees a small hole between two stones, smooth with use. Forcing her shaking hands to stillness, Tina pokes the tip of the lug wrench into the hole and hears a sharp 'click'.

A three-foot section of the stone wall pops out, and Tina levers it wide enough for her thin shoulders.

"I'm coming, Becca!"

The stone-lined tunnel is just wider than Tina's shoulders, which she is thankful for. As the floor dips down, her ankle is a constant pain. She props herself against the walls. A faint glow of flickering light far ahead allows her to make her way down the slope. She convinces herself that its tree roots brushing her hair as she passes and not skeletal fingers.

Tina's bare feet follow the well-worn tunnel down until she gets to the end and enters a large, circular cavern. The round room is at least forty feet wide and a quick glance shows the tunnel is just one of many.

It's like a hub of an old wagon wheel, and I just walked down one of the spokes.

The source of the cavern's light is four massive candelabras around a flat stone dais. A body clad in white robes lies atop it. Even from twenty feet away, the profile of the face Tina spent uncounted hours staring at while she was a teenager is plain to see. It's Becca on the dais.

"No! Becca!" Tina cries, and makes a stumbling run into the cavern.

Her eyes confirm what, in her heart, she already knew. Becca is dead, and from the look of the pale body, she has been for days, if not weeks.

"I tried Becca, I really did."

She collapses to her knees in front of the dais, the lug wrench clattering to the flagstone floor forgotten. Reaching out a scraped and filthy hand to the dead woman, Tina feels a sharp pain through her chest and looks down. A massive, leaf-shaped spearhead is poking through her t-shirt, staining the soiled fabric a bright crimson. The candles in the candelabras flare high, their flames crackling.

I wonder if that's the spear used to kill the animals displayed up in the bar, Tina thinks to herself before falling onto her side.

Her last memory is of the spear being pulled from her body, fiery breath in her ear, fingers in her hip pocket, taking the letter and Polaroid.

It was all a trap, the book, the sandwich, pretending Drew was pointing when he was already dead. All of it just to get the Polaroid back, and I fell for it.

I'm sorry, Becca.

MAKING THEIR WAY
By David Green

Hey Ma,

Got in a chase, couldn't shake 'em. Chet got shot, fuckin' blood everywhere. Windscreen shattered, poor sonofabitch screamin' for his momma.

Lost 'em on this old dirt road, said Route Thirteen. Broke as all Hell; Chet screamed something awful every time I hit a pothole.

He passed out before I found this place, some old motel. Whiskey Pete's. They took Chet, a girl called Stacey said she'd take good care of him, then they gave me a room. Stinks of shit, but better than an ol' cell. Told me to write you, let you know I'm okay. Got the money with me, won't let it out of my site.

Gonna lie low a while once they fix up my ride, head to Canada, maybe. I'll write you when I'm there.

Jesus, I hope Chet's okay. Heard screaming, then someone laughing a while ago. Drunks, probably.

Love you, Ma.

Waylon

TRENT
BY STEPHEN HERCZEG

Watching the boats racing on the Columbia River had me longing for the lost days of my youth. I remember a time when that was my life. Every weekend, I'd ride my bike from my home in Concordia down to the river and sail for most of the day. At times like these, I'd happily chuck it all in and do that again. It was a nice way to pass the time, especially on a Saturday.

Taking the final drag from my tenth cigarette of the day, I glanced up at the bright, blue sky and sighed. I knew I was moments away from spending countless hours in the car I sat on. Searching for clues, following leads and just trying to put pieces together.

Pulling the stub from my mouth, I dropped it to the ground and crushed it underfoot. A voice nearby snatched my attention away from the glorious scene before me.

"That's littering. Pick it up now."

A young punk police officer, uniform pressed and neat, strode up and stopped beside me, hands on hips in an attempt to give himself more authority. I took one look at that baby smooth face, then stared down at my foot. Scraping it across the ground to reveal the crushed remains of the cigarette lying among countless others, I shrugged.

"Pick it up, or I'll give you a ticket."

Putting on my best expression of disdain, I turned back to him. "You're new."

"So what? Doesn't matter how long I've been doing this job, that's *still* littering and I'm *still* going to give you a ticket."

He pulled out his ticket book, flipping it open to a fresh page.

Another blue uniform stepped up next to the rookie and closed the ticket book. "You won't need that, Collins."

The younger officer's mouth dropped open. "What are you doing, sir? This man is breaking the law."

"You have no idea who this is, do you, Collins?"

"No. Should I?"

Before the older officer could start to explain, the hood of the car rattled. Glancing down, I saw my phone bouncing around, screaming out *Bad to the Bone*. I smiled and snatched up the phone.

Holding it up to show to the officers, I said, "Sorry, could you two keep it down? It's your boss."

The expression on the younger officer's face was priceless as I saw his eyes take in the name 'Captain Mulroney'.

Tapping the answer icon and putting the phone to my ear, I said, "Captain. Been waiting for your call."

As I said, it was a Saturday. I seem to do the bulk of my work on the weekends. Sort of explains why I've never held onto a wife for any length of time. Name's Trent Porritt, ex-army, ex-police, all Oregon bounty hunter nowadays. They call me in when the trail's gone cold or the police have no more leads. I can do things that uniforms can't, go places they shouldn't show their faces.

Captain Mulroney and I go way back. Started as rookies together. He kept at it. I left the force.

Well, let's keep it at 'left'. May not have been my idea at the time.

Any time his officers get themselves stuck on a case, or can't run down an offender, Mulroney gives me a call. Most other times, I simply track down bail jumpers and drag their asses back. Hey, I gotta eat, and the cops are pretty good at their jobs most of the time.

I knew the call was coming after the debacle at the Portland courthouse yesterday. A lovely young lass by the name of Elane O'Donnel was being transported from County to the courthouse for sentencing. I use the 'lovely young lass' description with extreme sarcasm. O'Donnel was nowhere near lovely. Her crime was murdering her husband and three kids in cold blood. Prosecution said she'd got fed up with wifing and mothering and decided to finish them all off one night. Even her defense lawyers couldn't present contrary evidence.

Elane's excuse, "They had it coming. Always whining and asking for stuff. So's I ended it."

With that quote read throughout the courthouse, she'd pleaded "Not Guilty," forcing a full trial, which cost the state hundreds of thousands of dollars and ended up with a "Guilty" verdict, anyway.

Then, on her final trip back to court, she broke out of her handcuffs, killed a deputy, and stole the prison van. LoJack found it two miles away, along with a young woman she'd assaulted to steal her car. After a few hours, the car was tracked too, through CCTV, entering I-84 and heading towards Idaho. Ontario police were scrambled to set up a roadblock, but she never showed.

The last report had her filling up the stolen Dodge at a gas station in Baker City. The police tracked down the credit card of the car owner, but by the time the Baker City police showed up, she was long gone. She had them on the run, and I figured she was well over the state line before they even knew about the stop for gas.

That's where I came in. Oregon cops could call on the Idaho police to help, but then politics comes in, and it's an election year. Oregon leans Democrat, Idaho leans Republican, do the math. They ain't playing ball any time soon.

Picturing the state map in my head, I figured O'Donnel slipped off I-84 at Baker City and headed onto Oregon 86 through to Idaho. That's what I'd do, then head further inland, possibly on the old Route Thirteen. Not many folks use that one anymore, but it does connect up to US 95, which heads north to Montana. Eventually, she could cross into Canada and out of our lives forever.

After four and a half hours on the road, I pulled my old Mustang into the Sinclair gas station just off I-84. That area of Baker City looked pretty much only visited by travelers, with a run-down hotel nearby and a Micky D's across the road. There was a Shell opposite, but the Captain's info had O'Donnel using the Sinclair. I pulled in, filled up, checking the area to see if there were any cameras, or anyone around that might have been about the day before.

I realized O'Donnel was cleverer than I'd presumed. This was a high-volume place with a lot of customers passing through, most of whom wouldn't even raise the eyebrow of anyone working there.

I finished pumping and went in to pay. The shop was neat and clean, and could have been any one of the other hundred Sinclair's, especially when the cashier was wearing a baseball cap with the familiar dinosaur on the peak.

Pulling out my phone, I waited until the middle-aged woman—Carol, going by the tag above her left breast—finished processing my payment.

"Good afternoon Carol, I don't suppose you were on duty here yesterday afternoon?"

I pointed to my bounty hunter's license in my wallet. A look of suspicion crossed her face.

"You're not a cop then? They were here yesterday."

Shaking my head, I replied, "No, Bounty Hunter. Cops couldn't deal with this one, so they called me in."

"Well, I'll tell you what I told them. I was home with a sick kid. They already talked to Frank, the manager; he didn't know nothing either."

"Not a problem. Thank you for your time."

I thought that'd be the case. It wasn't Carol or Frank I needed to talk to.

After five hours in a car, there was one thing any human would *need* to do. I asked Carol about the restrooms and she thumbed towards the back. As I walked around the building, I scanned the area. There was one thing that struck me as strange. Elane would still be wearing the lovely, dark blue overalls supplied by the state. I doubted Frank would have blinked twice at a woman wearing blue overalls, even those associated with an inmate.

Around the back of the gas station, I found the two restrooms nestled together. The pungent smell of last night's meals from the nearby café wafted towards me from a nearby dumpster. Wrinkling my nose, I stepped into the men's room and surrendered several hours of storage to the waters. Stepping out, I noticed a house bordering the far edge of the parking lot. Washing on the clothesline in the rear yard blew in the light breeze, giving me an idea.

I hurried across to the front door and was greeted by a young mother with a babe in arms. Introducing myself, I asked the one question that had formed. "Have you lost any washing in the last day?"

Her expression turned to surprise. "About goddamn time the authorities took this seriously," she said. "That goddamn hobo that hangs around took a set of my sweats off the line, just last night."

"Hobo?"

"Yeah, smelly bastard. Hangs around the back of the café and goes through the dumpster for vittles. If I catch him in my yard again, I'll blow his goddamn head off."

Thanking the woman, who huffed that she'd never see those sweats again, I returned to the rear of the café and, as luck would have it, found the 'hobo' asleep under a cardboard box. He was the oldest, greasiest homeless guy I'd ever laid eyes on. I would have thought someone like him would have been in a big city, not in a tiny place like this. Regardless, I hoped he could help.

I prodded him with my foot, and amidst a series of coughs, groans and curses, he finally sat up and rubbed his eyes. As soon as his sight fell on me, he panicked, struggled to gain his feet, and tried in vain to shuffle away from me. Holding out a crisp twenty-dollar bill, I said, "Hey, I got something for you if you got some information for me."

The old bum stopped and turned back to see what it was. His eyes lit up, and a toothless grin filled his face. He trudged back towards me, holding out his hand and reaching for the bill.

Snatching it away, I said, "Not so fast, you here yesterday, round this time?" I could almost hear the wheels turning in his head. Finally, he nodded. "Okay, then, you see a red Dodge Neon?" I held up my phone with a mug shot of Elane O'Donnel. "Driven by this woman."

He looked at me. "You're not a cop?"

I shook my head.

Staring at the screen for a moment, he started to nod. "Yah, I seen her. She came round back, used the bathroom. Then headed off over to Nancy's place, hopped the fence, grabbed some clothes, and hightailed it back into the restroom. I figured she'd be good for money when she came out, but she just swore at me and took off." He shook his head in disgust, a strange reaction for someone that smelled so bad. "She waren't no lady, I can tell you that."

"Did you see which way she went?"

"No, she pushed past me and headed back round to the pumps."

I held onto the note a little longer.

"But I did see a little red car take off, a minute later." He pointed east along Campbell Street. "That car, one of them small Dodges I think, hightailed it east like the devil was after it."

I stared into his face and watched his eyes during the whole answer. Years of experience told me he at least thought he was telling the truth, which sometimes is all you've got to go by. I held out the note, which was snatched away and disappeared quicker than a prom night debutante's virginity.

"Thanks," I said, and hustled on back to my car.

Campbell Street led onto Atwood Road, which connected up with the 86. I had a bag of chips, a couple cans of cola, and a fresh pack of cigarettes. There was good rock-and-roll on the radio, so I was set for another long drive.

It was less than an hour when I reached Richland, and the 86 turned north. It was outside Copperfield that I finally joined the old disused Route Thirteen. I considered that Elane may have headed down the 71—a much better road, connecting with US 95 and headed back north to Montana—but if I was on the run for multiple murders, I'd be driving as fast as I could over the shortest possible route. One nobody else seemed inclined to use. That would be Route Thirteen. The road surface was almost dirt after so many years of neglect, and I'd heard legends of drivers never making it to the 95 over the years, but...

With the sun setting rapidly behind me, I turned east and headed across the Snake River and into Idaho, down Route Thirteen.

After an hour of rattling across the rutted, broken road that was Route Thirteen, I began to question my sanity. I'd calculated it was only thirty-five miles as the crow flies from Copperfield to US 95, but didn't count for the winding way the road cut through the gulches and gullies, over hills and around small mountains. The road hadn't seen maintenance since probably the last American walked on the moon and it showed. Short patches of broken tarmac gave way to longer stretches of rutted, dried mud and gravel.

My speed dropped sharply as the sun set and the light diminished. There were no reflective markers to catch my headlight beams, so each corner was a descent into madness that had to be taken at almost walking pace.

By the time I turned a longer, smoothly curving bend and saw a light up ahead, I was ready to pull over and give everything up as a bad joke. The light was a single bulb hung on a lamppost outside of a run down and crumbling general store. A faded sign above the porch roof said 'Pine Valley Store'. I don't even think I saw this place on the map when I studied it earlier, so seeing a store was even more of a shock. A welcome one though.

Checking my watch, I noticed it was seven thirty. I was hungry. The bag of chips and soda were long gone, and I'd been making do with smokes for the last hour. Pulling up outside the store, I noticed two good ol' boys sitting on the porch. They broke their conversation and turned their heads towards me, eyeing me with rheumy, watery eyes.

As I stepped up on the porch and reached for the front door, one of the boys said, in a raspy voice that had me thinking of throat cancer, "Help yourself, stranger. Leave the money on the counter."

Entering the store was like stepping through time. The only light was the dim bulb from a small, glass-fronted fridge at the back. I took out my phone and used it to light up the products on offer, recoiling at most of the goods. A lot of them belonged in a museum and probably had use-by dates that predated my own conception.

After a thorough search, I settled on a pack of Twinkies that were soft when I prodded them, a box of Reece's Pieces—I figured the candy shell should at least keep the chocolate slightly fresh—and a box of cherry-flavored Pop Tarts. From the fridge, I grabbed a couple of bottles of Coke, thinking at least they'd be cold. I totaled the sum in my head and left a twenty on the counter before heading back outside.

I needed any lead I could get, and these two men seemed to be welded to those seats. "Were you boys out here about this time last night?"

"Yep. We're out here every night. Got nothing better to do," the one that seemed to be the owner said.

"Did anyone go past about this time, or maybe stop off? A woman driving a small, red car, maybe?"

"Yep. Been talking about her all day. It's been so damn busy. What with you coming along now, we thought they'd opened up old Route Thirteen and she'd become a goddamn Innerstate."

I smiled at the thought that two visitors over two days was akin to an Interstate's continuous flow of traffic, but it's all perspective, I suppose. "Did she stop at all?"

"Yep. Bought a Pepsi and some chips. I tried to warn her about the chips. They be a little old, I reckon."

"She was purty," said the other one. "Like my Maisie."

"She was nothing like your Maisie. Your Maisie was blonde."

"Do you know if she kept going or turned back?"

"Oh, she kept going alright. She said something about trying to get to Montana. I laughed and says good luck with that. The way the road goes she'd be lucky to get to the 95 by morning."

"It can't be that far," I said.

The old man moved his head and stared deep into my eyes. The serious look that came over him was disturbing. "Oh, it ain't the distance you gots to worry about; it's what gets in the way. You watch yourself too, young feller. There's things out there that even a big lad like yourself would struggle with."

I don't scare easy, but these two were stirring something deep in my gut. "What? Bears or something?"

The man nodded, his friend joined in and said, "Something. That's fur sure, there's something out there."

I had what I needed. Elane had been here. Elane had gone on. I backed away before these two gave me the complete willies and made it back to the car, just as the store owner shouted out, "Take care, young fella. Take care."

Storming off into the night along the winding, broken road, I was about five miles away from Pine Valley when I finally started concentrating on the road ahead again. Just in time.

Something bolted out of the tree line and into the middle of the road. My mind must have still been spooked by the old men. What I saw lit up in my headlights was beyond anything I'd ever seen in my life. It looked neither animal nor human, but some strange being out of a nightmare. In the second or two that the creature was flooded in light, I swear I saw a hairless face with two huge, saucer-sized eyes staring from above a wide mouth filled with needle-like teeth.

In fright, I wrenched the wheel to guide the car away from the beast, sliding on the loose gravel of the road surface, and fishtailing towards the edge of the road and a large pine tree. My world was filled with the sound of grinding metal and the jerk of the seatbelt grabbing me and stopping my head colliding with the windscreen.

Shocked, I sat in the now silent car for a moment, before turning around. I stared out the rear window, trying desperately to snatch another glimpse of the strange creature, but the road was clear, just the wash of red from my tail lights.

Normally, I'm a very calm and stoic sort, but I could feel my heart thumping in my chest as if it was desperate to escape. Taking deep breaths, I closed my eyes and reached for the calm place within that always helped me in time of stress. The world was in utter silence except for the ticking of the cooling car engine.

Stepping out of the car, I realized just how dark the surrounding forest was. A chill ran up my spine as I stared into a darkness akin to some stygian abyss. My mind raced as sound began to infiltrate the silence. The cracking of sticks. The rustle of the brush in the light breeze. The mournful call of a night bird. The wheeze of my car as a cloud of steam billowed from the punctured radiator.

Turning back to the car, I assessed the damage as best I could in the gloom. My phone light only showed a small amount of the destruction. My mustang was an old Seventies model, all steel and chrome, but from what I could see, the bumper was bent back into the radiator, causing a pool of green, goopy fluid to form under the car.

My limited knowledge of mechanics told me it could still be driven, but not fast and not far. I reckoned I'd come about five or six miles from Pine Valley, which at a best guess put me around ten miles from US 95. I peered back to where I'd come, but shook my head. The good old boys at Pine Valley weren't going to be helping my car in any way, so it looked like I needed to head toward the main road and hope to come across a gas station or helpful passerby.

Sitting back in the car, I turned the key, forcing the old girl to cough and splutter in resistance. Finally, she fired up and, with a crunch and screech of metal, I reversed away from the tree.

Within a couple of miles, the steam cloud pouring out from under the hood thinned out, allowing me a better view of the road ahead. Unfortunately, I knew this was a really bad thing. The radiator was dry. Within another mile, the result was a lit-up Christmas tree on my dashboard. I needed water, and I needed it fast or the head gasket was gonna go.

With the temperature needle threatening to jump out the right-hand side of the dial, and the constant flashing from the overheating light bathing me in red light, I rounded a turn and saw sanctuary ahead.

Nestled amongst the thick forest of trees was my oasis. A run-down gas station and bar that looked like it hadn't seen a lick of paint since my car rolled off the assembly line. A few bulbs shone yellow light across the building and driveway, enough to guide my injured car in and park it next to the nearest pump. I glanced around the area. The place was called Whiskey Pete's. Wasn't sure if that was the bar or the whole place, but didn't really care.

The shop was dark, but I could make out movement inside. Rather than waiting for someone to come out, I jumped out of my stricken car and headed on in.

Behind the counter was a grizzled old gent that would have been well at home on the porch outside the store in Pine Valley. The name tag on the red overalls said 'Dale'. When I addressed him by that, he snapped back that he was Lorne, didn't have a clue who Dale was. I left it at that.

"I hit a tree when some weird animal ran across the road. Broke my radiator. You got a mechanic here?"

Lorne, Dale, whatever, stared out through the dirty windows at my car for a while, then back at me. "Had one. He...retired recently. Can help myself, but ain't gonna be tonight. I'm about to close up." He pulled a thick, blue leather-bound diary from under the counter and slammed it on top, raising a cloud of thick dust. Opening it with a creak, he licked a thumb and leafed through the pages until tomorrow's date showed. The page was empty. He nodded and said, "Yep, looks like I'm purty free tomorrow. Come by about nine and we'll see how she's a-going."

I grimaced. I needed to be gone way before then, but this seemed to be my only shot at getting the car fixed. "Fine," I said, putting my keys on the counter. I stepped away and pulled my phone out. The No Service icon displayed. Cursing under my breath, I turned back to the owner. "You gotta phone?"

He pointed to the far corner.

Putting the receiver to my ear, I was met with dead silence. Then I heard a voice from the counter. "Oh, it ain't worked none since Reagan was shot."

I placed the receiver down and bit my tongue. Stalking back to the counter, I asked, "You got any rooms here about?"

Sliding another open-lined book towards me, he said, "Stacey's gone for the night, but motel's out back." Pointing at the next entry, he said, "Name here. Write neat, eyesight's a bit gone." As I filled out the register, he turned and passed me the key for Number 9. "Best room we's got. Just go around the side. Ya can't miss 'em."

I glanced around the store at the racks of items that seemed older than at Pine Valley. Many were caked in dust so thick you'd have to wipe it off to see the name on the packet. Turning back, I asked, "Does the bar serve food?"

"Depends what you call food." Lorne let out a wet cackle that screamed serious illness. I stepped back, trying hard to disguise my disgust.

"Right now, I'd be happy with roasted four-day-old roadkill."

"Yep, I think that's top of the menu," the old man said, letting out another hacking laugh. Grimacing, I snatched up the key, thanked him, and headed out the door to retrieve my overnight bag from the trunk.

My job had brought me to some of the biggest dives in the United States, but the bestest room at Whisky Pete's motel was the worst. It was barely big enough to fit the bed lengthways. The window had been painted open, with years of bad weather staining the floor in front of it, and a thin gauze curtain flapping in the light breeze the only protection. There was no bathroom, just a toilet sitting mere inches from the top of the bed, and a sink above that drained into the cistern.

Dumping my bag on the bed raised a cloud of dust that had me hacking up a lung. I grabbed the lone glass on offer and tried to fill it from the sink. The brown sludge that resulted almost made me puke instead. A growl in my stomach sent me from the room in search of sustenance and possibly a large quantity of beer.

The cool night brought a light prickle of goosebumps to my bare arms as I skirted around the outside of the bar. As I walked, I realized the bare dirt area to the side was the parking lot. Unless I'd thought about it, I would never have known. It was devoid of cars and trucks, which left me with a feeling that the bar would be equally empty and possibly closed.

The reality was different.

The door let out a loud squeal of rusty hinges, but revealed a smoke-filled room with several people sitting around talking and drinking. A lone barman stood behind the counter, wiping glasses on a towel. The walls were adorned with the decapitated remains of creatures from the nearby forest, though none reminded me of the horror I had seen. A few patrons sat alone or in pairs in booths and at tables. A youngish man played pool by himself at a table covered in felt so old and worn it almost glowed white. In fact, the entire place looked like it had seen better days, about forty years ago. The old jukebox nestled against the far wall was the most alive thing in the place. *Freebird* by Lynyrd Skynyrd floated through the room, cutting under the background noise, but making itself known all the same.

Half-expecting a replay of every western ever made, I was surprised when nobody turned towards me except the barkeep. He eyed me up and down for a moment, before going back to scrubbing the glass in his hand. One eye stayed on me as I walked across the stained and faded carpet towards him.

I pulled out a stool and eyed the only other patron at the bar. He made Lorne in the shop look full of life, like a teenager. His long, spindly fingers, almost devoid of flesh, curled around the handle of a mug of beer that looked so flat and uninviting it may have been sitting in that glass for days. Wafts of long, white hair clung to his scalp like he'd walked through a cobweb and hadn't bothered removing it.

My observance of the ancient being was cut short by the bartender's question. "What'll it be?"

Turning towards the voice, I finally got my first good look at him. He was huge, standing well over six feet high, with a huge head that filled my vision. My gaze fixated on the steel-blue eye nestled next to the moss-green. Heterochromia, it's called. Unnerving is what it is, especially on a specimen like this.

"Beer," I quickly replied. "In a mug. And you got anything to eat here?"

The bartender pulled down a clean mug and set it under a tap. Reaching behind him, he grabbed and tossed an alfoil packet of beer nuts down in front of me. "Kitchen's closed."

My eyes dropped to the nuts, back to the bartender, then back to the nuts. I shrugged, tore the packet open and began picking at the contents. They weren't fresh, much like everything else in this bar. Even the beer was flat and watery, but at least it was wet.

I pulled my phone out and opened the picture of Elane. Calling the bartender over, I asked if he'd seen her pass by about seven o'clock the previous night. Watching his face for any obvious ticks or markers, he shook his head and gave me no reason not to believe him.

Disappointed, I looked around the room and sipped at the beer, trying hard not to gag or show any emotion towards it. If the barkeep didn't know Elane, then I doubted any of the other jokers here would know her. Except for one, maybe.

Placing my beer and nuts down on a nearby table, I turned towards the pool player. "You up for a game?"

He smiled widely, showing a mouthful of yellow teeth, before closing his lips again. "Sure. None of the old farts here can beat me."

I placed a dollar on the edge. "Let's see then."

His eyes lit up at the challenge. After breaking and sinking a couple of balls, his cockiness deflated a little. I made sure to mess up a couple of shots to make things interesting, but I could tell he was more talk than skill. Finally, I managed to turn the game and let him win. He was pretty ecstatic. I figured it wasn't something that happened often, but reckoned it was a way to get him on side. Slamming another note down as he racked the balls, I broke and while the balls skittled around, I asked the question I needed answered.

"Seen anyone new, other than me, around here of late?"

Lining up his first shot, he replied, "Well, yeah, as a matter of fact, we had us a fine-looking filly come in just last night."

His eyes went wide, and he froze in place. It seemed as if the whole place went quiet, except for a strong, deep voice from the bar.

"Joel, shut your goddamn hole!"

The tall drink of water dropped his cue on the table and skedaddled off to the back of the room, mumbling something about going to the restroom, and leaving me alone. I noticed every face now turned towards me, each one returning to their business as I glanced around. It was time to leave.

Back in my room, I gently peeled the dusty cover off the bed and dumped it to one side. I tried the old tube TV mounted on the wall. Nothing. Left alone with my thoughts, I just lay back and closed my eyes.

I was stuck in the middle of nowhere, chasing a phantom, but that phantom had been here. Where was she now? And how the hell was I going to chase her down? Pictures of Elane O'Donnel driving that little, red Neon ran through my mind as my eyes closed and I drifted off to sleep.

A woman's cry slammed into my mind and my eyes snapped open. Checking my watch, I found it was early morning. I listened for another sound, unsure whether it was my imagination or just some woodland creature.

Another cry came from somewhere in the dark. Anguish? Pain? Pleasure? I stared at the nearby wall. These rooms were divided by paper. Maybe there was a couple next door doing the wild thing.

Nothing.

Sitting up, I stared out into the night. Waning moonlight filtered through the thick canopy of trees behind Whiskey Pete's. There it was again. A single, high-pitched sob of pain, filtering through from somewhere deep in the forest. I picked the perceived location and memorized it. Part of me wanted to ignore everything and go back to sleep, but the hero, the soldier, the policeman in me, spurred me on to action.

Grabbing my phone and the small revolver I kept for protection, I crept out the front door and scooted around behind the line of motel rooms, finding mine, and orienting myself in the direction I heard the noise. Standing quietly, I listened.

Another sob. I had a direction.

Creeping through the obsidian darkness of the forest, I picked my way towards the source of the noise. The gloom closed around me like a cold, wet blanket. I shivered, but pressed on. Stopping until another gasp filtered through. I was getting closer. After another few minutes of stumbling, stopping, listening, and starting again, I came upon a small clearing.

There, in the middle, sat a small box cabin that could scarcely be more than a single room. A dull, yellow glow seeped out from a curtained window. Sidling up to the door, I listened.

There it was again. A single moan of pain.

Holding the gun in one hand, I pulled at the door with the other, and entered a world of nightmares.

Elane O'Donnel had stopped at Whiskey Pete's. My search was at an end, but our quest for survival was only beginning. Some sick son-of-a bitch had tied Elane's hands to a hook in the ceiling. She hung from a rope that chafed at her wrists, turning them to a bloody mess, her feet only just brushing against the dirt floor.

Blood ran from multiple wounds across her naked body. None seemed deadly, just superficial, more to extract a crimson flow and cause pain than permanent harm. Elane's head hung down, tears coursed down her face, making clean tracks in the caked blood on her cheeks.

"Elane?" I called.

Lifting her head, she looked at me through bloodshot eyes. "Kill me..."

I shook my head. "No, we got to get you out of here. Nobody deserves this. Not even you."

"Just kill me and get it over with. You've had your fun."

Confused, I said, "I didn't do this. I came to find you."

I searched for a knife or anything to cut the rope. Nothing. Glancing up at the hook, I tried to figure if I could lift her off it.

I put the gun away, and as I stepped forward to grab Elane, she screamed and spat at me. "Leave me alone or just fucking kill me!"

I reeled back. My eyes drew to the door as the hitch lifted. The figure that entered was a blur of motion, but the long, deadly knife in his hand wasn't. I stepped back and slipped in a puddle of Elane's blood, crashing to the ground, the gun slipping from my pocket and skittering away across the hard-packed floor.

My eyes saw the figure with the knife step towards me. Flight was my only answer. I crawled towards the far wall and the window there. Getting to my feet, I dove towards freedom, my belt catching momentarily on the window frame, a blinding bolt of pain erupting through my leg as I slipped through and crashed to the ground. As I gained my feet, agony flashed through my leg. I limped off into the darkness, glimpsing the figure filling the window, before a piercing scream filled the night.

I needed help. There was nothing in the motel room.

The shop? Telephone didn't work. Maybe the office in the bar? There's got to be one.

Struggling through the darkened forest, hoping beyond hope that I was headed in the right direction, I stumbled and hobbled through the detritus. Each bump and step sent shards of pain up my leg. I stopped briefly and grabbed at the area, felt the sticky ooze soaked into my pants. He'd got me, the bastard. He'd slashed my leg, and now he had my gun as well.

Cursing my own stupidity, I staggered on, almost falling through the last line of trees and onto the clear ground behind the motel. I stopped, glancing around the area, and listening for any noises behind me. Nothing. The killer hadn't followed.

I let out a long breath of relief. I was literally out of the woods, but I was far from safe.

I lurched to my right and carried on with a faltering step, skirting the dark motel rooms and finding myself in the empty parking lot next to the bar.

Confused, I stopped, questioning my own eyes. Sitting in the middle of the vacant lot was a red Dodge Neon. Elane's stolen car. I searched my memories, but there was no way it was there the last time I walked through this area. Shaking my head, I moved on, leg dragging behind me, ringing a chorus of pain through my mind as I shuffled on.

To my surprise, the door to the bar was unlocked. I entered. The area looked even older and more permanently locked into the past in that dim light filtering through the draped windows. I latched the door shut, using the tumble lock to secure it, and worked my way around the bar to where I presumed the office to be.

Luck was on my side. A door with a frosted glass window sat adjacent to the end of the bar. I let myself in and virtually collapsed on the floor. Silently pushing the door shut with my good leg, I lay there, sucking breath and trying to bury the pain in my leg deep into the recesses of my brain. After an age, I rolled to a sitting position and finally examined my wound.

The knife had gone deep. The slash wept copious amounts of blood. I tore off my belt and wrapped it around the top of my calf, synching it tight to stop the crimson flow. Black spots appeared before my eyes, but I sucked in air slowly to avoid losing consciousness.

I found I still had my phone and dragged it out to provide light.

The office was dusty and appeared unused for years. I lay on an old piece of the same carpet from the bar, which acted as a sort of rug. Behind me, an ancient dial phone sat on a desk pushed up against the wall. I reached up and snatched it down. Putting the receiver to my ear, I felt a hint of déjà vu.

Nothing. No dial tone. No nothing.

"Fuck," I swore under my breath.

A noise filtered in from the bar. I tapped off the phone's torch and stared wide-eyed towards the office window. I knew the sounds. The snick of a key slipping into a lock. The clack of the latch. The creak of the door opening. Heavy footfalls across the carpeted room.

My mind reeled. I was injured. I was unarmed. I was fucked.

I looked around in the gloom, trying to find a weapon. It was then I felt something beneath the rug. I tore it away and found the hinges and latch of a trapdoor cut into the floor.

Sanctuary.

I grabbed the latch and pulled the small, wooden door open. A rusted metal ladder disappeared down into the stygian abyss beneath Whiskey Pete's.

The clatter of the doorknob turning snatched my gaze. A dark shadow blocked out all light entering the office. I turned my sight back to the dark shaft and reached for the ladder.

Out of the corner of my eye, I saw the door burst open. The massive figure stepped into the office, floorboards creaking under its weight. I resisted the urge to look, concentrating instead on the dark void before me, trying to make out any shapes in the gloom below.

The figure took one step forward. Wood groaned underfoot. I lunged forward, ready to swing down and hope that there were rungs to receive my feet.

Another step. Creak.

I moved.

Suddenly, a long-fingered hand with deadly talons reared up from the gloom and clamped around my neck, the pain intense as the claws dug into my flesh. The hand pulled. I slipped, my momentum assisting my assailant.

My head was filled with the sound of my own screams as the darkness dragged me into its embrace.

NEVER GO BACK
By Patrick Winters

OH MY GOD, KELLY.

This Seattle trip has been the absolute WORST. The drive's boring as hell, Dad's being a total drag, and Joey freaking barfed in the car! Little worm spewed right on my shoes!

We had to stop at some pit called Whiskey Pete's to clean up. You think Duke's Dive is a dump? It's got nothing on this place. Grody to the max. I needed a shower just looking at it.

Some creep named Joe or Noel or something tried hitting on me when we went in. He thought he was Brat Pack material. More like Revenge of the Nerds! UGH! Dad, of course, loved the joint. Called it 'quaint'. Says we'll have to stop there again when we head home next month. I'd rather kiss Cujo than go back and see all the weirdos there!

Can't wait to see you and home again!

Love,

Nancy

DANI
By J.W. Garrett

Where the hell is she?

Dani Sutton tamped down her rising anger, mindset incongruent with the slow drip from the kitchen faucet into the sink. The place was quiet without her mom around, always moving from one thing to another so quickly Dani could barely keep up. Her energy livened up a room, encouraging everyone else to step up their game.

Harper Sutton managed a team of paralegals in Nashville, TN, where they lived. But that stuffy business suit and high heels didn't claim her for the time beyond nine-to-five. Mom excelled in work, but that's what it was—work. A means to an end.

In the depths of her heart, Dani's mother enjoyed her life and the people she surrounded herself with for the rest of the hours in the day. That's what kept her mom healthy and motivated—the relationships she fostered with people. Especially the one forged with Dani.

Maybe because it was just the two of them—not the typical nuclear family—or the fact that her mom gave Dani space to do her own thing, or possibly that when Dani confided in her mom, she really listened. All that made them feel more like siblings.

The numbing tick of the clock beat into Dani's brain in the silence of the cozy kitchen, feeling cold without her mom's presence to give it life. Every morning they shared coffee here, before her mom went to work and Dani headed to Vanderbilt. The upper-level classes were kicking her ass, but it'd be worth it to have an advanced degree in business from one of the nation's best schools.

When her mom had shared that she needed a week, no questions asked, to settle some 'old business' from her past, bells and whistles had shrilled a warning in Dani's head.

"It's only a week—Colorado and back—I'll see you again before you know it. You've got plenty to do with finals coming up. Hit the books hard, and I'll be back in time to bake chocolate chip cookies and siphon coffee into your veins while you study."

Dani had been so dead serious throughout the conversation that, when her mom's face lit up with a tiny smile, she'd returned it with one of her own. But the growing unease trickling through her had been on-target. Her mom was in trouble—the horrible, chilling, life-threatening kind— and Dani had let her walk out the door.

Damn it! Why hadn't she asked more questions? And what the hell was in Colorado that could tear her mom away from her daughter and the friends who adored her and the job she loved?

April 23. Now a week had passed since Dani had last heard from her mom. A missing person's report had been filed, but the police in the area hadn't seemed concerned. The Chief of Police had managed to reassure and condescend to Dani at the same time.

"Everything possible is being done to find your mother. Sometimes this happens around midlife. Adults want to get away. I realize this is hard to hear, but your mom might not want to be found."

Bullshit.

Frustrated, Dani confirmed from an app they'd both downloaded that the GPS on her mom's cell phone pinpointed an obscure locale close to Payette National Forest in Idaho. Not much else was close by, kinda right smack in Middle of Nowhere, USA. That would be Dani's destination too.

April 26. After arranging to take her finals early, Dani would leave town today. Sipping her coffee gone cold, Dani went through the to-do list in her head. Food, water, cash, emergency supplies—already in her car— along with basic necessities: a first aid kit, blankets, a flashlight, batteries, a map. Just needed to throw in a bag of clothes before she hit the road, after going through her mom's room one more time because the pieces didn't add up. Dani had missed something important. And the clues started there.

She headed for her mom's room. Neat as always, the room looked like Mom would stroll through the door at any moment and plop down in her reading chair near the window with a favorite book. So many hours Dani had spent here, curled under a blanket, listening to her mom read to her on a rainy afternoon.

Dani sifted through the miscellaneous items on her mom's dresser. Nothing new here... But the small jewelry box, which didn't house jewelry, had been left slightly ajar. The most likely explanation was that the key she always kept there had been recently used.

Hours later, lost in her thoughts, Dani loaded up her 1962 VW bug. Rosie was her baby, and she took good care of her, so she had full confidence that they'd get to her destination and back. Warnings spoken in her mom's voice echoed in the back of her mind.

"Well, I'm fresh outta options, mom. No more lectures. You should be home by now.

Keying her destination into her phone based on her mother's last GPS signal, Dani exhaled a long breath. The physical map laid out beside her showed no major city close by, just a lot of nothing. She'd circled the emptiness in red ink.

Shoving in the clutch, Dani turned the key and Rosie sputtered to life. "You and me, girl. Let's do this."

As she hit the freeway, Dani shifted into fourth gear, but her thoughts lingered on her most recent discovery. She shot a glance at the book underneath the map in the seat next to her and shivered. Things had quickly gone from bad to a helluva lot worse.

She heaved a sigh and began to digest what she'd uncovered to the repetitive drone of highway noise.

Dani hadn't been in the basement for years, even though her mom had taken her there often as a kid. Thinking back, that had probably been by design—to dispel the mystery of the dark, musty place.

When she'd been a teenager, it had been a cool place to hang out, play some pool, and drink beer. A tiny smile lifted her lips, as Dani remembered the last time she'd been down there and had beaten her mom at a game of eight ball. The celebration that had ensued following her win had been epic because she'd never won against her mother before.

The door to the basement was rarely locked, but it was today. She twisted the key and turned the knob, confronting total disarray. Papers cluttered the messy desk, several books thrown open, places marked haphazardly with pens or paper. Reminded Dani of cramming for a test, but for her mom, this scene sent a different message. Melted candles and jars full of various substances littered the room. When she'd opened one to check out its contents, Dani had gagged and almost puked from the overwhelming stench of God-knew-what.

Cups of coffee, half-full, had been abandoned on various surfaces, along with plates of partially eaten food. That, in combination with the clothes strewn across the couch, meant her mom had been spending a significant amount of time down there—and recently. An envelope postmarked April 2, from Portland, Oregon, had been left in the trash. Maybe the beginnings of this nightmare?

It wasn't the mess that bothered Dani. It was the chaotic state of mind characterizing the room that sent fear quivering down her spine. Mom had been rushed, scared, unprepared, grasping at straws from the looks of it. More books had been yanked from their shelves, other than the ones piled atop the desk, and these had been scattered across the floor.

Just being down there for a short time sent desperation seeping through her heart. Something had driven her mom away. Something that possessed power over her. More than the power Dani had. Something where the stakes were high, maybe even life or death.

Her good luck charm—a tiny thing—a silver sand dollar her mom had given her the first day of kindergarten; the tender memory tightened her throat. It had always served her well, and it warmed her pocket today. But life had been much simpler a few hours ago than now.

Dani shuddered. Given what she'd uncovered in the basement, the

Glock and extra bullets she'd stowed in her travel bag last minute felt like a necessary precaution.

Tossing one more glance toward the book that had occupied so much of her mother's time, Dani wondered how long the practices of the occult had consumed her mom's life.

Scrunched in a ball, Dani lifted her chin, meeting a cool breeze as it brushed against her cheek. She twisted in her seat and blinked at the harsh sunlight streaming through her partially rolled-down window. Wiping drool off her face with the back of her hand, she stretched, all her joints and muscles aching simultaneously.

Where am I?

She rolled down the window farther and stuck her face outside. No cars... Not a soul in sight. Only her and the snowcapped mountain peaks. Looked like she'd made it to Idaho? Or Oregon? Maybe?

Dani grabbed her phone from the console and swiped the screen. Dead...

Then, remembering her solar-powered watch, she checked that instead. Time: 11:00 a.m. Date: June 1.

Her hands trembled. *Okay... Calm down. Take a breath... June? How can that be?*

She'd left home April 26. Reaching into the back seat, Dani snatched her backpack and dug around inside for a battery pack to charge her phone. That done, she opened up a water bottle and eased back against the seat.

"Let's see... Has to be a reasonable explanation. I'm hallucinating. Dehydrated. Dreaming... Psychotic..." An icy fear worked through her veins. Normal humans don't lose track of a whole freaking month. "That's it... I hit my head."

But a brief search turned up no swelling. She didn't stop there, examining the rest of her body for injuries as well. Drops of red dotted one sleeve and stained the center of her T-shirt crimson.

Blood? Mine or someone else's?

Lifting her gaze to the rearview mirror, she took in her terror-filled gaze and resolutely slapped herself hard.

Tears spilled down her cheeks. "Son of a bitch, that hurt! Ugh!" Slamming her head against the headrest, Dani closed her eyes and blew out a breath. "Remember why you're here—for Mom. She needs you for once. So get your shit together."

Probably not psychotic, since Dani remembered why she was here. Wherever the hell *here* was.

A light flashed as her phone rebooted. Weak signal. No shocker there. But in the corner, the date showed June 1, validating her fears.

"All right." Her voice shook. "Abduction. Maybe I was drugged. An alternate universe..." She stifled a sob that came out as a laugh instead. "Oh, yeah. I'm stuck in an old episode of The Twilight Zone." Her teeth sunk into her bottom lip. "Maybe it's a bad sign that I'm talking to myself..."

Fishing in her bag again, she wrapped her hand around a granola bar and pulled it free.

"Okay"—she alternated between bites and swallows of water—"what would Mom do? She'd keep looking, that's what she'd do. Find me, no matter what it took." Swiping at her eyes, Dani stomped on the clutch and turned the key. Rosie sputtered, apparently not quite ready to continue the journey. "Stay with me, girl." Coughing smoke, the engine puttered and stuttered to life. "That's it. One in the win column."

The road to Nowhere, USA was eerily quiet, as she carried on the conversation with herself. Maybe the whole world was watching her gradually go insane. Her blood ran cold. Maybe she'd suffered an accident and was on life support in a hospital somewhere, and this was all a drug-induced dream.

Dani scanned the horizon as she drove on, anxiety gripping tight, praying for some sign of humanity. Twenty miles later, she got her wish.

The gas station was deserted. *No problem. I'll pay with my card, go inside to pee, and then be on my way.*

Problem—no credit card and only thirty bucks cash. Where had the $500 gone? And her ID?

Shit...

Dani scrutinized the gas pump, walked around to the other side. Her card wouldn't have worked anyway—nowhere for it to go. The pump looked ancient. After she pushed the hose in place and fiddled with the levers, the satisfying sound of gas filling the tank ensued.

As she opened the store's door, bells jangled cheerfully. "Hello?"

Silence...

Who leaves the door to a store open and just wanders off?

After a quick stop at the restroom, Dani picked her way back through the convenience store. A newspaper—yes! Tucking a copy under her arm, she pulled out a twenty and placed it on the counter for the gas.

Sliding into her car seat, Dani propped her copy of the Haven Chronicles in front of the steering wheel and read the headlines. Nothing unusual. Except again the date, meaning someone had dropped this stack of papers off today. A black-and-white flyer dropped out from between the pages.

Whiskey Pete's
Barbecue: All-You-Can-Eat Night
Come for the food.
Stay for the night.
And you won't leave.
Guaranteed.

Dani reread the ad. And you won't *want* to leave, she corrected. Two more words, big difference. Guess out here in the boonies typos didn't matter. People could get the wrong idea for sure. In small print at the bottom of the page, she spotted further info.

Directions: Ten miles ahead.

No address, no phone number. Strange... Add it to the growing list. If she could find some people though, that might mean getting answers to her questions.

Ten miles later—no Whiskey Pete's. Not surprising, though she'd been hopeful to find someone and perhaps eat something other than a granola bar.

The two-lane road narrowed ahead of a sharp turn. Unprepared, Dani muttered a curse and downshifted. Her little VW bug lurched, engine whining, lugging along with the change in speed. A huge canyon appeared around the next bend, and as Dani hugged the side of the road, she spotted the glowing neon sign and jammed the brakes hard—Whiskey Pete's.

She slowed and rolled to a stop, ducking her head for a better view. Nestled among towering trees rising up high in the rear of the building sat an old, beat-up motel. In front of that looked to be a bar attached to a store, and old-fashioned gas pumps front and center. Probably all empty, just like the last time...

It looked lifeless there.

Dani turned off the ignition, hoping her luck had changed, and that someone was actually here. Because being the last person on Earth would really suck balls. What a way to go.

She scrambled from Rosie, trudged to the door, and peeked inside. From her quick glance around, nope... No one. Pressing her nose against a window, she cupped her eyes for a better view, allowing her to scope out the area.

Yes! Someone there, and further back, off to the side, a pool table, a sign. Giddy, she hustled to her car, a plan taking shape in the back of her mind. Maybe things were looking up.

Or maybe she'd dreamed up this place to join in her crazy.

Inside the cramped confines of her VW, Dani wiggled out of her bloodstained clothing, 'cause looking like a murderer wouldn't do for what she had in mind. In its place, she slid into a tight-fitting jean miniskirt and a tube top that made her girls stand at attention. One more thing. Bending her body over her seat, she retrieved a pair of high heels and donned those as well.

Sitting back, she gave herself a once-over in the rearview mirror, scanning every detail with a critical eye. "Lip gloss..." After slathering on the stuff, she pursed her lips and popped a stick of gum in her mouth. "For you, Mom," Dani whispered, as she stuck a well-toned calf outside the car, then straightened. She shimmied, arranging everything in place, and with a practiced strut, strolled into Whiskey Pete's.

DANI

The door swung open, exhaling an old country tune, as Dani walked through. Captured by the time warp she'd stepped into, Dani almost slipped out of character. Her jaw fell open as she scanned the place, taking it all in. The bar screamed of decades long past, the '70s maybe? She scrunched her nose and sniffed.

Smells like the place hasn't had a good cleaning in almost that long.

The music she'd heard pulsed from an antique jukebox. Dani took another glimpse. No, it was just old, like everything else here.

Oh shit! What was that hairy thing hanging from the wall? A deer? An elk maybe? Looked like something had taken a bite out of it.

Arranging her face to a more carefree exuberance, she pranced to the bar and nonchalantly eased onto a stool. She cleared her throat. Waited... Cleared her throat again, staring into the broad back of a very large man, currently ignoring her.

"Excuse me... Uh, excuse me, please," she added a little louder.

"Yeah?"

"White wine please."

The bartender, whose name tag read Con, grunted and huffed a laugh. The rude, fat man would never be mistaken for attractive. Graying hair, large nose grabbing all the attention in a bad way, and Dani couldn't help staring at his eyes, which didn't match. Might have been interesting on someone else. On him, they looked sinister. Wrong.

Her smile remained plastered on her lips though, since he looked like he could squash her with his overbearing stare alone. Instead, she focused on the one other patron in the bar.

"Hi, I'm Dani." In slow motion, the old guy beside her turned his watery blue gaze to meet hers, like it took an enormous effort, his snowy hair trailing his struggle.

"Well, lookie here. Ain't you a sight for..." The man cocked his head, then nodded, as if having another conversation. Dani followed his gaze. But no one else was there. He turned his attention back toward Dani.

"Melvin," He dipped his chin. "Pleasure."

"Hello there."

"He's older than sin," Con interrupted, "and he ain't aged right."

What the hell did that mean? Dani tilted her head, studying the old-timer. Melvin's long fingernails clawed his drink. Her skin crawled. Seemed as if the guy had one foot in the grave already. Creepy as hell. In a slow, subtle movement, Dani shifted her stool further away from him.

Con grunted again from behind the bar. "White. Wine. For the lady," he mocked, sloshing the drink in front of her. Dani uttered a thank you, then took a sip and choked.

God... Nasty. Like everything else here, apparently.

"And, uh, where's the barbecue?"

"Huh?"

"I saw an advertisement at a gas station down the road from here for a barbecue tonight, here at Whiskey Pete's."

He chuckled, smacking his lips. "Ah... Barbecue. Sounds good..." He leaned in close to her and sniffed. "I'm hungry... I could eat..."

Con pinned Dani with a glare that had her squirming and digging into her wallet for the last of her money. She yanked out a ten and slid it onto the bar.

"Let me." An arm appeared from behind her, collected the money, and replaced it in her hand.

"This one's a piece of work." Con sneered. "I call her Whine..."

"Don't mind him. He never matured past his primate phase."

Attempting to get back in character, Dani let a giggle rip free for the man who had let her keep her last bit of cash, then swiveled to face him. She swallowed, hard. Was everyone here weird? Dani dropped her gaze, trying to control the shudder prickling across her skin.

"Thank you," she murmured, scrutinizing the man's cowboy hat and jeans that fit awkwardly in all the wrong places.

With a careful intake of breath, she lifted her eyes to his again and homed in on the pool cue in his hand.

"Name's Joel." He gave her a closed-lip smile. "And you are?"

"Dani." It's now or never. "Oh, do you play pool?" she drawled out, snapping her gum.

"I sure do." He puffed out his chest. "Pretty good, I might add." Joel eyed Dani's drink. "Yeah. I recommend the beer."

Dani wrinkled her nose and shoved the drink away. "I, uh, could never play as well as you. Now tell me. Where do you put all those balls again? And you whack them with that long stick of yours, right?"

He chuckled. This time showing an abundance of crooked yellow teeth. "Right this way. I'll show you a thing or two."

Snatching up this opportunity, Dani maneuvered ahead of Joel, glancing backward once, making sure she held his attention. *Bingo. Works every time.*

Pressing her body against the table, Dani retrieved a stray ball and rolled it around between her fingers. "What's this little ole thing done to you that you'd bang it all around this table?"

Joel's eyes widened, uncertainty flickering there as he pushed his thinning hair from his face. "How about I rack 'em and show you how it's done?"

Dani pushed up onto the table and crossed her legs, flashing a smile in his face. "Ohhh, sounds like fun." She batted her eyelashes as he leaned in close enough for her to smell his putrid breath. "Care to make it more interesting?"

"Well, that wouldn't be fair. You being a newcomer and all."

"I'm game. Let's do it."

"All right. Cash or something else?"

"Pay for my night's stay here, if I win."

"If you beat me, you can stay here long as you want, on me. And, if I win, I'll have the pleasure of a date with you. I'll choose the place."

"Done," she said, a little too quickly.

"You want to break?"

"Come around here and check my form first, and then I'll try. Would you?" she pleaded. His hands traveled along her hips to her waist, before finding and guiding the cue stick, instructions streaming from his mouth in a chorus of words she ignored, bobbing her head the whole time. "Here goes. Back up a little. I'm afraid I'll let go of this heavy thing."

Joel stifled a laugh just as she let loose.

Showtime. Rearing back, she glided her cue stick between her thumb and forefinger with practiced ease, aiming, once, twice, before connecting with a loud smack and pocketing three balls with her first shot. After making three additional successful shots and leaving him with little to shoot at himself, on her next turn, Dani made her shot and called it. Then she inched the cue stick forward and tapped the cue ball, barely brushing the left edge, sinking the eight ball in the side pocket.

A satisfied smile rose to her lips. "That's it."

He scratched his head. "Seems that it is."

Clapping sounded from across the room. Con laughed, an abrasive barking noise. "Man, you've been played by a girl."

Dani got the distinct feeling the man rarely laughed, and he shouldn't if that was what came out.

"Shut the fuck up, Con," Joel snarled, then propped against the wall, frowning, crossing one boot over the other.

"Yeah. Sorry. I really needed money for the room. You see, I'm broke. Actually, it's worse than that." She hesitated, all the fire from her act gone. "Much, much worse."

"Hmm..." Joel shared a quick glance with Con. "I did agree to front the money for your room. Give me an opportunity for a rematch, and I'll follow through."

She released the breath she'd been holding, relieved. "You bet."

"Follow me. I'll walk you to the motel."

Out a set of doors and through another, they crossed into a second building. She tossed a glance over her shoulder. Odd... Con and even the old guy had followed them inside.

Dark paneling confronted her as she passed through the lobby. She gawked. Peeling wallpaper covered one wall decorated with huge, black-and-white metallic gold flowers. Continuing on, her feet met carpet. It smelled like her grandma's basement in here—old, musty and foul—like the light of day couldn't penetrate the premises. The puke-colored carpet fit right in. God, she'd never be able to unsee this place.

"Stacey over there at the front desk will check you in."

"Thank you."

"No need. You'll more than repay me. I'm sure of it."

He left her pondering, as she stepped up to the check-in desk. Con and Melvin drifted toward Joel, engaging in conversation, and Melvin appeared… agile, animated in his movements, almost.

"I'll need some form of ID. Sign here."

"Oh. I'm sorry. Yes." Dani refocused. "My ID was stolen, along with my credit card. I have nothing."

Dani rummaged through her purse. Her troubled gaze met Stacey's. Turmoil swirled, framed within the woman's red hair, and it seemed eerily comfortable there. Finally, someone who might understand the chaos of Dani's day.

Not that she could tell anyone she'd lost her mom somewhere around here, as well as the last thirty days or so of her life.

"You'll need to give me something that tells me you're you."

The woman's deep, country-sounding twang irritated Dani. "I've got nothing," she said, before pulling out a plastic card, "but a library card."

"Hey, a library card… Fellas, we got ourselves a reader, all the way from Nashville."

The three men paused long enough to join in a laugh at Dani's expense.

"You're a long way from home."

"Yeah. I am. Not by choice, believe me."

Stacey held out a key. Their gazes locked, and the darkness billowing from the woman's eyes appeared to reach out for Dani too.

Scraping the key from her hands, Dani stumbled back.

"Out the door here, take a left, another left. Then up the stairs and a right to number fifteen."

"Left, left, right. Got it."

"Oh, and be careful out there. Head straight for your room. You're not in the big city anymore. Out here all kinds of monsters get confident in the dark. Wouldn't want you to run your pretty little self into any of 'em."

What the fuck?

Dani threw the key in her purse. The next second, she cringed and turned, a heavy grating sound freezing her in place. "Huh?"

When she spun around, she was alone. Stacey, Con, Joel—hell, even Melvin—had disappeared. Not one indication that they'd been right here. Gone. Like ghosts.

"Freakin' fantastic..."

Dani grabbed her bag and retraced her steps, creeping slowly, teetering on her heels, wishing she were anywhere else but here. Her feet brought her closer to the door and whatever hid inside the looming cover of night.

Left, left, right, she repeated. Gazing through the darkness that seemed to cling to her skin, Dani picked up the pace.

A man stepped out from the shadows and darted into Dani's path. Plastering herself to the wall, she shrieked. "Oh my God! Who the hell are you?"

"Late to be milling about, eh?"

"Uh. I'm just heading to my room, uh, Dale," she said, with a quick glance at his name tag.

"Name's Lorne. I manage things at the store."

"Oh. Okay, Lorne, but your name tag says 'Dale'..."

"Yeah."

"Well, I'll just be moving along. I'm tired. Long day. My room's just down the way here." She inched along, hugging the wall.

"Uh, huh. Key says number fifteen. You passed it."

"Right. Thanks." Even in the darkness the man's red jumpsuit stood out, that and his disgusting greasy hair. Goosebumps prickled her skin. Gross... "Bye."

"Didn't catch your name."

"Dani... I'm Dani," she mumbled over her shoulder.

"We don't like strangers around here. Best you git inside and stay put. Never know what could happen..."

"That's what I hear... Working on it."

Here we are: Fifteen. After fumbling the key into the rusty lock, she gave it a hard shove and ducked inside.

Taking a good, long look at the place, Dani shrugged. Why would this grungy room surprise her? The AC unit puttered along, stuttered, then heaved a groan, and ticked to a stop. The shag carpet felt stiff with accumulated crud, and through the dingy light of the one lamp, it was clear the room would have to work to achieve the status of a dump.

At least I didn't pay for it.

Suddenly remembering, she jerked the door closed and pressed her weight against it, wondering if she'd be safer outside than in even with the odd man Lorne—Not-Dale—loitering out there. Roaches scurried around as she gingerly picked her way across the room. With the nastiness here, it was no surprise they had the run of the joint.

But how would she sleep? The thought of lying on the bed, even with her clothes on, made Dani's insides shiver in disgust. Just imagining all the bodily fluids and moist flesh that must have pressed onto these beds fouled her skin.

Her Rosie would be a better option. Hands down. But traipsing outside again in the inky blackness wasn't an option she'd entertain. Not-Dale would find her again for sure.

Tiptoeing to the sink, 'cause she felt she'd absorb less filth that way, she quickly washed her face and brushed her teeth. Once beside the bed, Dani heaved a breath and pulled aside the covers. Tentatively she slid on top of the sheet, still fully clothed, and fought the urge to sleep with the light on. After all, bugs and who-the-hell-knew-what-else lurked about in here.

Slowly, her eyes drifted shut.

Flashes of scenes sparked to life in Dani's head. Snatches here and there... Fragments that wouldn't connect. Shapes shifted around her. Sucking in a breath, she attempted to slow the images, intuitively realizing their importance. Tall trees towered over her, gnarled limbs forming grotesque figures, inappropriate for the light. Mumbling voices echoed in the darkness that seeped through her skin, chilling her body to the bone, worse than any winter's day. The noise grew louder as others joined in, flickering candles casting the area in a ghastly glow.

From her limited viewpoint, she sought a leader who'd enlighten her—tell her why she was here. Instead, hooded forms crept along in the shadows, while others, adorned in what appeared to be animal skins and horns, raced about in frenzied bursts of action.

Homing in on the pairings, watching their smooth, fluid movements, their actions became abundantly clear. Averting her eyes, Dani found others similarly engaged, just beyond a growing circle of fire where revelers danced. She inched closer, and pushing along, got caught up in the merriment, but a harsh tug yanked her aside.

"Drink," someone commanded, a hood shrouding his face. The sticky liquid clung to her throat as she choked it down, gagging, the smell of iron saturating the air around her. Some of the concoction had spilled on her clothing, leaving a spotted crimson path.

Blood.

Focus... This is...important.

A hood shifted. Was that Stacey? And...Con?

The wind picked up, and stumbling forward, Dani fell in line with the others who moved forward. But her clumsy legs couldn't keep up. Con flashed a wicked grin and disappeared from sight. Scattered around the forest floor, others spread out. Easing against a tree, Dani dropped as her feet collapsed under her.

A haze descended upon her. The movement around her only vague shadows now. Her head ached, so heavy on her shoulders that it lolled to the side. But a familiar voice whispered close by, and through the clutter sweeping Dani's mind, she perked up, trying to piece together the broken conversation fighting for her attention.

"No, she will not. I've taken her place. She must never know..."

Mom?

"But she's been chosen... Belenus has spoken. For Beltane— Pure... One of us—Never—"

Hushed voices spoke with rapid inflection. And then, jostled and carried from the forest, still smelling of iron and wax, unable to hold on any longer to the fragments of speech, Dani's dream dissipated.

Dani flung herself upright, details swimming in her head as she evaluated, interrogating the strength of their validity in the harsh light of day. But the memories quickly faded, and as the last wisps of sleep drifted away, the vibrant scenes loosened from her grasp.

Could this explain the thirty days she couldn't account for? There had been a ceremony of some kind. Mom...

Dani felt her presence. Had been with her recently, somewhere close by. Why would her mom leave, abandoning her daughter for some...cult? Dani had learned from the book found in the basement that cults were mostly common with young adults, ones seeking acceptance, or adults who had distanced themselves from loved ones and had fanatical leanings. Mom didn't fit the profile, even though the evidence in their home attested to the fact that she'd been at this for a long while.

So, this group had importance in her mother's life, evidently ranking higher than Dani. Cringing as she stepped from the dirty bed to the filthy carpet, she yanked the drapes open.

In the distance, set away from the parking lot, tall trees greeted the gloomy morning. Evil resided there, nestled in that forest; she'd experienced its intruding presence last night during her dream or visitation, and it lingered around her still. The pull was powerful, and Dani believed the backwoods held her mom firmly in its grip.

While Dani didn't understand it all just yet, from the little she had pieced together from her dream, her mom's actions were an attempt to save Dani from some unknown fate. The possible options listed in her mom's book, too numerous to count.

Mind made up, Dani swallowed her lingering anxiety. Hopefully, in the light, the evil spirits had less power to evoke their magic. She needed answers, more concrete than a dream could offer. Narrowing her eyes as she focused against the weight of energy pulsing from the forest, Dani steeled her resolve. One way or another, today would bring resolution.

She gulped the last of the dark liquid masquerading as coffee and tossed the paper cup in the trash. That grossness was the best this two-bit motel had to offer—no cozy coffee shops close by here. If all went well, this hellhole would be a distant memory by nightfall.

She tightened the laces of her hiking boots, donned a lightweight hooded jacket, then straightened to check the items in her backpack: water, granola bars, Mom's book, a map, a small first aid kit, an additional pair of socks, and extra bullets for the Glock tucked in the back of her waistband.

Hopefully, she wouldn't need it.

Something—correction, many things—weren't right with this place. That fact became plainer with each passing breath. Shoving her hand in her pocket, she checked for her good luck charm, circling the silver sand dollar with her fingers. Dani needed that protection today.

The sky, overcast with hues of gray, fit her mood, and with a grim set to her mouth, she strode beyond the back parking lot of Whiskey Pete's toward the tree line, chomping on the last of her granola bar.

"Hey, where ya headin'? Might not wanna go traipsing through them woods without a guide."

Recognizing Joel's voice, Dani rounded on him. "Or what exactly?"

He shrugged. "It's easy to get turned around's all I'm sayin'."

Dani gave him a knowing nod, then laughed, the action feeling foreign in her throat. "I'll bet you have all kinds of stories about that kind of thing, from personal experience."

Joel made a sucking noise behind his teeth. "Sure. Got a tale or two, as a matter of fact."

Nothing made any sense... Her mom finding her way to this odd stretch of Hell on Earth. Dani following her here. Her loss of time. Her mom's research of the occult. It was almost as if they'd fallen into another dimension and they weren't on Earth at all.

"Where is everyone? This is a business, right? Why am I the only one here?"

"We have, uh...discriminating tastes, if you must know. Not everyone who passes through rates a stay." He chuckled. "But, by all means, suit yourself."

Well, that wasn't shady as hell. "How do you turn a profit?"

"Look around you, lady. We're barely scraping by. Other ventures keep us afloat."

"Other ventures..."

"That's right." Joel turned to leave.

She had a gun, and Dani could defend herself if she had to. But spending a day or night wandering, lost in those woods, wasn't an option she wanted to be forced to consider. "Wait."

"What?" he asked, tossing his attention to her again.

"You can come along, if you want."

With an 'I told you so' grin, Joel fell into step behind her, and their path darkened as they slipped into the additional shade of the trees. "Might help if I knew what you were looking for, or where you wanted to go."

"Looking for clues. I'll know one when I see one."

Dani hoped that was true. Willing last night's dream back to life in her head, she attempted to place herself in the midst of the nightmare, at the point where she'd sensed her mom.

The two walked deeper into the woods, Joel's earlier chattiness gone, matching the atmosphere that wrapped around them. The trees pulsed with energy—giving the feel of awakening life, like in her vision—but menacing with their tall, thick walls of bark that dwarfed her, sucking Dani into the heart of the forest.

As the wind whispered among the heavy branches, Dani lifted her gaze toward the canopy. What secrets were they telling, and how could she avoid being claimed by them? The earthy smell of mud, wet leaves, and other debris floated up from the moist forest floor, but a tang of something else was here as well. Something she couldn't quite place.

A flash of a picture—her dream again—crossed her field of vision, summoning with it chanting, fire, scenes of death and rebirth. When Dani blinked, the hallucination dissolved. But the odor was stronger now. The metallic stench of blood filled her nostrils.

"We're here. Don't you think?"

Joel grabbed Dani's arm and twisted her toward him. Along the sleeve of her jacket, he'd left a bright trail of red. Her eyes tracked dark crimson drops seeping from Joel's hand. His gaze bored into hers, and his contrived country-charm facade faded when he licked his pocketknife clean of blood and snapped it shut again. He muttered under his breath.

She stared at him in disbelief. "What are you doing?"

An icy smile ticked up his lips. "Calling up a few friends."

She inched her hand toward her 9-millimeter.

"I don't think you want to do that." Joel snatched the gun. "You have an innate ability. Just like your mother said. I can feel it rolling off you."

Joel shuddered as he reached toward her, like he could sense a higher power or essence she could not.

"How... How do you know what my mom said?"

"Heard it. Firsthand. Had a front-row seat."

Dani backed away, her gaze fixed on the cocky smirk stretching Joel's blood-smeared lips.

"Don't go." He loosed a savage laugh. "You're invited to the party. Hell, you *are* the party."

"Stay away from me..."

Her gaze frozen on his demonic face, Dani scooted farther away, arms splayed out, breath coming in small pants. She shivered, confusion and despair rippling through her in tandem.

Something was coming...

Mist smothered the forest, her reality suddenly altering...shifting...

evolving. She looked around. Where'd he go? Her mouth fell open, slowly forming words that wouldn't come.

Was she even really here?

She spun in place. Heat rushed her face. Fire had engulfed the woods, except for the bit of grass eroding at her feet. Plumes of smoke and ash billowed through the air, sliding into her mouth. She choked, gulping hot air. Before her, clumps of dirt and rock fell away, unearthing a pit. At the opposite end stood Mom.

Wrenching her gaze from the unfolding disaster, Dani focused on the perimeter and her mom. They were alone. Or so it seemed.

Dani's gaze stuttered, tracking the illusion as it morphed around her, changing shape and dimensions again. Tongues of flame sprang higher from the trees, the underbrush, licking at her exposed skin, singeing her hair, searing her throat, the conflagration consuming everything in its path. Was it real, or madness?

"Mom?" Dani's voice came out meek. "What's happening?"

"Go. You need to go."

"But I can reach you. I just need to step across."

"Dani, you can't. Look around you."

Dani looked. Nowhere else to go except the deepening abyss in front of her.

"Just like my dream..."

"If only it were, Dani."

"I'm coming."

"God, no." Her mother gasped. "All of it was for nothing..."

"What?"

"I'm not who you think I am. I'm not your mother anymore."

"No!"

Dani sobbed as her reality shifted once more, the fire gone, her mom's arms outstretched. She dragged a hand across her soot smeared face. Now was her chance.

Dani jumped, arms hurled forward with her motion, searching for purchase on the opposite side of the void, yawning open before her. But where her mom had been, a jet-black mass slithered just beyond the chasm, drawing Dani forward, hungering for her, greedy for her presence.

Hissing and snarling, the thing's tongue snapped out, dragging a slippery path over its thick, eager lips.

"Oh God!" Dani screamed, yanking her arms back, clawing only air.

Chanting filled the stretching seconds of her descent, her skin melting, then sliding away. And as the air was permeated with the pungent scent of her sizzling flesh and terror-filled screams, she heard the maniacal laughter and the roar of the furnace below.

LOST
BY J.W. GARRETT

Hi Dani,

My trip's taking longer than expected. Trust me, you don't want to be anywhere near this motel. I'm only staying one night—a place called Whiskey Pete's Bar & Grill.

Tonight's event is a life-changer for me...for us...otherwise, I'd be headed home because this place is hands-down the most backwoods, disgusting hole in the ground I've ever laid eyes on. Time forgot this rundown roadhouse somehow.

I definitely don't want you here.

Doesn't really matter though, I'll be gone by the time you get this. I'll see you soon. Hope finals went well! Take care and sit tight.

Love,

Mom

ZIA

By L.T. Emery

orking at the Haven Chronicles, I often get tips on a juicy story sent my way.

Most of the time they're from nutjobs looking for five minutes of fame. Just last week I had one wacko email me a picture of a piece of shit—I kid you not, an actual turd—all because he thought he saw Jesus in it. Guess it just goes to show, some guys can see meaning in any old bullshit.

Honestly, you wouldn't believe the stuff that hits my inbox. And that's the point I'm trying to make here, all of this stuff comes in via email. That's why this tip got my attention.

A manila envelope sat on my very cluttered desk—it's an organized mess, I like to tell myself. It had my name, and the address of Haven Chronicles, but no postmark telling me where it'd originated.

"Hey, anyone see where this came from?" I shouted to the bullpen, waving the envelope.

"The news fairy?" quipped Dylon Meyers, our resident junior photographer.

"Zip it, Meyers."

Everyone else just shrugged their shoulders or shook their heads.

Unperturbed, I cracked open the envelope and pulled out a bunch of old newspaper clippings, which I immediately dropped.

Something felt off with them. Paper shouldn't be cold to the touch, but these were. It was like they were shrouded in shadow. My curiosity got the better of me, and I scanned them. Mostly they were small stories, nothing front page; what the Boss likes to call 'filler'.

Only this was anything but filler; they were all about missing persons, or bodies found mutilated. One read, 'MISSING LOVERS' CAR FOUND', while another read, 'PODCASTERS MISSING IN DEVIL'S LADDER AREA'.

The stories had one thing in common. They all took place in or around Devil's Ladder, over in Idaho.

My interest was piqued. So many mysterious... I want to say crimes, but I didn't know that for sure. So many 'unexplained events' happening all in one region was odd, but the bigger question was, why send this stuff to me?

Haven's about 400 miles from Devil's Ladder. The story was way out of my territory; I cover Haven, Portland and the surrounding areas. The whole of Oregon at a push.

The reporter in me knew this could be a big story; if all of these events were connected somehow, we could have been in for a scoop. I had a hunch about them, and I wanted to know more. It was worth the eight-hour drive to go and take a look around, ask some questions, see what I could dig up.

There was only one thing for it. Take it to the Boss.

"Boss," I said, barging into Davey Teague's office without knocking.

My editor looked up, throwing his hands in the air, exasperated. "How many times I gotta tell you to knock first, Zia?"

"Not now, Boss. I think I have something."

I sat down and showed him the stories and the envelope. I walked him through my thoughts and finally asked him for permission to go down and snoop around a bit. A couple of days, max. If I came up empty-handed, I'd come back. The paper would be out some gas money and a night in a cheap motel. But if I found something, we could have a big story and even bigger sales numbers.

"Nope, not happening," Davey said, with complete finality.

"But..."

"No, Zia. You nearly got yourself killed the last time you got a hunch like this."

"That was different. Okay, maybe I shouldn't have been following a known mobster. But in my defense, when a PI gets shot, left for dead and—" I looked around and switched to a whisper. "When a PI gets shot, left for dead and there's some weird glowy light where he got shot, that only *I* can see? How could I *not* do some digging?"

"The only thing you dug was your own grave. You're lucky Wheeler missed, or you'd have ended up like your PI."

"Chill out, Boss. I'm fine, aren't I? And anyway, this time will be different. I'm just going to walk the trail, ask some locals about the area. I won't be taking on the mob."

I could understand his reluctance, and to be honest, I'm still touched by it. He's the closest thing I have to a father figure. He took me in when I was 16. I was shoplifting Slim Jim's from a convenience store and got caught. He stepped in, said I was with him and paid the teller. No harm done.

I was a scraggly thing then, on the run. I'd been passed around foster homes all my life. I'm an orphan, see. At least, I think I am. I was dumped, wrapped in a t-shirt for some saloon somewhere. I've looked for the joint a bunch of times; I figure if I find the bar I might track down my parents. My family.

Never have found it though.

Anyway, Davey put his arm around me, like I was his daughter, and we walked out the store. Outside, he talked to me. Not like I was some homeless kid on the run from the latest shitty foster home, the latest shitty foster parents who liked to settle things with fists instead of words. He spoke to me like I was an adult.

He was the first person to talk to me as an equal, and I listened. And I talked back. He offered me a job at the paper—well, an unpaid internship—but he also offered me his spare room and food and clothing. I've no idea why he took me in. Maybe because he never had his own family, maybe because he saw a bit of himself in me, I dunno. But I stayed, and I grew and I became a pretty decent journalist and I got a place of my own.

I guess what I'm saying is, Davey gave me a life, and I'll always be under his wing in some small way.

Davey sighed and sunk down into his chair. "You're gonna go anyway, aren't you?"

I gave him a big Cheshire cat grin.

"Fine," he said, the merest of smiles forming at the corner of his mouth. "But you're taking Meyers with you."

"Boss!" I yelled. "I can't take the kid!"

"You wanna go?"

"Yes."

"Well, Meyers is going too. That's the deal. Besides, you're gonna need pictures if this amounts to something."

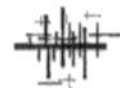

Neither me nor Meyers had a car, so the boss got us a rental. We left at 6am, which would get us to Devil's Ladder for somewhere around 2pm. That would give us a couple of hours to explore before heading to a little town called Chevron, where we had a hotel reservation for the night. Separate rooms. An early rise the next day, with the plan of poking around town, asking some questions and generally seeing what I could dig up.

I insisted that Meyers drove. An eight-hour drive left me with time to re-read the articles and do some research on the way to Devil's Ladder. After a few hours research, mostly a complete waste of time—I could barely find any information on the hiking trails of Devil's Ladder, let alone much more on the stories— I fell into a loose sleep, rocked by the music of the road.

Those stories had just flickered out before they'd got going. Like they'd been quashed. Covered up.

I dreamt. I dreamt of the forest, with flayed skin for bark. I dreamt of a cult, and a cavern; the victims all there watching me, looking at me like I could give them rest. The stories were gruesome, and clearly, things were getting to me.

When I finally woke, unrested and a little cranky, we were in the middle of some small—I hesitate to use the word—town. Really, it wasn't much more than a main street, with a few stores, a couple of bars and diners.

"Where the hell are we?" I asked Meyers, still a little groggy.

"Erm... This is Chevron."

"What the hell are we doing here? We're meant to be going to Devil's Ladder first," I shot back, wiping the dust out of my eyes.

"Hey, Sleeping Beauty! I don't know where we're going. You could've got Teague to shoot for a GPS for us. Or better yet, stay awake to read the goddamn map."

"It's one road, dumbass. Take the old Thirteen until you see signs for Devil's Ladder and turn off. It's not rocket science." I paused. "Wait, this backwater is *Chevron?*"

"I hate to say it, but yup. Well, at least we know what to look for when we come back later."

Meyers pointed to the lousiest looking hotel I'd ever seen. Least I'd be up early the next morning. Nothing like being eaten alive by bedbugs to put a spring in your step.

By this point, we'd already driven through Chevron and were back on the open road. "You better turn back so we can ask for directions."

"Directions! Nooooo," Meyers said.

"Oh god, you're not one of these dumb shit men that refuses to ask directions, are you?"

Meyers shot me a grin. "Maybe."

"Well, not on my watch. Turn around."

Just then a billboard showed itself on the side of the road: 'Carmody Chevron Motors'. Just below that, 'Turning in one mile'.

"We'll go in there to ask directions," I said, pointing at the billboard as we passed.

"Okay," Meyers said. "But only because I need the restroom."

I rolled my eyes and soon enough we were pulling into Carmody Chevron Motors. The place looked brand new; shiny new signage, and a fleet of top of the range 4x4s, soft-tops, hatchbacks, anything you could ask for.

"Who the hell is gonna buy these around here?" I wondered out loud.

"Not people from around here, that's for sure."

We walked into the air-conditioned showroom, which was a relief. It was hot, way above average for the time of year. The thermometer was tipping 100°F.

"How the hell can you wear that leather jacket in this heat?" Meyers asked, as we walked in.

"Zip it. It's what I wear." To be fair to him, I do tend to wear the same outfit most of the time. Black Dr. Martens, black jeans, black leather jacket over a t-shirt, but I didn't have to explain myself to some kid.

"Welcome!" a voice boomed.

We both looked up to see a big guy strolling over to us. I had to stifle a laugh, as we were pretty much watching Boss Hogg from Dukes of Hazzard—it was a show Davey made me watch over and over—walk over to greet us; perfect cream suit, white cowboy boots, topped off with a white cowboy hat. He even had a cigar poking out the top pocket of his suit jacket.

"What you laughing at?" Meyers whispered.

"Zip it," I whispered back.

"Welcome to Carmody Chevron Motors," the man boomed again. "I'm Garrett Carmody."

"Hi," I said. "This is quite a place you have here."

He guffawed, and I had to stifle another laugh. He sounded like fucking Santa Claus. This was just getting weirder and weirder.

"Thank you, Baby Cakes."

At that point, he immediately went from a novelty to somebody I loathed. Who the fuck goes around calling a complete stranger 'Baby Cakes'?

"Baby Cakes?" Meyers whispered, with a disgusted tone.

All credit to him for that. It stopped the rage I was feeling, so I bit back what I really wanted to say, and got down to business.

"Yes, well anyway, I wonder if you could help us? We're a little lost."

He guffawed again. This time it wasn't funny, just annoying. "Oh,

Baby Cakes, Garrett Carmody will always help a damsel in distress. Where are you and your boyfriend headed?"

I was gonna correct him there, but I didn't want this sleaze to think I was single and up the creepiness, so I pushed ahead. "Well, we're looking for Devils Ladder. We're going for a romantic hike."

Meyers shot me a confused look but went with it.

"Devil's Ladder doesn't sound too romantic to me, but look at her. Darkness is at the core of her heart and I can only beat to the same tune."

Internally, I retched at the cheese of it, but if it kept Carmody cool, then it was fine by me.

"Ah, Devil's Ladder. You want dark, you chose well. You overshot the mark a little, but if you go back to Chevron, then head north on the 95, you'll see a sign soon enough, turn off and follow the road. You'll soon be where you need to go."

"Great," Meyers said. "Would you mind if I used the restroom? We've been on the road a while..."

"Not at all, young man, go right ahead," Carmody said, pointing to the back of the showroom. He shot me a smile, which somehow didn't show in his hollow eyes. "What say I walk you around the showroom while you wait, Baby Cakes?"

"Erm, I think I'm good for a car," I said.

Something about the man made me nervous. The sleaze was too much; his eyes looked lifeless and cold. It made me nervous, hot and sweaty. So, I stepped back, unzipping my jacket to cool down, and started to turn to walk back to the car. His eyes immediately shot down to my bust, to goggle at my goods, but at that moment the creepy smile left Carmody's face to be replaced with a nervous look I didn't understand. I looked down at the t-shirt I was wearing. It was the one I was found in when I was dumped as a baby. Faded to hell over the years, but you could still make out the logo of a saloon.

Whiskey Pete's.

"You know this place?" I asked.

"Ah... Er... What place? No." Carmody took a step back, all of his cool gone.

I'm a reporter, I'm trained to read people, to know when they're lying, but even a child could see he was full of shit.

"You know this bar, don't you? Where is it? Is it nearby?"

I had a million questions all buzzing through my head. If I found this place, I could find out something about where I came from. I might even find my parents.

"You need to leave now," Carmody said, Baby Cakes forgotten.

"Where is it?" I pressed.

"You. Need. To. Leave." Carmody said, face starting to go red.

"Where—" I started, but was quickly cut off, as Carmody's expression turned from confusion to rage, but was that a moment of fear I saw come over him in between?

Before I could decide, he blew up.

"GET OUT!" he roared.

Just then Meyers returned from the restroom. "Whoa, what's going on?

"Get the fuck out of here!" Carmody growled, his face blood red.

"Dude, the hell is wrong with you?" Meyers said, then pretty much dragged me out of the car dealership and threw me into the car. Tires screeched as he hit the gas and we were on the road again and soon heading north on the 95.

"Just what are you expecting to find out here?" Meyers moaned.

I'd put thoughts of finding my parents to the back of my mind for now. We'd pulled into the parking lot at the Devil's Ladder Recreation Center. Meyers left the old Thirteen earlier than he should and got a little lost, but we made it safe and sound. It was empty, which I thought was a little odd for mid-summer. We grabbed our packs, which contained a few bottles of water, some protein bars, and some hiking basics—compass, flashlight, matches. Meyers, the boy scout, also had a small knife and first aid kit, as well as the DSLR camera hanging from his neck, complete with smiley face sticker. I added some insect repellent to my pack too. Then we walked…and walked.

"Just keep your eyes peeled. We'll know when we see it."

"We've been walking along this trail for over an hour. We've seen no one, and nothing apart from a few hundred trees."

"You've been looking at the trees?" I said, only half-joking. "We're here to look for something hinky."

"Hinky? Zia, look around you for a moment. Honestly, what's 'hinky' about any of this?"

He was young and it was bad news to judge a place by how it looked, but I could see where he was going. The trail was stunning. Firs and pine trees loomed up over us from each side of the trail. Bird calls filled the air. The rattle of a woodpecker echoed around us. Nature surrounded us, filling my senses with utter beauty.

Then a voice in the back of my mind reminded me of all the heinous atrocities that had occurred in the area. All the disappearances. Looking around, it was easy to see it wouldn't take much to get lost out here.

Or for someone to make you vanish.

"Meyers, I never thought I'd say it, but you're right. We're not gonna find anything on the trails. We need to go off-road."

I gave him an evil smile, waggling my eyebrows to add to the effect. Then I was off, walking between two trees, off the trail and into the forest itself.

"Oh, come on! That's not what I meant!" Meyers cried. "Did you even see the warning signs? There're mountain lions out here. There're bears, Zia. Zia?"

"Stop being a baby. Take some pictures. It's beautiful out here," I said, playing with him now.

"We'll get lost," he tried.

"We have GPS on our phones and a compass in our packs. Now keep up."

"GPS went out miles back," Meyers pleaded.

My drive to get a story can be a little…risky, shall we say. Following the mob, not a great idea. Running into uncharted forest, also not a great idea. It wasn't long before we heard the snap of a twig behind us. It was loud and piercing compared to the tranquil noise of the forest and it made us both jump.

"What was that?" I whispered.

"Probably a fucking mountain lion, like a warned you," Meyers spat back from the side of his mouth, trying to keep quiet. "Let's go back. *Now.*"

"That crack came from behind us. You wanna go back?"

Meyers ground his teeth and gave me a vicious glare. "Fine. Keep going."

Another five yards. SNAP. This time closer.

We spun around. Only trees filled our view. We gave each other a knowing, worried glance, but pressed on. Two more feet and the loudest crack yet echoed throughout the forest, quickly followed by the rustle of leaves and branches. We turned again and, ten yards back, a massive shape emerged from behind a bush.

Meyers didn't wait for the thing to step out; he just took off. He ran past me, screaming, "Bear!"

I didn't hang around. My heart was beating a million miles an hour and I followed right on his heels. Branches, leaves, God-knows-what whipped at my arms and face. The leather jacket protected my arms, but I felt scratches to my face and the warm trickle of blood down my cheek.

Then I ran straight into Meyers. He stood stock-still in front of a tree. My butt hit the deck, and Meyers stumbled forward. He screamed. Piercing my ears. I looked to see an eviscerated body—I think it was a young, black girl, but I couldn't be sure thanks to time and wild animals—and I joined him screaming.

Then a thud came from behind. The bear was still chasing us.

I got up, grabbed Meyers by the collar. "We gotta go."

Another ten yards or so, and we came out, somehow, to Devil's Ladder itself. The area's called that, after the rise at the middle. A huge, white, rocky scar in the earth looming up to a jutting peak. The trail was just across the way, and I thought if we could get to Devil's Ladder and climb, the bear may not be able to follow. It was a long shot, but it was all we had.

"Come on!" I screamed and took off.

The last thing I remember was Meyers shouting, "Wait!"

But it was too late.

"Fuck, fuck, fuck." A voice swam into my consciousness. "Zia, wake up."

My eyes fluttered open, seemingly of their own volition. A blinding, white light shut them up quick.

"Oh, thank god." It was Meyers.

I tried opening my eyes again and quickly realized he was shining a flashlight in my eyes. "Jesus, will you stop with the flashlight?"

"Oh, sorry." He swung the light away from my eyes and I got a glimpse of where we were.

"What the hell happened?" I asked, looking around. All I could see was bare, ragged rock.

"You fell through a hole in the ground," Meyers said. "We're in a cave, I think. Haven't really had time to look around."

"What about that thing chasing us?"

"Well, it didn't follow us down here, so I think we're all good."

"Good."

"Weeeell, it's not *that* good. I can't see any exit. Apart from the hole in the roof, which," he pointed up, to a flicker of daylight a good fifteen feet above us, "is a little too high to reach. It's a miracle you didn't break anything. Can you walk?"

I tentatively clambered to my feet, testing out my ankles and knees, and actually felt okay. I was lucky. Landing on a big pile of pine needles softened my fall.

"I'll live," I said, getting my phone out of my pocket. "We need to get out of here."

"Don't bother. No signal down here. Only one option."

Meyers pointed down a long, rocky tunnel.

I sighed, grabbed my flashlight. "Well, we better get moving, and hope and pray this leads to an exit."

"It will," Meyers said, but I heard more hope than surety in his voice.

We walked...and walked, like strolling through the forest all over again, but without the beautiful scenery and birdsong. It was pitch black down there, and surprisingly hot, so I tied my jacket around my waist. I'd always thought caves were meant to be cool places, but I guess I was wrong. I heard a trickle of running water, but it sounded like it was miles away. Every now and then, I would swear I could hear singing or chanting of some kind, but Meyers insisted I was hearing things.

"We should go back and shout for help," Meyers said. "Surely people hike to Devil's Ladder. Someone's bound to come along sooner or later."

"Don't be stupid. Did you see that empty parking lot? No one's coming this way any time soon. We need to make our own luck and find an exit."

"I'm not being stupid," Meyers shot back. "This is gonna make a great story for you. Isn't it? That's all you care about."

"Hey! That is *not* all I care about," while thinking it really *would* make a great story, and knowing I was being somewhat of a bitch. Luckily, we were saved. "Look!"

Up ahead was a junction where the tunnel broke off in two. Now we really did have a decision to make. We looked down both tunnels, and they looked exactly the same. We glanced at each other, knowing a truce was in place.

I knew we had to go left. I can't explain why, but I had another one of my hunches. Left was the way to go, but I threw Meyers a bone. "What way?"

He ran his hands through his short, messy brown hair. "Oh man, I don't know, Zia. How about—"

A low, deep growl came from back the way we'd come. Almost a groan.

"Fuck," he finished.

I decided for us and just took off running down the left tunnel. Meyers followed close behind.

Soon, the tunnel came to another junction, then another. Each time I went left. The growl continued from behind us. It seemed to be getting closer. Could've just been the acoustics of the place, but I wasn't taking any chances and carried on running.

"We're gonna die down here," Meyers cried behind me. Literally crying.

Another minute of running, and the tunnel changed considerably. From barren, rough-hewn rock, the tunnels became more of a structure. The walls were made of great, cyclopean rocks—they brought flashes of the architecture I'd seen in pictures of Machu Picchu. The ceiling became arched and smooth as butter. The rock floor evened out. There was even a camber in the center, so run-off water would flow down the sides into gutters. We were nearing civilization of some sort.

I was too breathless to say as much to Meyers, but we looked at each other, knowing in both our eyes. And that knowing pushed us on...

Until, up ahead, a light.

"Thank god!" Meyers screamed.

As we got closer, I saw the light was a burning torch made of a wooden stave wrapped in something and set alight. It looked ancient. I also saw we were running into a dead-end. The stonework abruptly ended, but the growling behind us only grew louder. Neither of us dared a glance back in fear we'd see whatever it was that was chasing us and freeze in terror.

"Fuck, fuck, fuck!" Meyers was hysterical now.

I looked closer and saw it wasn't a dead-end. The torch illuminated a metal ladder set into the rock wall.

I hit it full pelt and didn't wait to climb one rung after the other until I reached a trapdoor. I felt like I was in a horror movie and, as I pushed up, I expected it to stick, but it swung open easily. Above I saw only gloomy light.

I climbed through the trapdoor and into the place I least expected.

"Ow!" I cried, as I climbed out of the tunnel, banging my head on something hard above me.

"What now?"

"Jesus…"

I groaned, looking around, trying to get my bearings. My eyes stung as I came from the dark into the light, dull as it was. I was in a fucking bar, of all places. I crawled out and looked up to see what I'd banged my head on. It was the underside of a pool table.

"Chill out Meyers, I'm okay."

Meyers crawled out after me, and as he started to stand a black and white cat appeared from somewhere. It sniffed at his trainers, turned its nose up, like Meyers was a second-class citizen, then sprayed his leg with a stinking line of piss.

"Oh, Jesus!" Meyers cried, kicking out at the cat.

It doused all my fears immediately and I burst out laughing.

Dry, cackling laughter joined in, like something you'd expected to hear coming from a crazy old coot. I stopped and looked around to find just that.

He sat in a dark corner of the bar, laughing his head off and pointing at Meyers and me. He was old. Death-warmed-up old. His long, greasy white hair rolled down his face and over frail shoulders like languid seaweed. He clapped his palsied hands and pointed again, tears running down his face. He started to say something before he broke out in a wet, rough cough. It sounded something like "welcome home, stranger" or just "welcome, stranger" and I was about to ask what he'd said when a shadow drew over me.

"Take it easy, Melvin."

A handsome young man towered over me, pool cue in hand, the other held out in offer to help. I took it and he pulled me up.

"Joel Masterson, twenty-five. Nice to meet you."

As I got to my feet, I saw that he wasn't that good-looking at all. His brown eyes looked hollow somehow. 'A sandwich short of a picnic', as the boss would say. His smile was warm, but all yellow and crooked. As if he saw what I was thinking, he closed his lips, covering them up. I thought he looked like a Monet; from a distance, you saw a thing of beauty, but the closer you got, the more of a mess he looked.

A bit crass, I know, but so what, shoot me.

"Thank you, Joel Masterson, twenty-five. I'm Zia Bennett, twenty-two, and this is Dylon Meyers, eighteen."

Masterson didn't get my joke, and just carried on like it was nothing. "Now, I know you guys have got a story to tel—" He broke off, looked down at my t-shirt. "Oh shit! Welcome back!"

Welcome back? I thought. *I've never been here.*

I gave him a confused look.

"Whiskey Pete's," he said, pointing at my chest. "Welcome back."

"*This* is Whiskey Pete's?"

"Yeah, for as long as I can remember."

The air rushed out of me, and I felt suddenly woozy. I had a connection to this place, been searching for it all my life, and now I just *stumble* upon it. I staggered a little. Joel rushed to steady me and grabbed far too much of my boob and ass than was necessary.

"There now, little lady. Take it easy," he said.

"I'm fine," I said, brushing him off.

Meyers, to his credit, came to my rescue again. He seemed to have a knack for stopping sleaze-bags from taking a shot at me. "Let's take a seat," he said, and we grabbed a booth with leather-torn upholstery. "Hey," he shouted to the bartender, "can we get a glass of water over here?"

A minute later, two glasses of water slammed down on the table, both spilling slightly, accompanied by a grunt from the exceedingly chipper barman.

"Don't mind Con," Joel muttered, firing a frown at the other man's back. "Grumpy bastard."

"Joel, shut your goddamn hole."

I ignored them both and drank deep, downing the pint in one. Meyers pushed his over to me and I took another sip.

After a minute or two, I felt I was finally able to get my bearings proper. Whiskey Pete's was in need of some renovation. I felt like I was sitting in a 1970s time capsule. Even the jukebox was playing Bowie's *Diamond Dogs*. I looked over to the old man in the corner. He raised a glass to me and tipped his head. Joel had gone back to playing pool, but kept looking over at me every couple of seconds, smiling and winking. Gross. The barman, Con, had a face like thunder and stood wiping down the bar.

We sat in silence for a while. I had a million and one things running through my head. The tunnels. Was it really just them and bears that were the cause of all the weird goings-on in the area?

But now, Whiskey Pete's and my history came to the forefront. I watched Meyers fidget, nervously mucking about with his camera, picking at the smiley face sticker. Obviously, he had some questions of his own. I couldn't take it any longer, so I looked into his eyes, a sign I was ready to talk. He breathed a sigh of relief.

"Oh, thank god. Great. Glad you're okay. Now, what the fuck was that?"

"Meyers, slow it down," I said. "Before we get into this, we need beer."

"But—" Meyers started.

"Zip it. This isn't the sorta place where they ask for ID."

I strolled to the bar, feeling everyone's eyes on me. The old guy, Melvin, smiled and raised his glass again. I felt Joel's eyes on my ass. The bartender just looked livid that he had another customer to take care of.

"Two beers, and two burgers please."

He grabbed a couple of pint glasses and poured us two beers—Warden IPA, according to the tap. Then he walked through a door to what I assume was the kitchen, obviously not bothered about a tip. I grabbed the beers and walked back to Meyers.

The beer tasted like something the cat had just sprayed but I didn't care. My mouth was as dry as Joel's...well, you know what. A couple of minutes later, the barman dropped two plates on the table. The burgers looked good; fat and greasy, topped with onions, lettuce and pickles. No tomato, just how I liked it. I was impressed.

"Another?" Con said, grabbing the empty glasses.

Wow, he can talk, I thought.

"You read my mind."

And off he stomped.

I bit into the burger. It tasted heavenly. Grease ran down my chin, but I didn't care. By the time I'd finished my mouthful, the beers had arrived, and we were able to start talking while we ate.

"First things first, that was just a bear that chased us. Had to be."

"But the sounds it made—"

"It was just a bear," I said pointedly.

Meyers leaned forward like he wanted to get into it more, but then slumped back. For the sake of his sanity and mine, he dropped it. "Okay."

"Now, the bear..." I looked at him wide-eyed, and he nodded, "and those tunnels; that's our story right there. That's where everyone has gone missing."

"It was like a maze down there," Meyers said. "It's a miracle we made it here."

"I know," I said, neglecting to tell him about the force of the hunch that had guided me. "I hope you got loads of pictures."

"I did, although I'm not sure what the quality will be. I was running full-tilt and snapping over my shoulder."

"You get any of the tunnels?"

"Yeah, but again, I'm not sure of the quality without a flash."

"That's okay. A few atmospheric shots will add to the aura of the story."

"We're gonna need to get back to the car," Meyers said.

"Shit. I forgot about that," I said. Looking up to Con, I called, "Hey, where are we?"

He looked up and opened his mouth to say something. But Joel piped up from behind me.

"Duh, you're at Whiskey Pete's," he said, and gave a yokel guffaw I was pretty sure The Simpsons had trademarked years ago.

I just looked back to Con, who rolled his eyes, and with considerable effort said, "Speak to Lorne out front; he'll get you where you need to go."

"Thanks."

Now I just had the elephant in the room to deal with. I was dumped in the very t-shirt I was wearing. My hand gravitated to the faded Whiskey Pete's logo, the shirt now soft as silk. My parents must have been here at some point for them to have wrapped me in this.

I looked at the old man, Melvin. If anyone was around twenty-two years ago it would be him. The only problem I foresaw was the fact he looked about a hundred years old, and at that age, the mind tends to waver. Before my thoughts could wander any more, Meyers snatched my attention, coughing and spluttering.

"Jesus Christ," he spat, literally. He had a mouthful of burger in his hand and looked down at it, wide-eyed. "Fucking hell, I'm gonna be sick."

"What?" I asked.

"Fucking disgusting," he said, throwing the remains of the burger on the table in front of me. "That," he said. Pointing to a perfectly manicured red fingernail. "There's a fucking fingernail in my burger meat."

"Ewww," I said, and felt a little queasy myself. I pushed the remains of my burger to one side, and we both washed our mouths out with beer.

"I'm out," Meyers said. "Come on, let's get back to the car."

"You go. I'm gonna do some more digging here first. Besides, you stink of cat piss."

He flipped me the middle finger, then pointed at my t-shirt. "That?"

I nodded. "Pick me up when you've got the car?"

"Yeah, sure. You gonna be okay here, on your own?"

"Come on," I said, tapping my own chest. "What do you think? It's me."

"Okay," Meyers said, looking at his phone. "I'd call you when I'm on my way, but, shock horror, no signal out here."

"No worries. You know where I am."

"Okay," he said, rising from the booth. He pushed his second, untouched beer away. "I'll be as quick as I can."

Then, with a wave, he grabbed his camera and left, stopping briefly at Con. "You wanna tell your chef back there to wear fucking gloves. Public

Health is gonna get a call from me, I can tell you that."

I gave it five minutes before grabbing my beer and walking over to sit with Melvin to see what I could find out. Problem was, when I got there, his chin was resting on his chest, whistling out his nose as he snored.

Damn it...

I sat at the bar instead. Con didn't seem like a talkative man, but hey, I'm a reporter, I have some tricks up my sleeve.

"Another," I said, shaking the empty glass at him.

He nodded, grabbed an empty glass, and poured another pint before slamming it down in front of me.

"And one for yourself?" I offered.

He eyed me suspiciously, but shook a shoulder and grabbed a second glass.

"Thanks," he growled, lifting the cold beer in my direction. "Cheers."

I cocked mine back.

"So," I said. "How long has this place been here?"

"Built in the Fifties."

"Huh, it's had a good run then. Pete a relation of yours?"

Con laughed; one single, throaty "ha", then fell silent again. Like squeezing blood from a stone.

"You worked here long?"

"Long enough," he said.

I wasn't getting anywhere, so I went for a different tack. Head on.

"You know, I was dumped as a newborn."

"That right?"

"Yeah. I was wrapped in this very t-shirt."

"That right?"

"Yeah. You don't happen to remember anyone who came through here pregnant about twenty-two, twenty-three years ago, do you?"

I thought he looked a little uncomfortable for a second, but considering his demeanor I wondered if he just had some kind of social thing, like he didn't enjoy talking to the public. Odd for a barman.

Just then, Joel sat at the bar next to me and opened his mouth to start talking.

"Joel," Con said, with a hard stare, "don't even."

Joel retreated. "Fucking asshole," he muttered under his breath as he went.

"Lady, we have a lot of people come through here. I don't remember every motherfucker. Now, you want another drink, fine. If not, I got shit to do."

And with that he strolled off, grabbing our plates from the table, taking them into the kitchen.

I returned to the booth and waited, hoping Melvin would wake up so I could question him before Meyers returned.

An hour went by. An hour Melvin slept. I went to the restroom—I don't even want to talk about the horrific state of it—and when I came back, Melvin was gone. Damn it.

Another hour passed, and Meyers still hadn't arrived. I was getting worried. I checked my phone, but still no signal. I asked Con about a payphone, he told me the receiver had been ripped out during a recent fight. Typical. All I could do was sit and wait as the evening drew in. Con milled about, Joel played pool, Melvin never returned, a few other people came in and out, but it was pretty empty most of the night.

Finally, when it was around 11pm and Meyers still hadn't come back, I resigned myself to a night in the motel round back.

The motel receptionist, Stacey, hooked me up with a room and made me sign a registration book. The whole place oozed '70s. Threadbare carpet the color of vomit, wood paneling and peeling wallpaper, and worst of all, rotting taxidermy. A deer head stared down at me, skin pulling away, face an evil sneer.

"This place could do with some serious renovation," I said to Stacey.

She just chuckled, staring off into the distance like she was somewhere else. *Maybe she's high,* I thought.

"Oh, hey," I started, pulling out the envelope of stories from my backpack, "you don't happen to know anything about these, do you?"

I passed her the clippings, and she took a moment to thumb through them, her face completely expressionless.

Without looking at me she put them back in the envelope, put it on the counter and slid it back. "No, sorry. Devil's Ladder is a good eight to ten miles from here. We don't see too many hikers."

Eight to ten miles?!

She had to be wrong. We ran through the tunnels for no more than half an hour before getting to Whiskey Pete's. There was no way we went that distance.

"Ten miles?"

She nodded. "Give or take."

I wanted to press her, but what was the point? She knew the area better than me. I was about to go to my room when one more thought occurred. I lifted the envelope once more, showing her my name, my address.

"You recognize this handwriting?" I asked.

She looked, and her vacant eyes seemed to return, just for a moment, as recognition flashed across her face, but as quick as it was there, it was gone again. Her eyes glazed and Stacey looked at me, but not really. She looked through me into the middle distance.

"No." It came out as a coo. "I don't. Sorry."

This place just got weirder by the second. And to think my parents were connected, somehow. These characters—and that's what they felt like, just caricatures—seemed too spooky. Someone was hiding something, and wanted to find out what.

I waited for as long as I could in that crumby room; all shag carpets, stained sheets, ashtrays, and a tube television. I didn't want to even sit down in there. It was gross.

Come 2am, I was out of there. I quietly left the room, bag over my shoulder, and looked across the parking lot to the back of Whiskey Pete's.

A couple of dumpsters sat overflowing with trash. They'd make a good first hiding spot.

As quietly as I could, I walked across the gravel. Each footstep sounded like thunder in my ears, and I kept an eye out for Con or Stacey or anyone. Waiting to be spotted and questioned. I wear all black for a reason, and just then it paid off. The motel reception was dark, as was Pete's. Everyone was, as I'd hoped, asleep.

I stopped at the dumpster and checked my surroundings. 'All quiet on the western front,' as the Boss would say. So, I walked up to the back door and tried the handle. Not surprisingly, it was unlocked. Out in the sticks, there's no need to lock your doors, right?

I walked down a long, dark corridor. Doors lined one side. I was hoping to find an office, some paperwork—bills, invoices, orders, anything. To find the writer of my envelope.

I tried the first door. The creak was deafening. I froze, like a deer in headlights, and waited. Listening for the telltale sign I'd been caught, shouts or footsteps.

They never came.

I looked inside a janitor's closet. Mops, bleach and other cleaning goods. I gently closed the door and moved onto the next.

This door didn't creak. It opened smoothly to a set of stairs that led down into darkness. I pulled my bag off my back, stuck a hand in, and fished out my flashlight. After shutting the door, I clicked it on, and let it lead me into the darkness.

At the bottom of the stairs, I found just what I was looking for. A desk jammed with notes and receipts and all sorts of paperwork. I took my backpack off and laid it next to me on the desk, then pulled out the envelope full of newspaper cuttings. I started comparing the handwriting on the piles of notes from the desk with the envelope. No luck.

Then I saw something else, under a random silver sand dollar. Newspapers. All with stories cut out of them. Holy shit, someone *here* sent me the stories. Someone here lured me in. But why? I looked to the sky—or at least the ceiling—in hopes of finding an answer, and instead, all I found were more questions.

I saw a picture pinned to the wall of the office. It was beat up, edges fraying, and had the yellow look of age. The image was of Whiskey Pete's, and standing out front, everyone I'd seen today. Con, Joel, Melvin, Stacey, another man next to the petrol pumps who I assumed was Lorne, the man helping Meyers get back to the car. Once again, I hoped Meyers was okay.

There was another man in the picture too, short and fat, with his back turned and his arms raised as if in celebration. I envisioned him having the face of the Batman villain, the Penguin.

Then, bingo! Across the picture, two short sentences were written. 'The gang' and under that, 'Opening day'. The handwriting was a dead match. It didn't tell me anything I didn't already know, but when I hit the table in jubilation, something was knocked to the floor and the crash echoed out.

Again, I stopped dead, waiting for someone to come running, but no one did. I looked down to see what I'd broken and my blood ran cold. It was Meyers' camera, complete with its smiley face sticker.

"Meyers," I whispered, and swung my light around, looking into the unknown, hoping to see him standing there, smiling at me. Ready to tell me this was all some crazy joke, but what I found terrified me even more.

The basement was filled with luggage—hundreds of bags, suitcases, backpacks, duffels, handbags, saddlebags. There were piles of cell phones, from huge '80s bricks right through to the most modern smartphones. Piles and piles of clothes and shoes. A baseball bat leaned against one of the walls, a bloody nail sticking out of it. Next to it was a lug wrench and a small pile of handguns. There were even a few motorcycles.

Stolen? Only if the folks who owned them were still alive.

I turned to run back up the stairs and, at that moment, the door to the basement burst open, revealing the hulking silhouette of the thing that had chased us through the forest. Now I knew it wasn't a bear, but I still couldn't make out exactly what it was.

I had no time to hide. My flashlight had already given me away, and as the thing descended the stairs, I left my bag and ran for an exit. In the back of my mind I wondered if anyone would find my belongings, lying here among all the rest.

Between a pile of coats and a stack of laptops, I found another cyclopean tunnel. With the thing on my heels, I had no option but to enter it. As soon as I did, I heard the rumblings of a chant, some alien language, unknown to me.

My heart was beating out of my chest as I ran through the darkness, flashlight leading the way. I didn't need it though. Flaming torches lined the tunnels, leading me deeper, closer to the source of that chanting. Looking back now, it all seemed too convenient. Not just these torches, the ones before, leading me to Pete's from Devil's Ladder, the monster appearing and chasing me.

Guess I was too hot for a story. For answers.

I looked back and, although I couldn't see it, I heard the rough breath of my pursuer. When I turned back, the tunnel opened into a huge, cathedral-sized room. It was lit up like the Fourth of July.

Paralyzing terror overtook me. It was filled to the rafters with the monsters, like the one chasing me. They chilled me to the core, and I screamed, knowing my end was near. I turned, hoping by some miracle to find another way out, but when I did the monster following me filled the arched entranceway. It growled and panted, a sound I thought sounded like laughter.

It lifted a huge hand. I closed my eyes and waited for the killing strike. It never came.

I opened my eyes to see Garrett Carmody leering down at me.

"Baby Cakes," he said, walking by, and my terror briefly switched from fear to confusion. My gaze followed him back to where he took his place with all the others. All the monsters had taken their heads—their *mask*—off now. Men and women of all shapes, sizes and ages stood in the massive room. They faced the same direction, having averted their attention from me, looking up at something else.

"You..." I said quietly. "You led us here. Back at the showroom, it was all an act. Why?"

"Zia!" came a chilling scream.

It was Meyers. He was naked, lying across an altar hewn from rough stone, arms and legs tied at all four points of the compass. He had the hilt of a knife protruding from his abdomen. A line of blood dribbled down his side and onto the rock below. The altar sat on a huge, stone stage above the audience. The back wall was decorated in mind-bending patterns, wrapping around statues of horned demons. The torchlight flickered, making their eyes glow. Goosebumps erupted all over my body as those demonic effigies stared down on me.

"Zia, run!" Meyers screamed, through gut-wrenching sobs. "Get out of here while you can."

"Meyers," I whispered.

A voice filled the cavern. "Ahh... You made it, Zia."

The five people from the picture strolled out from behind it, surrounding Meyers. Con, Joel, Melvin, Stacey, Lorne. Then, finally, the last man from the picture took center stage.

My vision blurred, and I felt my consciousness start to ebb away, the terror too much to bear.

"Now, now," the voice continued. "Hold it together. We have a job for you. A job we've waited so long for you to carry out. So very long."

I focused on Meyers. I needed to get him out of there somehow, someway.

"Why all the games? Why not just pick up the phone? Why drag *him* into this?"

"You needed to find this place yourself, Zia. I needed to know you were ready. I gave you a little nudge, of course. You have a choice. Sacrifice your friend or be sacrificed along with him. Take that knife. Pull it from his abdomen, and slice open his neck. Spill his lifeblood and join us. Return home. Return to your family."

Home? My family? I looked up and focused on the speaker. Their features distorted like I was staring at the sun. Did I imagine a smile?

"Welcome home, daughter."

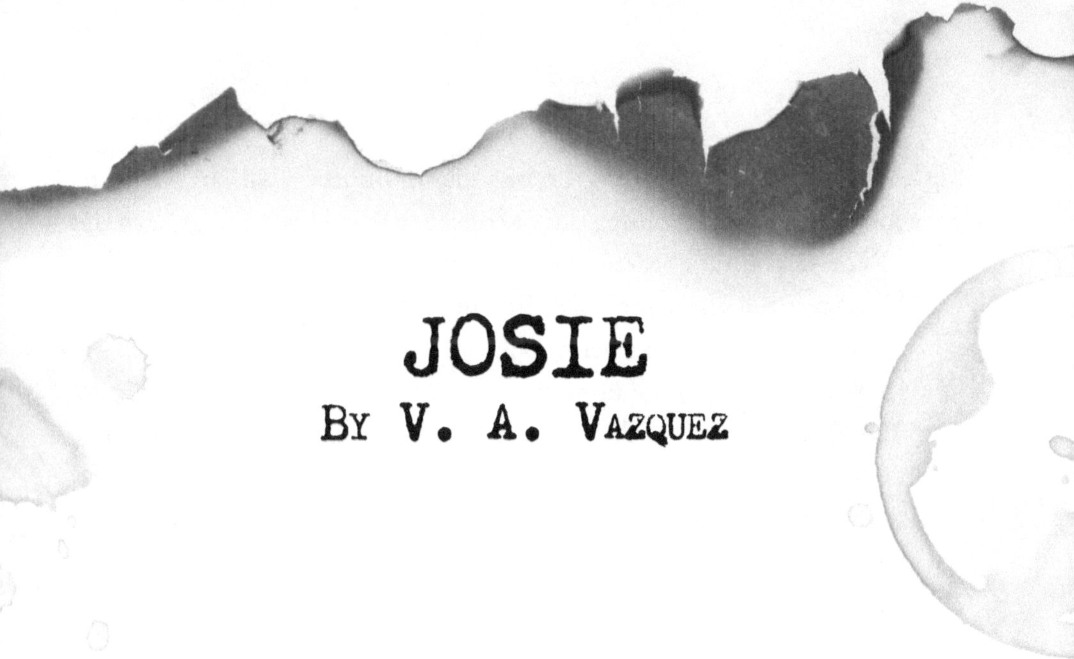

JOSIE
By V. A. Vazquez

"*Remember, you create your thoughts, your thoughts create your actions, and those actions? They create your reality.*"

Josie speeds down Route Thirteen. It's the middle of summer, and the air conditioning in the car has been busted since last year. The windows are all rolled down, but sweat still dribbles down the back of her neck and pools in the collar of her blouse. She grabs a handful of McDonald's napkins from the center console to dab up the sweat. As she reaches up, she notices dark splotches spreading underneath her arms.

"Damnit," she mutters, tossing the napkins onto the passenger seat.

It doesn't matter anyway; she's not going anywhere important—just some shitty little motel in the middle of nowhere. Same as the hundreds of other shitty little motels she's examined over the past decade. Each one, checkboxes ticked, questions asked and answered, a grade marked at the bottom, and a report filed with her department manager.

Ten years, you'd think she'd be the department manager by now. But that position's already filled by a baby boomer who insists he's just as energetic as the day he took the job. No retirement in his future, no siree, not even with the government pension waiting for him or the house he paid off in full back when real estate was still affordable. Josie's still repaying the student loan she took out to get her AAS in Hospitality Management from Lewis-Clark State College. She'd dreamed of working in one of the big hotels in Boise. A Hyatt maybe, or a Hampton Inn. Hell, she'd tried to get a job at the Super 8 coming out of college, but it'd been the peak of the Great Recession and her career hasn't picked up since.

What is it the magazines call Millennials? The Lost Generation?

She checks the GPS on her phone.

"Sure feel lost right about now."

There's no mention of this place on any maps, and when she'd stopped off in Chevron for gas, all the locals had shrugged and refused to give directions. Her boss had told her it was somewhere on Route Thirteen near Payette National Forest.

"What am I supposed to do with that information?" she'd asked.

"Keep driving until you find it."

"Everything you want is out there, just waiting for you to ask. Everything you want wants you right back. You just have to believe in your ability to ask the universe for it."

She'd bought the self-help CDs from a secondhand shop in Twin Falls. *The Law of Attraction.* Send those good vibes out into the universe; they'll manifest into everything you want and come back to you. Every morning, during her commute, she channels any scrap of positive energy left in her towards getting a new job. But thus far, nothing has manifested.

"Ask for what you want and be ready to get it."

Josie clicks the CD off as a motel looms into view—a rest stop for weary truckers that hasn't seen any renovations since her mother was in high school. Whiskey Pete's. The last E on the neon sign's starting to flicker, which means half the time it's Whiskey Pet's instead. Josie directs her Hyundai between the yellow lines of the parking lot and pulls the key out of the ignition. There are no other cars—just hers.

Clearly Whiskey Pete's hasn't been seeing a lot of business.

Her skin peels off the plasticky upholstery as she gets out of the car, picking up the manila file folder on the passenger seat and a ballpoint pen. She slams the car door shut and heads towards the convenience store. A tinny bell above her head rattles as she enters; no one's standing behind the cash register.

"Hello?" she calls, examining the shelves stocked with snack foods.

She picks up a dust-coated PayDay and checks the expiration date: October 2015. She uncaps the pen and jots down a note in her paperwork.

"You want that?"

An elderly man stands in front of her. His face looks like a topographical map of Payette: all bumpy hills and entrenched valleys. His stringy blonde hair has been combed over the bald patches on his scalp, the skin underneath red and shiny. His jumpsuit, which looks like it hasn't been washed since this place was first built, has an embroidered name tag on the front.

"Hello, Dale," she smiles, holding out a hand politely.

"Lorne." He takes her hand. There's crud lodged underneath his fingernails, and Josie yearns for one of those travel-sized bottles of Purell.

"Lorne." She doesn't ask who the jumpsuit belongs to or why he's wearing it. "My name is Josie Fisher, and I'm from the Eastern Idaho Public Health Department. We received a complaint about your facilities, but there's no Whiskey Pete's registered here in Idaho. This building doesn't look new. May I ask how long you've been conducting business?"

But Lorne's still stuck at the beginning of her speech. "A complaint?" he sniffs, mucus thick in the back of his throat. "Who filed a complaint?"

"We're not allowed to disclose that information."

"'Cause I gotta couple complaints of my own."

He picks up a chipped coffee mug from the counter and hocks a wad of phlegm into the bottom. As he puts it back down, Josie can see the accumulation of weeks of dark brown loogies congealed at the bottom. Her stomach flip-flops, and the Big Mac she ate for lunch threatens to make a one-way return trip.

He grabs a bag of potato chips from the shelf and shakes them in her direction. "You see these?" He waits for her to nod before continuing. "Taste like they went through a wood chipper. Think I got splinters in my tongue last time I tried to eat one."

"Um..."

"And take a gander at these." He walks over to the window, and Josie has no choice but to follow. The convenience store has one of those revolving dessert stands. The glass has never been cleaned; greasy smears mark where visitors have pressed their fingertips up against it. There's a dead fly trapped in the whipped cream on the key lime pie, wings bent at a forty-five-degree angle. "Those cheesecake slices are seven months old at least. Bite into one, and you'll end up shitting your intestines out. I can guarantee you that."

Josie uncaps her pen and starts jotting down notes. If this man wants to spill all the dirt on his employer, then who's she to stop him?

"What did they call you about? Was it the cheesecake? I keep telling them to order fresh, but—" Lorne wipes his palms on the thighs of his jumpsuit. "When's anyone ever listened to me?"

Josie checks the Post-It note stuck to the paperwork. "Someone reported finding a fingernail in their food." The words are out of Josie's mouth before she realizes how disgusting that is. She can't imagine biting into a chicken nugget and finding someone's raggedy old fingernail lodged in the meat.

And how does someone just lose a fingernail, anyway?

"Then you're going to want to drop by the bar." Lorne points to the building next door. Neon signs in the windows advertise Budweiser and Coors Light. "I'll introduce you to Con."

"Con?"

But Lorne's already halfway out the door, little bell rattling again as she jogs after him. She tries to keep her elbows pinned to her ribcage so no one notices the pit-stains on her blouse. Not that these folks are going to care. Lorne looks like he just pulled himself out of his own grave and wandered into work.

It's about as dingy as she expects inside. The bartender, who she can only assume is 'Con', slouches behind the bar with his arms crossed against his chest. There are stains on his shirt that might be from food, might be from drinks, or might be from the bathroom.

"Con," Lorne says, rapping his knuckles twice on the countertop. "Get this young woman a drink, eh? She's from the..."

He looks back at Josie, and she fumbles out her ID. "Josie Fisher, Eastern Idaho Public Health Department." She sets the ID down on the counter and isn't surprised when her fingertips come away sticky. Con stares at the photo on her ID, then stares at her, then offers up a guttural grunt that could mean anything from 'looks good to me' to 'go fuck yourself with a rusty crowbar, lady.'

"He don't say much." Lorne grabs a glass from the end of the bar and sets it in front of her: filmy residue, jagged chip along the edge. "Con, you know anything about a fingernail in the food?"

If Con's surprised, he doesn't show it. Just shakes his head and pours the remaining half bottle of beer into her glass.

She sees another Post-It note on the report and flinches. Talking sanitation sometimes gets heated, but nothing's worse than when you have to start talking money. "May I ask who's in charge of the finances here?"

Lorne and Con look at each other, but no one answers.

"Because you're not registered as a corporation here in Idaho, that means you haven't been paying taxes. It's not my department, but my supervisor instructed me to tell you that Whiskey Pete's has been reported to the Idaho State Tax Commission. You probably owe some back-taxes. Whoever's responsible for your accounting should be notified."

Lorne blinks once, eyelids saggy. "We don't really have anyone handling the backend right now."

"Oh?"

"We're looking for new general management." He nudges the drink closer to her. "If you know anyone who might be interested."

Josie's ears prick up like a border collie who's just heard a whistle in the distance. "You're looking for general management?"

Lorne nods. Con lets out another grunt.

She looks around the place with fresh eyes. It might be a hole-in-the-wall, but it certainly has character. Dark wood paneling, burnt orange jukebox in the corner. The felt on the pool table is ringed from the bottoms of beer bottles and singed from lit cigarettes, but that's nothing that can't be fixed. Whiskey Pete's has got that kitschy roadside appeal that's popular nowadays. Americana, they call it.

Everything you want is out there, just waiting for you to ask.

She could do some DIY repairs, the kind she watches on HGTV, and get this place back in working order. Sure, there are some back-taxes that need to be paid, but she's got friends over at the tax commission. They can work out an arrangement. And she can make sure they pass their health and safety inspection.

A sharp chittering sound comes from Lorne's pocket. It's familiar, but she can't place it until Lorne pulls out one of those old pagers from the '90s. He checks the message. "Gotta run to the shop a second. Be right back."

He high-tails it out of the bar, leaving Josie with her half-full glass of beer.

"You from around here?"

A man slouches against the counter, thigh resting on one of the bar stools. She gives him a once-over. There's handsome handsome, and then there's Idaho handsome. This man is Idaho handsome, but she's never lived anywhere other than Idaho, so what should she care? He's certainly better looking than her ex-boyfriend, but then again, she's probably not the best person to give an honest opinion. She'd thought Wesley might be the one; instead, he'd ghosted her last year. Men were always ghosting her.

"Not really," she says. "I'm from Twin Falls, about three hours out from here."

The man whistles, and she can see his teeth are a little crooked in front. He quickly covers them with his lips when he notices she's staring.

"That's one hell of a commute."

"You're telling me." She almost reaches for the drink before remembering how unclean the glass looked. It remains untouched on the counter. "I'm hoping to wrap this up quickly."

The man follows her gaze out the window. Lorne's still standing in the convenience store, chatting on the phone without a care in the world.

"You could do that," he says, stuffing his hands into the pockets of his jeans, "or you know we've got a motel out back? You could always spend the night."

She doesn't need to ask what spending the night means to him. And she's a little tempted. She's tempted to ask about the general manager position. She's tempted to stay and do a more thorough study of the motel, the bar, the convenience store. She's tempted to fuck this stranger who's just walked up to her in a dingy roadside bar.

The man leans forward and rests his hand on top of hers.

"C'mon," he says, giving her a cocky, little closed-mouth grin. "It'll be on the house."

There's a rumble from the back of the bartender's throat. "Joel—"

"Yeah, yeah. I know."

The man gives her a wink before going back to the pool game he appears to be playing by himself.

Everything you want wants you right back.

Lorne pushes the door open again. "Sorry about that." He must be from up North. He pronounces 'about' with the 'ou' in group instead of mouth. And thinking about mouths leads her right back to the man at the pool table's, still tipped upwards in a smile. His gaze settles over her like a weighted blanket.

"You have a motel?"

"Sure do," Lorne says. "It's right around back. You wanna take a look?"

She nods, picking up her manila folder and nodding at the bartender just to be polite. She gets half a grunt in response. Her sensible heels click against the cement as they cross through the parking lot towards the motel.

"So, how's business here?" she asks, hoping she sounds interested only as a public health inspector and not as a potential general manager. "You're right on the doorstep of Payette. You see a lot of hikers around here? Families going camping?"

There's an RV half-pulled around behind the building. It's not in one of the parking spots, but rather off to the side, on a patch of dirt with grass stringier than Lorne's comb-over. Maybe they do get some guests out here after all.

"Hikers, sure," he says. "There's a trail only a few miles from here. Can never remember the exact distance. Devil's Ladder. All kinds of stories about it, if you believe that sort of thing."

She's willing to bet Lorne believes in that sort of thing.

The motel's one of those long strip numbers with two floors chopped up by double doors, each one leading to a different room. The windows run floor-to-ceiling, although they're covered by curtains that have served the same purpose as the filter on a Marlboro cigarette. Still, good bones. This joint's got good bones.

Lorne opens the door, gesturing for her to go right on ahead. There's a woman standing behind the desk, flipping through the pages of the guest register. "Stacey, this is—"

"Josie Fisher," she says, holding out a hand. Stacey's is an improvement on Lorne's; her fingernails are freshly polished, and her cuticles are neatly clipped. "With the Eastern Idaho Public Health Department."

Stacey smiles blandly but says nothing.

"Can we get the master?" Lorne asks. "I'm going to show her around."

Stacey plucks a key off the wall behind her and passes it to Lorne. As they walk down the corridor, Josie notices the receptionist's still staring at the empty space where they were standing a few seconds ago. It's like she hasn't even noticed they've gone.

The motel's floors are covered in threadbare, orange carpet, and in some places, she can see the hardwood through the holes. Something's leaked out from underneath the door to room seven and left a dark stain.

"Is that..." She crouches down to get a better look. "Is that blood?"

When she doesn't get a response, she turns back towards Lorne. He shrugs.

Shit. They might have to call a biohazard team down here for clean-up. And then there might be a police investigation because lord only knows how many crimes have been committed here over the years. "How much do you charge a night?"

"Fifty dollars."

Fifty dollars. With those prices, she's willing to bet the folks coming through here aren't just hikers and campers. She can only imagine what else she might find in some of these motel rooms: stashes of narcotics, used sex toys and soiled condoms, maybe an unregistered handgun tucked behind a nightstand. She stands back up, shakes her head.

Just because the universe throws something in your direction doesn't mean you have to take it. You can always say 'nuh-uh, not today, Mr. Universe' and head right back to Twin Falls. Which is what she should be doing.

"You wanna see one of the rooms?"

Lorne sticks the key into the lock and turns it. They still have real keys, the kind you need to get cut in town, and Josie wonders how often someone slips one into their pocket as a souvenir. Who has to make the trek back to Chevron to get them replaced?

The door opens.

It looks like one of those picture postcards her mother kept in a shoebox. Like she just stepped back in time to when career women clacked away on typewriters and men wore polyester suits more flammable than a can of petrol. They'd need to do a lot of work, sure; all the linens would need to be replaced and they'd need a fresh coat of paint on the walls. But good bones all the same.

"What do you think?"

There are ways of marketing this place: a retro, roadside bungalow for those interested in the great outdoors. She has a photographer friend back in Twin Falls who still owes her favors for writing all his English 101 essays in college. After the renovation, they could schedule a photo shoot, get a website up and running. It wouldn't be that hard.

"It's perfect."

It's not. She knows there are objectively better hotels all over Idaho. That Super 8, for one. But how many times has she applied for managerial jobs at them and how many times has she been turned away?

As if on cue, Lorne says, "You know anything about running a place like this?"

Yes! she wants to shout. She knows *everything* about running a place like this. Well, maybe not everything, but enough to put Whiskey Pete's on the map. Her mind's a twelve car pile-up of all the things she wants to do here, and for the first time in god knows how long, she's excited.

"I might know something about running a place like this." She's trying to hold her smile back, but it spills out the corners of her mouth.

The smile drops when something heavy thunks into the window. "What was that?"

Lorne opens the window, which takes a bit more elbow-grease than it should, and the two of them peer down at the lifeless body of a crow—lying on its back, wings spread, feathers rustling in a sudden summer breeze.

"Huh," she says. "Maybe it got lost flying from Nampa?"

Lorne doesn't say anything. Just stares at the crow's glassy eyes reflecting the illuminated MOTEL sign and the smaller one right below, which reads VACANCY. Then he nods, as if he's come to a decision, and says, "Well, Whiskey Pete's might not be much, but we are looking for a new general manager, and if you'd be interested in applying—"

"I would."

The words are out of her mouth before she can second-guess her decision. Before she can count all the ways this might be a bad idea.

"Then why don't we introduce you to Pete?"

"Oh. There's a Pete?"

She would've thought, if there was a Pete in Whiskey Pete's, she would have been introduced to him before now. When a health inspector shows up on your doorstep, employees usually run to fetch the man whose name is above the door.

"There certainly is a Pete," Lorne says, showing her out of the room and walking down the long hallway towards a staircase at the end. "Opened this place almost seventy years ago."

"Seventy years? He must've gotten started young."

"Hmmm."

Lorne shuffles up the staircase, the untied laces of his sneakers clicking against the cement. He opens the door to the second floor and sticks the master key into the first door on their left.

A tidal wave of Pine-Sol freshness smashes into her as soon as she enters the room, causing her throat to spasm and cough. *Well,* she thinks, *at least we know one room's been cleaned recently.*

The administrative office—at least, she assumes that's what this room is—has a typewriter on the desk and one of those thick, glass ashtrays. Lorne plucks the freshest cigarette from out of the ashes; it's still smoking at the end.

"Must've just missed him." Lorne takes a lighter out of his pocket, holds the flame to the half-smoked cigarette, and takes a puff. "Still good," he shrugs when he notices Josie staring.

"I can wait," she says. "I have nowhere else to be."

It's true. She doesn't have to be back at the health department until tomorrow morning. She can spend the night, maybe with Idaho Handsome, and hit the road before dawn. Besides, now that she knows there's a Pete, she'd need to sit down with him anyway to go over his critical violations and discuss his tax situation.

"Good." Lorne pulls out an upholstered armchair that looks scratchy. "I'll take a look around and see if he's available for an interview today."

"Oh…"

Is she going to have to come back another day if he's not? She'll do it if it's the only thing standing between her and a motel management job, but she'd rather not make this six-hour commute again.

She'll have to refill her tank before heading back to Twin Falls. Better to do that tonight than tomorrow morning. After the interview.

If there is an interview.

Lorne steps outside and shuts the door behind him. There's a faint click-click sound, but she ignores it.

Josie takes out her cell phone and checks her email. Or *tries* to check her email. There's no signal out here, which is the first thing they're going to have to fix. If there's no cell service, then they at least need to make sure there's Wi-Fi available in the motel. Her sigh puffs out her cheeks, and she tucks the cell phone back into her pocket. That's when she hears it.

Thump.

Thump.

Thump.

It's the same dull thud as the crow against the window. Pulling back the curtains, she checks the sidewalk, half-expecting to see an entire flock splattered on the walkway. But there's nothing there.

Thump.

Thump.

Thump.

She tracks the sound through the office, skimming her fingers along the walls until she finally locates where it's coming from: a single, wood panel directly behind a potted plant. She shuffles the plant out of the way—so much dust sifting off its leaves, she can't help but erupt into sneezes—and then knocks a few times on the panel.

Knock, knock.

Probably rodents living inside the walls. It wouldn't be the first time she'd come across an infestation as a health inspector. She's good buddies with some of the best exterminators in the business. That'll be the first thing on her to-do list. Call the Everly Brothers and get them out here with—

Thump, thump.

"What—"

Josie stares at the wall. She's seen some clever rats over the years, but none that could communicate with her. She tries again.

Knock, knock.

Thump, thump.

There's someone on the other side of the wall. Maybe Idaho Handsome snuck into a custodial closet and is playing a trick on her. She tries not to enjoy the way her toes curl at the thought.

"Hello?" she calls, pressing her ear against the wood.

She thinks she hears a few muffled words, but that might just be wishful thinking.

Her fingers snag on something protruding from the wall, stuck in the seam between the two panels. A thin little hook... A latch, she realizes, looking closer. She grabs ahold and presses down as hard as she can.

The wall pops open.

The smell fills every nook and cranny in her nostrils, and she almost upchucks all over the office carpet. When her grandmother passed a few months ago, she'd shat all over the mattress—runny diarrhea that coated her entire backside and seeped into the fabric. The room behind the paneling smells a whole lot like that.

She nudges the panel open with her elbow.

And really, really wishes she didn't.

A man's zip-tied to a chair inside. Or at least, he's zip-tied at the ankles and around his chest. His right arm's been hacked off at the elbow, the stump sealed up tight with an ace bandage and the jack handle from someone's trunk. His left arm met the same fate up to the shoulder but it must've been some time ago because there's no makeshift tourniquet on that one. Whoever did the job clearly didn't have medical training; the left arm looks like it's been hacked through with a machete. The bone at the end's splintered and cracked. The flesh has been peeled away from the wound site in raggedy strips.

He's still intact below the waist, at least as far as she can see, but no one's been taking him out for bathroom breaks. Fecal matter has piled up around his ankles. No wonder the office smells like it's been doused in enough disinfectant for a germ genocide. Someone's trying to keep this hidden.

Is she a bad person because her first instinct is to close the panel and pretend she never saw? She can make her excuses and drive back to Chevron as quickly as possible. There, she should be able to pick up a cell signal and call 911. Get this man the help he needs. God knows there's nothing she can do.

She starts to back out of the room.

"Mmmph." The man protests with a groan, and he struggles to raise his head. There's a filthy necktie knotted across his mouth. His lips are cracked at the corners, and his chin's coated in spittle. That's why it takes her a few seconds to recognize him.

"Wesley?"

His eyes go wide as he recognizes her, too. Wesley Schneider. Her ex-boyfriend. The one who'd ghosted her. They'd met at a health and safety conference; he worked for OSHA as an auditor.

"Mmmph!" He jerks forward in his chair, and the legs make that *thump, thump* sound.

She can't leave now. It's one thing to leave a stranger behind for the police to help. It's another thing to leave her ex-boyfriend, especially since there's now a strong possibility he hadn't ghosted her last year. Instead, he'd come here to audit Whiskey Pete's and had been abducted and tortured instead.

She only just stops herself from sighing in relief.

Thank god. It really was him and not me.

"Just a second," she whispers. "I'm going to find some scissors and get you out of here."

She's about to start rifling through Pete's desk when she notices the stack of papers on the table next to Wesley. There's a Post-It note stuck to the first page, and she can make out the letters from here.

FOR JOSIE

They need to get out of here. There's no reason to stop and read the note left by whatever psychopath runs this motel, but as she comes closer, she sees the heading on the paper.

GENERAL EMPLOYMENT AGREEMENT

"What the hell?" She picks up the papers, despite Wesley's muffled protests and the sounds of the chair slamming against the floor, and rips off the Post-It note.

This General Employment Agreement ("Agreement") is made and effective August 4

BETWEEN: JOSIE FISHER (the "Employee")

AND: WHISKEY PETE'S (the "Employer")

IT IS HEREBY AGREED as follows:

1. DURATION OF THE CONTRACT

(a) The Employer shall employ the Employee in accordance with the Terms and Conditions of this Contract;

(b) This Contract shall commence from the date of the Employee completing a satisfactory job interview (see INTERVIEW);

(c) The Employee shall continue in the employment under the Terms and Conditions of this Contract in perpetuity.

Her eyebrows scrunch together. "In perpetuity?"

She may only have an AAS degree, but she thinks perpetuity means forever. Maybe it means something different in an employment contract. Like the contract's good for life or until she decides she wants to leave.

She can't stop herself from flipping to the section on compensation. She's only making $20,000 as a public health inspector and hasn't seen a raise in years. She just wants to know what she's worth; she *has* to know what she's worth.

4. COMPENSATION

A. Base Salary. As compensation for the services provided by the Employee under this Agreement, the Employer will pay the Employee $250,000 per year.

Despite the fact she's standing next to her ex-boyfriend who's been tortured for god knows how long, and despite the fact she's in the office of the man who's probably responsible, she re-reads that section a few times. Maybe the stress of the situation has made her hallucinate a few zeroes? She blinks, rubs any dust particles out of her eyes, but the numbers remain the same: $250,000.

A quarter of a million dollars every year to be the general manager of Whiskey Pete's.

Alarm bells go off in her mind, but they aren't the right alarm bells. The alarm bells that should go off are the ones signaling 'oh my god, what are you doing, there's a maniac heading upstairs with a machete to cut you both into little bits, you need to run get out of there now'.

Instead, she's only hearing: 'How can Whiskey Pete's afford that kind of salary?'

"Hmmph!" Wesley lets out another grunt and slams his chair against the floor. If she unties the gag around his mouth, he might scream and bring Lorne or Con or—if they're especially unlucky—Pete upstairs before they're ready. She crouches down in front of him.

"I'm going to take out the gag, but you need to stay quiet. We don't want to draw their attention, okay?"

Wesley nods so energetically, she's amazed nothing cracks in his neck.

The necktie gag's stiff with months of saliva. She lets it drop to the floor while Wesley opens and closes his mouth a few times. "Josie," he tries, the word coming out stiffer than roadkill. "Josie, what are you doing here?"

"Investigating a complaint to the Public Health Department. What are you doing here?"

"Investigating a reported OSHA violation. Or I was until someone knocked me over the head, and I ended up in here." His voice grows even more strained. "We need to get out of here. Now. They're fucking psychopaths, all of them. They've been—" He looks down at his hacked-off limbs as if just remembering they're not there. "They've been cutting off parts of me to use in some kind of ceremony."

"Like a cult?" Josie doesn't know much about cults, but she did watch that Leah Remini show on A&E.

"Yeah. I think." He yanks his ankles against the zip ties. "Find something to cut me loose. You drove here, right?"

"Yes."

"Great. We'll get to your car and head back to Boise. Get emergency help once we're there."

"We can just stop in Chevron—"

"No." She says nothing, just waits for an explanation, so he continues. "We don't know if they're in on it. Don't trust anyone in these little rural towns; wait until we get back into the city. Haven't you ever seen a horror movie? Don't be so fucking naïve."

She bites down hard on her lower lip to keep from saying something she'll regret. Opening the desk drawer, she starts rifling through the contents. *It's no big deal,* she tells herself. *He's been through so much.*

She pulls out a pair of scissors.

"Great," Wesley says, looking towards the office door. "Now cut me loose before they come back." As she approaches the chair, he keeps rambling. "I can't believe I'm finally getting out. It feels like I've been trapped here forever. What month is it?"

"August."

"Fuck me. Four months?"

Her hand stalls out right above the zip ties, the scissor blades open. Four months. He'd stopped responding to her texts over a year ago. Which means he *had* ghosted her. And now she was going to save the life of the asshole who hadn't even thought she deserved a text saying goodbye.

"What are you waiting for?" he hisses. "Hurry up."

Yes, she tells herself. *Hurry up. You're not actually petty enough to let someone get tortured and killed because he dumped you, right?*

And she isn't—she knows she isn't—but damned if she doesn't want to right about now. She sits back on her heels, accidentally knocking into the little table. The papers scatter to the floor, and she catches sight of a familiar section.

7. INTERVIEW

The Employee's interview will be deemed successful when, and only when, she has dispatched WESLEY BACHMANN to the satisfaction of the Employer. Upon completion of the Interview, this contract will automatically commence.

She re-reads the section while Wesley jerks back and forth in the chair, wooden legs scratching against the carpet as he tries to get her attention. What does that mean? Dispatched?

It can't mean what I think it does, right?

The scissors are still grasped loosely in her hand, blades wide open. Wesley's making a fuss, hissing and spitting like a rabid animal. She catches on little words like 'useless' and 'stupid'. It'd be so easy to jab the scissors straight into his neck and blame it on the psychopaths at Whiskey Pete's. Hell, maybe she wouldn't have to blame it on anyone; if the blood splatter downstairs is any indication, plenty of people have gotten away with murder here.

Remember, you create your thoughts, your thoughts create your actions, and those actions? They create your reality.

She snips the zip ties at Wesley's ankles and then the one around his waist. Josie could never kill someone, not even an asshole like Wesley Bachmann. She might want to—really, really badly—but that isn't the kind of person she wants to be. Wesley staggers to his feet, catching himself on the wall before he teeters to the ground. He's having a hard time keeping his balance.

"Let's get out of here," she says, grabbing him around the waist so she can help guide him from the office.

That's when the door opens.

Lorne's standing there with the master key gripped in his hand. Wesley physically crumples at the sight of him. The hallway looks darker than it did before, like one of the lightbulbs has burned out, but as she continues to watch, the shadows gather mass and thickness; they congeal like spoiled milk into something solid.

"Looks like the interview didn't go too well, huh?"

Josie doesn't say anything. Her muscles are trembling too hard for her to open her mouth.

"That's okay," Lorne shrugs. "This job's not for everyone. We understand. But regardless..."

She wants to scream, needs to scream, but all that comes out is a whimper as those shadows grow darker and thicker and closer.

"Pete's ready to see you now."

BEN
By Lynne Phillips

"There's cash for a room and dinner tonight. Report to Social Services tomorrow," the warden said, thrusting a wallet across the counter. "System says you're innocent, but with that temper of yours, I predict you'll be back real soon."

Fuck you.

Ben glared at him, knowing not to voice it. In five minutes, he'd walk out the gates a free man. After twenty years, serving a sentence for a crime he hadn't committed, Ben's bitterness overrode the joy of freedom.

The heavy gates clanged shut, signaling the start of his new life.

"Ben, over here!"

A solitary figure stood beside a small red car. The tension left Ben's shoulders; of course, Maryanne would be here supporting him, as she had for the last five years while they fought to prove his innocence.

"After all the highs and lows of fighting your case, I wanted to celebrate our victory," she said.

"How did you know it was today? They let me out early to avoid the press."

"I'm an investigative journalist, remember?" she said, smiling. "A friend of a friend contacted me. Not everyone in there thought you killed Lucy Carter."

At the mention of Lucy's name, Ben's face tightened, eyes betraying the depth of anger he felt over her death, his wrongful conviction, and the killer, still at large.

He managed a smile, grateful to Maryanne and her team. If she hadn't believed in his innocence, and convinced Pratt & Pratt Lawyers to accept his case pro bono, he would have either rotted in prison forever, or paid the ultimate price.

He shuffled his feet and looked at the ground.

"I'm glad you're here. Perhaps you can help me find a room and a meal; so much for prison rehabilitation."

"Come on, I've booked your accommodation," she said, taking his arm. "I'm sorry we haven't found the real killer, and there are some who still believe it was you."

A dark cloud passed across his eyes.

"I understand being angry, but you need to let it go. The state will pay for their mistake. It won't compensate for your pain, but there will be enough to establish a new life without you needing to worry about money again."

He scowled. "I want revenge. Not for me, but Lucy," he said, as he accompanied her to the car, still brooding, hands clenched deep in his pockets.

It felt strange sitting in the front of Maryanne's SUV. The traffic was daunting. So much had changed in twenty years. Neon lights flashed messages selling products he'd never heard of, and the sounds of blaring horns startled him and gave him a headache.

On arriving at his accommodation, Ben realized something. The room was too big. It felt overwhelming, but he smiled his thanks; it was a thoughtful gesture. Observing the traffic twenty stories below, he wondered if he'd ever pass a driving test and find a place in that bustling world.

"Sorry, Ben, I have to leave. I've put my contacts in this cell." She gave him a quick run through. "I'll be here tomorrow to take you to Social Services."

"Thanks, that would be great. I'm not sure where I fit anymore. This world's moved on over the last twenty years."

After Maryanne left, he paced the room. Other prisoners kept up with the outside world and the latest trends through television and computers, but he used the gym to vent his frustration and studied law, chasing justice.

Turning the television on and off, he paced again. *This is driving me crazy.*

He flicked through the paperback Maryanne left; at least it would take his mind off worrying about the future.

Room service delivered lunch and dinner as the day dragged on. The king-sized bed looked intimidating. He pulled the bedding off, carried it into the walk-in wardrobe, dumped it on the floor and climbed under.

Sleep came, filled with images of Lucy spread-eagled, face white as snow, contrasting with the gash in her chest, every heartbeat spewing bright, red blood onto the ground. He could see it soaking into the dirt as he tried to stem the flow, until her heart stopped and she lay still, whispering 'Ben' with her last breath.

He woke with a start, dripping perspiration, the images still vivid in his mind. It was only a dream. In reality, he'd found Lucy two weeks after she disappeared, by which time flies had staked a claim and vermin had desecrated the body.

"I know it wasn't me," he said, as if to reassure himself. "When I'm set tomorrow, I'm going back to Whiskey Pete's to find who killed her."

Maryanne arrived at ten the next morning bearing a backpack.

"Just essentials until you go shopping. Let's get this over with and I'll take you to lunch to celebrate your freedom." She looked around the room. "Did you sleep okay?"

He avoided eye contact, staring out the window. "Different from a prison cell."

Seeing the crumpled bedclothes in the wardrobe, she nodded with understanding.

Ben was glad Maryanne was there to help him fill out the forms at Social Services to gain a work permit.

"Your settlement will be paid in a few weeks. I've put an advance of five thousand into your account," she said, handing him a debit card and access details.

Lunch was delicious compared to prison food. A blonde waitress appeared at the table of the restaurant Maryanne had chosen. She could have been Lucy: blue eyes, curvy figure, an all-American girl. She smiled. "You enjoy your meal?"

For several seconds, she *was* Lucy. Ben's heart raced, sweat forming on his brow.

Oh, please, don't let me pass out here.

"Ben? Ben? Are you alright? Let's get out of here."

He stood, blindly pushing his chair back, rushing for the door, gasping for breath as he leaned on the wall for support, desperately trying to stem a panic attack.

He could hear Maryanne talking, see people staring as he collapsed onto the pavement, curled into the fetal position, wailing, "Lucy!"

Maryanne helped him to the car, his heart still racing, his head foggy. He recalled little about the trip back to the hotel.

"Are you sure you'll be okay?" she asked.

He smiled, trying to reassure her.

"I'll call you later," she said, as she left the suite.

He pulled back the covers of the newly made bed and slept for hours without dreaming of Lucy. When he awoke, he knew it was time to face his fears and head to Whiskey Pete's.

Squeaky hinges announced his entry as Ben stepped into the bar. The room looked as it had twenty years before. The same garish gold-and-black flocked wallpaper, threadbare carpet and strange stuffed animal heads, missing patches of fur, assailed his senses. Surprise on the faces of the occupants turned to indifference as he hesitated near the door before walking to the bar. The barman's craggy face glared at him.

"Strangers aren't welcome," he grunted, wiping a glass.

Ben glared back. He remembered the different colored eyes, the bulbous nose, the surly demeanor, but realized the barman hadn't recognized him, no longer the skinny eighteen-year-old who hung around the pool table.

"I just want a beer."

Con Muldoon assessed the muscle-bound guy holding his ground. He grunted, pulled a beer with too much head, and shoved it across the counter, scooping up Ben's money.

Taking his beer to an empty table in the far corner, Ben looked around. His eyes locked on a grizzled old guy, greasy hair, the name 'Dale' emblazoned on his red jumpsuit.

"Drink your beer and go if you know what's good for you. We don't like visitors. Bad things happen to strangers," the old guy said. "People who are sensible move on; they don't hang around."

The old guy looked familiar. Taking a photo of Lucy out of his wallet, Ben showed it to Dale. "Do you remember…" he started to say.

The old guy's face stared impassively ahead before his eyes flicked to Ben's face, ignoring the proffered photo.

"Never seen her, but I seen you around here, years ago. Skinny kid, ain't lost the scowl. You've muscled up since then. Better drink your beer and move on."

Ben felt his anger rise, imagining taking that scrawny throat and squeezing out a better answer, but he took a deep breath, shrugged and looked around.

Whiskey Pete's boasted a motel; he'd noticed the garish, neon vacancy sign, half-covered with grime, on his way in. It didn't look inviting, but he needed some place to stay. A sign at the end of the bar pointed towards a side corridor reception. A woman—petite, red hair, green eyes, full lips—stood behind the counter.

"Stacey," she said, looking past him.

As Ben approached the counter, maggots crawled out of her nose and eyes. Her red hair teemed with blowflies.

"What are you staring at?" she demanded.

"Lucy..." Ben gasped as he recoiled, body shaking, eyes wide. He backed towards the corridor leading to the bar. Bile rose in his throat; he felt he might vomit.

"Don't stand there like an idiot. Do you want a room or not?"

Ben blinked twice, took a deep breath, and the image shifted to reveal a woman about thirty, a vacant look in her eyes, red hair, nothing like Lucy. Fatter, older.

"I was hoping to get a room," he croaked.

"How long are you staying?"

"Not sure, a few days."

She gave a flicker of interest before the vacant look returned.

"Fifty bucks paid in advance. Room five, no refunds, no girls, and no eating in your room," she said.

She turned. Her head teemed with maggots. Ben stumbled back, trying to make sense of the situation.

"Get a grip," he muttered to himself, as he grabbed the key and escaped into the night air.

Flickering twice, the garish neon vacancy sign went black, causing Ben to fumble for the keyhole in the dark.

A double bed, with a lumpy mattress, filled most of the room. A dilapidated lamp and television that probably didn't work were the only other decor. A bathroom with stains and a sour odor Ben didn't want to recognize assailed his senses. Flocked, patterned wallpaper, torn and peeling in sections, told of historic cigarette smokers and the shagpile rug, curling at the corners, boasted unidentifiable smears.

He couldn't stay there. It didn't hold any answers for him.

As Ben walked back to the bar, the neon sign flickered on again, red hue giving the area an ethereal look, yet revealing hidden shadows on the periphery. A screeching owl swooped to catch a rat in its claws and other rats scampered across the empty parking lot. Ben quickened his pace, heart racing.

Con glared at Ben before disappearing into what he assumed was an office. A guy in the back avoided eye contact, pretending to be busy setting up the pool table. Stacey stared into space, recalling some memory that only she held, brow furrowed, and hands twitching. The old geezer in the red overalls was asleep in the corner. Only one pair of watery, blue eyes locked onto his. Ben couldn't believe the person was alive until he spoke.

"You're not welcome here, boy. I told you twenty years ago, and it still stands."

"I don't remember you, old timer; you must be confusing me with somebody else."

"You were a skinny kid from Chevron. Used to hang around the pool table…"

He stopped mid-sentence, staring into the past, cocking his head as if listening to someone, mumbling a tirade of words about fighting for the Confederates and ungrateful youths of today, before turning back to Ben.

"You ain't welcome here," he said again.

Ben held up Lucy's photo. "Do you remember this girl? She was a barmaid here."

Those blue eyes locked onto Ben's, ignoring the photo. "Never seen her, but you I seen. Had a short fuse, violent temper."

He stopped talking and stared into the distance again, mumbling about George Washington and the Civil War. Ben walked away.

"Ask Joel Masterson," the old man muttered at Ben's back. "He's the ladies' man."

Looking through the smoke-filled haze, Ben saw 'Joel' leaning on a pool cue, sardonic smirk covering the crooked yellow teeth, cigarette dangling from the corner of his mouth.

He ran his fingers through his lank, greasy hair as he watched Ben approach. "Pretty boy, did I hear my name used in vain?"

Ben almost turned, ready to ignore him. This mid-twenty-year-old would was too young to know Lucy, yet something familiar jarred Ben's memory.

"Do you recognize this girl?" Ben asked, showing him Lucy's photo.

"Man, so many girls fawn over me, they all look the same," Joel said, ignoring the photo.

Ben took a newspaper article out of his wallet. "Perhaps you've read this." He held out the article about Lucy's death and Ben's conviction.

"You ask too many questions. We don't like strangers asking questions, Pretty Boy."

Staring, Ben tried to recall having met Joel before; there was something familiar about him. Joel's skin started wrinkling around his wide-set eyes. His hair, while still lank, turned grey, and the hands holding the cue became marked with age spots. An older version of Joel held out the cue. Bewildered, Ben shook his head.

The younger version of Joel reappeared and said, "Challenge you to a game?"

Ben shook his head. "Maybe later, I used to be pretty handy with a cue, but I'm kinda out of practice."

As he walked back to his room, Ben shivered. *Someone just walked over my grave.*

It was an expression his mother often used. An icy feeling filled his guts. Hairs on the back of his neck bristled, making him turn, expecting to see someone watching him, but the darkness revealed no one. Still, the eerie feeling remained; goosebumps made the hairs on his arms stand on end.

The pine forest emitted strange sounds, some he could identify—a lone wolf, an owl hooting—but there were sounds that could have been voices, cries for help, moaning and shrieks that made the hairs on the nape of his neck stiffen. He strained to discern them, but the sounds changed, nothing distinct, just the wind whistling through the thick foliage. His hand shook as he struck a match and held the flame to a cigarette. Two long drags on it helped relieve the tension, but it was several minutes before the eerie feeling passed and he could relax.

Perhaps I'm just hungry, he thought, stamping on the butt and heading to the store. Walking released the sense of foreboding. Euphoria replaced it as the blood rushed back to his head. *I'm just imaging things.*

The shelves, sparsely filled, revealed nothing nutritional; a few dried, shriveled sandwiches, cans of beans, packets of chips, and Coca-Cola. He chose the chips and Coke from the vending machine, collected his change and left.

Whispering Pines—a long, curved forest—hid Whiskey Pete's from most angles, its thick rows of trees absorbing the sound of traffic and animals. On days with no wind, the trees even absorbed the silence. When the wind blew, the trees' song filled the air, whispering secrets, inviting exploration.

Ben and Lucy had known the forest well. They'd hiked the trails, making happy memories, Lucy laughing as she dipped her toes in an icy creek, plaiting daisies through her hair, and sharing a joke. Ben cherished those memories, but it was also where he stumbled upon her body, eviscerated, her empty eye sockets pecked clean by birds, maggots crawling out of every orifice, and gnaw marks on her beautiful arms and legs, turned black. He knew he would have to revisit Whispering Pines sometime.

Instead, he decided to hike to Chevron, a backwater town where he and his sister grew up, his dad working as a farmhand and his mum taking in other people's washing.

Russet tones of Fall trees brought back memories as he hiked the twenty-odd miles to Chevron. There was nothing there for him now. His father had died five years earlier, from a heart attack. Sarah, his sister, had gone years ago with the first traveling salesman that ventured into town the minute she turned sixteen. She wrote to him in prison, but after her second divorce and several moves, the letters ceased.

He wished her well, but he suspected Chevron, or someone in Chevron, had messed with more than her head.

Only Lucy kept him in the area once he'd turned eighteen. Lucy, who stole his heart and whispered his name with her last breath.

A rusty sign boasted 'Chevron: population 496' and nothing else. No welcome, no other information. Feeling his phone vibrating in his pocket, he stopped to answer it.

"Hello?"

"Ben, it's Maryanne. Where are you? You didn't check out of the hotel, and you've taken your backpack."

"Sorry, I should have told you."

"You haven't gone back to Whiskey Pete's have you?"

"I just needed to get away, get out of the city and explore the world outside my prison cell," he laughed, covering the lie, but even to him, it sounded hollow and false. "You don't have to worry about me, I'm planning to go hiking, enjoy some nature and breathe some fresh air."

"Well, keep in touch. I'll text you when your compensation comes through, it needs your signature."

"Thank you for everything, Maryanne, the city was just too hectic for me," he said, hating to be so deceptive. Maryanne deserved better, but the burning desire to avenge Lucy's death overrode everything else.

A bell above the door announced his arrival at the general store that doubled as a post office, but it was five minutes before an old woman bustled in, wiping her hands on an apron dusted with flour.

"Sorry, I heard you, but I was just making scones." She clapped her hands together and tiny motes of flour flew into the air, making Ben relax and smile. He remembered her name: Marion Clegg.

"We don't get many strangers around here, can I help you?" She peered at him over her wire-framed glasses. "You look familiar. Jed Marrison's boy, aren't you? I can see the resemblance."

Ben nodded.

"I thought you were in jail for killing that girl."

Ben's face darkened. He clenched his fists, forcing the rage back down. It wasn't her fault.

"They proved me innocent, I just got out."

"You know the shame killed your old man?"

Ben suspected as much.

"Anyway, how can I help you? A stamp, supplies, or are you just passing through?"

Ben chose muesli bars, chocolate, tinned food, juice, a candle, matches, and a couple of apples from the well-stocked shelves.

"There's nothing in Chevron but trouble for you, son. The Judd brothers took Lucy's death out on your pappy. He came in here one day, black eye, one tooth missing, and his arm in a sling. I wanted to call the police, but he wouldn't let me, said he deserved it for siring a killer."

"Well, he didn't have a killer for a son. My lawyer proved my alibi was true. I wasn't anywhere near Lucy when she was attacked. I found her body weeks after she disappeared."

"I'm glad to hear that, Ben. It's a pity your pappy didn't live long enough to know the truth."

Ben shoved his clenched fists deep into his pockets, a technique the prison psychologist taught him. He could feel the rage bubbling to the surface. *I'd better not run into the Judd brothers.*

"I suggest you move on. There's nothing here for you in Chevron," Marion Clegg said, waving him goodbye.

The crisp coolness of Fall caused Ben to pull his coat tighter as he walked along the gravel road, the russet tone of the trees contrasting with the occasional, vacant gray cottage. Neglected and boarded up, relics of more prosperous times when folks worked on Mr. Foley's farm. In the distance, red barns dotted the landscape.

At the end of the road, the house he grew up in looked forlorn; weathered timber, cracked windows, front door nailed up.

An old farm truck rattled past. No friendly wave.

Ben hesitated at the back door before giving it a hard kick, splintering the timber.

The room spun as memories washed over him. No-one had cleared it after his father's death. A filled pipe lay beside his father's favorite chair, dishes piled in the sink and newspapers strewn on the table.

"I wonder why Sis didn't take the old man's stuff," he said.

Perhaps she didn't even go to the funeral.

"Shit! What's that smell?" he said, gagging.

A dead raccoon, its bulging eyes the only part not gnawed by rats, lay on the hearth. He dragged it outside and washed his hands in the outhouse sink.

A small, portable gas stove allowed him to boil water for coffee as he ate cold baked beans from the tin by candlelight. Tired, he decided to stay the night. His old bed smelled musty, but he was too exhausted to care.

He fell into a troubled sleep where he dreamed the Judd brothers were beating his father to death.

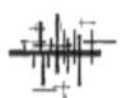

Bang, bang, bang!

"You'd better not be in there, Ben Marrison," a loud, slurred voice interrupted his nightmare, just when his father was taking his last breath, lying bleeding on the ground.

He wasn't dreaming; he was wide awake. Someone had tipped the Judd brothers off. Not Mrs. Clegg, no way. The farmer in the old truck? The front door shattered as Ben ran to the kitchen, grabbing his father's hunting knife and the tomahawk from beside the fireplace.

The Judd brothers had gone to fat, great jowls surrounded their piggy eyes, but they were just as mean as he remembered. Emboldened by grog, they came unarmed, relying on their combined brute strength, but Ben was prison fit and he knew he was fighting for his life.

"Pretty Boy, when did you get out of jail?" Jethro Judd sneered.

"We're going to make you pay for Lucy's death," his younger brother Jeremiah boasted, grabbing Ben by the throat and squeezing.

The one thing Ben had learned in a maximum-security prison was attack first if you want to survive. Thrusting the hunting knife into Jeremiah's chest, he ripped it upwards, blood splattering his face. Jeremiah's expression registered incredulity before he crashed to the floor, clutching at the knife. His body twitched as the light left his eyes. The older brother hesitated, moonshine-addled brain not believing what his eyes saw. His face turned red with rage. Grabbing a poker from the fireside, he charged at Ben.

"You're a dead man!" he roared. "Nobody hurts my brother and walks away!"

Ben knew there was no second chance. He swung the tomahawk, embedding it in Jethro's forehead, causing him to stagger back. The poker clattered to the floor as his hands frantically clasped the handle, blood making it too slippery to hold. Jethro's eyes rolled back in his head and he collapsed on the floor, joining his brother, their blood pooling together.

Blood Brothers, Ben thought, his mind verging on hysteria as he moved to the sink and vomited.

He'd been in a few serious fights in prison, sometimes ending up in the infirmary injured, or solitary confinement as punishment, but he'd killed no one before. Wiping the vomit from his mouth, heart pounding adrenaline, Ben stared at the carnage. He knew he had to get away. Rummaging through Jethro's pockets, he found keys, his hands accidently touching the pooling blood. Recoiling, he wiped it off on his clothes.

Finding a hammer and nails in his father's back shed, he boarded up the front door again. Wiping down all the surfaces he had touched, he cleaned away the remnants of his meal. He added a change of clothes to his backpack, along with a flashlight and the hunting knife, now wiped clean, then threw it in the truck and drove away from Chevron.

The thick trees of Whispering Pines closed around the truck, making it difficult for him to get out the door. Wiping away any fingerprints, he flung the keys into the tangled undergrowth. He changed clothes and buried his blood-splattered ones. After he'd hiked a hundred yards he looked back, pleased to see only dense forest, no sign of the truck. He hoped Whispering Pines still kept secrets.

The first rays of dawn were breaking as Ben entered his room. He crawled under the covers and slept until midday. Waking, drenched in sweat, he felt remorse, but he knew it was either him or the Judd Brothers who walked away. He didn't care if he went back to prison, but he wanted to find the truth about Lucy's death first, and he was sure Whiskey Pete's and its strange inhabitants were involved.

Eating an apple and a granola bar to appease his grumbling stomach, he crossed the empty parking lot looking for Joel for a game of pool. Ben noted his room was the only one occupied.

Joel stood, leaning on the pool table as if he hadn't left.

"Pretty Boy, you still here? Up to a game of pool yet?"

Joel thrust the spare cue in Ben's direction. He reached out. The hand that held the cue was old and gnarled, not that of a young man. When he looked at Joel's sneering face, it was unlined. He glanced back at Joel's hands. They were filthy, with long, yellow nails, but they were a young man's hands.

This place is eerie, Ben thought, reaching for the cue. *It's like it knows I know it. Back then. How it was and it can't hide itself from me.*

"It's been a while since I played, but I'm up for it."

They played three games. Ben won them all.

"Buy you a beer?" he asked, looking to the bar where Col was polishing glasses.

"Nah, I don't drink," Joel replied, avoiding eye contact with both Ben and Con.

"Bar's closed anyway," Con grunted, wiping down the counter, his eyes daring Ben to order. Remembering how disgusting the last beer was, Ben decided not to force the issue and wandered into the shop to buy more chips and Coca-Cola. He took them back to his room.

The television reception was non-existent, as he suspected, so he read the book Maryanne had given him before falling into bed exhausted. Despite that, he tossed and turned for hours until finally succumbing to sleep.

Something woke him. A shuffling sound. Someone or something was in his room.

"Who's there?" he mumbled, rubbing his eyes, trying to focus while reaching for the lamp beside his bed.

The switch didn't work. He fumbled for his cell phone, turning on the light, expecting to see someone in the room. The light revealed an empty room, but a message reading 'we have warned you' dripped down the far wall in large, red letters, slowly fading until they disappeared.

Unable to get back to sleep, Ben lay in the dark, trying to make sense of Whiskey Pete's and its inhabitants—the weird events, the empty parking lot, and the feel of an impending day of reckoning which permeated everything. He realized he was no closer to finding out who killed Lucy, although he was sure the answer was close.

When dawn filtered through the curtains, Ben checked the wall. There were no words, just a couple of dark stains that may have been blood on the edge of the carpet, but they could have been there for years. Pulling the carpet back, he discovered a trapdoor.

Maybe someone came into my room through there.

He dismissed the idea, because the trapdoor locked from his side. He placed the carpet back, vowing to check the trapdoor out later.

Maryanne's shiny red car looked incongruous parked next to the dilapidated Chevron General Store. A bell announced her entrance as she pushed open the door. A plump, pleasant-faced woman emerged from the back.

"We don't get many strangers stopping here," the woman said, peering at Maryanne over her wire-framed glasses. "Just passing through?"

"I'm looking for a friend of mine who grew up in Chevron. Have you lived here long?"

"All my life. Who's your friend?"

"Ben Marrison. Do you know him?"

Marion Clegg's eyes narrowed as she assessed the young woman waiting for an answer.

"Jed Marrison's boy? Yes, I know him. He was here three days ago, hiking with a backpack, said he was just passing through, checking out his past. He'd be far away now."

Maryanne's heart beat faster. *Ben really came back here.*

"How was he?"

"A lot of simmering anger, but he always had a quick temper. It was different now though. He was angry that his dad died before they proved his innocence."

Maryanne looked troubled. "I was the journalist who convinced the lawyers to pursue Ben's case. I'm worried about him. I talked to him three days ago. He didn't tell me he was already here then, and now he's not answering his phone."

"I warned him the Judd brothers were still around and wanted revenge. They're a nasty pair. Took their anger out on Ben's father. I hope Ben moved on like I suggested."

Paying for an orange juice and a chocolate bar, Maryanne asked, "Where's the old Marrison house? I'd like to see where Ben grew up."

"It's at the end of the gravel road. The last house. It's boarded up now. Nobody has lived there since Jed died."

The tires crunched on the gravel as Maryanne drove down the road, noting the open farming country dotted with red barns, a few painted, but most looking neglected.

The repaired front door was intriguing, her investigative mind racing ahead. Most wouldn't notice the hastily fixed damage, but she did.

Ben has *been here.*

Maryanne walked around the back. Someone had kicked the door in.

"Ugh, what's that smell?" she said, gagging.

Seeing a dead raccoon eased her mind until she noticed flies swarming into the cottage. Her heart raced. *Shit, I hope Ben isn't dead inside.*

She didn't think Ben was suicidal, but memories could have tipped him over the edge.

She stepped through the broken door. Flies buzzed around her, but many more flew into the next room. She steeled herself, expecting to find Ben's body. Instead, the bodies of two large, piggy-eyed men filled the small living room. *The Judd brothers.*

One man stared at the ceiling, a deep gash extending from his diaphragm to his neck, a tomahawk embedded in the skull of the other, the floor awash with blood, now congealing into a dark mass surrounded by flies.

A seething mass of insects crawled in and out of the Judd brothers' eyes and ears, their mouths appearing to speak as the flies transgressed their lips. More flies swarmed around both corpses, maggots already emerged, gorging on the rotting flesh, turning black around the edges.

"Oh, Ben, did you do this?" Maryanne said, gagging before rushing outside and vomiting until she was dry retching.

When her body finished convulsing, Maryanne washed her face in the outhouse sink. Finding a hammer and nails lying on the bench, she nailed up the splintered backdoor. She suspected Ben's involvement in the death of the Judd brothers, but she hoped it was self-defense.

Ben unlocked the trapdoor, pulling it back to reveal a black abyss with a steel ladder descending into the gloom.

Checking the flashlight was in his pocket, he climbed down, stopping every few meters to allow his eyes to adjust. The walls were dry; he could feel rough wood scraping against his body, getting narrower as he descended. A sulfuric odor filled his nostrils, forcing him to cover his nose and mouth with his shirt.

After thirty feet, he found solid ground. The shaft opened up into a series of tunnels. He contemplated what to do next while his shaking legs steadied. His breath was ragged and the smell of sulfur stronger. He decided to go back up.

With each step, the distance seemed to increase, his legs losing strength as he struggled to breathe. He was nowhere near the top when he realized there wasn't any light coming from the open trapdoor.

His flashlight revealed why. It must have fallen closed. Scrambling up the last ten meters he pushed against it, but it didn't budge.

"Hey, is there anyone up there? Open the trapdoor!"

The words echoed in the enclosed space. He pounded on the wood, but the hatch stayed shut. He looked at his phone, but there was no signal.

"Shit, what now?" he muttered, trying not to panic as it became more difficult to breathe.

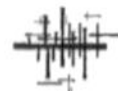

Maryanne drove away from Chevron, stopping on the side of the road to dial Ben's number without success.

A garish, neon sign up ahead announced gas and a motel. Thinking Ben might have checked in, she pulled in beside the pumps.

No one appeared to pump gas. Tooting her horn, she waited. An old guy with 'Dale' emblazoned on his overalls emerged, grumbling about being disturbed.

"Fill it up," she said. "I'm looking for my friend, Ben Marrison. Could be backpacking around here. Have you seen him?"

"You're the first stranger been here in years," the old guy said, avoiding eye contact. "That's twenty bucks."

Maryanne handed over a note and started moving towards the bar door. "I'll just ask inside."

Dale stepped close to her. "Missy, best you keep on driving. It's not safe for women to be alone around here. I told you you're the first stranger for years."

He touched her arm, sending shivers down her spine.

Maryanne wasn't happy, but decided not to force the issue by climbing into her car and driving away.

The old guy watched until she disappeared before he went back inside.

Maryanne didn't like being warned off. It made her suspicious. Ten miles out, she pulled over and dialed her friend Mike, who worked in telecommunications.

"Mike, I'm trying to contact Ben Marrison. Could you trace his phone for me?"

"Sure. Text him and I'll try."

Ten minutes later, Mike rang back.

"I couldn't get a response from Ben's phone. It's like he's dropped off the face of the Earth."

"Thanks for your help, Mike. I just hope Ben is long gone from here and he contacts me soon."

Ben descended the ladder again. The sulfuric smell abated, allowing him to take a few deep breaths. Halfway down, he realized the air was being sucked from the tunnel; he could feel the pull on his clothes, like a giant vacuum drawing the air down. The lower he went, the stronger the suction, pulling at his body, making it difficult to hold on to the ladder, the air getting thinner, harder to breathe.

He gasped, lungs heaving as they fought for air, brain panicking as his shaky legs reached the platform. Releasing his hands, he collapsed, semi-conscious.

Ben felt his body being dragged, bumping and grinding against a stony surface. Shrieks, moans and maniacal laughter drifted in and out of his consciousness, his oxygen-starved brain failing to send strength to his limbs. He was aware of heat from a furnace and saw lights filling empty spaces as something hauled him through a myriad of tunnels. The tunnels seemed to go on forever.

His battered and bruised body, no longer able to resist, lapsed unconscious.

Blinding light roused him as he was dragged out of the tunnels and deep into the pine forest. Intense pain gripped his chest as his lungs filled with fresh air, gasping for breath.

Something tore at his chest, exposing his heart, ripping it out of his body, the agony overriding the pain in his lungs. His screams were absorbed by the dense pine trees as his heart continued to pulse, pumping blood onto the ground where it seeped into the mat of pine needles.

His blood-starved brain's last thought: *I'm sorry, Lucy. I failed, and I've ended up just like you...*

BAD INVITE
By L.T. Emery

Brother Dude,

I met the grooviest girl, man. She lives for the high! Itz been two dayz and I swear I'm gonna marry this chick. Her namez Stacey and shez spaced out 24/7, dude. The acid is righteous! I'm tripping ballz with her! It got a bit heavy last night tho, I bummed this trip when Stacey cut the heart out of this kid! But, hey dude, who hasn't had a bad trip once or twice. You gotta come met her. We're at this bar called Whiskey Pete's, it's on the old Route thirteen.

Peace out,

Dan

AUDREY
By Holley Cornetto

When she reached the top of the peak, Audrey flipped up the hood of her sweatshirt and offered a hand to Seth, pulling him onto the ridge beside her. From there, the view was stunning. The forest was thick with evergreens, littered with boulders and piles of rock. She'd seen pictures of places like this, but never experienced them firsthand.

Mom would have loved this, Audrey thought, and wiped the dampness from her eyes.

Her mom used to talk about going on vacations and getting closer to nature, but the cancer had stolen those memories before they'd had a chance to make them. Of course, if Mom had been there, they wouldn't be on this trip—to meet Audrey's soon-to-be-stepmother's family in Boise.

"Hurry up, slowpoke!" Dad called from ahead.

It had been his idea to hit up every tourist trap and landmark on the drive from Spokane. He'd been so excited about hiking Devil's Ladder that he'd mapped out their entire route.

Audrey turned to check on Seth. "We aren't all boy scouts, you know."

Jodi crossed her arms. "Perhaps if you'd dressed appropriately, you wouldn't have such a hard time keeping up."

Audrey's smile drooped. Jodi was nothing like Mom. She was worse than a replacement—she was an intruder, bent on changing everything. Audrey rolled her eyes and shrugged past the woman.

Jodi turned to Seth. "Are you okay, sweetie?" she asked, in the baby-talk tone she always used with him.

Audrey scuffed some pebbles with her boot. "Don't talk to him like that. He's not a baby."

"Tom?" Jodi asked.

Dad lowered the map. "Audrey's right, hon. It isn't good for him."

Audrey bit her lip to suppress a smile. She knew she shouldn't use her brother to get under Jodi's skin, but she'd earned the right after being there for him for thirteen years. Jodi didn't care about them. Not really. Audrey had overheard the conversations at night. Jodi wanted to start a family, and have children of her own.

"I need to visit the ladies' room." She'd be damned if she let Jodi see her upset.

Dad swept his arm around in a dramatic gesture. "Pick a rock and duck behind it. We'll keep an eye on the trail and whistle if anyone's coming."

Audrey headed down a beaten path that led off the trail to the left. Though the morning sun was high in a cloudless, blue sky, the boulders and dense forest canopy provided a shadowy cover. The ground had frosted overnight and gave a satisfying crunch beneath her feet. It would be perfect if not for Jodi.

She followed the path to a ring of old growth trees, and walked around a massive boulder to the left, running a hand over its smooth surface. It was strange to think how many years the rock had been there.

"Wonder how many hikers have peed here?" she asked aloud, suddenly aware that the forest was quiet around her.

She undid the button of her black jeans and had them half unzipped when a faint tinkling sound, like a bell, made her freeze. "Shit," she whispered, tugging the zipper back up. She held still, straining to hear.

The sound came from the right this time. She turned fast enough to glimpse black fur slinking around the boulder. A cat?

They'd hiked for miles. The cat would have to be lost to be way out here. Maybe someone had left it? But if it had a bell, it would have a collar, and maybe a tag with a phone number. Audrey crouched to make herself smaller and inched forward. "Here, kitty, kitty…"

A handsome tuxedo cat that looked as if it had never missed a meal rubbed its side against the bark of a tree. It watched as she crept closer, but otherwise didn't acknowledge her presence.

Closer now, she saw the bell on its collar. The cat had stopped rubbing against the tree, content to watch her approach.

"Hey, little guy. Come here," she coaxed, slowly reaching out her hand.

The cat bumped its face against her knuckles. Audrey saw her opportunity and made a grab for the collar. It rebuked her with a startled yowl and skittered a few yards away.

She lifted her hands, palms outward. "Okay, okay. I'm sorry."

The cat stepped deeper into the wood.

Audrey looked back in the direction of the trail. Dad was going to worry, and Jodi would be pissed, but she couldn't just leave the cat out there. If she went back to get the others, it might wander off. With cautious steps, she started towards it again. "Where are you going, buddy?"

The cat wove its way through the giant evergreens and lichen-covered rocks. Despite the close trees and thick undergrowth, a clear trail cut through the wood, and the cat stuck to it.

She closed the distance between them, creeping closer. The cat nuzzled her leg, then skittered out of reach again. "Damn cat…"

How far have I wandered from the trail? She glanced behind and saw a wall of thick trunks, as though the forest had filled in behind her. The slightest hint of fear crept in. Forget the damned cat—if she got lost out here, who would save *her*?

As she started back toward the trail, a playful *mrrrrow* made her jump. Audrey spun to see large, golden eyes staring back at her. The cat was so close she could nearly touch it.

"One last try," she assured herself. "Then I'll go back."

As Audrey inched forward, the cat twitched its tail lazily, daring her to catch it. She coiled like a spring…and lunged.

A root grabbed her ankle. The cat leapt nimbly aside, and Audrey slammed into the leaf-strewn ground.

"Shit," she cursed, brushing away dirt with a bloodied palm.

The cat stood about ten feet away, looking over its shoulder at her.

"I tried," she said to the cat. "I really wanted to help you, you know. Save you from bears or marmots, or whatever the fuck lives out here. Serves you right if a coyote eats your ass. I'm out."

It was the smell she noticed first. A smell like a rotting corpse. She stepped forward and scooped the cat into her arms. The game was over. It was almost as if the damned thing had led her here on purpose.

"What have you found?" she asked, moving towards the smell.

The stench came from a rock shelf, about three feet high and littered with an odd assortment of junk. Much of it was harmless—cheap plastic jewelry, pretty stones and twenty-five cent toys in cheap, plastic bubbles—but mixed among the trinkets and toys were more ominous offerings. Small animals sat in various states of decay, from bare heaps of feather and bone to corpses fresh with writhing maggots.

A few bones looked too big to come from an animal. And were those human molars? Audrey shivered.

The centerpiece of the collection was a pair of grotesque little dolls, with pine cone bodies and blank, acorn-cap eyes. Audrey didn't know much about altars, or shrines, or whatever the fuck this was, but if the dolls were in the middle, they were important.

She lifted the female-shaped figure to inspect it. Dark, wet spots of blood dripped from her wound, staining the doll. Another offering, she thought with revulsion. She shouldn't have touched it. What the hell was she thinking? And now her blood was all over the damned thing. She dropped the doll onto the altar and took a step back.

What kind of twisted creep would leave all this shit in the middle of the forest? It could have been children. She'd done some weird shit as a kid. She'd often wandered around the lawn with a stick, collecting rocks and leaves she liked—a collection she'd later show her mom with pride. But Audrey's had been the innocent trophies of a child, not this macabre collection of death and plastic.

The air was heavy with mist, and the thick canopy of trees shut out the sunlight. She hugged the cat against her chest. This wasn't the work of children. Children wouldn't be wandering around alone in this forest. Children wouldn't be killing animals and leaving them here, and she needed to get the hell away before she met whoever did.

A prickling sensation on the back of her neck made her feel watched. Had all of her clunking drawn the attention of some animal? A twig crunched to her left.

She clutched the cat to her chest and ran.

Branches and roots clawed her arms and legs as she tried to navigate her way back to the trail through a forest that felt as if it were closing around her. For one terrifying moment, she thought she heard the rustling of branches behind her. She sped past a lichen-covered boulder. Was that where she'd first seen the cat?

Audrey burst from the side trail, almost bowling right into Dad and Jodi. She gasped for air, trying to speak, but words wouldn't come.

"For God's sake, where were you?" Jodi's tone was all frustration, no concern.

Audrey gulped in a breath. It felt like she'd never have enough air again. "I..."

"Are you okay? What do you have there?" Dad asked, stepping closer. He placed a hand on her shoulder.

"C... Cat," she wheezed.

"Slow down, sweetheart. Take a breath." He wrapped his arm around her.

"We can't take it with us," Jodi said. "It's probably someone's pet."

"I, uh..."

Audrey searched for words to describe what she'd found in the woods. How could she tell them of the shrine, or altar...or whatever that horrible thing was? The tingling sensation on the back of her neck persisted, as if whatever had followed her through the woods now watched them all.

Dad sighed heavily. "Does it have a collar? A tag?"

Audrey nodded and turned the shiny brass tag that hung from the cat's collar. "It says: Whiskey Pete's, Route Thirteen."

"That's all?" Jodi pulled the cat from Audrey's arms and checked the tag.

As if I'm too stupid to read it myself, Audrey thought.

"What do you think we should do, Tom?"

Dad couldn't hide the disappointment in his sigh; he'd been looking forward to this hike for weeks. "I suppose we should head back and look for this Whiskey place. We can't leave the little guy out here alone."

Despite her guilt at ruining the hike, Audrey was relieved. The forest seemed to crawl with restless shadows, creeping always at the corner of her vision, and she couldn't leave it soon enough.

A small hand grabbed Audrey's, nearly making her jump out of her skin. Seth gazed up at her, his face a mask of worry. He reached down to the ring of cards he wore around his neck—the cards he used to communicate. He flipped through until he found one with a large yellow face with a bandage across it: Hurt.

Audrey plastered on the best fake smile she could muster. "I'm okay, buddy. Everything's going to be alright."

Dad let out a low whistle as he pulled the Volvo up to the gas pump of Whiskey Pete's. "See, kids? This is real America. Backroads and hidden gems. This is why it's important to take the road less traveled. You never know what you're going to find."

Whiskey Pete's hadn't been easy to locate. It wasn't in the GPS, and internet service was too spotty for a Google search, so Dad found a road atlas, and drove around until they spotted a sign for Route Thirteen. The old-fashioned way, he'd called it.

Audrey pressed her face against the backseat window, only half-listening as Dad rambled on about the dark age of his youth. The glass felt cool against her forehead. Each time she closed her eyes, she was back in the forest. Her mind ran circles, trying to explain what she'd seen. The altar. The bones.

She'd wrapped the cut on her palm in gauze she'd grabbed from the medic bag, but it was already starting to bleed through. The cut throbbed. The metallic scent of blood mingled with the corpse stench of the forest.

Dad glanced at his watch. "Looks like a good place to gas up. Why don't you go in and look around, and I'll see if I can find who Kit-Cat here belongs to?"

He gathered the cat in his arms and climbed out of the car, headed towards the side of the building. Seth flipped his deck to the card with a candy bar and displayed it to Audrey.

"Good idea. I could use some chocolate, too."

She opened the door and slid out of the car, taking a moment to stretch her legs.

A flash of movement caught her eye as a scrawny, greasy-haired old man approached the car. The embroidered patch on his red coveralls identified him as 'Dale'. She instinctively stepped in front of Seth.

"Fill 'er up?" asked the old man.

She exhaled sharply. Was she really scared of grungy old men now? Had the forest fucked her up so badly that she was jumping at every shadow? Seeing danger where there was none?

Jodi leaned across from the passenger seat and called out the window. "Yes, and wash the windshield too."

The man shot Jodi a look that said she could wash her own goddamned windshield.

Audrey grinned at his reaction as she and Seth walked past him to the store. She could have sworn the old geezer winked at her.

Inside, the shelves wore the dust of years, like a place forgotten by time. She looked down at Seth, whose eyes were wide. "Do you remember when we went to Cracker Barrel, and there was all that old-looking stuff inside? Like fake antiques?"

Seth tilted his head, listening.

"It kind of reminds me of that, except actually old. The kind of place Dad would love."

Seth pointed to the card with the candy bar again.

"Oh yeah, sorry. I forgot we're on a mission." She glanced across rows of shelves until she located one with candy and chips. "Over here."

Seth wandered down the aisle, inspecting every chocolate bar, but Audrey knew how this would go. Her brother, a creature of habit, would buy the same thing he always did—a plain Hershey bar.

She took a moment to glance around the store before movement in one of the large convex mirrors caught her eye. Her body went rigid with the memory of being stalked through the forest. Could something have followed her here?

When she summoned the courage to look again, she saw a raven-haired man in the mirror's reflection. He was watching her and Seth.

She exhaled a deep breath and tried to ignore the fluttering in her chest, like she'd had too many cups of coffee. *Maybe he works here, like the other guy.*

Seth came back with a pair of chocolate bars, and to her surprise, they weren't his usual. "What the hell is a Marathon bar?" she asked, holding out a hand. "Let me check the expiration date on them, okay? The wrapper looks old."

Seth clutched them against his chest and shook his head.

"Okay, fine." She held up her hands. "Go put them on the counter and I'll pay."

The old man from the gas pump stood behind an ancient-looking cash register. "Will that be all, then?"

She nodded. "Hey, you wouldn't happen to know how old those candy bars are, would you? I've never seen that brand before."

He shrugged. "Chocolate's chocolate."

She passed him a five-dollar bill, and as she slipped the change in her pocket, a withered, leathery hand landed on her arm. She tried to jerk free, but the man's grip was firm. "Let go!"

He stared straight through her when he spoke. "You have no idea what you've done. What you've disturbed..."

Audrey's body went cold. What she'd disturbed? An image of the altar flashed through her mind, and a creepy little doll with acorn cap eyes. How could he know?

"Don't let the sun set on you here, little missy. Walk if you have to, but don't—"

"Lorne?"

The man she'd seen reflected in the convex mirror now stood propped in the doorway. With his tight jeans and raven-colored hair, he had an air of danger about him. A large tuxedo cat dangled from his arms.

"I think Pete wants a word with you."

The old man—Lorne?—jerked his hand away as if he'd been electrocuted. He grumbled something under his breath, and brushed past them, moving much faster than she thought a man his age could.

"Hey there, sugar," said the man with the cat. He was handsome enough, from a certain angle, in a certain light.

"Me?"

He winked. "Yeah, you. I heard I've got you to thank for returning my pussy cat. Can I buy you a drink?"

Was he flirting with her? "I... I'm underage."

The man shrugged. "Con don't card folks noways. I'm Joel."

"Nice to meet you, Joel. I'd love to take you up on the offer, but I'm with my family. We're not staying, just passing through."

"We'll see." Joel smirked and slunk out of the doorway.

Audrey turned to Seth, who flipped through his cards and stopped on a large happy face with a black line through it: Don't like.

"Yeah, me either. Something's weird about Whiskey Pete's."

The place smelled like the altar in the forest. Mildew, rot and death.

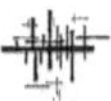

"What do you mean 'it won't start'?" Jodi squeaked, a few octaves higher than usual.

Dad turned the ignition again. "I mean, nothing's happening." He let out a heavy sigh. "Look, I'm going inside to see if they know of a garage nearby."

"Well, what are *we* supposed to do?" Jodi asked.

"Why don't you go in and sit down for a bit? It looks like there's a restaurant connected to the building."

Audrey looked at the flashing neon signs in the window. "I think it's a bar, Dad."

He flashed her a grin in the rearview mirror. "If they serve food, it's a restaurant."

She looked over at Seth, who'd unwrapped his Marathon bar and was now sporting a chocolate mustache. "What do you think? Want to see if they've got any real food?"

Seth nodded around the chocolate bar.

"I'm not going in there," Jodi grumbled. "It looks like one big health department violation."

Audrey bit her tongue. There wasn't time to argue. Dad would never get the car running with Jodi nagging him to death, and Audrey didn't want to spend any longer than she had to in this shithole place with the creepy old lecher who'd tried to terrify her with gibberish warnings. Tall, brooding trees loomed all around them, creeping almost to the buildings—a tendril, perhaps, of the same forest from the hike.

She plastered on the same fake smile she'd used on Seth in the woods. "Come on, Jodi. We might as well make the most of it. You never know. It might be fun."

Audrey placed a protective hand on Seth's shoulder as they entered the bar, Jodi a few steps behind. The place was just as dingy and dated as the service station. The walls were lined with the stuffed heads of creatures that might have been identifiable thirty years ago, but now sagged, sad and shapeless. She wasn't sure if they were supposed to be quaint or menacing, but to her, they were a grim reminder of the animal remains on the altar. A man sat on one of the vinyl-covered stools at the bar, nursing a pint of watery beer the color of piss.

The beer reminded her of the days when Dad would let her taste the craft brews he brought home. She'd felt like an adult, listening to him talk about the bitterness of the hops, or explain the differences between a stout and a porter.

That was, of course, before Jodi scolded him about the evils of underage drinking. Dad didn't really talk to Audrey about much anymore, except to ask her to take care of Seth. She felt like one of those things hung up on the wall—forgotten and ignored.

The trio settled into a booth in the corner. Seth's eyes lit up when he saw the old, orange jukebox in the corner and he tugged Audrey's sleeve, pointing. His face was still rimmed in chocolate.

The man from behind the bar approached the booth with a small notepad in his hand. He stood beside them, looking down without comment.

Jodi was first to speak. "Do you serve food here?"

The man grunted.

"Do you have a menu?"

Another grunt.

"I don't suppose you have anything gluten-free, do you?

Audrey failed to suppress a giggle. Here they were, in the middle of nowhere, something evil in the forest, and Jodi was worried about gluten. It all seemed so ridiculous. She had to laugh, otherwise she might burst into tears.

Jodi glared at her from across the table, which made Audrey laugh harder. "What?"

"We'll take two burgers and fries," Audrey choked out through laughter, "and can my little brother get a root beer, if you have it?"

Jodi cleared her throat. "I'll just have a plain salad. Dressing on the side, and no croutons, please."

The man made a few scratches in his notepad and lumbered away.

Jodi reached into the folds of her designer bag and lifted out a handful of coins, offering them to Seth. "Look what I've got. Why don't we go take a look at the music selection?"

Seth slid out of the booth and followed Jodi to the ancient-looking jukebox in the corner.

Audrey jumped at the sound of Joel's voice behind her. "So, you decided to stay after all?"

Had he been watching her? Waiting for her to be alone?

"Car trouble," she replied.

"Is that a fact? I'd say that's too bad, but..." He was interrupted by the opening guitar riff of Norman Greenbaum's *Spirit in the Sky*.

The ancient man on the barstool lifted his pint glass in an imaginary toast and swayed back and forth to the beat, sloshing his beer onto the floor.

"Ahem," Jodi said, returning from her cheap ploy to win Seth over with music. She looked Joel up and down, disapproval written plainly on her face. "If you'll excuse us, please."

"Of course." He winked at Audrey. "I'll see you later, sugar."

Audrey watched him retreat to the pool table. He moved like a predator, which both fascinated and frightened her. It reminded her of the forest, and the feeling of being hunted.

Jodi's voice cut through, bringing her back to the present. "Men like that are only after one thing."

Audrey shivered.

"Yeah, he skeeves me out too."

Audrey shook her head. "It isn't that. I didn't want to say anything earlier, but I saw something weird in the woods this morning. I don't know, it freaked me out."

She was interrupted by the bartender, who banged their plates down on the table. The burgers were gray, the consistency of deflated tires. Jodi's salad looked even worse, just a bowl of shriveled brown and white iceberg lettuce.

"Uh, thanks," Audrey managed, before he turned and left with one final grunt.

"He seems nice," Jodi said, cracking a smile.

"He forgot the root beer," Audrey added, with a grin.

"Think we should leave a bad review on Yelp?" Jodi asked, and together they broke into a fit of laughter.

Audrey felt a familiar tug on her sleeve. She looked over at Seth, who was holding up a card with a large, yellow smiley face on it: Happy.

Audrey couldn't bring herself to say more about the macabre scene in the forest. They might not believe her. Or worse, they might want to go back to see it for themselves. Best to tuck it away until it was a distant, faded memory.

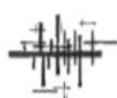

The motel's receptionist was pretty, but there was something oddly familiar about the jewelry she wore. She'd given them rooms one and thirteen. The only vacancies, she'd told them, in an absent tone.

Dad had enlisted the help of Lorne and Joel to push the car into the motel's desolate parking lot until a truck could tow it to a garage in Chevron.

Audrey took the key to room thirteen and grabbed her bag from the car, Seth tagging along behind. One glance over her shoulder told her it was going to be a long night. The only one brave enough to eat the food from the bar, Seth was doubled over, holding his gurgling stomach.

She turned the key in the lock and pushed the door, but it didn't budge. "Shit."

She checked the tag on the key. It was the right room. Seth's stomach made another grumble of protest. She turned the key and slammed her shoulder against the solid door. It swung open with a pop.

"Just drop your bag and go!"

She sidestepped as Seth dashed past her into the bathroom. The room smelled like cheap air freshener, sprayed to cover up the death stench that had followed her out of the forest. She tossed her bag onto the bed closest to the door. The sounds from inside the bathroom intensified, making Audrey grateful she hadn't eaten her own burger.

She grabbed her phone from her bag and lit up the screen. She wondered what the internet would have to say about this place. Maybe there was paranormal activity in the woods, or cultists. Possibly Bigfoot. Anything that might explain that creepy altar.

It was the mystery, she reasoned, the not-knowing what it was, that wouldn't allow her to let it go.

No signal here, damn it.

She sighed dramatically and settled back onto the itchy comforter. Five knocks rapped on the door in a familiar rhythm: Dad's knock.

"Come in."

The knob turned, and the door swung open with a thump.

"The door sticks."

Dad rubbed his shoulder. "You aren't kidding." He pushed the door back into place, leaving it slightly ajar.

Since he and Jodi had gotten serious, he'd grown a beard that didn't suit him and wore expensive flannel shirts with vests. Lately, he looked as if he'd stepped straight out of a Land's End catalog.

"Do you think we could request a different room? One with a door that actually works?" Audrey asked.

"The receptionist said these were the only two rooms available."

"There were no cars in the parking lot. I didn't see any other guests either. Did you?"

He shook his head. "Hey, where's Seth?"

"The bathroom. His stomach was making weird noises."

Dad glanced towards the bathroom door, then around the room. "It's vintage, huh?"

Every surface of the room was colored with burnt oranges and olive greens that looked like shades of vomit and old reruns of The Brady Bunch. "If by vintage you mean 'hasn't been redecorated in decades', then yes. How does Jodi like it?"

He grimaced. "She's gone to find the manager."

Audrey rolled her eyes. "Sounds about right."

The bathroom door creaked open and Seth walked out. Streamers of sweaty hair framed his face.

"Are you okay, Sport?"

Seth shook his head, holding his stomach.

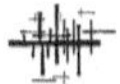

Audrey placed the comforter from her bed over Seth, who lay trembling beneath the blankets.

"He feels cold," Dad announced, hand pressed to Seth's forehead. "Did he seem sick to you earlier?"

She shook her head. "It's probably food poisoning from that disgusting burger he ate."

Dad nodded and rose from Seth's bedside.

"Hey, Dad?"

"Hmm?"

"Do you mind if Seth stays with you and Jodi since he's sick?"

He frowned. "We only have one queen-sized bed. There isn't enough room."

"You could sleep in here."

"I don't know if Jodi and I would fit on that little bed."

"You could sleep with Seth, and Jodi could have—"

"He said NO," Jodi said from the doorway. "I swear, Tom, you've got to start putting your foot down. You let her walk all over you."

He lifted his hand. "It's okay. I've got it under control, Jodi."

"Should've closed the door all the way," Audrey mumbled under her breath.

"What was that?" Jodi demanded, arms crossed under her chest.

"I said calm down, Karen."

Jodi hated being called Karen. Partially, Audrey suspected, because she knew it was true.

Jodi's face contorted. "You need to watch your mouth, young lady. You can't just disrespect me like that. If your mother had taught you better manners—"

"Don't you EVER talk about my mother, you stupid bitch!"

Audrey felt the sting of her hand against Jodi's cheek before she even realized she'd crossed the room.

Dad pushed between them, steering a stunned Jodi towards the door. He looked over his shoulder at Audrey. "I'll speak to you about this later."

The door stuck, not completely closing behind them.

"Well, screw you both then."

Audrey threw herself back down onto her bed. She'd expected as much from Jodi, but Dad? How could he stand by and let Jodi talk shit about Mom? Why didn't he care more that Seth was sick? It was Jodi's fault. Clearly, there was no room in her new family for Audrey and Seth. She was driving a wedge between them, and Dad was letting her.

Other girls her age were going to parties, or looking at colleges, or losing their virginity, but she was stuck taking care of her brother because Dad couldn't be bothered. It wasn't fair.

It was irresponsible of her to leave Seth alone when he was sick, but that wasn't her fault, really. Seth wasn't her child. He wasn't her responsibility. Dad should be looking out for him, not running off with that home-wrecker.

Well, if Dad could be irresponsible, so could she. Audrey grabbed her purse, and pulled the door shut behind her. What was it Joel had said earlier? Con don't card folks noways.

She headed for the bar.

In the dim light, the dingy bar could almost pass for quaint. She straightened her shoulders, trying to look more confident than she felt.

The man from earlier was still on his barstool, nursing another drink.

She glanced across the room. Joel looked up from the pool table. When their eyes met, his face widened into a Cheshire Cat grin. He dropped the cue and walked forward, never breaking eye contact. She felt a shiver down her spine.

"You came."

She inclined her chin slightly in affirmation. She didn't want to look too eager.

"How about I get you a drink?"

"I'd like that."

Audrey hung back for a few awkward moments while Joel chatted up the bartender. Unsure what to do with herself, she wandered to the pool table. Like the rest of the place, it had seen better days. The felt was torn, and looked as if someone had tried to glue it back into place.

Joel returned and offered her a pint glass. "You play?"

"Not really, no."

"I can teach you." He placed his glass on the edge of the table and passed her a cue.

Audrey leaned over the table, lining up the cue with the ball. She felt hot breath on her neck as Joel wrapped his arms around her from behind, guiding her hands. He smelled of beer and cheap cologne.

"Like this." His thigh pressed against her hip.

Audrey squirmed and closed her eyes. She knew she should push him away, but this was what she'd wanted, wasn't it? To be treated like an adult? She shifted her position, pushing against him slightly, and tapped the cue ball. It missed the other balls on the table, hit the side, and landed somewhere in the middle.

Joel tsked. "That's too bad."

She handed him the stick, then picked up her drink. He'd brought her a beer of the watery piss variety. She turned it up and swallowed hard, ignoring the stale, skunky taste.

"Damn, girl. Slow down," he teased, taking a shot. His was no better than hers had been. It simply pushed the cue ball around the table.

"Sorry." She wiped her mouth with the back of her hand. "I've had one hell of a day."

"Oh yeah? Tell me about it."

He propped the cue on the table and lifted his drink, brushing back a strand of greasy, black hair from his face.

She upturned the drink. The fizz tickled her nose, and she detected a bitter, chalky aftertaste. She had no reason to trust him, but she had to tell someone, and after today, she sure as hell wasn't going to tell Dad and Jodi.

"Our family was on a hiking trip. Up by Devil's Ladder. Do you know the place?"

Joel nodded to the man behind the bar.

"I wandered off the path, and I saw...something. There was this... I don't know what it was, an altar? It was covered, like people had left things on top of it. Trinkets, toys, gifts, offerings... I don't know what."

She waved her hand, as if she could conjure the image from her memory.

Joel noticed her bandage and pulled her injured palm towards him. "You're hurt."

"Yeah, I fell and cut myself."

He lifted her palm to his mouth, and kissed the bandage. For a moment, she thought he sniffed the wound. "Did you tell the others? What did they make of it?"

"No. I didn't say anything. I was scared. I felt wrong, like someone was watching me. And then, after we left the forest, we came here and there was the cat, and the car trouble, and now my brother is sick and I just..."

He slid an arm around her waist. "Shh. It's okay. That stuff in the woods is probably just some people fooling around trying to scare hikers. I mean, I've heard rumors about weird shit going on up there, and then there have been some people go missing on the trails, but I doubt it's got anything to do with—"

"JOEL, SHUT YOUR GODDAMN HOLE!" The bartender slammed their drinks down onto the nearest table, then spat on the floor.

"Can't you see I've got a lady friend here, Con? Watch your language, you miserable son of a bitch."

Con grunted and turned back to the old man on the barstool.

"You'll have to excuse him," Joel said. "He's got shit for manners. Shit for brains too."

"It's okay. I..."

In the corner, beside the jukebox, was a vending machine. The kind that, if you put a coin in, would spit out a small plastic bubble with a toy inside. The kind she hadn't seen since she was a kid.

No, that wasn't right. The kind of toys she'd seen on the altar. Suddenly, Audrey realized why the receptionist's jewelry looked familiar. It was the same plastic junk that'd been on the altar.

She felt as if someone had placed an ice cube against her neck. Was this place connected somehow with the forest? She needed to think, but her thoughts were hazy. She was almost certain she hadn't drunk enough to justify the blanket of fog that had descended upon her consciousness.

"I need to go and check on my brother." She over enunciated each word.

"You sure? The party's just getting started."

"Yeah. He wasn't feeling well."

The words felt thick and clumsy on her lips. She lurched through the doorway on her way out of the bar, and laughter followed her out towards the hotel. She fumbled through her purse for the room key. A familiar tinkling sound came from ahead.

"Cat?" she asked, stupidly.

The cat walked out of a room, brushing its body against the doorframe. Not a room, she realized with horror. *Her* room.

She ran the last few paces, almost tripping over the cat. The door stood wide open.

Shit. I closed it. I know I closed it.

She rushed over to Seth's bed and jerked back the blankets. There, in Seth's spot lay a grotesque little doll with a pine cone body, and eyes made of acorn caps. Seth was gone.

I'm dreaming. I must be dreaming.

She grabbed her inner thigh between her thumb and forefinger and pinched herself hard. "Fuck!"

She had to find Dad and Jodi. She was in a shit-ton of trouble, but maybe Seth had woken up to find her missing and gone to their room. Maybe he'd found a doll in the forest too. Maybe...

She glanced at her bed. A second doll lay on her pillow, this one stained with her blood.

She felt tears threaten as she stepped closer. She was drunk. She was seeing things. None of this was real. She reached the door to Dad and Audrey's room and banged her fist against the door. No one answered. Nothing stirred.

The gas station attendant's words of warning raced through her mind. *Don't let the sun set on you here...*

A sob escaped her throat as she staggered away from the hotel room door, and into the night.

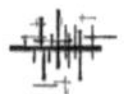

Audrey blinked against the darkness. She tried to rub her eyes, but something tethered her wrists together. The doll with the acorn cap eyes had been placed in her lap—the one she'd stained with blood. Something warm and sticky was draped around her shoulders.

Her head pounded to the tune of her pulse. Is this what a hangover feels like?

She was outside, sitting. Why was she outside? She listened for a moment, and heard low, rhythmic chanting all around.

She strained, turning her head left. She was in a forest. *The* forest. It must have been a nightmare. She was somewhere safe, sleeping off the alcohol. She'd be in trouble, but she was safe. The last thing she remembered was going to her room to check on Seth.

Seth...

She inhaled deep and looked to her right. Seth was posed in a sitting position beside her, on a rock shelf about three feet high. The other doll lay in his lap. Something warm and damp was spread across the top of the altar. It smelled sharp and metallic.

As her vision focused, she saw Dad and Jodi strung up against two giant slabs of rock. Jodi's eyes were closed, her head lolled to the side. Gaping wounds like open mouths revealed the emptied caverns of their abdomens.

Her stomach lurched. "No..."

Audrey looked down at the warm wetness that covered her and realized, to her horror, what was spread over her and Seth like garlands.

Voices spoke in a chorus. "We give thanks for all we have received."

She and Seth were surrounded. More figures stepped out of the forest, pressing around them. She tried to look at their faces, but beneath the hooded robes were masks fashioned of straw and acorn caps.

"We hope you will accept this offering in return for your bounty." One voice this time.

"Please," she pleaded. "Why are you doing this? I don't understand."

She saw a flash of metal. Tears streamed down her cheeks.

"It is only right that you atone for that which you destroyed."

"Take me then. Let him go!"

The blade sang through the air, and all went dark.

CONTENDER
By Peter J. Foote

Dear Mr. Masterson,

We have received your handwritten letter requesting admission to the World Pool-Billiard Association (WPA). Unfortunately, we have chosen to refuse your membership at this time.

For future reference, we do not accept applications for membership written on the back of bar menus, and I personally consider this an affront to the noble sport of pool. We also do not recognize 'reigning champion of Whiskey Pete's Bar & Grill' as a suitable marker of skill.

Please do the world a favor and put down your cue.

Best regards,

Mr. Alfred M. Stockley III (World Straight Pool Champion, 1972)

JASPER AND HUCK

By Abigail Lindhardt

"**M**ake sure you get my new haircut in good light," Huck said, with a wink and a smile as Jasper danced around a hole in the rotting floor. "And get one side with my blue eye and another shot with my green. Keeps the viewers guessing."

His friend tried desperately to keep the camera on Huck as they walked through the abandoned house's halls and around its corners.

"You're walking too fast," Jasper grunted, taking a wide step over a suspicious white patch of wood while holding the large camera on his shoulder. "And it's like three in the morning. It's dark. No one can see your hair."

Huck stopped so suddenly Jasper almost ran into him; he clutched the camera, losing his balance from trying not to run into Huck.

"Cut," Huck snarled, so that he'd know where to edit the video later. "What's the point of our 100K subscriber special and the new camera if they can't see me? Good thing this isn't a livestream episode."

Jasper patted the new piece of tech on his shoulder, looking at it lovingly. "I guess I could mess with the settings. See if your black hair will stand out in this black house."

Huck didn't smile back. He motioned for Jasper to start recording again.

Jumping right back into his part, Huck smiled broadly and gazed into the lens. "It's almost three in the morning and if legend holds true, the ghost of Lady Wentwal will appear sometime within the hour. The locals say she took her life on the top floor." He looked down the dark hall to the winding Victorian stairs dramatically. "We have a ways to go. And with all the rot and mold, this is a dangerous journey, with or without ghosts."

"What are you doing?" Jasper groaned, dropping the camera from his shoulder.

"Narrating for our viewers?" Huck shrugged, smoothing his plucked eyebrows. "Trying to build suspense? What are *you* doing?"

Jasper sighed and rubbed his eyes violently, looking away from his co-host into the dim light from the window. "You're doing something weird with your lips and squinting too much."

"It's called a look," Huck argued, making sure his t-shirt was untucked just right from the side of his designer jeans. "Makes my cheek bones look sharper. And it makes me look boyish." He smiled at Jasper and pointed finger-guns at him. "Subscribers!"

"The stuff we capture on camera gets us subscribers." Jasper reached forward to adjust the mic clipped to the front of Huck's shirt. "Just like always."

Huck scoffed. "Maybe I'll think about quitting again? Leave you and your scrawny ass to film, investigate and edit alone?"

Jasper didn't even flinch at the threat. "I know this whole ghost hunting thing is a joke to you, but my thing is honesty. I need your stupid face. We finally make a living doing this. Can you at least pretend you like your job like the rest of the world?"

Just then, Huck's phone vibrated, and he jumped at the opportunity to look at the alert rather than face his best friend's disappointment.

Scrolling through the text from his twin brother made his thumb ache. Huck groaned, only catching bits here and there. His brother was reaching out for conversation, trying to soften the hard times, but he was going on and on about the drinking, leaving home, all that other stuff.

You need to figure this out, bro, he typed back. *I can't do it for you.*

He looked up at Jasper's face as he pocketed the phone again. His friend had a way of looking sad, eager and pushy all at the same time.

"You know I'd never leave you alone," Huck smiled. "Let's go find the lady of the manor, shall we?"

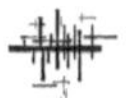

The sun splashed a deep purple and orange across the sky as the boys loaded up their new static cams, mics, and other equipment. The dew made the air taste clean, fresh.

Huck went to his side of the car and stood in the open door. Remembering the text from his brother, he opened his phone and skimmed it again. A tiny trickle ran down from the nape of his neck. His hair stood on end. He'd felt similar sensations when a supposed spirit or ghost made something move or spoke in the spirit box while they filmed. The feeling didn't always accompany those instances. Only sometimes.

Those were the times he hated most.

"What is it?" Jasper asked, leaning over the car roof. "Excuse the colloquialism, but you look like you've seen a ghost. Are you sick?"

His gut turned like it did when he ran a red light. A surge of adrenaline raced up his spine. He swallowed hard and looked over at Jasper. His friend's eyes danced across his heterochromia.

Closing the door, Jasper came to his side. "What the hell, dude? What's the text about?"

"Wait," Huck whispered. His lungs wouldn't take in air. "Something's wrong."

Around them, the crickets and other night creatures faded into the rising mist. Silence fell.

A jolt ran up Huck's arm from his phone and he screamed.

"The hell!" he cursed. The vibration tingled his too-sensitive fingers. The screen glowed with the name 'Mom' followed by a heart and the eye-roll emoji.

Jasper sighed, growling loudly. Shaking his head, he returned to his side of the car.

Huck took a couple of breaths before answering the phone. He laughed off the fright and sat in the passenger seat. "Hey, mom," he wheezed, running his hand through his thick, black hair.

"Huck, baby?" she managed between gasping sobs. "I need you to come home, okay? Mark, he... Hun, your brother, he...”

It didn't matter. His lips went numb and he couldn't reply. His arm, though it was heavy as a bucket of stones, didn't drop his phone. It wouldn't move from his ear as his mom continued to beg him to come home. Eventually, he hung up. His throat went so dry he could barely reply to her.

“What is it, Huck?” Jasper whispered.

He hadn't started the car yet. The pressure in Huck's face had tricked him into thinking they'd been moving at high speed for the entire conversation with his mom.

“I have to go to Idaho,” he croaked. He looked down and touched the dark screen of his phone. “My brother died.”

Jasper reached out and put his hand on Huck's limp arm. “Damn, Huck, I... I don't know what to say.”

Huck sucked in his lower lip and nodded. “Say you'll come with me.”

“Yeah, of course.”

“Bring the equipment.”

“What?”

“If I remember right, there's a place over there that will make for some great views. Haven't been there since I was a kid, but...”

Jasper stammered harder than before. “W-wait, what?”

Huck shrugged, eyes fixed on the rising sun. “May as well make good use of a huge ass trip like that. Get some filming done.”

“The fuck, Huck? Isn't it a memorial or a funeral? Your brother—”

“I get it!” Huck snapped, finally meeting Jasper's eyes. “Shut up and drive.”

“There's probably a gas station in this town,” Huck sighed, looking down at this phone.

“Can you search?” Jasper asked, unwilling to take his eyes off the road winding through the national forest.

“Service sucks too much. There's something there though. Think that might be a city or something."

The two boys sank back into the silence that had dominated their trip so far. The long drive from Ohio to Idaho had only been broken by calls from Huck's mom and older sister, and the stops they made along the way. The memorial had been a blub-fest and Huck couldn't stand it. They asked him to say something, since he and Mark were close, but he refused. He looked back down at the last text his mother sent him.

So accusatory.

They passed the boundaries of the forest and ahead, the darkening sky glowed with the white light that only came from a city in the middle of nowhere.

"See?" Huck smiled. "Chevron. Let's get a place to sleep and get our bearings. Service is better too."

"Hey," Jasper piped up, voice rising more than it had since they'd left Ohio. "You know, we're on the right side of the country now. Maybe we could check out that paranormal private investigator in Oregon? For the show, I mean."

He pulled a colorful sticky note out of his pocket. Huck rolled his eyes.

"That message was *so* shady. I can't believe you're bringing it up. No one with their sanity still intact calls themselves a 'paranormal private investigator.'"

He leaned his head back and closed his eyes, but Jasper wasn't done.

"We deal in shady," he pointed out. "What the...?"

Huck opened his right eye and looked sidelong out his window. Then he sat up, quick. "Fuckin' hell!"

The hills that rose up to the right dissolved into white mist, seemingly oozing up from the earth. The trees barely peeked out from the sudden haze. Both boys leaned to the right and squinted to get a better look.

"Jasper!" Huck screamed, pointing out the front.

In a moment of sheer terror, Jasper screamed and cranked the wheel to the left, spinning out on the damp asphalt. The car spun twice, tires screaming and burning rubber, before it jolted to a stop. Their panting filled the silence.

"You saw him?" Jasper gasped, grabbing his friend's arm.

Huck didn't answer. His eyes danced back and forth between the high beams before them. He couldn't say yes.

Yeah, Jasper, I saw a dude with a camera completely made of white smoke hit the hood of our car before beaming up into the sky like they abducted him.

"No, I don't know," he managed. Twisting in his seat, he fixed his eyes on the misty hills again. Were those three lights passing behind the trees? "What are you doing?"

Jasper flung open the car door and ran to inspect the front. "We hit something," he called. He leaned in, the beams illuminating his pale face. "There's a dent."

It's not real, Huck thought to himself, eyes glued to the hovering lights. The shadows of the trees flipped past them on the ground, almost looking like a car passed behind them.

"What are you looking at?" Jasper asked, turning to face the misty hills.

Huck wiped his palms on his jeans. Jasper didn't see them?

"Nothing, I guess. Get the fuck back in the car. Let's go."

The sensation took him. A metallic tingling down from the nape of his skull. An involuntary shiver. He all but saw something watching them from the trees. His brain said eyes were on him, but he couldn't see them.

"We start in the morning," Huck whispered, once Jasper re-entered the car and the doors closed. He pushed the lock. "In daylight."

"It was a cannibalistic cult possessed by the ghosts of aliens!" Jasper pleaded, chasing Huck around the back of the car.

Huck tossed their bags in the trunk and stared up at the old-as-hell hotel where they'd stayed the night. They'd driven in circles looking for a place to rest and found it by chance. The sign on the way into town said 'Chevron', but nothing else was signposted, going in or coming out. No way to even know which road they were driving out on.

"That's too many boxes to tick," Huck said. "And this one-road town is giving me the shivers. I don't like the way the people just stare out of the windows at us. Remember that movie, House of Wax? That's exactly what this feels like."

Jasper stopped. His hands fell to his side. "Why did you even drag me all the way out here then? You're a god-awful, stubborn skeptic."

To avoid answering, Huck glared at Jasper over the top of the car. "Stop trying to make me feel bad."

The shiver that accompanied his lies cooled his flesh. He knew he could easily manipulate Jasper that way. It worked.

"You're right. I'm sorry. Let's head down the road. Devil's Ladder is nearer that national forest. We can get some filming in before our night session."

More than once on the drive, they pulled over to rub mud off a road sign to see where they were. Every one claimed they were on Route Thirteen but it wasn't on the map. The boys got turned around again and again, every time they thought they were close. Before they knew it, noon came and went.

Finally, Jasper suggested going back to Chevron for directions. Annoyed, and tired of being in the car, Huck agreed.

But they couldn't find it.

"These damn trees!" Huck shouted, pounding the trunk of the car when they pulled over, near five in the evening. "We can't see anything."

Jasper took his pack out of the trunk. "Let's walk. If we don't find anything in an hour, we can turn back."

"Sun sets in an hour and a half," Huck sighed, checking his phone. "And it's supposed to rain tonight. Temperature will drop."

Jasper shrugged. "We'll sleep in the car. C'mon, Huck. Go on an adventure."

Something inside Huck turned a cog. Looking into Jasper's pleading green eyes, he suddenly got the feeling that if he said no, he'd regret it for the rest of his life. He could give his friend this. This one boon. Almost smiling, he shook his head and opened his mouth to reply.

He froze. If he said yes, he'd never see Jasper again.

No, that was weird talk. He didn't believe in that kind of feeling or vibration or whatever. He was just creeped out about the events from the night before.

"Fine," he smiled, heaving his pack onto his shoulder. "Into the woods to look for alien ghosts."

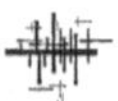

"I see neon!" Jasper crowed in delight. The sun had gone down about half an hour ago, and Huck didn't care enough to argue with his friend with the cold rain starting to soak their clothes. "That has to be a gas station."

"Good, I'm dying of thirst," Huck sighed.

They broke through the trees and came into a gravel clearing. A neon sign several yards away read 'Whisky Pete's', with a vacancy sign blinking half-heartedly. Blocking their view of whatever lay beyond was thirteen grimy windows.

"A motel?" Jasper offered, starting to track around it.

Every window only offered a black square of nothing. No light. Not even a set of yellowing blinds. The back side of the motel was so dirty and falling apart, Huck doubted it was operational. He followed Jasper around front, their footfall overly loud on the gravel, echoing up into the cold night air.

"It *is* a gas station." Jasper's tone was way more delighted than it should have been.

The structure in front of the motel was indeed a gas station. Some sort of roadhouse was attached to the general store. The lights inside somehow looked on and off at the same time. No movement came from the inside. No steam rose from the stacks. Not so much as a muffled rock anthem came from inside.

"It looks really dead, Jas," Huck mused.

Despite saying that, Huck found himself drawn into the motel lobby. The door opened, not so much as a bell signaling his entrance. The air inside was colder than the November chill outside.

"Hello?" he called.

In the corners of the room, cobwebs gently lilted on the draft.

"Two?"

The high, ecstatic feminine voice made them both jump. A short woman with near-glowing green eyes and full, smiling lips appeared from a back room.

"One room, if it's ok," Jasper asked, still cringing from the scare.

"Sure," she smiled. "It's easier that way."

Huck frowned.

"Oh my gods, I cannot *believe* there are two of you," she said again, handing them a dusty set of keys. "What a year it's been." She smiled at Jasper. "You're not bad."

She spoke energetically, but her eyes never focused on either of them. Like she saw past their flesh to the souls beneath.

"Right." Jasper gingerly took the keys. "Do you know anything about the history of this place? We're looking for Devil's Ladder. You may have heard of us? We're Team Darkfront."

Her eyes glassed over even more, her teeth showing behind a false smile.

"The web series?" Huck supplied. "Ghost hunters?"

The girl shrugged. "Try the guys in the bar."

Huck scoffed and looked at the empty, dark parking lot. "Thanks, lady."

Once inside their rooms, Jasper dumped his pack out and immediately prepared his equipment. "Did you see this place!" he gleefully hissed. "There is no way someone has not been murdered here." He handed Huck the laptop. "Do a search. See what you can find."

"There's no service," Huck said, after trying a few times to connect to anything remotely close.

Jasper's face lit up. "That's perfect. Roll the camera, show our phones and get some shots of the motel room." He pulled out his spirit box and a smaller camera. "Let's go to the bar when we're done."

"It looks really empty," Jasper said for the fifth time, as they trekked across the gravel to the bar. "There are no cars out here. We need to find ours."

"You live for this stuff," Huck sighed.

"But I don't want to die for it."

Ignoring his friend's remark and the tingling at the base of his skull, Huck pushed the door open to the bar. The ancient metal blinds on the back of the door clanged. A heat wave and *Carry On My Wayward Son* by Kansas blasted into their faces. The sound of pool balls clacking snapped over the chatter and ruckus. A couple of eyes turned to look at them.

The man behind the bar, staring disdainfully at a tray of glasses, looked up. His blue eye glimmered in the yellow light from the over-hanging lamps. His green eye continued to glare. A man at the pool table quickly ran his hand through his long greasy hair, glaring at Huck.

"I'll chat to the guy in the Canadian tux," Huck whispered. "Guy playing pool is giving me the death stare."

"He's just jealous of your good looks," Jasper said good-naturedly.

They split up, each heading to their designated interviewees. Huck sidled up to the bar and opened his mouth before he knew what to say.

"I'll have a beer, shaken not stirred." He grinned at the bartender as if they shared a secret joke.

The man's glower deepened, killing Huck's smile. "ID?" he grunted, barely opening his lips.

"Really?" Huck sighed.

"Try me."

He pulled his wallet out of his back pocket and tossed his driver's license onto the bar. The man picked it up, glaring down his bulbous nose at the offending piece of plastic.

"Eighteen. Only just." He sighed, tossing it back. "Shame." He turned around and grabbed a beer. Slamming it down, he growled, "I'm not shaking it."

Huck looked into the man's mismatched eyes with his own. "Don't see that often," he offered, more humbly than before. "My dad used to tell me it was a mutation. My mom said it meant I was gifted."

To his surprise, the man didn't turn away. He watched Huck half-heartedly as he spoke. Huck started by talking about the web series and said they were just there to get some shots. The longer he spoke, the more the bartender seemed uninterested, but would not break eye contact.

"What you boys yapping about?"

The man from the pool table, who Jasper should have been talking to, joined Huck at the bar, once again flipping his hair back.

"Not a thing that concerns you, Joel," the bartender growled, green eye glaring again. "This one's mine."

Huck set his beer down. "Sorry?"

"You ever done anything nasty, kiddo?" the man named Joel asked, with an oily grin.

"What do you mean?"

Joel smiled and picked at something between his front teeth. "We like a certain crowd that's all. And, phew! Your friend is a saint."

A rumbling drew both Huck and Joel's eyes back to the bartender. *Was he growling?* Huck thought. Joel threw his hands up in mock surrender.

"Um, yeah. Jasper's the better half." Huck shrugged. "I just like to look out for number one. I don't sugarcoat things." A new guilt welled up inside him the more he spoke. "I could be nicer."

A gravelly chuckle emitted from the bartender. "Don't say that. We like 'em tough. You gotta be to make it by."

"Right," Huck smiled, relaxing a little.

"Do whatever it takes to survive."

"Yeah." Huck pushed the beer away. What was he thinking? He'd never drank before. The front of his brain fogged over and, for a minute, he thought the barstool he sat on swayed. "Where's my friend?"

The bartender put down the too-clean glass he'd been wiping. "Good question. Lorne?"

He looked over Huck's head outside, towards the gas station windows.

"What a creep," Jasper said, out loud so his camera could pick up his voice while he filmed the outside for his future viewers. "Way too touchy. And he smelled, guys, I'm telling you."

He stopped, focusing in on the gas station. An old man with enough years on his shoulders to make him shorter than even Huck hobbled a little too quickly out the back door towards the motel.

"The fuck?"

Jasper walked over the dark gravel parking lot, still void of cars, to the motel lobby, where the old man ducked inside. Crouching low, he skittered below the front window and tried to figure out how to get his bulkier camera up to see.

"Something's going down, guys," he whispered. "That old man was walking way too fast and way too shadily."

He held his breath when he heard the man call for Stacey in a strangled hiss.

"There's no car," she hissed back. "Must have broke down. They came through the woods."

The older man grunted. "That's a positive and a negative. Harder to escape."

"Their room's full of recording equipment," Stacey replied. "I went through all their bags."

Getting dizzy, Jasper realized he hadn't breathed yet. But now he couldn't. *Harder to escape?*

"You better get in there," Stacey went on. "I hear Con has already put dibs on one of them. That other one—with the blond hair?—he can't stay. He's a giver for sure."

"A fine one to sacrifice on the bloody altar."

Hyperventilating now, Jasper clutched his camera. He wanted to run. Find Huck. But if he got up, they'd see him sprinting away. Without his car to run to. They knew that.

A blinding light erupted into Jasper's eyes. He'd hit the light on his camera, flooding his face and the space above him with the mounted bulb. Instinct kicked in and he bolted up, not caring if they saw him now. He ran hard, slipping in the gravel. His camera tumbled down, smashing the lens and the light.

"Shit!" he gasped, palms burning from the impact. Looking over his shoulder, he saw Stacey staring out the window, blank-faced, shoulders drooping. "Where the hell is—fuck!"

The old man, Lorne, leaped towards Jasper like a monster. His head swayed side to side with every step, fueled with murderous intent. "C'mere, boy!"

Chucking his camera with all his might into the old man's face, Jasper got to his feet finally and ran behind the store into the motel room. He slammed the door so loud he prayed Huck heard it. His breath came in shuddering gasps as he closed the blinds and locked the door. His hand shaking, he dug his cell out of his pocket. He punched the button to bring up his recent calls and Huck's name.

"Fuck, Huck, pick up!"

No sound came from the phone. Not a ring. Not a dial tone. Not a "please hang up and try again." Jasper lowered the phone and looked at the black screen. His own terrified, white face looked back, ready to cry.

It was just lit up!

Holding his breath, he pressed himself against the wall and looked out the window. The old man and his Regan-from-The-Exorcist impression was nowhere to be seen. Jasper had just made up his mind to sneak out the back window when a haggard, claw-like hand burst through the glass. Without a second to pull back, the old man's nails dug into Jasper's face as he reeled, prying at the vice-like grip.

"Huck!" Jasper screamed, as loud as he could around the wrinkled hand.

"Can't hear you while he's inside," the old man cackled, crawling through the window.

With a high scream, Jasper brought his foot up with all his might, crunching the old man's family jewels. With a howl like a wolf, he doubled over, releasing Jasper. Taking the chance, he grabbed his lanyard with his keys on it and ran into the bathroom. The single window was barely big enough for him to get through. Not caring how much he hurt himself anymore, he punched it out and lifted himself through. He went headfirst and fell halfway out, cutting his stomach and thighs as gravity pulled him.

Jasper clutched his wounds, groaning. Looking behind him, the woods stretched out for miles. Somewhere beyond them, the car waited. Safety. He could run now.

"Huck," he whispered. "I can't leave him."

He stood up. The old man's crazy eyes laughed at him, peaking over the broken bathroom window. Jasper screamed, leaping back. The old man ran his tongue over the glass, licking it clean of his blood.

"That's not foul at all," he cawed. "You're the good one, all right."

Jasper's spine throbbed with adrenaline as he ran away from the window, around the motel. "Huck!" he screamed as he pounded towards the bar. "Ah!"

With a hard tackle, the old man was on him, pinning him to the ground. The impact knocked his sight into double vision and his head rang. Something dug into his hip wound, using it to grip him tight. The pain seared through his entire body, paralyzing him. He reached out towards the back door. Any minute now, his best friend would emerge.

Short and strong, Huck could make it out. He'd come. He'd save him.

The door didn't open.

"Huck!" Jasper screamed again.

"This place has tunnels, you know," Joel, the pool player, said.

The bartender glared at him.

"Yeah?" Huck asked casually. "Could be cool for a few shots."

"What's this?"

Joel leaned a little too close to Huck and prodded at his spirit box.

"Picks up EVP," Huck explained. "Means Electronic Voice Phenomenon. I think it's kinda kitschy, but Jasper's a big believer in this kind of thing. He's kinda a kook really—"

Both men suddenly stood up, pushing away from the bar. Huck looked around, unaware of whatever drew their attention. Without warning, they all filed out the front door, leaving him alone.

"Ooh-kay," he sighed.

With them gone, he decided to look for the tunnels. He might think everything was a big crock of malarkey, but Jasper would love it if he got some shots of a tunnel under an old roadhouse. He took his camera and the spirit box, and started to snoop around.

He didn't find a tunnel, but he did make his way down to what he thought were the offices. The cramped space reminded him of his grandma's basement. It even had an eerie, invisible darkness hanging over it.

Curious, he whipped out his spirit box and turned it on. The white noise filled the basement. He carefully stepped over a few odds and ends until he found a set of stairs leading deeper underground.

His hair stood up and the tingle buzzed at the nape of his neck.

"Is anyone there?" he asked, more quietly than he normally would.

The spirit box continued to scratch. He was about to turn away when it skipped.

"What?" he asked the darkness again. His ears pricked up.

"We... down... ere..." the staccato reply came over the box.

"You're what? Give me a sign, or whatever the fuck Jasper always says."

"Ee... r... own... ere..."

"'We are down here'?" he asked.

The pit of his stomach dropped away. The box droned on with its white noise, but he heard beyond it. Underneath the static and skips, a sound rose. A cry of a thousand voices behind a thick, black veil.

His senses kicked in like never before. A force inside him shouted for him to leave. Yes, someone was down there, but he needed to go. Now.

"Go!" all the muffled voices screamed.

This isn't real! he screamed in his mind, but didn't take the chance.

Turning, he bolted back up the stairs, cold sweat making his hands slippery.

At the top of the stairs, he pushed the door open back into the bar. He stopped dead in his tracks.

The room was full again, all eyes on him. None of them moved or spoke. A single sound cut the silence. Someone panting in sheer horror, choking on blood. Joel, the pool guy from before, stepped aside. Huck's mouth went dry.

Lying across the table was Jasper, bloody, crying.

"We don't typically do this," the bartender said, with a grunt.

"And we'll get in trouble for it," Joel said, crossing his arms like a sulking child.

"We like dark souls. And yours has blood on it."

Huck took a step back. "I've never killed anyone."

An old man hobbled up beside Joel. Dried blood painted his lips bright in his pale face. "Lies."

The bartender reached back and pulled Jasper forward by his hair. His friend cried in pain. "Tell him, kid. Who'd he kill?"

Terrified, Huck locked eyes with Jasper. "I'd never!"

Joel snickered. "He is a dirty soul. Not even asking if you're ok." He patted Jasper's bloody face.

"Huck…" Jasper whispered feebly.

"What do you want from me?!" Huck shouted, eyes darting behind the gang to the windows. The door stood ajar.

"Tell us who you killed," the bartender grunted softly. "I'd love it if you did."

Shaking his head, Huck clutched his spirit box, the voices still echoing in his skull. "No one. Never. I'm just a kid!"

"M-Mark," Jasper managed to say. Saliva and blood dribbled from his mouth.

Ice filled Huck's veins, stopping his heart, rooting him to the spot. "My brother? I didn't! He killed himself!"

"That's what I want to hear!" the old man cheered. "Time to go now, boy."

They wanted to kill him. Then it happened.

Black blood oozed slow and thick from the corner where the ceiling met the wall. It stretched down until it pooled on the old wood-paneled floor. Huck's eyes snapped from the creeping blood to the inhabitants of the roadhouse. Their flesh moved before his eyes: stretching, snapping until it was pulled so tight he could count every rib. Their gaping maws opened in silent, hellish screams and their eyes flamed, turned to red pits like endless tunnels to hell itself. Around them swarmed hundreds of black shadow people, flickering.

One of them—almost indistinguishable from the others now—snapped his fleshy, skeleton face towards him. "See something ya like, kid-do?"

The voice sounded like a hundred damned screams and a chorus of devils all at once.

Huck blinked and it all vanished. The oldest man caught the change in Huck's eyes and squinted maliciously.

"Fuck me," Huck shouted, and turned.

"Don't run, boy!" the bartender roared, for once raising his voice.

Huck bolted down the stairs the way he'd come. He ran so fast his gasping cut out the snapping and static from the spirit box, but once he reached the office again and flung open the doors to the creepy basement, he realized it had just stopped.

The network of tunnels froze him for only a minute. They'd know them better than him.

Right... the voice of a young man whispered from nowhere.

Bodiless voices guided him through the twists and turns. A new one chimed in every now and then. He didn't want to stop and think about it. He just wanted to get out. If he stopped, something behind him would catch up. Something shapeless. Something that wanted him and his screams, to bring him pain. Something that wanted him to believe he'd killed Mark. He could smell the shapeless black. Like burning, molded eggs.

Without warning, Huck ran headlong into something solid. It knocked him off his feet. Looking up in the darkness, he made out the rungs of a ladder. He gripped it, ready to climb.

"Don't leave me!" Jasper's voice cried out from the tunnels. "You always only look out for yourself."

It's not him! the ghostly voices whispered from every angle. *Go!*

Digging up the last of his strength, Huck climbed. He would swear later something grabbed the hem of his jeans and tried to pull him back down.

Breaking the surface, he found himself in the woods again. Knowing the car was close, he scrambled to his feet and ran. He ran until his lungs burned and his legs went numb. He prayed to any god that would listen that he wouldn't see the lights in the woods again.

The trees remained dark.

Screaming in agonizing relief, he caught sight of the car on the side of the dirt road. He didn't slow down, allowing himself to smash into the driver's side door before pulling it open and getting inside. He locked the door and started the car with his own set of keys. He gripped the wheel, shaking, breath a rasping quiver. He sat, waiting for the shapeless black to appear.

For the first time in his life, a feeling like black chalk coating his skin covered him. Guilt. Pressing his forehead onto the wheel, he allowed himself to sob.

"I'm sorry, Jasper," he moaned. "They wanted me. I should've been the one on that table."

The tingling he'd felt since going into the basement subsided. He didn't like it. That was the spiritual gift his mother always talked about. He bit down hard on his bottom lip, denying it as hard as he could in his own head. This was not how he wanted to live his life. Not with this. Seeing the nightmares that others only had to witness in their dreams.

Maybe that's what drew them to him? The...thing...inside him was what they wanted. Not what they claimed: his foul soul.

"I'm not foul," he pleaded, hitting the wheel until his palm hurt. Jasper would tell him he wasn't. His friend's bloodied, terrified face loomed before his shut eyes. He sat up, opening them into the sun.

Should he call the cops? Would there be any use in it? Could they find the devilish roadhouse? He couldn't even tell them where it was. Down some road in the woods. His arms wouldn't stop shaking. He closed his eyes again, trying to conjure the roadhouse again. Was there a road? Could someone get back to it?

The sun's first rays peaked over the hill and through the branches. As if this was the green light, Huck shifted into gear and sped down the hill towards the city of Chevron. A bright slip of paper in the seat next to him caught the morning sun. Looking over, he saw the sticky note with Jasper's handwriting on it. The name of that paranormal private detective was written on it.

Nick Holleran.

Clenching his teeth, he grabbed the note and stuffed it into his jeans' pocket, taking the turns quickly, speeding away from the sunrise, into a darker tomorrow.

THE TOMB OF NICK CAGE
By Missy Mooney

Hey Tanner,

I have some bad news about that Idaho gig, and you are just going to have to understand. You know The Tomb of Nick Cage normally doesn't pass up an opportunity, but you should have known something was wrong when you booked it.

That dude over at Whiskey Pete's sounded way shady and only gave us a landline contact.

WTF.

The guarantee sounded sweet, but when we started down Route Thirteen, I swear it went got so foggy we could barely see. The trees looked weird, man. There was something trailing the van that made a god-awful yipping.

When we finally slowed by the venue there was nobody there except for an old dude in red overalls standing by the pumps. That was it, you know? No cell service out here and I honestly don't want to talk about it.

Sorry again - but no way.

Kym Trailz

NICK

By David Green

"Route Thirteen?" I ask, screwing up my face. "The one running through North Carolina? That's a little outta my wheelhouse, kid."

Name's Nick Holleran and my life's complicated enough—in fact, it's a downright sonofabitch—without driving to the other side of the country.

"Naw," the kid replies. "There's another one, it ain't on any map, but if you search for it, you'll find it."

"Right," I say, racking my head for the kid's name.

He's got different colored eyes—one green, the other blue. He ain't that young either, I'd guess mid-twenties, but I've been wrong before. Man, so *very* wrong.

I rub at the three scars under my black t-shirt. They still ache, every damn day.

He caught me going up the stairs, back to my office after I'd come out for a bit of fresh air. Big mistake. There's more of *them* out here, just wandering around like it's no big deal, which is why I'm fixed on the guy's mismatched eyes. What's his name? Rhymes with f—Huck! That's it.

I hear the phone in my office ring upstairs. Great. Busy day.

"So where's this uncharted Route Thirteen, kid? Enlighten me."

He bristles when I call him kid. Look, it amuses me and I get little in the way of laughs these days.

"Idaho," he bites out.

"Huh." I study his face. I used to work as a private investigator—guess I still do, in a way—and I've seen plenty folk spooked, for want of a better term. This guy's shitting bricks. "Think I'd have heard of that. Done a lot of work there, being our neighboring state and all."

"Work?" he asks, an eager light in his odd stare. "Like...paranormal shit?"

I sigh. My scars itch, and I glance down the street. A washed-out looking old-timer—all grays and dirty whites—watches. But he doesn't see us. He stands there every day, morning, noon and night, for the last year. Staring.

He's dead, but I see him. I see 'em all, every goddamn place I go in Haven. This city's name's a joke if I ever heard one. This place is Hell, and I mean that in every sense of the word. I look at Huck, and the kid flinches, so I push my dark thoughts from the forefront of my mind. For now.

They always return, like the baddest fucking penny ever created.

"No," I mutter, "before that."

He takes a step closer to me.

"Before you could see?" he whispers, glancing from side-to-side.

I nod. Upstairs, the phone's ringing stops. Not missing a beat, my cell vibrates in my jeans pocket. Listen, I work for myself, I can dress however the hell I want, even if I'm pushing forty and wearing a black-tee and converse. Sue me.

I ignore the cell.

"You've done your homework," I say instead, raising an eyebrow. "What do you know about me?"

Kid gives me the side-eye again, like he fears someone overhearing him. If only he knew.

"That you're a paranormal PI," he says in a rush. The words just tumble out on top of one another. "That you changed gears to the supernatural about a year ago, after you got mugged in some alley and left for dead. Is that when it happened?"

The cell stops, and the phone upstairs rings again. It ain't often I'm in such demand, but I wanna hear this kid's story. My eyes flick over his shoulder, and the reasons, plural, stare back at me. I wonder if he knows.

"Yeah," I say, thinking of no reason to hide it. "It's like this. I died, Huck. Then I came back and let me tell you, everything you've heard about? Heaven, Hell, God, demons, vampires, ghosts—shit, Bigfoot himself, for all I know—all real. Except for one massive difference they don't teach you in elementary or Sunday school."

I take a cigarette outta my jacket pocket, take my sweet time lighting it. I ain't above milking a moment.

"What?" Huck asks. He's eager, leaning forward. Maybe I shoulda taken up acting.

"Hell ain't below us, Huck," I reply, blowing smoke into his face. I can be a dick too, when I'm in the mood. "We're living in it. They're all around us. I'm learning the ropes still, but here's what I've picked up. Some are benign. Shit, a whole lot of the sorry sons of bitches don't even seem Aware at all. But the others are, and the things they're capable of..."

I shake my head, nice and slow, blow out another mouthful of silver silk. Gimme that Oscar.

"So, why'd you come looking for me?"

Huck's turned as white as a... Well, you know. From the deep breaths he takes, I reckon he's just about holding back tears. I glance over his shoulder again, and my intuition tells me the kid's either fucked up bad, or running from something awful. Good chance of both, all told.

"You may not believe me about the old Route Thirteen, Holleran, but it's real. There's a place there, an old motel called Whiskey Pete's, like something ripped from a fucking time-warp. It's out between a town called Chevron and a place called Devil's Ladder. My buddy and me, Jasper, well, we have a YouTube channel, Darkfront. You know, for ghost hunting? It's kinda famous."

I nod and try not to laugh at the name. Sounds like something an edgelord would come up with. I've never heard of it, and I stream a lot. Huck's rambling, building up to something. He looks more boyish than before, and I reckon the kid's just a teenager. I'm sickened by the pang of sympathy I feel for him.

"We were out there in November and, well, Jasper didn't make it. That place, Holleran, it gave me a feeling the entire time. Like, pressure in the back of my head, made my stomach turn. It always happened whenever we came across somewhere *actually* haunted. For real, not just an act for the show. I can't shake the feeling, not since Whiskey Pete's. Didn't think anyone would believe me, but Jasper looked you up before..."

Tears flow. A catch in the throat. Without thinking, I grip his shoulder and give him a smile. I'm uncomfortable right away, but I hold on and peer into his eyes. The blue and green stare back, and I nod. He's not like me. He can't see the truth, but he can *sense* it. A natural 'gift' some would say, though not me.

Not by a long shot.

"What else aren't you telling me, kid?" I ask. "Something else happened, didn't it?"

A tear trickles down Huck's cheek. I cough, let go, and look away. Look, I ain't macho or anything. Emotion is fine, but this kid is one breakdown away from curling up in a gutter and dying, and I don't wanna be responsible for that.

"My brother," he whispers. "My twin, Mark. He died, and it's my fault. My best friend, too. I just left him. I ran, Holleran."

I look behind him and nod, mind made up. The kid's telling the truth. In the meantime, my office phone and cell have taken turns trying to snatch my attention, like a technological synchronized swim. They ain't missed a beat, one stops and the other starts.

"What's your cell?" I say, pulling out my phone.

I've a bunch of missed calls from a number I don't recognize and one I do. Rosa. The woman who kept me alive when three bullets to the chest tried their damned hardest to kill me.

"You're taking the case?" Huck asks, breaking into a grin.

"I'll check it out, is all I'm saying," I reply, handing him my cell so he can punch in the digits. "I've got some clients in Haven first. If I've time, I'll dig into Route Thirteen, Idaho. But I ain't cheap."

"Thank you," Huck says, looking up into the sky. Light Oregon rain drizzles down on us. "Didn't think you'd believe me."

"Kid, I just wanted to see if you'd tell me the truth. I knew from the moment we met you were into something deep."

"What? How?"

I spin him around. They're watching us, and I'm pretty sure two of them are Aware. Can't tell for sure, but I'm guessing...Jasper? The other one is the image of Huck, which makes him the twin. Two ghosts following one kid around. The deaths he's responsible for.

"That nagging sensation you're getting? You've got two spirits on your tail. They ain't doing anything. Yet. The recently deceased just linger if they don't have a ticket for Heaven, or if they've other business. At first, they're tethered to a location, or a person. These two? They're fixed on you. Maybe you reaching out to me is their unfinished business, maybe it ain't, but kid? Take my advice. Make your peace with how they wound up. Or they'll haunt you till the end of your days." I point at him for added effect, like I'm Han Solo. "I'll be in touch."

Tears stream down the kid's face as he reaches out with feeble fingers. I give him a last pat on the shoulder and race up the stairs to my office, hoping I've done the right thing. Huck seems a decent sort, and God knows we all make mistakes. It's better he knows the truth.

My office overlooks the street, and the phone's ringing again. I'll call Rosa after. We've a date tomorrow, and our relationship, like my life, is complicated.

I crash through my office door, intent on grabbing the phone. I lied to Huck; I don't have other clients and money's tight, too tight to mention. So much so, I don't enjoy calling people back unless I have to. Costs too much.

There's a check tucked away in my desk, but I don't want to cash it unless I'm desperate. In fact, I don't even want to think about it. It's blood money, even if the blood belongs to me.

"Holleran," I bark down the receiver, a little out of breath. Look, like I said, I'm pushing forty and I've three bullet wounds in my chest. "What can I get ya?"

A pause, before a deep male voice, one I recognize, asks, *"Nick Holleran? The private detective?"*

"Don't do that anymore, Davey."

Scowling, I twist the phone wire across my desk and drop into my seat. I regret it, because now my attention's drawn to the corner of the room. Suppressing a shudder, I swivel in my seat and glance through my window. Huck's climbing into his car. The two ghosts are already sitting in the backseat. Funny how they do that. Beats floating behind the rear bumper, I guess.

"At least, I don't investigate the kinds of cases that would interest the editor of the Haven Chronicle."

"You want to hear about the case before you turn me down, Holleran?"

"If the price is right."

"Money's not an issue."

Music to my ears, but maybe I can drive up the price. A bit of work that isn't of the supernatural flavor appeals, so long as it doesn't involve the mob. My scars itch thinking about that. The cigarette's still between my fingers, and I take a drag.

"What's the skinny?"

A sigh of relief blows down the receiver. I used to hear that a lot. *"Reporter of mine went missing back in July 2020."*

"Go to the police. They like that sort of thing."

"Didn't happen in this state, Holleran. Idaho."

I glance out of the window. Huck's finally pulled into the street. What are the chances that Idaho of all places has become a hotbed of activity? Idaho!

"Huh..." I say. "FBI, then?"

"They said they'd look into it. Five months ago."

"And?"

"They came back with nothing."

I lean forward while trying to avoid looking in the corner of my office. "Davey, I fail to see what I can do here. If the FBI can't help, how can I?"

A beat.

"It's not like they can't help, Holleran," he says, voice hoarse. *"They won't. They're saying they've got records of my missing reporter leaving the country, back in July."*

"So she ran away," I laugh. "Didn't think you were that bad to work for, hoss."

Another beat.

"I wanted to believe it. Zia's had a rough life. Maybe she found something new. Only, it wasn't just *her. A junior reporter went with her, Dylon Myers. The FBI found his passport used too. I figured that was case closed. Maybe they eloped. Couldn't have pictured it myself, but whatever. Then, this morning, I received something in the mail. A postcard."*

"Nice." A wrinkle in the story. I love a goddamn wrinkle. "Anyone you know?"

"Yeah," Davey replies. *"Zia Bennett. She used to wear this t-shirt, of a place she could never find, one her adoptive parents found her wrapped in when she was a baby. You know what the t-shirt said?"*

My blood runs cold. I know what he's going to say. Without thinking, I blurt it down the receiver and regret having a voice instantly. One day, I'll learn how to keep my mouth shut.

"Whiskey Pete's."

"You've heard of it."

It isn't a question. I'm experienced enough to notice a statement of fact when I hear one.

"Just this morning. Lemme guess, the postcard's from the same place."

Davey Teague replies with a low chuckle, devoid of humor. *"Holleran, the postcard had your name on it. That's it. Nothing else. Now, I think it's time you drop the wise-guy act and come see me. Else, this piece of evidence goes to the FBI and I'll tip off the local PD that you're wanted for kidnapping. How does that sound?"*

"Sounds like I'll arrive at the Haven Chronicle within the hour."

The phone clicks, and a dead line hums from the other side. I leave it off the hook. I don't feel like taking anymore calls today. In the corner of my room stands a young girl. She's been there since I returned to the office, after my 'death.' For all I know, she coulda stood there for decades. The girl doesn't talk, doesn't so much as twitch. Gave her a name. Darcy, I call her. Spun her around once, and I still have nightmares about what I saw. Empty sockets where eyes should have been, gray blood covering her cheeks.

Still, she's someone to soundboard off'f.

"Looks like I'm going to Idaho," I say to her back. "Or leaving the fucking country. I hear New Zealand's nice."

The girl doesn't reply. Why would she?

I fire up my computer and start googling Idaho, Devil's Ladder, Chevron and Whiskey Pete's. Even goddamn Huck, Jasper and Darkfront. I've a little time before I meet Davey Teague and I want to prepare.

My cell vibrates and I almost fall out of my chair.

It's Rosa.

"Hey, Nick," she says, sunny voice making my stomach sink. She has that effect on me. I care for her, I do. Sometimes, I think there's something there, a chance for happiness. Then, when I look at her, I see her panicked face peering at me as she held the blood in my chest. Rosa is the reason I'm still alive, and that makes things—yeah, you guessed it—complicated.

See, when I died, I saw Heaven. Damn near had my fingers on it and then Rosa dragged me back. A stranger who passed the alleyway where I lay dying and rushed to help.

Part of me resents her for it, even though I try to bury it deep down. She's great. Better than great; she's more than a schmuck like me deserves. But...let's just say these mixed feelings get in the way.

I put her on speakerphone so I can continue my research. "Hey."

"We still on for tomorrow night?" Rosa asks, and just when I think my stomach can't sink further, it does.

"Shit," I say, and I can't decide if I'm regretful or relieved to have this excuse. "Just caught a fresh case. Sounds like it's gonna be a rough one. Think I'll be out of town for a spell."

"Right," she replies, but doesn't hang up. That ain't her way, no matter how many times I mess her around.

"Sorry," I say, and I'm surprised that I mean it. Guess I wanted to see her after all. "Listen, there was this kid and he was crying and..."

"Nick, there's always a kid, or some guy wearing concrete shoes in the reservoir, or a woman with her throat cut. Didn't you used to have a work-life balance before?"

Anger rises, and I speak without thinking. "You think I want ghosts on my ass, day-in, day-out? I didn't ask for this. I could have been kicking back in Heaven right now, but I'm stuck here instead and they're *everywhere*!"

Silence. I regret my words even before I finish snarling them. Like I said, one day, I'll keep my fucking trap shut. But clearly not today.

"Sorry you feel like you're stuck," Rosa whispers. "I was just trying to help. Maybe you missed out on Heaven, but are you sure you're not missing out on a real life? Just...think about it, okay?"

She hangs up, and I fight the urge to bang my head against the desk. It's a losing battle, but I'd deserve the pain. My eyes drift to the girl in the corner, and wonder what she makes of it all, if she can even hear me chasing away the only good thing in my life, time and time again.

"A trip to Whiskey Pete's is just what the doctor ordered," I say with a sigh, turning to the computer screen. "Work two cases at once, get out of town, try to stay out of an FBI holding cell. Guess I'll try to make it up to Rosa when I come back."

I fish my notebook from my desk drawer and get to work.

Time's ticking.

I knew it before I met with Davey Teague, but someone really wants me at Whiskey Pete's.

The meeting confirmed it.

The postcard is in my raincoat pocket and it's exactly what I thought it would be. The front shows Whiskey Pete's—a carbon-copy mid-century truck stop bar, store and motel. The backside has my name written in a bold hand, and Haven Chronicle's address.

Teague ain't certain if it's Zia's writing, or the guy she left with. He showed me their pictures. Dylon's handsome in a coltish way, but in my experience, pretty ladies tend to stick in the mind more, so I'll use her as the lead.

Meeting didn't last long. Teague blackmailed me, said he'd go to the Feds if I didn't look into it. Like I needed much prompting. If someone wants me there so bad, they won't stick to sending postcards. Still, I put my newfound acting skills to work and got him to pay twice my going rate plus expenses. All in all, Davey Teague is a crappy blackmailer.

Instinct tells me he cares for Zia, deep in his bones. He's concerned for Dylon, but Teague and Zia have a relationship that goes beyond employee/employer. He doesn't have any daughters, but I get the feeling he wanted one.

I packed a bag soon after and filled my model-green 1994 Ford Mustang convertible with gas. She's a classic. The money I've spent keeping her roadworthy over the years is crazy, but worth every cent. One of the more recent mod-cons is the radio, which has a USB port—vital for keeping my cell charged, for music, and for GPS.

My research didn't turn up a peep about Whiskey Pete's or old Route Thirteen, but I found plenty of mentions of Devil's Ladder in Idaho, and Chevron. Missing persons, random acts of unexplained violence, and mutilated bodies turning up in the wild.

I ain't a chump. I packed my gun.

And a few other things too. If Davey Teague alone had reached out to me, I might have treated this like my old work. I've searched for plenty of missing persons, and most don't want finding or all that's left is a corpse. But with Huck's visit, and his mention of my new line of work, I've decided to come prepared. I brought an Expunger.

See, most ghosts of Hell just let the living go about their, ah, 'lives'. Others leave when they attend to some unfinished business—to Heaven or maybe some other layer of Hell, like Dante wrote about, but I ain't seen or heard anything to say that's true—and some need to be *made* to leave... and that gets messy.

I have a contact, made through a bar called the Styx in Haven. Guy called Harry, and his ghost wife, Maeve. Nice couple. He got me wise to a few of Hell's finer details, including Expungers. They're special items that burn a ghost or demon from existence; it removes them from reality, like they never existed. It's dangerous, and shouldn't be used too often—a thing exists, and telling the universe it doesn't, and never did, is awful confusing.

Plus, they're a bitch to make, and involves pissing off a certain Queen of the Fae. Yeah, you better believe Lilith's real too.

I drove through the rest of the afternoon and into the night, stopping for a few hours shut-eye at a rest-stop on the way. Aiming for Devil's Ladder on the longest GPS route, I came across Route Thirteen easy enough, though I almost missed the turn.

Looked like I was the first driver on this route in forty-odd years. It's narrow, winding, rough and dark as...Hell. My spirits lifted when I discovered road signs for the town of Chevron, and I figured I'd swing through, check it out after hearing so much about it and take a little rest from all the driving.

Anyway, I just left Chevron. Straight up swung the Mustang around and headed back to Route Thirteen. I thought about stopping, but one glance out of the window told me all I needed to know about the place. 'Hills Have Eyes' country. It doesn't bode well for Whiskey Pete's.

One weird thing. No ghosts, no demons. No nothing.

Like I said, I see things everywhere I go. Chevron, and the strip of Route Thirteen I'm on, heading to Devil's Ladder, it's like they exist in a void. To be honest, it freaks me out. It should come as a relief, but I know that shit ain't right.

Tall pine trees surround the road, and a light mist sits heavy on the asphalt. It's 10am, and I reckon I'm close. Huck said Whiskey Pete's sat midway between Chevron and Devil's Ladder, and I haven't taken my foot off the gas for an hour.

The road bends, and through the fog I see the flicker of neon. Nestled against the trees is Whiskey Pete's, and a thousand voices scream out to me as one. Their cries pierce my ears, and I slam the breaks, trying to keep my hands on the wheel. The Mustang slides, crunches over gravel and comes to an abrupt, jolting stop.

The screaming ends. Silence deafens. I open my eyes to see the fog has vanished.

"That was some entrance, bucko. You some kinda streetcar racer?"

I turn with such speed, my neck aches in protest. Maybe it's just a whiplash.

To my left is one of the ugliest looking men I've ever laid eyes on. He's leaning through my window as he stands next to the gas pumps I somehow slid up to. His fingers, nails caked in filth, grip my car door through the open window, which I have no memory of winding down. My eyes flicker over him; he must be seventy, though his pruned face and lank, greasy hair could add years to his total. And he has a Canadian accent.

"Not a racer, no." My eyes flick to his name-tag. "Got lost is all, Dale. Been driving all night. Guess I almost fell asleep at the wheel."

"Name's Lorne W. Petersen. Who the Hell's this 'Dale' folk keep yammering on about? You want fillin' up or not?"

I glance at his name-tag again but decide to let the matter drop. Truth be told, I'm shook. That screaming... Never experienced anything like it. I can feel death, but a quick scan of my surroundings shows nothing of the Hell I've seen every goddamn day since I died.

And yet, I *heard* them.

"Maybe I'll get gas later."

Lorne hocks and spits a shower of phlegm onto the gravel. "Good. Hate pumping gas."

"Right..." I toss my head to Whiskey Pete's. "Take it coffee's available? Could do with a hit before I get back on the road."

"Coffee? Con can sort you out with something stronger. Where you headed, boy?"

Boy? Suppose I am compared to this fella. And something stronger? I look at the Mustang's clock. It reads 2:51pm.

Somehow, I've lost almost five hours.

"Shit... I mean, Devil's Ladder. Sorry, pal. That swerve has me shook."

Lorne glances behind him, sweeping his gaze up and down old Route Thirteen. "Yeah, near-death experiences will do that to ya. Seen plenty myself over the years."

The old coot straightens up and walks towards the road without another word or a backward glance. He heads straight across and into the tall pines on the other side, as if it's the most normal thing in the world to do.

A giggle escapes me, one filled with disbelief. "What the fuck?"

For a second, I consider starting the engine. Heading back the way I came. Telling Davey Teague I tried my best, but discovered not a goddamn thing, try as I might. Call Huck and tell him to move on and forget all about Whiskey Pete's.

I think about it for more than a second, truth be told. The postcard though. Someone wants me here, and I mean to find out who.

My old Ma always did say my curiosity would get me in trouble.

I leave the Mustang where it's sat, parallel to the only working gas pump. There ain't any other vehicles here, and I don't recall passing a single car this side of Chevron. Even before, as a matter of fact. If anyone runs into Whiskey Pete's yelling for someone to move the ol' model-green '94 outta the way of the pumps, I'll lay a golden egg.

Huck's right, by the way. I'm expecting that people in there are wearing bell-bottoms and listening to the Bee-Gees. It's like I've stepped into the land that time forgot. Or, from the complete absence of the paranormal, the land that Hell ignored.

I sling the raincoat over my shoulders as a light drizzle falls from the sky, right on cue. Standing there, in the empty gravel pit, I stare at the postcard and compare it to the actual thing. I'd say Whiskey Pete's has seen better days, but even in the picture it looks ripe for demolition.

I jam the postcard back into my jacket and take two items from my duffle bag—my Ruger Blackhawk, which I slide into the ass-band of my jeans, and my Expunger. The iron disc fits into the palm of my hand, and I slide it into my front pocket where I can grab it in a fix. My fingers tingle from touching it; they don't affect the living, but I'm a dead man walking.

Drawing a deep breath, I approach the store side of Whiskey Pete's, figuring I can listen in on the bar from there. That sense of nothingness nags at me again. It isn't how I felt before I died, before I knew Hell and Earth existed as one. It's more like I'm in a bubble; Hell still exists, but out there. Whiskey Pete's is its own thing, and that strikes me as worse.

Much worse.

"Hello?"

Store's empty. Smells rotten too. Stench almost makes me gag. A refrigerator with a blinking, buzzing bulb catches my attention. The cartons of milk leak green sludge and I almost add a stream of vomit onto the liquid dripping onto the floor. I see a dark corridor beside the counter and guess it leads to the bar.

The edges of my vision shift. Moving my eyes makes it stop. It's like the room I'm in wants to change whenever I'm not focusing, like the details are still forming around me. There's a pressure here, like fingers delving into my brain, sifting through my memories.

I tell it to fuck off, and the store settles.

It's older. Decrepit, even more run-down than when I first walked in. Makes me wonder what anyone else would see. Something a little different for each person, I reckon. Shitty, bargain-basement glamour.

High-tailing it back to the Mustang sounds pretty good, but the postcard's burning a hole in my pocket.

It's quiet. Not too quiet, like they say in the movies, but there's an absence of sound, like Whiskey Pete's itself is holding its breath. I fight the urge to pull my Ruger—better yet, the Expunger—and face the corridor to the bar.

I walk into the darkness.

"Can I help you?"

The voice is female, monotone, and scares the living shit outta me.

A light blinks on, and a woman sits behind a small side desk in the narrow corridor, like it's cut into the wall. I see an office behind her, and the tinkle of glass echoes from the direction of the bar.

"You enjoy startling people?" I ask, a little too loud in the breathless hush even for my own ears.

"Yes," she says, in a tone that suggests she's never enjoyed a single thing in her entire goddamn existence.

She's got a Southern accent, the type I enjoy, but right now all I can think about is Kathy Bates in Misery. And her eyes... She stares through me, like I don't register to her all that much. Like *nothing* does. She's gorgeous, ain't no denying it, but it's like something ripped her soul right out of her, leaving nothing but residue behind. Something rotten.

"Bar that way?" I thumb down the corridor. She keeps up the thousand-mile stare, like she's peering into some horrifying past. Or terrible future.

"I'm Stacey, welcome to Whiskey Pete's." A switch flicks behind her eyes, and the sudden smile makes my skin want to peel off onto the floor and slide right outta the place. "We've rooms available at a cut-rate price. Special offer, sir."

"Uh, sure," I mutter.

"Oh, sir!" Stacey almost screams in delight. "Why that's wonderful news! That'll be twenty dollars, and y'all can pay when you check out. Sign in the book, please."

She pulls a heavy book from beneath the counter and spins it my way, and I'm thinking things are too easy—it's a perfect chance to leaf through the ledger, an opportunity to determine if Zia or Dylon ever rocked up at this joint. My luck ain't in; pages upon pages are missing, torn out with little in the way of hiding the fact.

I pick up the pencil in the spine's crease, spying an opportunity to pry. "Any other guests?"

Her face changes again, back to that pretty, blank canvas framed by red curls and she says nothing. I scrawl a name into the empty column.

"Kurt Francis," Stacey intones, without even looking at the page, like I've etched the name right into her brain. Too bad it's not real. Made it up from the singers of two of my favorite bands. "Enjoy your stay."

"So the bar's that way, right?" I repeat.

"I never wanted to come here," she whispers, and we share the briefest eye contact. Her face flickers and her features age by at least forty years. Instead of a thirty-something woman, a grey-haired septuagenarian sits in front of me, terror etched into her face. Then Stacey blinks, and the vision fades. "I never wanted to stay. The bad things I did, before I came here... It spoke to him, and he whispered to me. Sometimes I remember myself. I never wanted to stay."

"Then leave."

Tears leak from her emerald eyes, but she doesn't move. Stacey stares, and try to imagine what might be looking back at her.

A voice in my head screams for me to follow my own advice.

"Zia Bennett."

Stacey doesn't look at me, but the fact she stands up, turns around and disappears into the office tells me she knows the name. I almost shout mine after her too. My real one. After all, I'm expected.

Besides, she didn't give me my goddamn room key.

"...save the South, God save the South. Her altars and firesides, God save the South!"

The singing tugs on the edges of my hearing.

"Is that...a fucking Confederacy song? Are you shitting me?"

It's coming from the bar area. The words drift to me and grow stronger as I approach what must be the oldest looking man that ever walked the planet. Dude looks like a skeleton with parchment instead of skin, wearing clothes that were out of fashion back when my granddaddy wore diapers. The old-timer's clawed fingernails tap on the table of the booth he's sitting in as he sings in a too-firm voice. His watery, blue eyes, shallow pools in black pits, bore into mine.

"...freedom or death! Chanting our battle cry, freedom or death!"

I lean over him. Guy's tall. Even though he's sat down, I can see he'd top me by a good six or seven inches if he were on his feet. He falls silent as I stare into his eyes, until his mouth creaks into a rotten grin. His skin melts away, snowy hair shedding and a living skeleton leers at me with those weak, blue eyes.

"You see too much, son," the skeleton whispers, though its jaws don't move. "This ain't gonna end well for you. We've all seen too much, but we just can't help ourselves no more. Like we ever could."

Without thinking, I reach out to touch the skull, fascinated and repulsed in equal measure.

"Hey, you leave old Melvin alone," a youthful voice shouts. I look around, and a fella brandishes a pool cue at me. "You gotta problem, take it up with me, ya hear?"

The old man, Melvin, has found his skin again. What's left of it, anyway. I drop my hand and back up. He cocks his head, as if listening to something only he can hear.

"Run while you can, Kurt Francis," he says with a sly grin. "What was it Rosa said, 'you sure you're not missing out on a real life'?"

"And how'd you know what Rosa said, *Melvin*?"

Melvin hums to himself, eyes getting that faraway look that seems to be all the rage around Whiskey Pete's. I glance over at the pool table. The young fella's eyeballing me. Trouble, and misplaced arrogance, ooze from his pores.

"Ignore Joel, the dumb bastard. You ever hear of George Washington?"

I blink. Melvin's looking at me, eyes narrowed. I take it the pool guy's Joel. Suits him. Never met a Joel I liked.

"Who the Hell hasn't heard of George Washington?"

"Yeah, old Georgie taught me some classics, *Nick Holleran*. Hollered 'em night and day, he did. Hollerin' Holleran."

My blood's ice. I rack my brain, trying to remember when I used my name. I'm convinced I never fucking did.

"Sorry, Melvin," I say, in as low a voice as I can, hoping the young buck by the pool table's hearing ain't so great. "Name's Kurt Francis. Think you've got me mistaken with someone else."

Melvin's laughter tears from his throat, thin shoulders shaking with mirth. I take a step backwards, and he stops and cocks his head again.

"Twelve months into thirteen. A special one for each occasion with a few more for good measure. This place don't work on you. You can see. But you made it in time, sonny. Enjoy the show."

A weight drops on my shoulder, buckling my knees. A heavily muscled man, thick body fattening and sagging from age and misuse, stands behind me. A little taller than me, but twice as wide, and I reckon he could snap me in two without a second thought.

"Coffee?" he grunts.

Like Huck, he has mismatched eyes—green and blue—though he's doing his best to avoid eye contact. Without another word, he heads for the bar, which I'm only noticing for the first time.

"How'd you know?" I ask.

"Lorne," he grunts. Behind the bar now, he nods his head to the side. Lorne's sitting at the end of the bar, Stacey beside him.

"And you are?"

"Con." The big man breathes the name instead of speaking.

I whistle, tension making it shrill. "Really chatty, Con."

I feel a presence behind me and see Melvin move with impossible, cat-like grace to sidle up alongside me at the bar. Joel approaches, pool cue in hand. He's wringing it, no doubt imagining it's my neck.

"Fellas," I say, spreading my hands, adding a smile I don't mean. "Why do I feel we've got off on the wrong foot? Coffee sounds just swell."

"You hear too much, Nick Holleran," Lorne says, his voice loud. It rings and echoes as if a hundred Lornes are all speaking at once.

"See too much," Stacey drones.

"Know too much," Melvin whispers, a murmur like a waterfall.

"Who sent you here?" Con growls, eyes glittering with malice.

"Ya might as well spill," Joel snarls. "You ain't leaving this place alive, Holleran."

Joel's nearest to me, close to the corridor to the office. Fuck me, but I have to think fast. I smile, placing my hands on my hips. My fingers are close to the Ruger's grip.

"Well," I say, thinking I'm Clint-fucking-Eastwood all of a sudden, "it's like this. I died before and don't quite feel like doing it again."

I pull the gun free and spin, slamming the muzzle into Joel's nose. Blood spurts and I feel cartilage crunch. I slide behind Joel and wrap my arm around his throat, sticking the gun to his temple.

The regulars of Whiskey Pete's—Joel excluded—stare at me, unmoved. The lights flicker, and they *change*. The other Stacey and Melvin leer back, older, skeletal. Con and Lorne are the same, aged in a blink. Joel's raven colored hair is grey and thin and feels like sun-bleached crab grass beneath my fingers.

"One move, and you'll see the color of your buddy's brains." I cock the gun as I try to keep my hand steady. I can hear three gunshots echoing in a dark alleyway and I struggle to keep my nerve. "Me and Joel are going into that office back there, see if we can't talk this shit out. I dare y'all to follow."

They laugh, a chorus of wheezes and grunts, but they don't move as I edge Joel backwards.

"Pete's hungry," Melvin calls. "You hear, Holleran? You'll meet him real soon."

I snatch the pool cue from Joel's limp grip as I push him into the office and slam the door. There's a lock, but I jam the cue through the handle and pull a table against it for good measure.

Then I breathe.

"What the fuck just happened?"

I don't get an answer. Instead, Joel rams into me, sending me crashing into my makeshift barricade. My head hits the table with a sickening thud. The Ruger slips from my fingers and slides across the floor, and I thank Him upstairs it doesn't fire on impact. Lights flood my vision. I feel hot blood trickle down the side of my face. Joel's on top of me, beating at me with his fists. I shove him away with both arms and shake my head, trying to clear my eyes. Crouching across from me, he's young again, but he has the strength of a child—or a decrepit old man.

I bare my teeth, and he flinches. Joel knows he can't take me in a fight. His eyes slide to the side and narrow.

The fucking Ruger.

Joel dives for it, and I throw myself on top of him. His reach is good; his fingers lace the gun's grip.

"No, you don't, pal," I growl.

Joel's grip tightens, and he swings the business end towards me.

With a growl, I grab his wrist and twist. It's an aikido move Rosa showed me and goddamn it works. I feel the bones snap and Joel screams . The Ruger fires, and I feel the bullet scorching my blonde locks as it whizzes by and punches a hole in the office wall.

I'm not a brutal man, but this guy, whatever he is, just tried to kill me. I pull the Ruger from his limp grip and smash his busted nose with the butt. He howls and I backhand him across the face, sending blood and rotten teeth flying from his mouth. His eyes are unfocused. He's whimpering for me to stop.

But as I stare at him, as we lock eyes, I see what's happened here at Whiskey Pete's.

Death. Murder. Sacrifice. And Joel and his band of freaks stand at the center.

You see too much...

It all hits me in a wave, that absence of Hell, and I realize the truth. They hide it somehow. Control it, maybe. I glance around and see ghosts the Whiskey Pete's regulars have hidden from me—suppressed somehow—filling the room. A white man beside a black woman, holding a newborn child. A woman in a business suit. A tall man with a haunted-look, even for a spirit. There's even a tall figure dressed in a fucking Santa outfit. There's a family with a woman standing slightly apart, estranged even in death. Bounty hunters. Private investigators. Frat boys. Young and old. Innocent and guilty.

They crowd me and their deaths hit me one by one. The pain makes me gasp, makes my stomach lurch, sends hatred coursing through my veins. Hatred for the sick fucks tied to Whiskey Pete's.

Yeah, they're tied here, victims themselves in a way. Probably started as cultists, doing wrong like so many others. But they caught the attention of something else. Something serious. And like old Melvin said, they just can't help themselves no more.

A young man with a camera pushes to the front. Him I recognize. It's poor Dylon Meyers. But I don't see Zia.

They point at Joel. No, at a space of floor *beneath* Joel. A trapdoor.

I place the muzzle against Joel's head and the barrel scorches a circle between his eyes. He flinches, whimpers. Beneath the blood, he's an old man again.

"Joel, I'm gonna level with you. I'm new to all this paranormal shit, but I've seen my fair share of shit to hazard a guess at what's going on here. You and your pals found this place deserted in, I'm guessing, the Seventies. You all had the same end game, maybe a bunch of you were even from around these parts, and the dark influence drew you all together here. You looked at this joint, reckoned it was a nice secluded spot to carry out your depraved business in peace. Only, the previous owner didn't leave. It slept. You woke it up and made a deal with it. Everlasting youth and life in return for blood." I cock the gun. Joel trembles. "How about it? Getting warm?"

"Fuck you, Holleran," he growls, blood flicking from his mouth.

I hear that a lot.

"Well, I reckon, even after all the sacrifices, you and your buddies are still basically human. You break and bleed like the rest of us. Guess there's only one way to find out for sure. A bullet to the head'll tell us real quick, don't you think? And if it don't kill you, I reckon it'll hurt like fucking hell. Still got five bullets in this thing. You as curious as I am?"

Damn. Might as well ask the son of a bitch if he's feeling lucky...

"Pete!" Once Joel starts, the words come quick. "Reckon he's the devil himself. There are tunnels below, running all over. To Devil's Ladder, the forests, Chevron. They all lead here. Pete protects us all. Keeps us safe. Strong!"

"Yeah, you're looking plenty strong right now, fella. Where's Zia Bennett?"

Joel giggles, blowing blood bubbles on his thin lips.

"You'll see her soon enough. One more sacrifice, that's all Pete needs. You arrived just in time, Holleran."

A heavy weight crashes into the office door, and I decide.

"I'd say sorry," I mutter, whipping Joel on the temple with the butt of my Ruger, knocking him out, "but you're a real sack of shit."

I pull him off the trapdoor the ghosts are all pointing at. The door trembles again. I yank the hatch open, revealing a ladder descending into darkness. Glass shatters, and I twist. The Whiskey Pete's regulars leer at me through the door's smashed window.

"Reckoning's coming," Con grunts, throwing a finger in my direction. "You're a dead man, Holleran."

I glance into the darkness beneath my feet.

"Yeah. So they tell me."

I drop, spinning onto the ladder. As I pull the trapdoor down behind me, I see the ghosts rush forwards. Noise explodes above me, and something crashes onto the trapdoor, sealing it shut. I slide down into the shadows.

All I hear is my breathing. Ragged. Panicked.

"Pull your shit together, Nick. Gonna have to keep it level if we're getting out of here alive."

An epiphany strikes me. It ain't as painful as it sounds. All this time, since my death, I've struggled with what I missed out on. Heaven. Having it within my grasp. I resented Rosa for saving me, but now, alone in the impenetrable darkness of the tunnels beneath Whiskey Pete's, with a murderous undead cult above me and God knows what ahead, I want to live.

Very fucking much.

I laugh and just like that, some gloom leaves my soul. The Ruger's grip feels good against my palm as I thumb in another bullet. The Expunger's weight is comforting in my pocket.

"You've got this, Nick. You've fucking got this."

The trapdoor creaks above, and I flee into the darkness.

I don't got this.

Throwing my free hand out in front of me, I feel my way forwards with frantic fingers and unsteady steps. My heart tries to escape through my throat when my fingers trace across fur, but it feels fake. Like a costume. There's a hint of cinnamon in the air, it's hotter than Lucifer's nutsack and, in this darkness, I'm blinder than Mr. fucking Magoo. A pit could open up in front of me, and I'd plummet down, blind, towards death.

"Think," I hiss. "They want you dead. You heard 'em. One more death. Don't give those freaks what they want."

I slow down, crouch, and listen to the silence surrounding me while I get my hammering heart back under control.

Holleran...

I've haven't shit myself since I was in diapers, but hearing my name whispered in my ear brings me very goddamn close.

Her essence penetrates the darkness. She isn't washed out and dull like a normal ghost. More like she's a soul ripped from her body. Davey Teague showed me her picture, and she's the one I'm looking for.

"Zia. Got your postcard. Try not to give me a fatal heart attack too."

She smiles. Always nice to have a hunch proven correct.

"Take it you ain't quite dead yet? Thanks for dragging me into this. How the Hell did you find out about me? Nice place you've got here. Been on better blind dates, truth be told, but it ain't one I'll soon forget."

Look, I babble when I'm nervous.

What's this, twenty questions? Zia grins. Reckon I like her. *Sending you the postcard got me stuck like this. Pete and his cult said they couldn't trust me when I refused to kill Dylon myself, and ripped me from my body. Ready for the ritual. A couple of kids got drawn here a few months ago—*

"Huck and Jasper? We've met."

But Jasper died... Understanding floods her eyes. *He's following Huck, isn't he? They talked about you. Thought about you. I don't know how, but I knew they did. I hear so much when I'm down here. I got the chance to sneak above and smuggled out the message. I hoped you'd bring back up.*

"Sweetheart, most people don't believe in the paranormal. Hell, half the time, I'm not even sure I believe it. You're lucky I'm here at all. You have a plan or what?"

Zia glances down the tunnel. Either my eyes are adjusting to the gloom, or her light is chasing it all away, but I can make out the walls. Costumes line it—your basic cult monster starter kit—furry bodies and big claws and fangs designed to frighten teenage campers. Hokey shit.

But there's symbols etched into the stone and they ain't hokey. I don't recognize them, but they send a shiver on a return trip along my spine.

Pete—that ain't his actual name, by the way—he's...my dad.

"Well, fuck me."

Maybe some other time. Look, I didn't know. Pete inhabits his children's bodies so he can go out into the world. He's done it for centuries. His last one died, and he meant to use me as his vessel. Only, someone stole me away. Guess he knew I'd come back, and he and his thralls had prepared for it. Since then, he's been tied here. He can appear every now and then, looking like a person from someone's memories. It's why the place shifts and changes so much. He delves into everyone's minds. It lulls people into a fugue-like state, makes them sloppy. Anyway, they need one more sacrifice, and he'll take my body. He's tethered to this place, but after today, after one more death, he can do whatever the hell he likes.

I scratch the stubble on my chin with the barrel of my Ruger. Zia looks at me like I've lost my mind. Maybe I have.

"We have a problem here," I say, lowering the gun and pretending nothing happened. "Can't kill the host—sorry, your—body. That'd still give him the juice he needs to take a body, mine or anyone else's. It might not be perfect for him, but it would do. We can't rule that out. Guess the bloodline makes you first choice, or maybe it makes him stronger, but I'm guessing he's a demon of sorts and with enough sacrifices any sack of meat and bones will do. So that means I can't let anyone die. There's a way, but you're gonna have to help me. Guessing your body's in some kind of ritual chamber?"

Yeah.

"Course it is. Well, I'm gonna start shouting real loud. Wait for me in there, but hide. Let no one see you. When I say the word, I need you to grab whatever Pete is and do your goddamn best to hold onto him."

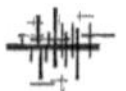

It didn't take long for them to find me after I started raising Hell. I do my best to look like a man who's regretting his life choices, who knows he's beat.

Con, Stacey, Melvin and Lorne walk in silence, the barkeeper's meaty grip on my bicep. Joel's elsewhere. They took my Ruger, but didn't search my pockets. The Expunger's safe for now. They all look like they did when we first met, but if I stare at them any longer than a glance, they change. The truth, revealed.

I shouldn't, but part of me feels sorry for them. They're sadistic murderers, but once they were folk too afraid to die, glamored by some malevolent demon and forced to live a mockery of a life. Tethered to Whiskey Pete's in thrall of their master.

Maybe I'm being generous. Gotta remember, these guys are a cult, and were long before they came across Pete.

I wonder if they know the truth? That if they died, they'd be stuck here anyway. In Hell. These folks haven't a notion of entering Heaven now, and never did.

Done some thinking, piecing together what I've seen and what Zia told me. Pete's a Kashgar.

Now, that's the name of a place on the Silk Road in China, but they got the name from the type of demon I'm dealing with. There's evil, and there's a Kashgar. They derive pleasure in suffering and sow misery wherever they tread, and the world's got plenty enough of that as it is. They thrive on control, manipulation. Memories, especially of the unhappy sort.

"Just so you know, I'm leaving the worst review you'll ever get for your bar. Didn't even get a key for my motel room when I checked in. Or a coffee."

Con grunts.

"You ever get sick of all this?" I ask, just for my peace of mind. If my plan works, this won't end well for them, and look, I've a goddamn conscience.

"No," Lorne says. He grins at me, and his face shifts, revealing his true, rotting self.

Melvin chuckles. "Rather all the sorry sons of bitches that wind up down here than us, boy."

Stacey shrugs. "A part of me wanted to leave. A long time ago. I regretted coming here, but the woman I was is almost dead, too, and now I don't mind so much."

I feel a little better. Like old Melvin says, rather those 'sorry sons of bitches' than me and Zia.

We reach an ornate set of double doors that swing open as we approach. I whistle at the sight. In the center of the wide room stands a twenty-foot statue of a crouching, horned, fork-tailed creature. Hooved, menacing and meant to represent Pete. I reckon it's bullshit. Kashgars look human, just without the humanity.

Robed, hooded figures surround the room, and Zia's body lies on a dais in front of the statue like Sleeping Beauty in leather.

I see her soul flicker, letting me know she's there, worry etched into her luminous face before it disappears. I wink as she does. So long as Pete don't see her, we've got a chance.

Two things occur to me. One, these guys, for all the killing they've done over the years, are a bunch of amateurs. They haven't bound, gagged or searched me. Means they're stupid, lazy or both. Overconfident for sure, but that leads to my second point.

And that is, this cult is bigger than I thought. There's at least a hundred people down here, watching, waiting for their master's arrival. Reason for the lack of restraints. One blow-in fresh from the road ain't gonna take down over a hundred sickos, right? Right.

Maybe it's the pessimist in me, but I'd never take that chance.

The Whiskey Pete's mob pulls me over to Zia's body. She's pale and slight, but breathing. Alive without her soul.

"So, which of you does the killing?" I ask, as they lean me over Zia's body. Melvin's long nails cut into my scalp as he grabs a handful of my hair and wrenches my head back, exposing my neck. I hear the snick of a blade.

"Con? I'm guessing Con."

"Joel likes doing the women and children," I hear Stacey's monotone murmur, "but they leave the men for me when it's up close and personal. Other times, we like to have a bit of fun with them."

"When you've killed as many as we have, you want some variety," Con rumbles.

Melvin's grip slackens a touch. Reckon he's shocked. That's probably the longest sentence Con's uttered all year.

The room holds its breath, and I face the prospect that these are my last moments. I stare into the space where Zia should be and think of Rosa.

I ain't ready to die again just yet.

A shadow, a sliver of darkness, slithers from behind the statue and congeals into the shape of a man. A normal, pale, dark-haired, black-eyed man. The others, except for Zia's soul, can't see him unless he wills it, though they feel his presence. Melvin's grip on my hair tightens again, and Con chuckles.

Pete, the Kashgar, sneers at the cultists then caresses the cheek of Zia's body. I can see the family resemblance. He doesn't look at me at all. I'm just more blood, a means to an end. Zia's eyes appear, locked on mine.

"Now!"

Pete looks up, understanding registering in his demonic eyes. "No!"

As Zia's soul launches itself at him, I stomp down on Melvin's foot and throw my head back, connecting with his eye socket. With a grunt, he lets go. Stacey and her knife could be close, but I don't wait to find out. Zia's got Pete trapped, for now, right on top of her empty vessel. That's all I care about.

I pull the Expunger from my pocket—that small, cool piece of iron that sets my fingers a-tingling—and throw myself at Pete.

Pain lances my ribs as the knife's blade scores them. Screaming, I slam the Expunger onto Pete's forehead. His eyes grow so wide I think they'll pop.

"Tell 'em Nick Holleran sent ya, you sonofabitch."

I grew up watching '80s action flicks. Sue me.

Pete sizzles. He vibrates under the Expunger as it removes him from reality. Around me, the regulars scream. They see what's happening, and they're powerless to stop it. Melvin grabs me by the shoulders and I bring my fists up, ready to strike. I don't have to. With a withering scream, his face sags and turns to paper over ancient bones. Then he disintegrates into dust, his age catching up to him all at once. I wipe him off my jacket sleeves.

The Expunger melts, searing into Pete. Confusion floods his face as he unravels, like someone caught a loose thread in him and started tugging. Zia lets go as she fades too, alarm filling her expression.

Nick! she screams.

The other yells drown her out. Hundreds of them, as Pete's thralls age on the spot. Some turn to dust, some collapse and wither. Others, like Stacey, curl into a ball on the ground and cry. I glance around; Lorne's dead, a skeleton already, grinning up at me from the ground.

Con. Where the fuck is Con?

The answer hits me. Literally.

"You son of a bitch!" he growls, knocking me off my feet with a shoulder barge.

He's aged, a loose, leathery, withered sack of skin covering his bulk, hair white and sparse, but those mismatched eyes glitter with malice.

I gotta tell ya, didn't think Con looked all that young before, but now he looks about eighty-five. A fucking strong eighty-five.

My legs take over from my brain, boots kicking out into Con's shins with as much force as I can muster. The brittle snap, and his grunt of pain, is music to my ears.

Bastard falls on top of me, and the air in my lungs evacuates.

"You're gonna fucking die, you little shit!" he snarls, decrepit face in mine, gnarled fingers searching for my eyes so he can dig into them. The fucker wants to pop my head like a grape.

"You first, hoss," I bite out, slamming my forehead into his nose. I ignore the sick, hot feeling of fresh blood and snot spurting across my face.

My knee finds his ball sack, and old man Con's in a world of pain. Heaving, I throw him off me and he slams into the altar, blood smearing.

Might as well add more to it. I grab his head, feel the thin bones beneath my fingers. The sudden strength's left him. Con knows he's done. Old. Finished. He's too used to being immortal, being eternally young. He's spent his life picking on the weak and powerless at Whiskey Pete's. All that power and he used it to become a supernatural playground bully.

I don't like killing, even evil shits like him, so I'll make it quick.

His head slams into the stone, temple to corner. One swift blow, and Con's dead before his body hits the ground.

Then I hear a new sound. A crack, followed by a rumble.

The fucking statue's coming down.

"Well, shit."

I grab Zia's body and throw it over my shoulder, knees buckling with her added weight. My head pounds after my collision with the table upstairs, and the blood leaking from my side saps the strength from me, but I struggle on.

I haven't come all this way, battled cultists and a Kashgar, to let her die under a fucking piece of stone.

I ain't too thrilled about the idea myself, for that matter.

Staggering through the doors, two thoughts collide in my mind, one more important than the other: I left the Ruger behind, and I have no fucking idea where I'm going.

Screams, cracks, and rumbles echo around me. It's fucking pandemonium, and if I don't get crushed, I reckon I'll spend the rest of my short days lugging Zia's body around those endless tunnels.

I throw a pleading glance at my surroundings and see something ahead of me. More than one something. Many fucking somethings.

Ghosts, sweet spirits, some of which I recognize from Whiskey Pete's office. They're lining the walls, showing me where I need to go.

"Thank you," I whisper.

Each one I stumble by fades, a look of hope and gratitude on their washed-out faces. Their purposes met. The nightmare over.

"Thought you'd never wake up."

Chevron's behind me. The GPS is back, and I've still got enough gas to get me a few hours away from Whiskey Pete's. My headache is a dull throb, and the knife wound's superficial. Everything's coming up Holleran.

"Where am I?" Zia mumbles, groaning as another vehicle's headlights startle her.

The sight's welcome to me, it's the first car I've seen on the road since emerging in the forest, across from Whiskey Pete's.

"In my Mustang, on our way back to Haven. You remember me?"

She wraps her arms around my chest and that's all the answer I need.

"Easy there. I got sliced, remember?"

Zia laughs and slides back into her seat. It's a good sign. She's seen some shit, and that changes a person. I should know.

"You did great back there. Really stuck it to your old man."

"Is he gone?"

I glance at her. Zia's determined. She wants the truth. Of course she does. It's what got her into this trouble in the first place. No wonder Teague wanted her back. She's a hell of a reporter.

"What I did to Pete, there ain't no coming back from that. The others? If the tunnels didn't collapse and crush them all, some of them might have survived. Even without Pete's glamor, cops could search those tunnels for the next three lifetimes and never find 'em. So let's hope geology does us a favor."

We fall silent, and I turn up the radio. *U-Mass* by The Pixies blares through the speakers, and I feel great, despite it all. A while back, before Zia woke, I sent Rosa a text. Asking if we could talk.

She said yes.

"So, what now?" Zia asks. "Life goes back to normal? Is that it?"

"No," I say, shaking my head. I turn to her and smile. "We find a new normal."

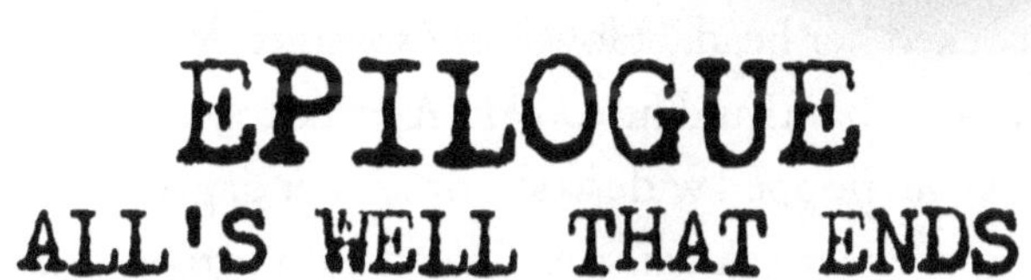

Stacey pushed her way into Pete's office. She knew the tunnels better than anyone. She'd led what survivors she could back to the surface. They made poor time. Age had caught up with them all. She glanced at herself in a shard of glass and grimaced as an old, grey-haired woman peered back.

Stacey might not have her youth anymore, but she held knowledge. Pete wasn't the only one of his kind out there. She'd find another. Or draw a better master to her location. Whiskey Pete's had its charms, after all. Blood in the foundations and bones in the basement.

Whiskey Pete's: Under New Management. Got a ring to it.

Joel lay on the floor, a broken, bloody mess. And old, just like the others. He breathed though, and that brought a smile to Stacey's lips.

She kicked him in the ribs, earning a grunt and groan for her troubles. "Wake up, you useless sack of shit."

His eyes fluttered open.

"Fuck, you got old."

"So did you, dick-for-brains."

Joel pushed himself onto his elbows, grimacing. "Where's the rest?"

"Dead."

"Pete?"

Stacey shook her head. "Gone."

Joel's bottom lip trembled, and Stacey pushed down the urge to slap his pathetic, beat-up face.

"What's gonna happen?"

Stacey cocked her head. "How 'bout we start over?"

She held out a hand and he took it. A smile took her lips as she pulled him close. His eyes popped wide as she drove her dagger into his heart. His last breath was a wheeze. A whisper. She wouldn't go out like that.

Blood poured between her fingers, dripping off her arm and Joel's chest, leaking through the floorboards and into the collapsed tunnels below.

Seeds.

In his glassy eyes, she saw her hair thickening, reddening, her youth returning. The beauty she saw looking back from the shadows, reminding her of everything she had to gain, everything she had to lose. She smiled.

"Something will hear us. I'll *make* 'em hear us." She thrust the knife into Joel one more time, just for good measure. "Then, I'm gonna find Nick Holleran and make him pay."

THE END.

ABOUT THE AUTHORS

Holley Cornetto

Holley Cornetto was born and raised in Alabama, but now lives in New Jersey. She holds a Master of Fine Arts degree in Creative Writing from Lindenwood University and a Master's Degree in Library and Information Science from San Jose State University. Holley writes dark speculative fiction, which has appeared in over a dozen magazines and anthologies. She is also a reviewer and regular contributor at The Horror Tree.

She can be found on Twitter @HLCornetto.

L. T. Emery

L. T. Emery is a British author, with a love for Horror, Sci-fi and Fantasy genres.

He is the proud father of one and husband to the love of his life. Outside of family life, he is an avid reader of novels, genre magazines, comics, manga and just about anything else he can get his hands on. With a particular love of long form fiction, he is currently working on a fantasy novel which he hopes to publish in the future.

He can be found online at https://ltemery.wixsite.com/home and twitter.com/ltemeryuk

Peter J. Foote

Peter J. Foote is a bestselling speculative fiction writer from Nova Scotia, Canada. Most of his stories are within the genres of Science Fiction, Fantasy, and Horror.

Outside of writing, he runs a used bookstore specializing in fantasy & sci-fi, cosplays with his wife, and alternates between red wine and coffee as the mood demands.

Believing that an author should write what he knows, many of Peter's stories reflect his personal life and experiences.

As the founder of the group "Genre Writers of Atlantic Canada", Peter believes that the writing community is stronger when it works together.

Follow Peter:
Newsletter: https://www.subscribepage.com/c3j4h4
Facebook: www.facebook.com/peterjfooteauthor/
Twitter: https://twitter.com/PeterJFoote1
Amazon: https://www.amazon.com/-/e/B077M7JJ9B

J.W. Garrett

J.W. Garrett is a multi-award-winning author. Initiated into fantasy after reading The Hobbit in elementary school, she has been hooked ever since. She writes speculative fiction from the sunny beaches of Jacksonville, Florida, but loves the mountains of Virginia where she was born. Her writings include novels, short stories, and poetry. Since completing Remeon's Crusade, the third book in her sci-fi fantasy series, Realms of Chaos, she has been hard at work on the next installment. When she's not hanging out with her characters pounding out words, her favorite activities are reading, running and spending time with family.

Website: www.jwgarrett.com

David Green

David Green is a writer of the epic and the urban, the fantastical and the mysterious.

With his character-driven dark fantasy series empire of ruin, or urban fantasy noir nick holleran, david takes readers on emotional, action-packed thrill rides.

Hailing from the north-west of england, david now lives in County Galway on the west coast of Ireland with his wife and train-obsessed son.

When not writing, david can be found wondering why he chooses to live in places where it constantly rains.

Newsletter: https://tinyurl.com/y6ah8brp
www.twitter.com/davidgreenwrite
www.davidgreenwriter.com
https://www.facebook.com/davidgreenwriter

Stephen Herczeg

Stephen Herczeg is an IT Geek, writer, actor, film maker and Taekwondo Black Belt based in Canberra Australia. He has been writing for over twenty-five years, completing two novels in the mid-nineties, that even he doesn't like to talk about, plus sixteen feature length screenplays and dozens of short stories, micro-fictions, and scripts.

He has had over ninety short stories and eighty micro-fictions accepted for publication. He has featured in anthologies from Hunter Anthologies; the Australasian Horror Writers Association; Oscillate Wildly Press; Things In the Well; Dead Set Press; Dragon Soul Press; Fantasia Divinity; Monnath Books; Battle Goddess Productions; The Great Void Books; Blood Song Books; Black Hare Press; Raven and Drake; SweetyCat Press; and Black Ink Fiction.

His Sherlock Holmes and Solar Pons stories have been published through MX Publishing and Belanger Books, and his first collection of Sherlock Holmes stories, The Curious Cases of Sherlock Holmes, was published in mid-2021 by MX Publishing.

His first novella, After the Fall, was published by Black Hare Press in July 2021.

He lives by the creed, Just Finish It, and his Mum is his biggest fan.

Amazon: https://www.amazon.com/-/e/B07916SQQS
https://www.goodreads.com/author/show/17100782.Stephen_Herczeg
Facebook: https://www.facebook.com/stephenherczegauthor
Twitter: @HerczegStephen

Abigail Linhardt

Abigail Linhardt is a dark fantasy author who dabbles in sci-fi. When she's not live streaming her cringe-worthy gaming skills or writing monster-filled tales of magic, she can be found watching documentaries on cadavers or spoiling her ferrets.

You can follow her at www.abigaillinhardt.com

Beth W. Patterson

Beth W. Patterson was a full-time musician for over two decades before diving into the world of writing, a process she describes as "fleeing the circus to join the zoo". She is the author of the books Mongrels and Misfits, The Wild Harmonic, and a contributor to over sixty anthologies.

Patterson has performed in nineteen countries across five continents. Her playing appears on over two hundred albums, singles, soundtracks, commercials, and voice-overs (including eight solo albums of her own). More than a hundred of her compositions and co-writes have been released. She studied ethnomusicology at University College, Cork in Ireland and holds a Bachelor's degree in Music Therapy from Loyola University New Orleans.

Beth has occasionally worn other hats as a body paint model, film extra, minor role actor, recording studio partner, record label owner, producer, and visual artist. She is a lover of exquisitely stupid movies and a shameless fangirl of the band Rush. She lives in New Orleans with her husband Josh Paxton, jazz pianist extraordinaire.

You can find her at www.bethpattersonmusic.com
facebook.com/bethodist

Lynne Phillips

Lynne Phillips lives in the Northern Rivers area of New South Wales Australia. Her stories have been published by Zombie Pirate Publishing, Black Hare Press, Fantasia Divinity Publishing,Our Wonderful Anthology, Black Ink Fiction, and in various online magazines. She enjoys exploring the craft of writing stories and the challenge it presents. Her priority is spending time with her family while her passions are reading, writing, keeping fit and spending time at her farm.

Connect with her on https://www.facebook.com.lynne phillips.505

Austin Shirey

Austin Shirey's fiction has appeared in Silver Blade, Orca, All Worlds Wayfarer, Stonecoast Review, and in anthologies from Eerie River Publishing. When he's not busy writing, he's probably reading or enjoying time with his wife, Sarah, and their daughters—and cats!—at home in Northern Virginia. He holds an MFA in Creative Writing from Lindenwood University.

Find him online at www.austinshirey.com and follow him on Twitter @ tashirey87.

Joshua D Taylor

Joshua D Taylor is an author from Southeastern Pennsylvania who never stopped playing make-believe. He enjoys gardening, comic books, ska-punk music, Disney World, and traveling with his wife and infant son. Raised during the weirdness that was the late 20th century Josh's eclectic interests produce eclectic works. He loves to mix-n-match things from different genres and story elements to achieve a madcap hodgepodge of the truly unexpected.

amazon.com/author/joshuadtaylor
facebook.com/authorjoshuadtaylor

V.A. Vazquez

V.A. Vazquez comes from New York City where she has previously worked as a theatre producer, an arts educator, and a ghostwriter for famous fashion editors (which you wouldn't be able to tell from looking in her closet). She writes psychological thrillers and occasionally dabbles in more fantastical horror.

www.vavazquez.com
www.twitter.com/vavazquezwrites

Patrick Winters

Patrick Winters is a graduate of Illinois College in Jacksonville, IL, where he earned a degree in English Literature and Creative Writing. His work has now been featured throughout several magazines and anthologies. A full list of his previous publications may be found at his author's site, if you are so inclined to know:

http://wintersauthor.azurewebsites.net/Publications/List

More from Eerie River

We want to take a moment and thank you for purchasing this copy of **Last Stop,** by Eerie River Publishing. We hoped you enjoyed the stories and the horrors and thrills that were captured within them. Please consider taking a few moments and reviewing this story on Amazon, Goodreads or wherever you obtained your copy. Reviews and recommendations are the cornerstone of small press publishing.

Without you, there is no us.

Eerie River Publishing, is a small independant publishing house that is devoted to releasing quality dark fiction books and anthologies.

To stay up to date with all our new releases and upcoming giveaways, follow us on Facebook, Twitter, Instagram and YouTube. Sign up for our monthly newsletter and receive a free ebook Darkness Reclaimed, as our thank you gift.

https://mailchi.mp/71e45b6d5880/welcomebook

Interested in becoming a Patreon member?
Patreon membership gives you exclusive sneak peeks at upcoming books, early chapter releases, covers art as well as free ebooks and discounts on paperbacks.

https://www.patreon.com/EerieRiverPub.

ALSO AVAILABLE FROM
EERIE RIVER PUBLISHING

NOVELS
Dead Man Walking
Devil Walks in Blood
A Sword Named Sorrow
Storming Area 51: Horror At the Gate
In Solitudes Shadow
SENTINEL

ANTHOLOGIES
It Calls From The Forest: Volume I
It Calls From The Forest: Volume II
It Calls From The Sky
It Calls From The Sea
It Calls From the Doors
Darkness Reclaimed
Last Stop
After
With Blood and Ash
With Bone and Iron

DRABBLE COLLECTIONS
Forgotten Ones: Drabbles of Myth and Legend
Dark Magic: Drabbles of Magic and Lore

COMING SOON
Kindgom of Fire and Stars
The Void
NOTHUS
Vengeance

www.EerieRiverPublishing.com

Get more Nick Holleran in this special edition of Devil Walks In Blood, a paranormal detective series. Dark, gritty and everything Nick.

www.EerieRiverPublishing.com/NickHolleran